KU-352-945

GYPSY BRIDE

En route to Cranleigh Castle to meet the eligible Earl of Greystone, Lady Angelica Winsford was forced to stop for the night. As she settled in her room, a shadowy stranger appeared. He said the gypsies called him Gitano and his plea for refuge touched Angelica's soul. Even after they had gone their separate ways, Gitano haunted her dreams. Now promised in marriage to a man she secretly feared, she despaired of ever again knowing the passion Gitano had shown her....

DOM

≋ Hounslow

Special Services Library
Hounslow Library Centre
24 The Treaty Centre
High Street
Hounslow TW3 1ES
Telephone 0181-570 0622

0	1	2	3	4	5	6	7	8	9
740 131		665 383	303 14	265	0786		3958	579	
7920		812 0653		6418	6496		338 149		
861	582	673	3404	1265	516		2548 839		
		6343	0784	995	996		809		
		6503		88	516		2067		
861		7773		745800			6489		
					196		3499		
						3308			

P10-L-2061

C0000 001 566 268

GYPSY BRIDE

Gypsy Bride

by
Anne Hamilton

LIBRARY AT HOME SERVICE
COMMUNITY SERVICES
HOUNSLOW LIBRARY
CENTRESPACE
24 TREATY CENTRE
HIGH ST. HOUNSLOW
TW3 1ES   TEL: 0181 570 0622

Black Satin Romance
Long Preston, North Yorkshire,
England.

British Library Cataloguing in Publication Data.

Hamilton, Anne
  Gypsy bride.

A catalogue record for this book is
available from the British Library

ISBN 1-86110-007-8

Copyright © 1995 by Anne Hamilton

Cover photography © Margaret Penwarden

Published in Large Print August, 1996 by arrangement with
Kensington Publishing Corporation.

All rights reserved. No part of this publication may be
reproduced, stored in a retrieval system, or transmitted in
any form or by any means, electronic, mechanical, photocopying,
recording or otherwise, without the prior permission of the
Copyright owner.

L. B. HOUNSLOW
LARGE PRINT COLLECTION

SITE	DATE
1 *DOM*	*1/98*
2	
3	
4	
5	

Black Satin Romance is an imprint of
Library Magna Books Ltd.
Printed and bound in Great Britain by
T.J. Press (Padstow) Ltd., Cornwall, PL28 8RW.

ONE

It was 1860—the year Angelica was to become engaged—just as soon as she could find a fiancé. In America, civil war was threatening; in Europe, France and England were enjoying a lasting peace.

Spring was on its way and the hunting season would soon be over—that is to say, the *fox*-hunting season—but the real hunting season was just beginning—the husband-hunting season, more delicately referred to as the *London Season*, when all of society gathered to show off their diligent, darling daughters, whose sole job it was to run to ground the suspecting prey—any rich and well-placed scion who was not quick enough on his feet to outrun the pack.

This year, the London Season was to have a prize catch: the Prince of Wales, the would-be heir to Queen Victoria's throne. His Royal Highness had matured into a witty, good-humoured and high-spirited dance partner with, as all of Society observed, remarkable stamina. His endurance allowed him to cavort with his partners across the ballroom floors of the great houses well into the small hours. The over-worked musicians, to say nothing of the hostesses, were left exhausted and deprived of their beds until the Prince finally cheered them—by going home.

This exercise—of dancing with the Prince—was bound to bring a healthy glow to the cheeks of marriageable girls and make their mothers flush with triumph. The well-developed royal charm made dancing a quadrille with the future king a not unpleasant honour which fell only to the select number of young ladies who, by birth or financial considerations, made up the year's covey of debutantes.

As a duke's daughter, Angelica, who had just turned eighteen, more than qualified to be presented at court and receive the Queen's perfunctory peck on the cheek bestowed only upon young ladies of the aristocracy. The daughters of rich merchants had to content themselves with kissing the Queen's plump, briefly proffered hand. Shared equally by all the debutantes—in white clouds of tulle over satin, floating across the polished floor like swans on still water—was the near impossible task of scuttling backwards from the throne room. This was the feared moment when the swan could suddenly revert to an ungainly, beached cygnet, whose disgrace would come if she tripped over the steel wire of her crinoline which, instead of holding her vast skirt out behind her, could bend inward and catch her ankle with the sure, slick finality of a poacher's snare. Any hapless young lady who was unlucky enough to stumble, while the hundreds of pairs of fishy eyes were upon her, wished the floor would divide and she could sink below it like a blushing Venus returning to the refuge of the waves.

In spite of being high born, Angelica had approached the Season aware of an obstacle more considerable than the hazardous whimsies of fashion. Her grandfather, the sixth Duke of Winsford, had pitched the vast family fortune into disastrous and ill-advised investments, leaving his heirs penniless. The sixth Duke's profligacy meant that his only son, Angelica's father, inherited nothing but the title and crushing debts. The young Duke and Duchess had been brought to an early demise as their energies and spirits were sapped by the lost battle with creditors, leaving their orphaned daughter to the charity of relatives.

An impoverished state did nothing to diminish a young lady's social standing during the London Season. It did, however, make it devilishly difficult to finance this expensive, complex, but necessary launch into society. Fortunately for Angelica her aunt and uncle, Lord and Lady Avery, had taken on the task of giving her a debut that befitted her having been born to the purple. And now, after a wonderful stay in France with her cousin, Count Chénier and his family, she was crossing the English Channel to engage in the serious business of securing a rich husband.

'There are endless details to attend to,' Angelica's aunt was saying. 'Lord Avery's agent has finally found a suitable house in London and, although it is in Belgrave Place instead of Belgrave Square, it will do very well. Your uncle has never seen the need to have a house in London as we go there so rarely. I

9

have been there perhaps a dozen times since my London Season and that, my dear, was a fair few years ago.' Lady Avery pulled her cashmere shawl more tightly around her shoulders and she seemed to wrap her whole self around the frail glass of cordial she was sipping from, convinced that it was the only thing that stood between her and sea sickness. Angelica, watching her aunt, was reminded of a gentle, greying hedgehog rolling itself up into a protective ball, safe from disturbances. Lady Avery sipped at the cordial and said, 'These Channel crossings do so get me down. I feel queasy for days afterwards. It is just twelve hours of pure torture for me.'

The bevelled glass and mahogany of the first-class saloon had a warm glow and the spitting, swaying gas lamps cast a flattering sheen on Angelica's soft burnished curls. As they had the gently swaying room to themselves, Lady Avery spoke loudly as if addressing a meeting. 'The first thing we must do when we get back to Ickworth is pack up for London, and that will be a grotesque effort, except in your case, my dear, as we've neglected your clothes so badly. You've hardly a stitch! But you know what country bumpkins we are, me with my gardening and your uncle always so busy with the estate.'

'You know I've never taken a great interest in clothes, Aunt Clarissa,' said Angelica good naturedly directing the draft from her fan towards her aunt who was looking alarmingly pale.

'I know, bless you,' confided Lady Avery in

a whisper. 'You're too pretty to have to worry about dressing up your looks, but too artless to realize it. But the first thing we do, the minute we are settled in Belgrave Place, is rush off to the dressmakers in Bond Street and order your gowns. Lady Saddleworth brought out her daughter, Constance, last year and she has given me a whole list of things that must be done. I am sure these things were not so complicated in my day! In any case, Lady Saddleworth says that we are very late getting in, but that we did the right thing stopping at Mr Worth's in Paris to order the gown which you will wear to be presented to the Queen. Lady Saddleworth says Mr Worth will be absolutely, colossally famous one day and I have to admit she may be right—your dress will be a dream!'

Lady Avery earnestly sipped again at her cordial and resumed with eyes wide as if imparting some shocking tidbit, 'Do you know that Lady Saddleworth told me they waited a full *four hours* to be presented to the Queen! The line of carriages wrapped all the way round the Palace, and once inside they stood waiting for at least a half a decade! The young equerry assigned to escort Constance was such a dull fellow that by the end of the day they were ready to scream! He hardly said a word and did not even have the courtesy to hide his boredom! Really it is too much, after all the trouble and expense one has to go to!' Lady Avery bristled at the thought of it all which restored some colour to her cheeks.

Angelica toyed with her teacup and restrained

her impulse to side with the callow equerry. She was dubious but resigned to the whole complicated social process, which was solely devised to assist young ladies in the necessary business of securing a suitable husband. Despite her own natural reticence, Angelica made a show of enthusiasm as her aunt and uncle were going to a great deal of trouble and expense on her behalf. She smiled encouragingly at her aunt. 'I am sure Lady Saddleworth and Constance were just unlucky. I am positive we will fare better.'

'We are terribly far behind with preparations. We will be hard pressed to get everything done. At this rate, a seamstress will be finishing your gown in the carriage as we make our way down the Mall to the Palace!' Lady Avery snorted out an unamused laugh. 'And Count Chénier's insistence that we extend our stay has put us even further back!'

Angelica always adored staying with her French cousins who had a confection of a château overlooking the Loire. She had spent her happiest days with Count Chénier and his numerous, boisterous children. Her brief visits were the nearest thing to the normal family life she had been deprived of. Although she loved being a surrogate member of the Chénier family, she was always aware of her role as an outsider. She was reminded most of this distance when the Count or Countess handed out scoldings to their often ungovernable offspring; after they had berated their own *enfants sauvages*, they would smile at Angelica to show that she was exempt from their anger. But she longed to be included in the force of emotions that parents lavish on their children, no matter what form it took. She adored the Chéniers, their rowdy ways and escapades, and she always found it difficult to tear herself away from the Chénier *ménage*. Even this time she was loath to depart, in spite of the taunts she received from her cousins that she was far too grown-up to be any fun any more. Plump little Cousin Mumu had teased her relentlessly about her coming London Season. 'You will now have to find a wealthy husband to look after you,' she had said before collapsing into a heap of giggles and blushes without understanding the truth of her words. Angelica's parents had made a love-match much frowned upon by both families in the light of diminished fortunes on both sides. This, and their early deaths, formed an inseparable issue in Angelica's mind.

Angelica was lost in thought and unaware that her aunt had manoeuvred the conversation around to her favourite topic—gardening. 'Do you know, those cuttings Madame de Grasse gave me are *in* the hold! *The hold*, I say!' she ranted and her colour was now completely restored. 'I specifically ordered that they should come to my cabin, and now they say they cannot retrieve them until we land. They are a completely new species from Brazil and I am the *first* to bring them to England! It is a beautiful ornamental herb with darling white spotted leaves—*Caladium schomburgkii*. The sea air must be dreadful for them as they are tropical! I am quite beside myself when I think of it!' And, as usual, Lady Avery's hands fluttered like a flock of startled pigeons whenever she became agitated.

'Good evening, Lady Avery,' the ship's First Officer said, appearing suddenly beside their table. 'The Captain asked me to present his compliments.' The tall, handsome young man, his fair complexion tanned and his hair bleached almost white by the salty sun, looked at ease in his crisp boiled-wool uniform, in spite of the fact he was almost standing at attention; he bowed slightly as he delivered his message. Then, with less formality, he could not help smiling at Angelica whose open expression seemed reserved, yet unforbidding, unlike many well-bred young ladies of her age. He was delighted when she returned his smile but, fearing the aunt would think him forward, he turned the beam of his charm upon the older woman who gratefully basked in its rays. He added, 'Won't you be joining everyone on deck, Lady Avery? There is a full moon tonight and it will make a wonderful sight when we reach Dover's white cliffs in a moment.'

'Ah, so that is it!' snapped Lady Avery, half serious and half in jest. 'I wondered why the saloon was deserted. I thought perhaps the "abandon ship" had been sounded and you were coming to take us to the lifeboats!' Her ladyship liked to remind everyone how much she hated ships in hopes they would think her very noble for even contemplating a sea journey.

'No, ma'am, all is in order, I can assure

14

you. In fact, it is a remarkably calm night and I am sure you will be quite comfortable on deck. May I assist you with your wraps?' Lady Avery consented wearily to the young officer's ministrations and permitted herself to be fussed over, helped into her cloak, and delivered to the saloon door like a more pliable hedgehog about to set off on an adventure. The first officer radiated another dose of well-practised charm, uttered a few more pleasantries to her ladyship and Angelica, and bowed them out onto the deck.

As she and Lady Avery left the First Officer, Angelica thought to herself, now there is someone in a similar position to mine. He is probably a second or third son of a good family, born like myself to a position in society, well-educated, but because of a trick of birth—penniless. And that is where the similarity ends. While the younger sons inherit nothing, they are encouraged to find a vocation—a good regiment, the Navy, the Church. But we titled ladies who are born without a fortune or, as in my case, without a farthing, we must marry before we are too old and our looks fade. And all that just to keep us from starving, and she laughed to herself without bitterness at the whole quandary of life.

Lady Avery interrupted Angelica's train of thought, 'I have only come out on your account, Angelica. I knew you would like some air. However, you are far too robust and I hope you will always do your best to disguise it when you are in company. It is very unbecoming in

15

a young lady to appear too hardy.'

'Yes, Aunt Clarissa,' said Angelica, concealing her amusement at this nit-picking reprimand which indicated that her aunt was feeling more her old herself and finally getting her sea-legs, although rather too late in the voyage as land was in sight.

'I suspect your uncle is in the smoking saloon playing backgammon with Lord Bewick. He should amuse himself like that more often. He has become quite obsessed with estate business and I must speak to him about it. He is almost in danger of appearing eccentric, not permitting his agent to conduct his business for him. There was a time when that sort of behaviour was unheard of, and I certainly disapprove of it. Mr Slocombe is a very capable agent and is well paid for his efforts. Lord Avery should remember his position and behave accordingly.' She puffed out her cheeks in disdain until she resembled a blow fish and then exhaled sharply. The blow fish vanished and Lady Avery continued. 'I must confess that since your grandfather lost his fortune it is not surprising if there are displays of nerves amongst his fellow peers, not wishing to entrust their fortunes to anyone but themselves. Your grandfather's ruin was a terrible shock to everyone, but it was years ago now...' and Lady Avery sadly heaved a weary sigh, but, then, empowered by a prickly little resentment against her husband, she went on, '...but I have to say it! It was truly the *absolute limit* when Lord Avery spent almost our entire sojourn with Count and Countess Chénier tinkering with some...some French scheme. I do not pretend to understand these financial things, but I am cognizant of how a person of breeding should behave.' Lady Avery finished unburdening herself before they came within earshot of the other passengers.

A veritable menagerie, Lady Avery was now resembling a tortoise as she hunched with cold inside her wraps, gulping and surveying the world from heavy-lidded eyes with a wet, dismissive gaze. As they made their way along the deck, Lady Avery exchanged warm or cool greetings with some of her acquaintances depending upon their standing in society. It would be wrong to call Lady Avery a snob; it would be more accurate to say that she was very aware of the correct order of things and scorned and resisted any deviation. Aunt and niece soon found a quiet spot out of the mainstream of activity and Lady Avery said, 'Let's stand here, Angelica. I start to feel rather hemmed-in at sea if I am surrounded by a crowd.' So they stood on the leeward side of a mast where they could observe the general bustle about them on the great expanse of deck.

With blissful cries, some unruly children ran past, pursued by their long-suffering, po-faced nanny who trailed in an undignified fashion after them; the hem of her serviceable grey poplin flew about as she ran revealing the sanctity of the top button of her laced ankle-boots. At this sight, Lady Avery gasped and could not forbear, with the expertise of the childless, from commenting that it was pointless having a nanny who could not control children. She added that, had she been blessed with offspring she would have known how to deal with such lapses in domestic arrangements.

The First Officer had not exaggerated; the high white chalk cliffs and the full moon combined to create a spectacular show. The Dover cliffs glowed under the moon like gigantic curtains of light. They seemed to float upon their own reflection in the dark sea and rise up like a shimmering wall of white organza with nothing to make them seem real except occasional flickering lights from the windows of the distant harbour cottages.

The ship was making discordant but reassuringly rhythmic creaks and groans as it moved slowly towards the port. It was a windless night; the sails were reefed, allowing the steam engines to carry them smoothly into the harbour and the ship gave an occasional shudder as the turbines changed speed. Phantoms of escaping steam fled into the night sky high above Angelica, who loved the feeling of mystery and freedom that ships carried with them. The sound of water cascading from the giant paddle wheels mixed with the chatter of the passengers languidly promenading the deck. 'This is beautiful, Aunt Clarissa,' said Angelica enthusiastically. 'Aren't you glad we came out to see it?'

'Yes, I suppose I am, Angelica dear, but I must confess I will enjoy nothing until we dock and I can rescue my priceless cuttings from that filthy hold!' And she began to deliver a diatribe on the evils of all shipping agents.

Angelica was not listening; the scene before her was magical and it consumed her totally. The moon was shining so brightly that the lamps lining the deck seemed dim by comparison. The faces of the other passengers glowed with an unearthly pallor in the silver light and the effect was heightened by the contrast with their sombre travelling clothes. Traces of white linen appeared disembodied as cuffs and handkerchiefs seemed to float miraculously across the dark background.

As the ship turned slowly to meet the harbour entrance, Angelica scanned the scene and watched the play of moonlight on the railings and rigging. With the ship's changing position, the moonlight slipped playfully along the deck, casting into light what had been in shadow moments before, and Angelica noticed a dark figure standing in the shadow of a lifeboat away from the other passengers.

He was tall, young, powerfully built, his dark hair somewhat dishevelled. And that was all Angelica could make out as his cloak collar was turned well up across his face so that, even if there had been a brighter light, he would still have seemed more a part of the shadows. She idly mused that she had not seen him before amongst the passengers. For no reason in particular she let her eyes rest on this mysterious figure for a moment, safe in the knowledge that he could not see her from where he was standing.

The moonlight, pouring through the lattice-work of rigging, danced across the pivoting ship.

One minute there were deep shadows and a second later they were banished, only to return as the light moved on. For an instant, a bright shaft of moonlight fell across the man's face; as his eyes were revealed to Angelica, a tremor shot through her and she later wondered if it had only been the undulating vibrations of the ship's thrumming engines. She tried to recall if she had really gasped or had she imagined it? The only thing completely clear to her was that, even in that split-second view of the stranger's eyes, she had seen the kindest and saddest eyes she had ever known.

Leaving her no time to reflect, at that very second, the unruly children raced past again and a woman's terrible scream lanced through the calm air.

'The child! The child!' the nanny's sobbing voice shrieked. Taking up the cry, the crowd of passengers surged to the railings. All was chaos; Angelica could only see hysterical passengers and crew running aimlessly about the deck. A young boy had been playing chase with his brother and had dashed behind a lifeboat; not realizing that there was no safety rail there, he had tumbled into the pitch-dark sea. Angelica looked around in helpless panic at the mindless throng swarming the deck. Her eyes raced across the scene and she only caught fragments of what was happening.

Almost at the instant of the woman's first cry, the stranger in the shadows threw off his cloak and dived into the icy water after the child. He moved with such speed and there was so much confusion that only Angelica and the few people nearest him saw him leap over the railing into the dark void.

The shouts of passengers and crew were mixed with the piercing cries of the boy's mother. 'My darling! Please God, spare my baby!' she poured out in pathetic agony, while a commanding voice barked from the bridge above, 'Lower a boat! Lower a boat!' Women were sobbing and others supported the swooning mother as sailors clambered into a lifeboat just as it was abruptly and erratically winched down into the water by a flurry of panicky hands.

Somewhere above, in the jungle of rigging, a sailor's melancholy voice was sounding the alarm: 'Man overboard!' and then a low and terrible groan racked the ship as an explosion of unwanted steam mushroomed into the sky, rendering the ship powerless and bringing the engines shuddering to a stop.

Lady Avery, instantly dismissing her dislike of crowds and all things maritime, grabbed Angelica by the arm and propelled both of them into the swarm of passengers racing towards the stern. No one was quicker than Lady Avery in claiming a space for herself and Angelica at the railing. The crowd was straining against the mahogany rails and peering down into the foaming water—churned by the last rotations of the ship's now idle paddle wheels—trying to see the fate of the child and the young man swimming strongly towards him.

Someone cried out, 'He's got him! He's reached the boy! Get to them with the boat!'

Without knowing it, in the excitement Angelica was clinging to her aunt's arm; equally unconsciously, she in turn was holding fast to Angelica's wrist with such ferocity that her grasp was strangling the circulation. Like everyone witnessing the drama, Angelica was weak with anxiety; she was aware of a sickening hush falling over the crowd as the sailors, with outstretched hands, grasped and hauled the limp figure of the child into the lifeboat from the arms of the swimmer who had been holding the tiny boy's head above the waves.

For what seemed like an eternity, Angelica watched the small lifeboat in the near distance idly slipping up and down the moon-streaked slopes of the undulating waves; the silhouetted figures of the sailors slid the child's small body over the gunwales, out of sight, into the bottom of the boat and then they stood motionless looking down at their forlorn cargo. Angelica felt time was standing still; after what felt like hours to her—but which was really a matter of seconds—the swimmer hauled himself up by his arms onto the side of the lifeboat and shouted something at the sailors. They responded by unceremoniously picking up the little boy by the heels and pouring the sea water out of him. Horrified, Angelica turned her frantic gaze to the swimmer, half in and half out of the water, who, roughly scraping his dripping hair out of his eyes, could only wait like everyone else, in hope and dread for the child's life. Vaguely aware of a numbing sensation, Angelica suddenly realized that she and everyone else had stopped breathing and the only noise was the softly chafing rigging high overhead; it sounded unreal and distant as if in a dream. Just when Angelica was finding the stillness and uncertainty unbearable, the silence was broken by the shout of the massively built bosun in the lifeboat who, standing up and cupping his hands to his mouth, bellowed towards the ship, 'The lad's all right!'

With this the crowd at the rail went wild with delight and a great cheer rose up. People were laughing, crying, clapping their hands and shouting, and a couple of tipsy men, who had been compelled from the bar by the commotion, celebrated by throwing their expensive, beaver toppers high into the air. After hovering for an instant, the hats fell into the sea with a *plop*. Even Lady Avery was so caught up in the excitement that, although she was not one to encourage displays of affection, she surprised herself by clasping Angelica in a fervent hug.

The child's mother was helped along the deck to where her errant offspring was being lifted on board. Her shaking voice could be heard saying, 'Thank you...thank you...' over and over again to no one in particular as she embraced the sodden bundle wrapped in a rough woollen blanket.

Helping hands quickly ushered mother and child below where hot sweet tea and a warm bed were being made ready. Almost unnoticed, the swimmer quickly scrambled back on board, up a treacherous rope ladder, and he seemed oblivious to the congratulations and praise from his fellow passengers. Slipping by them, without a pause, he disappeared below to his stateroom.

'Well, that was the *most* remarkable thing I've ever seen!' Lady Avery exclaimed, overcome and clinging to the rail for support. 'What bravery! What heroics!' she announced theatrically. 'Oh, it's been too much for me, I must sit down.' Angelica was only slightly more composed as she helped her aunt to a deck-chair next to one occupied by the corpulent Marchioness of Bewick, who was also in a posture of near collapse. Administering to the Marchioness was her married daughter, Lady Harriet, who, although plain, had a fortune that had fetched her a fashionable marriage to the influential, but dull, Sir Henry Buckle. Lady Harriet insisted upon compounding her plainness by wearing the most unflattering and outdated hair fashion, a ringlet at each temple which, in her case, looked like two oily, mouse-coloured sausages framing her face. Lady Harriet was obligingly dabbing her mother's temples with a handkerchief moistened with cologne from a small silver bottle.

Trying to catch her breath and turning to the Marchioness, Lady Avery demanded, 'My dear Lady Bewick, have you *ever* witnessed such a thing? I thought I should faint clean away with the suspense of not knowing if that little child was drowned dead!'

The Marchioness was not to be topped in her suffering brought on by extreme over-excitement and—more accurately—an over-tight corset. 'I thought my heart had stopped completely! *Truly* I did! And now it is beating so fast I feel it will never be calm. I wonder if I should have the doctor, Harriet?' she enquired doubtfully, turning to her daughter for an answer but then not waiting for one. 'No, perhaps not, he will be attending to the child. I have just sent my son-in-law, Sir Henry, to find out *who* that gallant young gentleman is. Do *you* know, Lady Avery?'

'I don't think I have ever seen him before, but I could hardly see his face. Did anyone see him properly?' Lady Avery was wheedling for any morsel of gossip, her eyes darting suspiciously across their faces like a hardened Spanish Inquisitor determined to miss nothing.

The deck was buzzing with similar little groups speaking of nothing else and asking exactly the same question.

'I don't remember seeing him on the crossing. Perhaps he was in his stateroom for most of the voyage,' suggested Lady Harriet, 'but truly I didn't even get a peek at him, there were so many people *pushing* and crowding the rail.' And at this, Lady Avery wondered if the Marchioness and Lady Harriet flashed her a duet of pointed looks.

'I think he was standing by that lifeboat, over there,' volunteered Angelica, as confounded by events as the rest, 'but I can't be certain, it all happened so suddenly.'

'Here's Henry now!' announced Lady Harriet as her husband approached. All eyes turned eagerly towards Sir Henry Buckle, hungry for the news of the stranger's identity. 'I've failed you miserably, dear ladies! Apparently no one knows the gentleman's name, and no one saw him on the crossing. But, the most remarkable thing has taken place! Naturally the boy's father sent a message to the chap's cabin saying that he wished to call upon him to thank him for saving the life of his son and heir. Well, I gather that the gentleman sent his servant, a rather grotesque and foreign-looking individual, back to the father to say that it was unnecessary to thank him or to honour him with a visit.'

'What *extraordinary* behaviour!' the Marchioness said with a sharp intake of breath, and her eyes widened with interest.

'I'd call it downright churlish!' Lady Avery announced, wearing her most scandalized expression. 'Are you *quite* sure the person *is* a gentleman?' she speculated disdainfully.

'That he definitely *is* a person of breeding is the only thing anyone knows for certain. It was obvious. And an old Etonian at that. You know one has an instinct for these things, having been to Eton oneself. However, the face was not familiar. Probably in a later year to me,' assured Sir Henry, twirling his pale, thin, waxed moustaches with an air of satisfaction.

'Really, Henry!' laughed Lady Harriet scornfully, 'How can you say the gentleman is an old Etonian when all you or anyone else could see was the figure of a soaking wet man, dripping with sea water in all but darkness! The fact that his clothes were well-cut might not have been totally disguised by the infiltration of half an ocean—that he bore himself with breeding—and that his brave act was the act of a gentleman, may add up to the probability that he *is* a gentleman. But to say that he is a fellow old Etonian! It is really too far-fetched!'

Sir Henry was totally uncrushed by this condemnation of his observations and continued to stroke his moustache. The Marchioness took his side before he could defend himself. 'Now, Harriet, if Henry says the gentleman is an old Etonian, you must not dispute it! Your father and your brothers would confirm it, I am sure. It may not be something that you or I can understand, but I accept it as a fact.' And then, turning to Sir Henry, she purred, 'I know you are infallible in these things, Henry, and I rely on all you say, but it still seems very odd behaviour for the stranger to refuse to see the child's father.'

Sir Henry only nodded his agreement, but Angelica, who had been weighing up the arguments in her mind, said, 'He must have had a very good reason, but what could it possibly be?'

'Oh, I do hope we find out, I hate mysteries,' Lady Harriet moaned.

'That is precisely what it is! A mystery!' said the Marchioness, with narrowing eyes. 'We must solve it! I shan't rest until I know!'

The ship had docked unnoticed by the preoccupied passengers; therefore the captain, descending from the bridge to take up his usual place at the gangway, found his progress much impeded. Passengers wishing to know if he was privy to the stranger's name interviewed and questioned him at every step.

'Do please put us from our quandary,

Captain!' Lady Avery pleaded as he approached. 'Please tell us the identity of the gentleman with no name!'

'I am afraid I am just as ignorant of the gentleman's identity as everyone else. I should very much like to know it as the entry in my log, and the report I must file to the company office, will look very bare without it. All I have been able to ascertain is that he was travelling alone, apart from his servant, and that he was the first person to leave the ship the moment the gangway touched shore.'

'Oh, he's gone! And we are still in the dark. Well—there is nothing for it but to go ashore,' said the Marchioness with resignation.

Too new to Society to be aware of the importance of juicy gossip, Angelica's mind was unfashionably still on the fate of the half-drowned child. 'And the little boy will he be quite well?' she asked the captain.

'Yes, I am happy to say!' he responded, relieved to find the conversation turning to a subject to which he could offer answers. 'But the little lad will have a very sore throat from swallowing all that sea water, and a headache to boot. But a good night's sleep and some bed-rest will see him right in a few days.'

Lord Avery had missed the night's public excitement while embroiled in a little drama of his own. Closeted in the smoking room with the Marquis of Bewick, he had won a hundred guineas at backgammon on a lucky throw of the dice. Lord Avery later wished that he and his opponent had abandoned their game to investigate the loud commotion they had heard coming from above decks, but nothing short of an in-rushing sea would have moved the Marquis away from the gaming table. The Marquis in turn recouped his hundred guineas and then relieved Lord Avery of seventy guineas more. It was an ill-tempered Lord Avery who rejoined the ladies, and then they made their way down the gangway to where Lord Avery's coach was waiting on the busy quay side.

Emerson, Lord Avery's butler, who, when travelling with his lordship often combined the duties of butler and valet, was left behind on the quay to oversee the copious amounts of baggage into a second coach. Once the footmen had handed the tired passengers into the coach, they were taken at breakneck speed the short distance to the Grand Hotel where Lord Avery kept a suite of rooms which he found a great convenience for his frequent trips to France.

'Too fast, Avery! Really too fast!' complained Lady Avery halfheartedly. In reality her ladyship was thankful for anything speeding her to her bed, as it would be the only piece of furniture she had encountered in fifteen hours that was not suspended on waves or wheels. Angelica was silently revelling in the speed and the crashing sound of the horses' hooves against the cobblestones.

The Grand Hotel's manager, Mr Arbuthnot, was on the steps of the ponderous, white stucco hotel to welcome Lord Avery's coach. Flanking him were half a dozen elegantly turned-out under-managers and a battalion of hotel staff lined the steps. Rows of maids, in black dresses and freshly starched aprons and caps, were outnumbered by scores of valets, porters, and footmen, virtually all of whom were off duty at this late hour and pining for their beds. Mr Arbuthnot always made a great show of Lord Avery's arrival. As someone who retained one of the hotel's largest suites for the purpose of visiting perhaps no more than fourteen days a year, he was an invaluable patron.

Simpering and twittering his welcome, Mr Arbuthnot led the weary little band up the sweep of stairs while the domestic honour guard bobbed and dipped with curtsies and bows.

Angelica lay between the cool linen sheets that night going over the day's events in her mind. She found them complicated and confused and they insisted upon swimming about in her head. Too tired to make order of her thoughts, she closed her eyes to sleep. As she drifted into slumber, she suddenly started and opened her eyes. What she had seen when she closed her lids were the eyes of the stranger just as she had seen them revealed by the moonlight for that brief instant on the ship. She found this phenomenon rather disturbing but not unpleasant. She decided it was just a reaction to the excitement of the journey and finally, she fell into a peaceful sleep.

TWO

The next morning Angelica was awakened by Sarah, the maid, pulling open the heavy velvet curtains. Angelica stretched languidly for a moment and then, suddenly filled with excitement, she sprang from her bed and raced to the windows to view the day. The sun was casting its pure white, morning light on the gelid, grey sea, making the waves glitter like a million stars too bright to look at.

Knowing that she was embarking on the beginning of her adult life gave her a sense of exhilaration, but it was tempered by a sense of apprehension. For all its obvious shortcomings, being a debutante during the London Season would have entertaining aspects. Floating from sparkling ball to glowing party in an array of beautiful gowns, which might tempt even her simple tastes, would doubtless be fun, but she felt ill-equipped to cope with what lay ahead. She had until now spent her days in country pursuits and apart from her relatives she had not met many people. In her most honest moments, Angelica listed her fluent French and her education as her only two assets and she found this dismaying.

Angelica really did not feel she had much to offer any suitor, but she was determined to try to be charming and agreeable to all the eligible gentlemen whom she would meet. And perhaps, she thought, someone rich and kind, whom she could admire and respect, would ask for her hand. Although penniless, she would be able to give in exchange her loyalty and obedience, but she could not bring herself to add love to this list. Love was an emotion she had learned to scorn because it had been the cause of her parents' financially-unwise union which had resulted in heartbreak. The memory of her parents' anguish at the loss of the family estate, after so many generations, and their constant struggle to honour the family's debts, hung over her like a spectre. Her father had been a broken man, haunted by the burden of knowing that he had brought his beautiful and loving young wife to live a poor and mean existence. The strain had ruined his health, and he had soon died.

Both families were shocked at the young Duke's death; he had been too proud to let anyone know how truly desperate matters had become. Lord and Lady Avery had immediately taken in Angelica and her ailing mother, who had exhausted herself nursing her husband day and night. She never recovered her health and died three months later. Even at the age of seven, the child understood that her mother had died of a broken heart. All these considerations whirled around in Angelica's thoughts as she merely picked at the light breakfast Sarah had brought on a tray.

Sarah had spent the morning dashing between Lady Avery's room and Angelica's room. She was really Lady Avery's maid, but her ladyship thought it was much more practical to share a maid when travelling. Sarah was the daughter of one of the gardeners on the Averys' estate, Ickworth. She was only a few years older than Angelica, did her work with a willing manner, and Lady Avery was well pleased with her. Returning to Angelica's room, Sarah could not contain her curiosity any longer and burst out, 'Please! Please! Now tell me what happened last night, Lady Angelica! We could not see a blessed thing on that ship from where we was! You promised last night you would tell me all about it this morning. You must have seen the whole thing, you being on the deck and all! We was below decks and we saw nothing. Oh, do *please* tell me everything! Nobody was drowned?'

'Well, in truth,' said Angelica, 'although the moon was very bright it was very difficult to see anything, and the crush was terrific. People were running about in a great confusion.'

Not content with these meagre details, Sarah demanded more, 'Who was the young gentleman what saved the lad? He had a very strange manservant who was rather standoffish. I know 'cause Lady Finnlow's butler, Mr Baxter, tried to have a conversation with him. The stranger's manservant was very ugly and fierce-looking, with scars all over his face. Not a bit like an ordinary manservant. And he was foreign-looking. Anyways—' Sarah continued, not waiting to draw breath in her determination to share her gossip, '—Mr Baxter tried to chat with the manservant, just to be friendly like, but he got a very chilly snub. Well, some people say the nameless gentleman isn't a gentleman at all, but a *fantasmically* (Sarah often mispronounced long words she had heard Lady Avery use) rich prince, *foreign,* mind you, who is travelling in secret to see the Queen! He's on some important mission or some suchlike matter! Affairs of state they calls it. As I figures it, this prince is travelling without all the usual fuss and servants and the like, so that no one will notice him!'

Angelica listened intently to Sarah's theories, but this last pronouncement sent her rocking with laughter and she almost upset the tray and the small Sèvres teapot shaped like a strawberry. 'But really—I am sure you are wrong, Sarah. There must be some very simple explanation and no mystery at all.'

'Well, why is it, then, that nobody knows the gentleman's name?' asked Sarah stubbornly defending her theory.

'I have to confess, that does remain a puzzle,' granted Angelica, moving across to the dressing table and sitting down, 'but you must help me with my hair or I shall be late for Lord and Lady Avery.'

Sarah had only just begun drawing the silver hairbrush through Angelica's full mane of honey-coloured hair when Lady Avery burst through the door in a state of agitation, 'Good morning, Angelica dear, I am beside myself! I sent a servant this morning to see to my cuttings and they are all wilting terribly! Madame de Grasse will *never* forgive me if they perish at my hands! I should never have tried to bring

34

them back with us. I should have waited and had a servant follow on with them after they had been properly packed. I am desperate to get them back to Ickworth, and now Lord Avery has decided we are to have a change of plan and we are not going back to Ickworth at all!'

She swooped about the room in her turmoil, toying agitatedly and absent-mindedly with the multitude of diamond and sapphire rings that punctuated her stout fingers. 'The Earl of Greystone has invited us to stay with him at Cranleigh Castle and Lord Avery is determined that we should go, as he has been concluding some business for Lord Greystone in France. This means we will be even later getting to London and making preparations for the Season. I do not know what Lord Avery has in his mind, but he insists that we go—so *go* we must!' Her voice dropped from its crescendo and she began muttering plans to herself. 'That means I must send a servant straight back to Ickworth with my cuttings and I must write out instructions to the head gardener on how to deal with them properly. No time to waste! I must make arrangements!' and she sailed from the room, calling over her shoulder, 'The carriage will be round at ten! Send Sarah to me as soon as she has you packed, Angelica dear!'

'Quickly, Sarah, help me dress and go straight to Lady Avery. She has far more to do than I,' said Angelica as Sarah slipped the last hairpin into place.

Sarah's lace cap was already starting to slide over her left ear and her wiry tangle of brown

35

hair looked in need of hairpins far earlier in the day than usual. Angelica read this as a sure sign that it would be a traumatic morning—and it was.

Due to the sudden change in plans, Mr Slocombe, Lord Avery's agent, hurriedly arranged for a third carriage to take the baggage that would not be needed at Cranleigh Castle back to Ickworth. Normally a wagon would do, but Lady Avery wanted her cuttings to get to Ickworth quickly and she had persuaded her husband to lash-out on the extra expense of a fast vehicle. The baggage—trunks, shoe boxes, dressing-cases, valises, hat-boxes, parasol cases, and bandboxes—had to be sorted out and Emerson was on the verge of being short-tempered with the footmen as he hated these whimsical alterations to his lordship's itinerary. Baggage was shifted from coach to coach until the right pieces were in the right places. Their departure was even further delayed by the elusiveness of a yellow, pigskin document case that Lord Avery had given to Emerson with the strict instructions, 'I will carry the document case in my hand, Emerson. *Do not* permit it to be packed.' But a footman or a hotel servant had scooped it up and bundled it into a coach boot and everything had to be dismantled again until it was found and delivered into Lord Avery's anxious hands.

'Our departure is so late now that we cannot finish the journey today. It is too dangerous to try to make any progress after dark,' bemoaned Lord Avery to her ladyship who was reclining

36

in a chintz chair fending off the vapours with a cup of tisané. His lordship rang for Slocombe and instructed: 'Send a servant by post to find us accommodation at a country inn of good repute and then onward to Cranleigh Castle to express apologies to Lord Greystone. We will be a day late.' Slocombe listened to this, wearing a very downtrodden countenance after the frantic morning, and then shambled off to obey.

Angelica had slipped out of the bustle of activity and had found a quiet corner on a sun-warmed, glazed veranda overlooking the hotel's gardens; she had installed herself in a large wickerwork chair and was contentedly reading a book until Sarah, whom Lady Avery had sent to find her, interrupted her solitude. 'Lady Avery says it's time to go now, m'lady.' A new topic of gossip had already taken over Sarah's fertile imagination. 'There was a murder at this 'ere Cranleigh Castle, and not that long ago neither. One of the footmen told me, and it sounds right spooky, m'lady! I know I shan't sleep a wink! I hope his lordship isn't planning to stay there for long. I don't think my nerves will stand it!' Sarah rotated her eyes heavenward in dismay.

'You must stop listening to gossip!' Angelica laughed as she flew down the stairs to join her aunt and uncle.

When the party was at last in the coach, the coachman and the footmen in their places on the precarious, exterior seats, and the second coach carrying the servants and the baggage was in order, they were finally ready. Mr

Arbuthnot and his troupe of under-managers were standing at attention on the steps. Before he would permit the esteemed guests to depart, Mr Arbuthnot insisted upon oozing a few words extolling Lord Avery's great virtues and his condescension. He could not but mention how fortunate the Grand Hotel was to have his lordship and their ladyships as guests. To all this verbiage Lord Avery muttered, in a disinterested tone, 'Yes, yes...quite! Goodbye!' and they finally made their getaway.

The galloping horses made short work of the journey to The Royal Oak, a coaching inn on the Ashford road and recommended by Mr Arbuthnot. Although the few hours by coach had gone quickly, the departure from Dover had been so protracted and torturous that Lord and Lady Avery were tired. Angelica was remarkably 'hardy,' as her aunt had observed and could have travelled all night without a thought. But she was delighted to stop at the little inn with its rustic, thatched outbuildings, low ceilings, and curious white crosses painted on the stone floor before the hearth—an old precaution continued by some country people to keep the witches from coming down the chimney.

'Good eventide,' the fat, rosy-cheeked inn-keeper said, rubbing his hands on his apron as they stiffly unfurled themselves from the coach. He could not believe his good fortune in capturing such venerable guests. 'I am truly honoured your lordship has chosen my humble inn to honour with his presence.'

'Yes, quite...quite...' muttered Lord Avery in response, finding all these sycophantic utterances dulling to the senses. The innkeeper's face was aglow with pride as they entered his vine-encircled door.

'Emerson, see to everything. We will have an early supper in a private room and retire early,' commanded Lord Avery. The innkeeper was rather put out that his plans for showing off his great prize were curtailed as they were to dine in private and be hidden from the admiring view of his other guests.

Still, their host produced a creditable meal and a well-laid table, although Emerson fussed about, as butlers do, in a disapproving manner, as things were not to the grand standard he always provided for his lordship at Ickworth. However, Lord Avery seemed well-satisfied. 'A fine drop of ale this, landlord!' he said cheerfully, having regained his good humour with the substantial meal.

The landlord puffed himself up for a good boast: 'It is the local brew, m'lud, and a finer ale cannot be found anywhere in England. It is of course the Kentish hops, from right round 'ere, properly managed, that make it such a rare refreshment. And I treat it with respect and make sure the cask is not disturbed for a full fortnight before it is tapped. It makes all the difference, 'deed it does!'

'You have mastered your art well, sir, and I congratulate you!' responded Lord Avery generously as the serving girl refilled his tankard.

Lady Avery was not enjoying herself. She

forlornly waved away the mutton, the blood-red roast beef, the rabbit pie, and the plump partridge, saying, 'I really couldn't eat a thing,' Looking slightly greenish, she continued, 'I am still feeling the effects of the crossing,' and dabbing the beads of moisture from her upper lip with a corner of her handkerchief, she implored Emerson, 'Just have them bring me some clear soup and a drop of cordial, I couldn't possibly face anything else.'

Of the three, only Angelica was not thinking about food. She was absorbed in memories. Not since her parents had been forced to move into a tiny cottage near the family's defunct estate, in an attempt to 'live on nothing a year,' had Angelica stayed in such informal surroundings. She was thoroughly enjoying it and found it restful and appealing after living in the opulent wake of Lord and Lady Avery. 'It is very pleasant here, Aunt Clarissa. It must be wonderful in summer when the garden is in bloom. I love the simplicity of the uncluttered wooden furniture, and the unbleached muslin drapes. They create such a...homey atmosphere.' And she looked around admiringly at the frugally decorated room.

Lady Avery gave her a pregnant look and said with unusual severity, 'Don't you go getting any girlish ideas about retiring to some country idle to be a milkmaid. Marie Antoinette could play those games, but she was a queen. You haven't been letting your French cousins fill your head with any silly ideas, I hope!'

Angelica had to laugh tolerantly at this

outburst, as it was so unlike her aunt. 'Aunt Clarissa, you know me better than that. I know where my duty lies. You know I am not foolish and I would never do anything to disappoint you and Lord Avery.'

'Oh, I am sorry, my dear,' said her aunt, softening, 'I am not myself tonight—too much rocking about on that ship, and far too much bouncing about in that coach...' She had to stop her vivid description of undulating motion as it was making her giddy again. Patting Angelica's hand, she said, 'Don't pay any attention to me. I know you are dutiful, with a proper head on your shoulders, and let that be an end to it.'

When the meal was over and Lord Avery had consumed as much ale as he dared—under his wife's watchful eye—they retired to their bedrooms.

Lady Avery returned from her dressing-room prepared for bed, her plaited hair under her nightcap. 'You know, Avery,' (her ladyship always called her husband by his surname when she was feeling well-disposed towards him) 'I was very cross this morning about this sudden change of plan you threw at me at the last minute. But now that I've had time to reflect upon it properly, it might serve as an opportunity for Angelica.'

Lord and Lady Avery did not always see eye to eye on important issues, which was of no great import to his lordship, as he prided himself on being the master of his own house. However, on the few occasions when his wife praised his decisions, he was ready to congratulate himself on his wisdom and natural talent as a diplomatist, as on this occasion: 'I am glad to hear you say that, Clarissa, because, although that was not my original intention in seeing Greystone, it will certainly do the girl's chances no harm. Greystone is someone she will meet during the Season anyway, and a fine catch, if I do say so, for any fortunate girl.'

'Are you absolutely positive that Lord Greystone has not set his cap at anyone?' inquired her ladyship eagerly.

'Absolutely no doubt,' said Lord Avery emphatically, as he tied the neck laces of his voluminous night shirt. 'Greystone's totally unaligned. I know it! Bewick is a close confidant of Greystone's, and he told me over backgammon on the ship.' The ale had left Lord Avery filled with such self-admiration that even the memory of his lost seventy guineas could not dispel his good humour. 'Greystone has been too busy sorting out affairs at Cranleigh to even think of marriage. But he will have to get a move on. He may be a Duke soon, and guaranteeing the succession will start to weigh upon his mind.' Lord Avery fixed his wife with a canny twinkle. 'I would say he is ripe to be picked.'

'We shall see,' Lady Avery said doubtfully. 'Angelica hasn't a sou, I need not tell you that, and although you will settle a generous dowry upon her, it may not make her attractive enough for someone as well placed in the world as Lord Greystone. However, Angelica has a very appealing and honest nature and she, I

42

am sure, will make herself pleasant enough to Lord Greystone, and if he does not think she will suit it will be no fault of hers.' Lady Avery, too, was in a self-congratulatory mood. 'I think it is not out of place to do myself the honour of saying that the Prince of Wales himself will not find Angelica wanting in any of the social graces. Nor do I think I go too far in saying that His Royal Highness could not find better qualities in any prospective consort than Angelica possesses. If the rumours are not true that the Queen has already contracted him in marriage to a foreign princess, Angelica's success in that quarter would not unduly surprise me. I may compliment myself that I have done rather well at seeing that that poor orphaned girl has learned to conduct herself with the bearing of a lady of breeding, especially in the light of the amount of time she has spent with those rowdy French cousins of hers.' Lady Avery huffed her shoulders up in despair as she said, 'All Count Chénier's children riding about the countryside like a...like a band of gypsies!' Her voice rose in distaste.

'They are very high-spirited, that is for certain, but Chénier is really very strict with them and would never permit his children to overstep the mark. He rather enjoys seeing that great brood of his larking about.' His lordship occupied himself by having a luxurious scratch and a stretch.

Her ladyship sniffed: 'Well, although I have nothing but admiration for Count Chénier, I am quite convinced that the French have no idea of how to bring up children. I can only say that it is a blessing that Angelica has turned out as well as she has, despite some of the influences she has come under.'

Settling himself into bed Lord Avery said through a yawn, 'We were far too old to take on that little sproggett when her mother died, and you said so yourself at the time, but goodness knows what sort of life Angelica would have had if her impetuous parents had lived. They were too proud to take any kind of charity, so who's to say what would have become of the child. One really cannot afford to be proud where money is concerned...' He yawned broadly again, and then gave a little shake like a damp dog. 'It was very lonely for her at Ickworth with no other children. It was just as well that Chénier was willing to take her for great long spells. Surely you remember how you used to let out a sigh of relief whenever she would go off. It meant you could stop fretting about whether or not the governess was going to insist on taking up your mornings discussing curriculum when you were hoping to get back to supervising the digging of your ornamental lake.' His argument was very convincing now, as he desperately wanted his sleep.

Lady Avery was bound to agree that her garden was the paramount thing in her life and replied, 'I suppose you are right. We really had no other course of action. I will stop complaining. Good night, Avery,' she said, but his lordship was already snoring tunefully.

THREE

Angelica had been asleep for about an hour when something made her stir. The thin and fleeting dream images drifted away and evaporated as she surfaced from a comforting sleep; her mind swayed for a few seconds in unworried confusion as she wondered where she was. She let her eyes roam the unfamiliar room with its plain whitewashed walls and then she realized she was in the little bedroom at the coaching inn. What had awakened her? She vaguely wondered if she had heard a noise. Still more asleep than awake, she again raised her sleep-heavy lids to take in the surrounding darkness which was sliced into by a column of moonlight casting crisscross designs onto the counterpane.

After a moment, she became aware of a dark shadow in the room. She blinked again to try to resolve the image. What was it? A trick of the light? As she peered into the darkness beyond the moonlight, she tried to bring into focus an elusive shape. Suddenly she became fully awake with a jolt. Her heart leapt and the noise of it surging in her ears blanked out all other sounds. Her sharp intake of breath was the prelude to a scream, but it died instantly when the shadow reached out and gently placed the tips of two fingers on her lips, and said softly, 'Please don't make a sound. You are perfectly safe.'

As the figure leaned forward, towards her, the shaft of moonlight crossed his face and she knew his eyes, dark, sad, and kind. They were the eyes of the stranger on the ship.

Her terror died instantly and it was replaced by a inexplicable calm, and this phenomenon poured more confusion into her whirling brain. How could one moment her heart be bounding with fear and then, at that second of meeting the gaze of those kind eyes, have all fear replaced by utter stillness? Before any of this could assemble itself into organized thought, he spoke to her.

'Forgive this intrusion,' he whispered, still leaning over her, 'but I slipped in the first open window I came to, and I am sorry to have frightened you.'

Angelica, eyes large with bewilderment, stared up at him and then the frantic sound of men running in the courtyard below shot up through the window. A man's voice was shouting: 'Don't let him escape! Search everywhere!'

The stranger slowly took a step back from the bed, his face and dark cloak again hidden by the shadows, but his voice, low and reassuring, drifted to her. He said, 'I am afraid my journey has been temporarily interrupted. I am sorry to impose upon your hospitality like this.' He might have been conversing in a smart drawing-room, murmuring only to avoid disturbing the thin raspings of a small, string ensemble.

Forgetting for an instant the unconventional aspects of their téte-â-téte, Angelica was seized with curiosity and compassion. She sat up in bed, absently clutching the bedclothes to her throat in an unconscious gesture of modesty, and whispered, 'You're the gentleman who saved the child from drowning last night!'

He leaned towards her a little, and again his face came into the column of light; she could see the grey eyes smiling at her with a puzzled expression. 'How do you know that? Were you on the ship as well?'

Her voice was hushed. 'Yes, and everyone wanted to thank you, but you disappeared before anyone could speak to you.' Again hearing the heavy footsteps of the men, this time stamping about somewhere below in the public rooms, she asked urgently. 'Why are these men after you?' She gave a fearful tremble; she knew instinctively that the enemy was not this man before her, but the men below, and they were getting closer. Doors were banging somewhere nearby. 'Who are you?' she asked.

He hesitated slightly. 'I am called...Gitano... and I can only say that I shall be forever in your debt if you do not divulge my presence. The search party is getting closer and I would rather not meet them.'

'What will happen if they find you?' she asked.

He gave a slow, easy shrug. His manner was so relaxed, it was more fitting to a gentleman at a smart soirée than one fleeing in the night, and he answered, 'Well, I am rather afraid they plan to kill me.' At this she gave a little gasp of horror, so he said, 'Dear lady, I am sorry to upset you, but please believe the truth, which is that I am innocent of any crime. However,

I have enemies who would like to see me condemned.'

'I saw you save that child so I know you are not capable of any evil...' Her whisper faded as she heard the men getting closer.

A din of heavy boots and shouts of 'Open up! We're constables!' boomed in the corridor a few feet from Angelica's door. The men were pounding unceremoniously on Lord and Lady Avery's door and the voice of Lady Avery, shrill and angry, cut through the male voices as she emerged from her room hurriedly pulling on a wrap. 'How dare you knock on a lady's door in the middle of the night! No, you may *not* come in! What presumption! I don't care *who* you are!'

'Angelica!' Lady Avery's voice was coming closer as she sailed down the hallway towards Angelica's room. *'Angelica?!'* Her ladyship was now standing just outside the door. 'Angelica dear, can you hear me?! Are you all right?!'

Flinging back the covers, Angelica swung her bare feet onto the cold floor boards and flew to the door. Gitano stood motionless as he watched her dart away like a startled bird, a flurry of nightgown and golden tresses as she flitted through the moonlight. Was she about to give him away? Cry for help! He made no move. Angelica was at the door now and breathlessly called through it, 'Y-yes, Aunt Clarissa! I—I was awakened by the noise.'

'Are you all right, my dear?' demanded her aunt.

'Yes! Perfectly.' Angela turned and Gitano

48

was now standing next to her, looking down at her with a grateful and amused grin. Angelica leaned her back against the door and he stood over her, bracing one hand against the door above her head in case the men decided to force it, and as they waited there, so close together, separated only by a few inches, she could feel the warmth pouring off his body, filling the tiny gap between them with an intoxicating heat and energy.

Again Lady Avery's voice boomed through the cracks in the wooden door panels. 'My dear, there is nothing to worry about—' the octaves were rising by the syllable, '—it's just some ruffians who will pay dearly for their behaviour! Under *no* circumstances may you open your door to anyone!' With this pronouncement Angelica and Gitano exchanged a silent, laughing glance, sharing the joke and the relief at Lady Avery's decision not to enter Angelica's room.

Lady Avery continued to berate the interlopers. 'And you call yourselves constables? What on earth do you mean by going about at night out of uniform? Tell me that, will you? You look disreputable and a disgrace to the constabulary! What is the meaning of this?'

'We have our orders, ma'am! We're to search every room!' retorted the largest man who seemed to be the leader. 'So if you will permit me, ma'am...'

He made the mistake of trying to push past Lady Avery to get to Angelica's door, which only resulted in sending her ladyship's glass-cutting tone even higher. 'Take your hands off me, you cad! And take *that!'* and she struck him a sharp blow on his already bulbous nose with Lord Avery's gold topped cane, which she had been holding at her side all the while. 'Now be *off* with you, and let God-fearing people get their sleep!'

Admitting momentary defeat, the men moved off down the corridor, their leader cradling his damaged nose in a ragged handkerchief. Lady Avery wandered back to her own room, muttering something to the effect that Lord Avery could sleep through a battle. The men descended the stairs and their heavy footfalls could no longer be heard.

Even now that the danger had momentarily passed, Angelica and Gitano remained where they were, sharing that same tiny space by the door, with no inclination to move apart. She stood with downturned eyes, her golden hair spilling to her waist. She looked tiny as she stood barefoot on the chilly floorboards, the many intricate folds of her long, virginal-white bedgown enveloping all but her delicate, tapering hands and feet. She reminded him of an angel in a Renaissance painting as her shimmering hair and heart-shaped face caught the moonbeam that played on the wall. He was struck by her beauty and serene manner which almost made him wonder if she could really be of this world.

She could feel his eyes upon her and could not account for her own self-possession in that impossible situation. Her sheltered and often lonely upbringing had little prepared her for the everyday terrors of social etiquette; but she now found herself standing in a dark room in her bedgown in the middle of the night with a complete stranger, and she felt no fear.

When the men had moved further out of earshot, Gitano spoke her name quietly, 'Angelica,' and it sounded softly musical in his mouth. He brought his face down to hers to whisper in her ear. 'So that is what you are called. You are indeed an angel for not giving me away. You must be my guardian angel.' She could feel his warm breath on her cheek and it tickled her ear in a way she had never experienced.

She raised a finger to her lips. 'There is still danger. We should be silent.' As she spoke, she caught the naked fragrance of his skin and it sent a tremor through her. They were so near; nothing shielded her but the mere gauze of her bedgown, and yet he made no attempt to touch her. But even if he had slid his strong arms around her tiny waist, then and there, and had drawn her into the source of that heat, he could not have held her more firmly than she was being held at this very moment by his presence. Her young body ached with natural but restrained longings. Again his face was next to hers, and again his curving lips were there, inches away, about to whisper something into her ear. Trying to control her maddening urge to taste a kiss from those softly serious lips, and trying to shake off the power of the compelling desire his closeness was engendering in her, she gave a little shudder.

51

Thinking this was a sign that she was cold, he scooped up her cloak, which was lying across a chair, and he draped it round her, taking great care not to so much as even brush her shoulder with his hand. He brought his lips to her ear again, and again she could feel his breath brush her cheek, the sensation as potent as any embrace. He said, 'If you will allow me to stay a moment longer...I must wait for a signal.' By way of answer, Angelica nodded. If she was near swooning with the headiness of his proximity, it was taking every ounce of Gitano's forbearance not to scoop this delightfully unexpected and unpredictable nymph into his arms. Her translucent bedgown swept down and round her breasts and thighs, nestling into the contours, hiding so little and suggesting so much. If Angelica could have seen beyond his supposedly calm appearance, she would have realized that the booming pulse she could feel and hear was not just her own, but was shared by the night, condensed and distilled in that minute space they occupied as they waited for the danger to ebb.

They remained silently looking at one another; the only sound was their soft, rhythmic breathing. In the half-light of the room, she studied him. He was tall, and perhaps six or seven years older than herself. His shoulders were broad, and his face remarkably handsome. And there were those eyes that embodied so much kindness. When he smiled, a small straight scar became visible on his left cheek.

As she looked into his face, a different sort of

flame flickered within Angelica. Taking it for the first spark of infatuation she abruptly dowsed it with common sense. How absurd you are, her sensible self scolded, to lose even one heartbeat over a penniless fugitive even if he is obviously a gentleman and charming! The little fire was instantly smothered—or so she believed.

So unpracticed were the workings of her heart, a process took place without her knowing it. This light whirlwind that passed through her went quite unrecognized as the first symptom of love. She had forsworn love so often she believed she was totally immune to it and all its strains of infection. All this passed by Angelica unheeded.

As the old inn fell into a sleepy silence, Angelica again dared whisper and again he brought his face down to hers to catch her elusive words. 'I think I understand now...' her voice was so steady that it made her wonder at her own composure, '...when you were on the ship you were travelling incognito to prevent anyone from recognizing you. That is why no one saw you on the crossing until we were almost in port. But when the child fell overboard, and you went in to save him, you revealed your identity to an enemy. You endangered your life in more than one way when you dived into the sea, because you knew there was someone on board who would recognize you.'

A look of wonder came over his face. 'How is it possible...?' he began, but checking himself, he said with a lazy smile, 'I see that I am right...you are an angel, and you see and know everything.'

They then stood again gazing at one another in silence for a long moment until the hollow, reedy call of a tawny owl floated through the window and broke the spell.

'That is my signal to depart. Thank you for your kindness. Farewell, dear Angel.' His dark eyes were fixed on her all the time, and Angelica wondered how someone so seemingly good came to have such sadness in his gaze. He took her hand, or she took his, she was not sure which because that touch seemed the most natural thing in the world. Their hands just seemed to come together in the dark; slowly he raised her fingers to his lips and she felt a sharp stab of agonized delight, and then he was gone—a shadow crossing the window sill.

For a few seconds Angelica stood, still wrapped in their shared warmth, not quite sure if she was awake or if she had been dreaming. The encounter had happened so quickly she felt it might have been her imagination. Then she felt a slight chill akin to loneliness and loss. Rushing to the window, she looked into the unyielding darkness and listened for any sound that might confirm the truth of what had happened. The tawny owl hooted again, then she could hear the faint sound of horses' hooves cantering away into the distance on dew-damp grass. It had all been real. He was real. Trying to recapture the elusive sensation, she put her fingers to her cheek hoping to rekindle the fire of the fleeting brush of his lips, and for a second it was as if he was there again, enclosing her in a phantom embrace. Still wrapped in the thrill of the encounter, she went to her bed, and when sleep finally returned she was cloistered with her dreams which were new and delightfully disturbing.

The next morning Angelica was already dressed when Lady Avery came to her room. 'I don't think I slept for a moment,' her ladyship announced and, since she was short and round, her tired eyes made her look a bit like a sleepy creature emerging after a long hibernation. 'I have convinced Lord Avery to send a letter to the Chief Constable to complain about last night's unforgivable intrusion,' she said, stifling a yawn. 'Did you sleep at all...?'

'I slept quite well, thank you, Aunt Clarissa, but I did have a...very curious...dream, after I was awakened by the noise. But I feel quite rested now.' Angelica realized that there was no point in telling her aunt of the nocturnal visitor. As it would only upset and alarm her ladyship, Angelica remained silent on the subject. Fortunately for her own peace of mind, Angelica was far too naive for it to occur to her that the night's encounter might be construed as scandalous.

She found herself thinking through everything that had taken place the night before, and although the experience had awakened something new in her, the memory of it was vague and elusive like a dream. If she had not seen the stranger on the ship she might have been willing to just consider the night's occurrence as

55

a trick of her mind. And his name—Gitano—it was familiar to her somehow but she did not know why.

'Angelica, you are *already* dressed!' declared Lady Avery with astonishment, as if she had not been standing before her for a full five minutes. 'I remember what I came to say—forgive me—I'm all at sixes and sevens this morning and I cannot concentrate—I mean to say, I think that dress you are wearing is starting to look a bit worn. You had better wear your brown silk—I want you to look presentable when we arrive at Cranleigh. And don't put on your bonnet, your 'pork pie' is much nicer. I'll send Sarah to help you change.'

Returning to her husband, Lady Avery reported, 'Angelica seems no worse for wear after last night's disruptions—which is more than I can say for myself. My nerves are in a frightful state. However, it must be disconcerting for a young girl to awaken in the middle of the night in an unfamiliar place with all that rumpus going on. Really, Avery, this is the last time I shall ever venture to a low place like this!'

Lord Avery, upon awakening from his night's rest, had been enraged to hear that her ladyship had spent the night fending off a raggle-taggle band of country constables stalking a criminal. By mutual, unspoken consent, to maintain marital equilibrium, a veil was drawn over his lordship's ale-induced state which had rendered him totally oblivious to the events of the previous night. To help deflect from this topic, his lordship flew into a fury about their host's lack of security and, still in his nightclothes, he sent for the hapless landlord.

Lord Avery's face became puce as he gave the landlord a severe dressing-down, the gold tassel of his nightcap bouncing about as if punctuating his words. His lordship's eyes looked ready to pop right out of their sockets, and Lady Avery bade him calm himself. He vented his spleen by giving the quaking and profusely apologetic landlord a lecture about allowing such goings-on under his roof. So chastened by Lord Avery's bombast, the landlord had retreated from the irate guest's bedchamber muttering something about not requiring payment for the rooms—only the board. Lord Avery latched on to these softly spoken words like a magnet scooping up iron filings and he told the landlord *that* arrangement would go a *small* way to repairing the damage.

This tight-fisted attitude of Lord Avery's explains why he was so rich; he was careful with his money; apart from a little gambling or a flutter on the horses, he guarded every farthing with care. Therefore, although a tiny sum by his standards, he was delighted that they would be saving the cost of their night's accommodation.

After the landlord departed, Lord Avery turned to his wife and said, 'This is a very uncivilized part of the world!' Removing his nightcap and running his fingers through his thinning, grey hair, he observed scornfully, 'It is a veritable nest of smugglers and worse! But really, I had not the slightest idea their

57

constabulary was in such a shocking state! Totally devoid of manners and not even in uniform, you say? *Most* irregular! Bring back the militia, I say, at least they had military discipline. Some of these county forces have only been established for a few years.' His lordship massaged his temples, hoping that the effect of the ale would soon wear off. He added, 'We are fortunate that we live up in Essex, as our policing has been much longer established.'

'But you will write to the Chief Constable to complain, won't you?' encouraged Lady Avery. 'It is really up to people in positions of responsibility to make these shortcomings known. *Noblesse oblige,* my dear Avery.'

'Yes, yes, of course,' his lordship responded, and putting his words into action, he rang for Emerson knowing that the sooner he got the letter off the sooner Lady Avery would leave him in peace. Emerson appeared and obeyed his lordship's offer to bring his writing case.

Lord Avery was so alert to his duty that he did not even bother to dress before beginning to compose the missive. He scratched away laboriously with his pen for a short time under Lady Avery's approving eye. Then, moistening the nib on his tongue and glancing up at his wife, he asked, 'How many "Rs" in garötté...?'

In the meantime, Sarah was helping Angelica change into the brown silk and chatting away in a state of high nervous excitement. She had never had such prime gossip to contend with at one time. 'Those men what came last night! What a noise! I thought I'd die of fright all alone in that attic! At Ickworth I usually sleep with Violet, the housemaid, but I was frightened something awful on my own. I just hid under the covers. I didn't know what was going on! This morning, Mr Emerson said they battered on all the doors downstairs and went into all the rooms where the footmen were sleeping. They even tried to get into Mr Emerson's room, but he said he saw them off! If they had come up to the attic where I was I don't know what I would have done! I could hear Lady Avery giving them a good telling-off and I felt better after that, but I still didn't know what had happened until this morning. I lay awake all night quaking and praying for dawn. I've never been that frightened in my life. Mr Emerson says that the landlord is not at all sure they was constables, but they looked terribly mean and he didn't dare enquire too close. He took fright. They said they was looking for somebody, but I don't believe it myself. There's talk that they was bandits come to rob his lordship. Were *you* frightened, m'lady?'

Angelica could not help smiling a little to herself at this but she had no intention of sharing her secret with Sarah or anyone else. Neither secretive nor dishonest by nature, Angelica was surprised to hear herself say in very believable tones, 'I did wake and it was frightening, but, as far as I know, they did not go into anyone's room near me.' Then she slid her elegant arms into the brown silk bodice that Sarah was holding for her; Angelica had been a coltish child but had grown to be slim and willowy, moving with a natural unstudied grace.

Fastening the multitude of hooks and eyes at the back of the bodice with nimble fingers, Sarah huffed and puffed with discontent and said, 'I don't know if my nerves will stand it after last night, and now we are going to this 'ere castle where there was this *murder!*' She went on to arrange Angelica's hair; to her credit, Sarah could rattle off gossip at a great rate and still make an excellent job of dressing hair all at the same time, and she adjusted the brown velvet hat on Angelica's intricate coiffure. 'The landlord 'ere knows all about the murder at the castle and I think that Mr Emerson does, too, but he was pretending he didn't. I'm not sure why. Maybe to get the landlord to tell him more. But all I do know is that I am not going to sleep a wink at this 'ere castle place and what if there is a ghost and I bet it will be cold and draughty and I'll be miserable!' Sarah wailed and almost swallowed one of the hairpins she was holding between her teeth.

Angelica started to wonder if there was some truth in what Sarah was saying and thought she might ask Lady Avery about it. 'You must calm down, Sarah, you are just tired after losing sleep last night and after all the travelling. I am sure that Cranleigh will be perfectly agreeable and you must trust that Lord Avery would never ask Lady Avery or myself to go anywhere unpleasant. Please rest assured you will be perfectly all right.'

Seeing the sense in this, Sarah relaxed a little,

but not so much that she could not enjoy the *frisson* brought on by a good scare. Turning her attention to her handiwork, she looked at Angelica's reflection in the mirror and said, 'There! That looks lovely, m'lady. You do look like a beautiful picture in that hat.'

'Thank you, Sarah, I hope I will do,' answered Angelica in a tone that lacked confidence because she was completely unaware of her own beauty and never thought about it. However, at that moment, there was someone who was thinking about her heart-shaped face and sparkling blue eyes. He was wondering how all that golden hair would look lit by a warming summer sun; he was wondering, because he had only seen Angelica once, and that was by moonlight.

FOUR

Fortunately the departure from the Royal Oak was a much simpler matter than the departure from the Grand Hotel in Dover. Emerson completed all the arrangements, the packing went without any hitches and, much to everyone's relief, the landlord alone bade them farewell. Directing a shower of bows and waves and good wishes at his departing guests, he kept bending at his ample waist like a clockwork toy until the coach was out of sight.

Returning a sober little wave to the landlord

as the coach pulled away, Lord Avery said out of the corner of his mouth, 'All this bowing and scraping sometimes makes me feel like a potentate on a pilgrimage.' Lady Avery covered her mouth with her gloved hand and gave a remarkably girlish giggle, 'Tee-tee-tee,' and then scolded, 'Really, Avery, you must not make me laugh at your nonsense! We have a position to keep up, and if you do not remember your duties then it all falls to me.'

Lord Avery's coach was roomy, but even in its comparative comfort it was almost impossible for two ladies to sit side by side with the current fashion for crinolines. The skirts, over their extensive hoops, rose up at the back and telescoped out to the sides, taking up an inordinate amount of space. For comfort and equanimity Lord Avery sat next to his wife and permitted himself to be partly submerged by her copious skirts while Angelica sat across from them.

After a few moments on the road, Lady Avery fixed Angelica with an enquiring stare and asked, 'Do you know anything of the history of Cranleigh Castle?'

'Nothing, Aunt Clarissa. I have never heard of it before and I only know that you said the Earl of Greystone lives there,' replied Angelica.

'I thought you might have heard some servants' gossip about it, and I did not want you to have the wrong impression of the place. It has a very complicated background and you had better know the whole strange tale, as you will only hear an inaccurate version from the servants—although I know you don't listen to below-stairs tittle-tattle.' Her ladyship absently gave her bonnet ribbons a little plumping up with her gloved hand.

'The Earl of Greystone's family estate is actually Crowood,' continued Lady Avery. 'It is a fairish estate which marches on Cranleigh, on the west side I believe. Cranleigh Castle and Cranleigh Estate is, in fact, the seat of the Dukes of Stanforth who have lived at Cranleigh since the time of William the Conqueror. Lord Greystone is the first cousin of the last Duke of Stanforth. About eighteen months ago the most terrible tragedy struck. The Duke of Stanforth was brutally murdered right at Cranleigh. It was such a terrible business. The young Duke, Edward, was gentle and well-loved. He had always been very wise and even as a boy he was never unruly like most children but rather studious and serious. He was unlike his younger brother Lord Anthony who was two years younger than Edward and had developed into a gadabout-town. Young Lord Anthony did a lot of larking about and got into many a scrape. But, in contrast, the young Duke devoted all his time to running Cranleigh estate which he loved. A bit like you, Avery,' she said, patting her husband's hand, but he was dozing intently and didn't respond.

'Yes—as I was saying,' she returned to her story, 'the young, murdered Duke was a model to us all. He was quite young when the old Duke died and he succeeded to the title. No one thought such a young man could cope with such vast responsibility but Edward seemed to manage beautifully. His mother, the Dowager Duchess, who died a few years ago, once told Lady Saddleworth how delighted she was with the way Edward had taken on his duties and that the old Duke would have been proud of his son. The young Duke was thrifty, thoughtful, kind to the servants and the estate workers. If anyone on the estate was ill he would always see that food and clothing were sent down from the castle. He always sent a doctor and would take it upon himself to pay the doctor's fees.'

Angelica listened in intrigued silence. Never before had her aunt confided such a remarkable story to her and this was the first time Angelica had been exposed to such a tale in real life. She had never been to the theatre but she had come across such events in books—books that Lady Avery would have disapproved of; books that would make her ladyship shudder if she knew Angelica had read them; books like *Jane Eyre.*

Lady Avery, like a fancy moulded jelly swaying slightly with the movement of the coach, continued, 'The young Duke was clever with his running of the estate and his kindness always got the best from the workers.' Lady Avery chatted on. 'The estate thrived, and his horses and cattle were renowned as the best for many a county. He was an absolute paragon. His younger brother, Lord Anthony, however, was more interested in spending his days horse racing and going about in Society. He was very worldly and as far as anyone could see he had not found a vocation for himself as younger sons are meant to do. Oh, they say he did not always have an evil nature, but he spent his days in pursuits quite opposite to his brother's—and he fell into bad company. The prodigal son, if you like. They even say he had gambling debts that the young Duke cheerfully covered for him. In fact, some people say that the Duke encouraged his brother's wild and fancy-free ways because he liked to see him enjoying the freedom that comes with not being saddled with an estate and all that it entails.'

Lord Avery nodded out of his slumber. 'Really, my dear, if anyone could hear you rattle on like that, they might accuse you of being a gossip.'

'Come now, Avery,' continued her ladyship, 'you must confess that absolutely every word I say is true! In any case it is important for Angelica to know these things, as we will be guests at Cranleigh for some days. She cannot be kept in the dark.'

'True, true,' responded Lord Avery without much conviction and, lapsing again into a light doze, his head nodded forward onto his chins and he snored softly as if humming a repetitive tune.

'Because of the seeming closeness of the two brothers,' Lady Avery went on, 'it makes the story almost too sad to relate. As I said, about eighteen months ago the young Duke was brutally murdered. It was during a shooting party he was giving at Cranleigh Castle. As I understand, the Duke and his guests were about to sit down to a beautifully prepared luncheon somewhere in the castle parkland and a message arrived for the Duke saying that some urgent matter was in need of his attention. So the Duke excused himself and returned to the castle. Shortly afterwards servants in the castle heard a pistol shot and they rushed to the Duke's study and there he lay dead! Standing near the Duke's body was his brother, Lord Anthony, and at his feet, the pistol with which he had *killed* his brother!'

'Oh, what a sad tale!' cried Angelica, her kind heart moved, 'but why would anyone kill such a fond brother?'

'*Greed,* dreadful as it may sound, it was simple greed!' Lady Avery sighed for the whole of humanity's failings. 'Lord Anthony killed his own brother to steal the family jewels, a fortune in themselves. He fled with the jewels as soon as he was discovered. Perhaps there was a falling-out over a gambling debt or some other wrangle over money. No one will ever know the truth of that aspect of things.

'There has not been a trace of Lord Anthony from that day to this. He simply *vanished!* It is said that he fled to the Americas or that he is dead. The detestable thing is that with his brother's death, the title of the Duke of Stanforth passes to him, but of course being a common murderer, if he is still alive, he will never enjoy the title. Ever since that ill-fated day, Lord Greystone, as the nearest relation, has been heroic in his efforts to keep his dead cousin's estate and house in running order. He has spent week upon week at Cranleigh managing the estate, sometimes to the detriment of his own estate, Crowood.'

Lord Avery, feeling rested from his sleep, now took an interest. 'You do have to admire the fellow, you know! Greystone, albeit the first cousin, will inherit Cranleigh eventually—but until a court proves that Lord Anthony is a murderer and he is executed for his crime, or until he is dead from any cause, Cranleigh is in a state of limbo. So it is very good of Greystone to spend such a great deal of time keeping Cranleigh in good fettle.'

'What happens if Lord Anthony is never found?' enquired Angelica.

'That is the rum part of it for Greystone,' continued his lordship. 'If the younger brother is never found, under the law he can be declared officially dead after seven years. That means Greystone could stand to have a seven-year wait until he can officially take over Cranleigh and the title. I think it is hard on Greystone, who has done so much in the memory of his murdered cousin.'

'You will like Lord Greystone, Angelica,' said Lady Avery brightly. 'He is extremely distinguished and decidedly entertaining. He is always enquiring about my garden at Ickworth.'

Their journey continued in a lazy silence induced by the swaying of the coach. As Lord Avery had not been convinced that the railways were more than just a fad that would disappear after the initial flutter of interest, he had directed his coach builder to produce a large and substantial road coach ideally tailored to long journeys. It allowed his lordship and his guests to travel in excellent comfort in all weathers. Lady Avery, however, felt that the coach was a little too...well fitted-out to be quite *nice* and, when all the seats on top were occupied by servants and baggage, the only thing that distinguished them from the *hoi polloi* of the Edinburgh public coach was the distinctive periwinkle paintwork and his lordship's coat of arms on the doors. She kept her own counsel on this, not wanting in any way to denigrate the design of the coach, much of which was his lordship's own inspiration. All the same, she found a way of arranging matters so that she might travel in elegance as well as comfort.

After the coach had been in Lord Avery's possession for only a short time, Lady Avery had said, 'Avery, my dear, I really do feel it is unfair to ask the household servants to ride on top in all weathers. Emerson is dreadfully inclined to catch a chill, and we simply could not afford for him to be ill. We would be in hard straits without a butler. Just think! The household would be in a state of total disarray. And Sarah—if Sarah was ill her father would never forgive me, and he is my *best* gardener and if *he* were out of sorts think how my dear sweet garden would suffer! So you see, my love, it really is such a *good* investment to have a second coach follow with the servants and the baggage.' And so happiness abounded. Lord Avery gained a reputation for benevolence towards his servants by assuring that they travelled in comfort; Lady Avery was transported in style in a coach uncluttered save for the requisite liveried coachman and footmen, and the household servants retained their health and escaped windblown, ruddy complexions.

A short halt at a post-house for a change of horses and for her ladyship to refresh herself with a hurried cup of tea was the only real interruption in their journey. The post-house kitchen had run out of milk for her ladyship's tea and, unseen by the travellers, the kitchen maid was dispatched in a great rush, feet flying and pitcher in hand, to the stables to coax a little milk from the perplexed cow who wisely knew it was not her proper milking time. However, with bovine equanimity, she chewed her cud and graciously presented the kitchen maid with enough of the bubbly warm liquid to meet the emergency. Whenever Lady Avery travelled, which was far too frequently for her liking, she was in the habit of sniffing at the milk jug to make sure it had not gone off. It was a wise and dreadful habit, and she had once forgotten herself and sniffed at Countess Chénier's silver creamer when she and Lord Avery were guests at their château. The look on the countess's face, as she watched this sinful lapse in good manners, could have slain a battalion of Wellington's army. But in this case, at the little posting house, Lady Avery's insistence upon sniffing the milk resulted only in gladness as she complimented the landlord's wife upon the freshness of the milk. The ladies then rejoined Lord Avery who had chosen to spend a few moments ruminating with his pipe over a glass of stout in the tap room.

The coachman, having obtained detailed directions from the job-master at the posting house, was confident of finding Cranleigh Castle. Good directions were essential as signposts were sorely lacking in spite of the busy roads. The new team of horses were of a high quality: a showy, matched bay four-in-hand, always insisted upon by Lord Avery whenever he had to make an appearance anywhere. As Cranleigh was one of the most elegant houses in England, he did not want there to be anything shabby about their entrance into the great courtyard.

Their progress was swift and nothing could overtake them, with the exception of the mail coach which had right of way over all other traffic. Lord Avery's coachman slowed and pulled his team towards the side of the road while the racing mail coach flashed past in a red blur and a shower of dust. 'We've been caught napping!' cried Angelica as she sprang forward and pulled up the window against the gritty clouds rolling in. 'The air had been so nice up until this moment. I wonder why we didn't hear the mail guard's horn behind us? Aren't they bound to give fair warning that they are about to overtake?' she asked her uncle.

'The wind must be before us,' Lord Avery said, coughing at the dust. 'The noise of those "yards of tin" can be swept away by the slightest breeze.'

'Oh, Angelica! Look at your dress! It's covered in dust!' Lady Avery moaned in dismay. 'Nothing shows the dust like chocolate silk, and just look at it! Let me try to dust you off with my handkerchief—' but, failing to reach across the expanse of their skirts, she passed the square of lace to Angelica. 'Oh, here, you'll have to try for yourself.'

Angelica flicked disinterestedly at herself with her ladyship's hanky. 'It doesn't matter, Aunt Clarissa, I can change as soon as we get to Cranleigh.'

'I know, but I especially want you to look nice when we arrive.' Lady Avery simpered out a sweet smile.

Angelica glanced quizzically up at her aunt. Something in her ladyship's tone gave Angelica the impression that her aunt's simple statement was ponderously heavy with meaning.

'Now, why are we slowing down?' Lord Avery grumbled as the coach came nearly to a stop on the open highway. He banged sharply with his cane on the roof for the coachman's attention. Hearing Lord Avery rap, a footman dropped from his perch above the boot. In a couple of long, bounding strides alongside the moving coach, he managed to slip between the lethal, spinning wheels and, catching hold of one of the lamp brackets, swung himself onto the small foot plate below the coach door. With this, his face suddenly appeared at the window and Lord Avery lowered it to speak to the footman. 'Why have we slowed down again? What is it *this* time—not another mail coach?'

'No, m'lud, there is a caravan of gypsy wagons moving very slow, going in the same direction. There's only about a dozen of 'em, yer lordship, but there are so many horses and goats wandering in the road they're blocking the way. The coachman is trying to overtake as best he can,' said the footman, giving a remarkable rendering of a bow despite his precarious perch.

Lord Avery, still feeling jaded after the previous evening's excesses, was losing his patience and snapped, 'Well—tell him to make short work of it!'

Lord Avery's coach moved slowly forward until the exotic, trundling caterpillar of caravans and wagons was alongside taking up more than its fair share of public thoroughfare. 'Aren't the caravans beautifully decorated!' cried Angelica. 'We saw an immensely long line of gypsy caravans crossing France from Spain last year when I was staying with Count Chénier. It is marvellous how their slow steady progress seems, in the end, as effective as all the speed in the world.' She didn't say aloud what she was thinking: how she envied their total freedom to come and go as they pleased. 'Someone must go to a great deal of trouble painting all the flowers and designs on the caravans. Look at that green one, Aunt Clarissa! It is just like a little cottage on wheels with latticed windows at the back, and shutters!' Angelica laughed delightedly. Her aunt only snorted in disinterest. Undeterred by the slight elevation of Lady Avery's nose, Angelica continued excitedly. 'I've never had such a close look before. You can even see that they have chimneys, so there must be some sort of grate inside...no, that would be impossible, a stove perhaps? And at the front where the driver sits—it is like a canopy or a veranda, to keep off the weather, I suppose. They are rather clever, don't you think?' She glanced at her aunt, who was looking out the opposite window seemingly fascinated by a landscape empty but for a flock of crows. Getting no response, Angelica wondered aloud. 'But I would love to know why they have the bow tops, and they seem covered in a heavy green fabric?'

'I am told,' said Lord Avery, taking pleasure in rendering some knowledge, 'that the green bow roofs are fashioned in that way to help the caravans blend in with hedgerows and woodland enabling the travellers to camp undetected. It would allow them to encroach on a landowner's property without being noticeable. Rather sly, I'd call it,' and he raised a fluffy, grey eyebrow to emphasize his disapproval.

'They do look charming, all the same. I would love to peek inside one to see how they are arranged,' said Angelica.

His lordship speculated in a careless moment: 'You will go to the Derby this year as part of the Season and they have gypsies there telling fortunes. Perhaps you will have an opportunity there to see inside one.'

'Well! *Really,* Avery!' choked her ladyship, giving him a piercing look. 'Have you gone quite mad! I do wonder sometimes! It is bad enough that Angelica should show an interest in such low things as...as those people! But you actually *encourage* her! It really is too bad. I will

73

have no more of it!' She turned to Angelica and snuffled while dabbing at invisible tears with her handkerchief. 'You do worry me sometimes, Angelica, really you do!'

'Please, please, Aunt Clarissa, I won't say another word,' implored Angelica. 'I'm sorry I upset you...I was only trying to make the journey pass more quickly with my harmless prattle. I meant nothing by it. You know what a goose I can be sometimes.' Lady Avery seemed placated and Lord Avery took his scolding like a man and retreated into slumber.

Angelica continued to look out of the oval window at the caravans which were clattering steadily along. Some of the goats had bells suspended from wide leather neck straps. The ringing of the bells mixed with the clinking of swaying pots and pans, suspended here and there by bits of frayed rope, and it all gave the procession a shambolic musical accompaniment. The gypsies' horses were varied. Some were sad, bony-looking things with scrub manes and tails, others, large sleek steeds, were obviously their owner's pride and joy.

Frolicking children with unwashed faces tried clinging to the side of the coach for an instant until the footmen saw them off by threatening to box their ears. The children then turned somersaults and raced alongside showing off their agility. Angelica wanted to throw them a few coins in return for their performance, but knowing that Lady Avery would get into a tizzy, she refrained. Strong-featured women, wearing multicoloured skirts and shawls, were

74

either sitting next to the powerfully built men who were driving the caravans, or peering out through the small windows. The gypsies watched the passing coach. From every weathered face stared suspicious, almond-shaped eyes; they looked sidelong and unblinking at the passing capsule of elegance, and Angelica was too fascinated to do anything but return their stares unabashed. The coach finally overtook the little parade and sped on its way again.

The approach to Cranleigh Castle was through a high stone arch surmounted by the Stanforth family crest carved in stone; the ornate black and gold iron gates were opened by the keeper who had been at his dinner when he was alerted by the coaching horn and clatter of hooves. He emerged from the gate house at a run with a large napkin still tucked under his chin. Although he had forgotten to remove his bib he had remembered to snatch his hat from the hook behind the door and doffed it repeatedly as he laboriously heaved, grunted and finally swung aside the heavy gates.

Following the long curving drive that meandered through beautiful parkland, the coachman walked the horses. Lord Avery had issued instructions that the horses were to be spared on the last leg of their journey to insure that they would have energy enough to be whipped up into a showy and spirted arrival at the castle door.

This slower pace gave Angelica time to admire the ancient trees and giant, gnarled rhododendrons. The sound of the coach disturbed a large herd of deer. Rising up from their resting-place, they trotted off into an endless sweep of green landscape. A massive stag with a crown of antlers stood his ground and watched the intruders until the rest of the herd had moved to a safe distance. The drive ascended and ran along the crest of a wide ridge for what seemed like miles. They could see through an opening in the trees a lake where a small, domed Grecian temple was reflected in the water, which was broken into slow ripples by a flotilla of Tufted Ducks as wild-eyed and cocky as naughty, little boys swaggering off to do mischief.

At last, Cranleigh Castle came into view on a rise ahead of them. It was the most magnificent house Angelica had ever seen. It was no longer the fortress which had been built on the site during the reign of Henry I: it had been rebuilt in about 1700 by Sir John Vanbrugh, the architect. As the coach approached the final gentle curving slope, the coachman whipped the team into a flashy trot. As the coach followed the curving lane, Angelica could see ahead a second set of high black and gold gates which at that moment were being swung wide by two liveried servants. These gates opened into a vast cobblestone courtyard which was enclosed by the house on three sides. Angelica thought, as she looked about in wonder, that the courtyard was large enough to accommodate a hundred carriages. The coach flashed through the gates onto the cobblestones with a great show and clatter just as three arrogant peacocks strutted unmindfully across the path of the flying hooves; too haughty to ruffle their feathers in an unseemly show of flight, they escaped unhurt only by inches.

'Here at last!' Lady Avery said thankfully, her hands fussing at her bonnet. 'I must look a wreck but I am pleased to say, Angelica, my dear, you look as fresh as ever. You will make a good impression on Lord Greystone.'

Looking sympathetically at her uncle, Angelica was thinking it must be doubly difficult for someone of his years and suffering from gout, to put up with the rigours of coaching. Lord Avery sat in his corner, crumpled and boneless, like a rag doll that had lost most of its stuffing during the journey. 'I do hope Greystone hasn't a whole posse of people here. I really don't think I want to sing for my supper quite yet. All this travellin' about has made a mince of me,' complained Lord Avery. 'I've sat here so long I wonder if my legs will ever unbend again. Can't wait to stir myself!'

'I know you, Angelica,' said her ladyship, drily, 'if you had your way you'd have us all riding about the countryside for miles on end on horseback.'

'It's true, Aunt Clarissa, I adore it. It is the only way to get about in comfort!'

The Earl of Greystone appeared at the top of the stairs just as the carriage door was opened by the footman. With jocular good humour he came bounding down the steps to greet his guests. Tall, fair, and slim, he was dressed in the height of fashion and had a muscular physique which was flattering to anything he wore. As Lady Avery had been predicting, he looked very distinguished, but with his easy charm and beautiful manners he instantly put his guests at ease. His smile was friendly and welcoming and made him seem younger than his thirty years.

When Angelica was presented to the Earl, he was immediately taken by her beauty. She looked the image of simple modesty in her unfussy dress and uncluttered velvet hat with its single small feather. The shimmering brown fabric showed off her blonde hair and delicate complexion to their best advantage. The Earl was attractive and appeared agreeable in all ways and Angelica immediately took pleasure in his company. She politely returned his greeting and dropped a small curtsy as he bowed slightly over her hand. Angelica happily returned his smile and looked into his violet eyes for the first time. Still holding her fingers in his, he felt her shiver slightly so he said:

'Your ladyship must be cold. There is a sharp breeze from the east today. Do please come in and get warm by the fire.'

Angelica thanked their host and walked up the steps to the entrance with the others, and she was too preoccupied by the magnificent surroundings to wonder what had made her shudder.

Cranleigh Castle was even more beautiful than Angelica had first imagined. It was light, airy, and huge windows looked out on beautiful views in every direction. Rotund cattle grazed just beyond a ha-ha bordering the south lawn;

from the house's elevated position, the new arrivals could see a river and, across the west terrace, the gardens which were full of graceful statues and stone urns. Angelica immediately fell in love with Cranleigh and she experienced the previously unknown sensation that she was somewhere that completely fitted her personality and taste. She laughed at herself for her arrogant whimsy of thinking that, given the opportunity, she would arrange a great house to look exactly like Cranleigh in every detail.

FIVE

After dinner on their first evening, the Earl was entertaining his guests in the yellow drawing-room. 'I will do my best to see that you do not get too bored,' he was saying. 'You will have to forgive me for not getting up a house party, but as I am really only an interloper here at Cranleigh I don't really feel it would be proper if I had a large gathering. Cranleigh does not belong to me, yet. It would be rather unseemly to do any lavish entertaining, don't you think, Lady Avery?' he said, giving her a soulful look.

'You are absolutely right, sir,' confirmed Lady Avery. 'As usual your judgment is impeccable. I am sure the whole world admires what you are doing here at Cranleigh in going to such enormous trouble to preserve your late cousin's estate. We shall be very happy just amusing ourselves—you must not spend a moment of your precious time looking after us! For myself, I shall be happy exploring Cranleigh's many gardens, and Lord Avery can use the imposed rest.' Leaning towards the Earl, she said confidentially, 'Do promise not to let him talk estate business!'

'There will be one distraction for you, if you are of a mind to take advantage of it,' said the Earl, 'My neighbour, Lord Revelstoke, is giving a ball next week, and I do hope you will stay for that. We are expected to spend the night at Revelstoke's and it promises to be a very grand affair.'

Lady Avery's mind raced with the same razor-sharp clarity as that of a calculating merchant haggling over desirable yard goods, weighing up the pros and cons of what was on offer. With the speed of light, her ladyship computed whether or not it was worth delaying their return to Ickworth even longer, and thereby delaying their preparations for the Season, so that they could attend the Revelstoke's ball. Lady Revelstoke (née Beauclerk) was very well-connected, as her sister, the Marchioness of Droitwich, was a lady-in-waiting to the Queen. Yes! *Decidedly, yes!* Lady Avery concluded; it might be altogether a good thing for Angelica to have friends in that quarter, and she answered instantly as if there had never been any bargaining going on in her mind. 'There you are, Angelica!' trilled Lady Avery ecstatically, '...your first ball! *Of course* we will stay, Lord Greystone! *How delightful!*'

'I wish there was more to entertain you, Lady Angelica,' said the Earl, turning his full attention to her.

'I am sure it will be impossible to be bored in this wonderful house,' she replied earnestly. 'I shall enjoy having time to read. I saw the library before dinner. It looks extensive and I understand Cranleigh has a famed collection of paintings. That will interest me enormously.'

'Good heavens, Greystone!' interjected Lord Avery with wine-enhanced humour, 'haven't you any horses about the place? That's what Angelica would really like to know, I'll wager. Don't you know you have as a guest one of the most accomplished equestrians in England? All she needs to keep her occupied for hours is a horse that has the stamina of an ox. Anything weaker and she'll ride it into the ground,' and he laughed in his usual hardy and unfortunate manner which sounded like an attack of whooping cough, *'Whoop-whoop-whoop!'*

'Stop it at once, Avery!' chided her ladyship, laughing with mock gaiety in an attempt to hide her real disapproval. 'I absolutely forbid you to go about telling people that our dear, little Angelica is some sort of...of Amazon,' and simpering at the Earl she confessed, 'It is true that Angelica loves riding and she is *very* accomplished.'

'That is good news,' said the Earl, turning to Angelica with one of his infallible smiles. 'There is a stable full of my late cousin's exceptional horses, and not a soul to ride them. I'm far

81

too busy running both this and my own estate to find a moment for recreation. I will give you a tour of the stables myself tomorrow and you must ride any horse that takes your fancy.'

Delighted at the prospect of a day riding, Angelica turned to the Earl and said, 'That is kind of you, Lord Greystone, but please don't trouble yourself on my account. I am very grateful for your offer, but I am quite happy to wander about the stables on my own as you are kind enough to let me ride one of the horses.'

'It will be my pleasure to accompany you, if you will allow me, Lady Angelica,' said the Earl, settling the matter.

When Angelica retired to bed, she sat reading for a short time, and then she put out the lamp and began to slide below the covers, but something made her sit very still for a moment and listen. Her eyes soon became adjusted to the dark, and she could see that the moonlight, which was being shut out by the thick drapes, was peeking through a small chink where Sarah had not drawn the heavy fabric together properly. Angelica thought she could hear the call of a tawny owl, so, without relighting the lamp, she rose and made her way to the nearest window, drew open the curtains, and let the moonlight pour in. She opened the window and leaned on the sill as the fragrant, cool air tumbled in around her. Below, the parkland swept into the distance and the giant old oaks cast long and deep moon shadows. She thought she saw something move next to one of the trees, and guessed it was a deer settling itself for sleep. The tawny owl hooted out its mournful cry again, and she hurriedly scanned the monochrome scene trying to detect where the call was coming from, but she could not see its hiding place. Then she remembered why the tawny owl held so much fascination for her. The night before, it had been the signal calling Gitano away from her.

She remained, leaning on the window ledge, scanning the night, waiting...waiting... Suddenly, fully aware of what she was doing, she stepped back from the open window, snapped the drapes shut, and berated herself for wasting time even thinking about the gentlemanly fugitive. She refused to let herself become ensnared by a pointless infatuation. Silently scolding herself for her futile romanticism, she returned to bed and fell into a restless sleep.

Across the moonlight, and through the open window, a dark and friendly shadow visited her as she slept, but this time she was not surprised to see him. His kiss drew the breath from her and his touch was as gentle as she had expected. He was whispering in her ear, so softly that his words were tiny vapours which were so elusive she strained to catch them. He folded her in a firm embrace and kissed her again, more deeply than before, then let her down on the bed again and turned to go. She opened her eyes and put her hand up to touch his cheek, and the shadow was right there before her, but the room was empty. He had been only a dream. Racked by a sad ache, she turned her face to the pillow and willed herself back to the dream world.

The following day, as promised, the Earl escorted Angelica to the stables which were in a grove of trees off to one side near the front of the castle. The architect had planned it in that way as the trees would hide the stable buildings and thereby keep the view of the house uncluttered by outbuildings.

The sun was making an effort to appear through the sullen grey spring sky; its rays were slanting sulkily through the stable windows. With a little more effort from the elements, it would turn into a fine morning. The grooms had recently been wielding their besom brooms over the stone floor and the dust hung in the air capturing the light. Now the grooms worked quietly around the horses and doffed their caps respectfully as Angelica and the Earl passed along the corridors of stalls.

Walking up to a box stall, the Earl said, 'Here is a nice little chestnut mare that has been ridden side-saddle before and is reputed to be very gentle.'

'She looks...very pretty,' responded Angelica, trying to hide her lack of enthusiasm as she was thinking the mare was virtually a pony and rather smaller than the horses she was used to.

Wandering slowly down the long corridor, they chatted in a desultory way while glancing from side to side at the beautifully turned out horses which were standing with their heads lolling over the open tops of the stable doors.

They came to a stall which seemed empty. As unexpected as a lightning bolt on a clear day, the peace was suddenly shattered. A terrifying scream cut through them as a huge black horse suddenly crashed against the stall door and flew at them with teeth bared and eyes rolling back, showing only the whites. With an ear-splitting scream, it lunged for the Earl and just caught the shoulder of his coat, instantly reducing the seam to tatters. The Earl responded by lashing it furiously across the face with his whip.

'Back, you devil!' shouted the Earl, cracking the whip violently, but the horse was like a creature possessed. It battered against the heavy door which barely restrained it, first crashing against it with its massive chest, straining to catch the Earl again in its jaws, and then swinging around to kick the door until it seemed ready to explode into a thousand splinters. The whole building shook with the horse's crazed frenzy.

The Earl's face was twisted into an angry snarl, and with his whip he struck out again and again at the horse. Angelica had fallen back in terror at the horse's first assault, but now the sight of the Earl lashing out at the horse made her feel ill. She could not bear to see any horse whipped and was about to cry out for the Earl to stop when he turned away and shouted for a groom.

'Binstead! Come here!' the Earl raged fiercely as the alarmed head groom came running towards him. 'Haven't I told you dozens of times to keep this monster properly locked up!

That beast is going to kill somebody one of these days.'

Binstead, a strong, stocky man, slammed shut the top half of the stable door and threw the iron bolt. 'I-I'm sorry, m'lord!' he stammered, looking shaken, 'I didn't know yer lordship was coming to the stables or I would'a locked him up proper like!'

Looking at Angelica and seeing that she had grown pale, the Earl, in a kindly voice, said, 'I'm sorry you had to see that, Lady Angelica—a very frightening experience for you. The beast is completely mad! No one can ride it and it is a danger to anyone who comes near it. I really should have it destroyed. I can see this has upset you.'

'Well, I must confess it came as a shock,' breathed Angelica truthfully; and she had been shocked, not by the horse's attack, but by the Earl's striking out at it so savagely with his whip. Her mind suddenly went back to that moment of their first meeting when she had looked into his eyes and had been shaken by a little shudder. Was there some connection? Had she somehow sensed this violent streak in the Earl?

His rage had vanished as suddenly as it had come and he was again all pleasantries and concern for her comfort. 'Would you like to sit down for a moment?' he enquired gently and then, with a sharp edge to his tone, he called to the groom and demanded, 'Binstead! Bring a chair immediately!'

'No, no, please,' Angelica protested, 'you are very kind, but I am perfectly all right. I was just...surprised. That's all.'

A discreet cough made them all look round. Hibbard, the Earl's servant, had arrived during all the commotion and had been standing silently and unnoticed until this moment. This was how Hibbard always appeared. No one ever heard him coming or knew how long he had been eavesdropping on a conversation. Angelica was to imagine on several occasions that it was as if he was spying. He was a string-bean of a fellow who dressed far too grandly for his position as the Earl's major-domo. The cut of his coat was a measure too sharp, the cloth too expensive; his batisté shirt cuffs, fastened with gold buttons, were far too elegant; his cravat, of the finest weave, was flawlessly folded and fastened with a stick pin that glittered like a real topaz. Hibbard lorded it over all the other servants except for Park, the elderly butler, whom he seemed to avoid. 'I am sorry to interrupt, m'lud,' Hibbard said, 'but there is an urgent matter which may require your lordship's attention at the castle.'

'What is it that cannot wait, Hibbard?' the Earl demanded sharply.

'Your lordship required me to tell you when your emissary to the Americas arrived. I have asked him to wait in the library.' Hibbard's delivery of these words was accompanied by his irritating habit of lowering his eyelids when speaking. His eyes closed slowly like window blinds being unfolded and he punctuated everything he said with a small, crooked, sycophantic smile.

87

'Please forgive me, Lady Angelica,' said the Earl apologetically. 'This is a very pressing matter, and I am afraid I must attend to it. May I walk you back to the house?'

'I have taken too much of your time already, Lord Greystone. If you don't mind, I should like to continue to look around the stables and perhaps ride,' she answered.

'Whatever you wish, Lady Angelica. You may have the pick of the horses and take out anything that catches your eye,' said the Earl. Then, turning briskly to Binstead, he ordered, 'See that her ladyship is given every assistance and saddle whatever horse her ladyship wishes to ride.' The Earl offered Angelica an apologetic little bow and strode off, with Hibbard following a few deferential steps behind.

'What is wrong with this horse?' Angelica asked Binstead quietly as they both strolled back to where the black horse was locked up. It was pacing back and forth in its stall, sweating and breathing heavily.

'There ain't really nothing wrong with that horse, yer ladyship, 'cept he sometimes don't like certain people. He just 'bout tolerates me to feed him and brush him but that's 'bout all. I'm the only one who can ever get near. All the stable lads are frightened to get close,' Binstead cautiously reopened the top half of the stall door. The horse's coat shimmered like the richest black satin and now, more subdued, he put his head over the door and looked warily at Angelica.

'He is very beautiful,' she said, certain that he

was not mad at all, and she produced an apple from the pocket of her riding habit. Approaching the horse slowly, with an outstretched hand, she offered him the tempting red fruit. The horse seemed cautiously interested. Still keeping his distance, he sniffed keenly at the apple and, after a moment's indecision, snatched it up and devoured it gladly. Angelica moved closer, talking softly all the time. She slowly raised her hand and tried to stroke his neck, but he flinched sharply away.

Standing perfectly still, she talked to the horse in a calm voice. She slowly reached out to stroke his neck, and this time he stood still; she could feel his nerves tremble violently under her gentle touch as he watched her suspiciously every instant. After some minutes he permitted her to stroke his face and eventually his ears. Angelica knew that horses love to have their ears pulled very gently, especially to warm them in the cold. As she did this the huge horse lowered his head submissively. Angelica stood patiently for ten minutes speaking reassuringly in a soft voice, until the horse shut his eyes as if asleep.

Binstead watched dumbfounded and said in a hushed, disbelieving tone. 'Well...I'll swear! Oh! Beggin' yer pardon, m'lady! That's the first time I've seen that great fellow nod off like that. He's acting just like a pet tabby. There's no doubt, that horse likes yer ladyship.'

'What's he called?' whispered Angelica as she continued to run her hand through the silky mane.

'He's got a whole string of fancy thoroughbred names, but Lord Anthony—'cause it was his horse—called him Prospero.'

'What a perfect name,' said Angelica, stroking the horse's head. 'Shakespeare's sorcerer. He does look as if he has special powers. Did you say Prospero belonged to Lord Anthony? Wasn't that the Duke's brother? The one who...' she hesitated and didn't finish the sentence.

'Yes, m'lady, Lord Anthony, the Duke's brother. It's a tragic business,' Binstead shook his head sadly, 'but you never can tell with people. They're just like horses. You never can tell what they'll do. It's hard to believe Lord Anthony could kill his own brother...but there it is. Park, the butler, saw it happen. Them lads was that close as boys, too. I'd never seen brothers what got on so well together. Maybe that was the trouble. Maybe Lord Anthony got confused about what was his and what was his brother's. As yer ladyship knows, younger brothers inherit nothing—maybe Lord Anthony didn't like it. It wouldn't be the first time somebody killed for money. But it still rankles with me something awful. If anybody told me Lord Anthony could kill his brother I'd called him a liar. But there you are. You never can tell. People are just like horses. One day they're fine and the next day something snaps and you got a mad or bad one on your hands.' Binstead gave a forlorn shrug, stared at the floor and then, as his thoughts drifted inward, he murmured to himself in a disparaging whisper, 'Nope...you never can tell...' Angelica watched sympathetically as he relived some private sorrow.

He stood for a moment lost in thought. Then, more to himself, he laughed quietly but looked up at Angelica and said. 'You never saw a happier lad than Lord Anthony the day he first rode this 'ere horse. He had him as a foal, he did. He was with this 'ere horse every hour of every day. And now since he's disappeared there's been no one who can ride Prospero. Won't let a soul near to ride him. Kicks like a wild thing, he does, if anyone gets near him with a saddle.'

'What a shame,' said Angelica quietly. 'It can't be doing Prospero any good not getting out for a gallop.' After a thoughtful pause her face brightened and she announced, 'Binstead, I am going to try riding him. He seems to like me—I *must* try.'

Alarmed, Binstead protested, 'Please, yer ladyship, there ain't been nobody on that horse for a long time! It's dangerous to try! In any case, Lord Anthony was the *only* person whatever rid' that horse!'

'I am determined to try. Please bring me a side-saddle and a bridle,' she said firmly.

'His lordship, the Earl...may not like it and if something happens I'll be in for the jump, m'lady,' said Binstead, pleading for his own hide.

'Don't worry, if anything goes wrong I will tell Lord Greystone it was all my fault. I will tell him I ordered you to let me ride Prospero. You have my word.'

Binstead, a practical man, thought to himself: her ladyship's sentiments might be in the right place, but what if the girl breaks her neck? She won't be around to make any explanations to the Earl or anyone else! He asked himself pointedly: And then what would I do for a job and a home? I'd be out on my ear! But that was not the sort of thing a groom could say to an aristocratic lady without getting a sharp reply, like an iced, 'How *dare* you be insolent!'—or worse. What Binstead did not know was, if he had said such a thing to Angelica she would have fixed him with an honest look and replied, 'You are right, of course, Binstead, but if I *do* break my silly neck you'll have the satisfaction of knowing I got a good comeuppance!' and they would have both laughed. Unaware that in her presence he could have spoken his mind, he simply protested politely, 'This 'ere horse never been rid' side-saddle, neither, m'lady.'

'I understand that, but he'll learn quickly,' she retorted, smiling faintly at his countless protests.

Binstead, finally realizing that she would not take 'No' for an answer, started to warm to the idea or, in truth, the sportsman in him smiled on the idea. 'It would be a fine thing to see this grand horse under saddle again. But I'm worried—with respect, m'lady—that he might be too strong for yer ladyship. Bound to be a bit too fresh not being rid' in so long!'

'I know you are perfectly right, Binstead, but I am settled on taking the chance. There isn't another horse in the world as beautiful as this, and I want to try. Besides if the horse is exercised properly it will calm him down.' This was the real key to Angelica's desire to ride the horse; she was horrified by the Earl's comment about having the horse destroyed and it occurred to her that if ridden regularly the horse would become more tractable and therefore eliminate any reason for it to be put down. Brushing aside all further protests, she said resolutely, 'Now please—fetch me a saddle.'

Binstead obeyed and was surprised that, albeit after a long, nerve-racking spell of coercing Prospero, he accepted the saddle and bridle, and Angelica led the nervously prancing, sweating horse from the stable. Binstead, feeling he had to make some effort to help, offered to hold the horse's head while she mounted.

'Maybe it's better if you don't. I don't want him to think we are trying to bully him.' Angelica walked Prospero up to the mounting block where, to her surprise, he stood perfectly still. He was trembling with controlled energy, but he made no effort to rear up or lash out. Binstead, standing at a respectful distance, was conscious that he might have to lunge forward and attempt to grab the bridle if the horse bolted. Angelica walked up the steps of the mounting block, speaking softly all the time, and slid into the saddle in one easy movement. Waves of nerves rippled across the powerful horse's back as he contained his excitement and the strangeness of being under saddle again. Angelica firmly encouraged him to walk forward.

Binstead had been joined by a little group of eager spectators. Word had spread quickly amongst the stable lads that some foolhardy soul was attempting to ride the most notorious horse in the county; their jaws dropped with astonishment when they saw that the misguided person was hardly more than a slip of a girl. They grinned knowingly, elbowing each other in the ribs, as they watched; it was quite obvious that Prospero was totally unused to having a side-saddle on his back. His ears twitched in all directions. Neck arched, feet dancing nervously, he flew off to the right like a startled crab. He was finding the side-saddle confusing as he was unused to having most of the rider's weight on the left. He didn't understand what he was supposed to do, and trotted in place like a steel spring winding up. Angelica urged him on with her weight and gave him the occasional light tap with her left heel.

'There is going to be an almighty explosion any minute now!' smirked one of the grooms; the little group watched and waited expectantly for the unpredictable horse to bolt or rear or, in any event, deposit his passenger very roughly on the ground. 'Somebody's in for a fall,' gibed another lad.

'I ain't so sure...' disagreed Binstead with a mischievous glint in his eye, remembering how the horse had responded to Angelica a few minutes earlier in the stable. As Binstead's grandfather had been an Irish horse-tamer, he had grown up hearing tales of near-magical relationships between people and horses. He was convinced that he was now witnessing just such a thing.

'Don't suppose you'd be interested in a small wager?' challenged one of the cocky grooms.

'Aye! Yer on, laddie!' said Binstead with the bravado of a gambling man, and a flutter of bets went round the impromptu gathering. The odds were heavily weighted against Angelica and in favour of the horse at 2-to-1 on.

Angelica was now guiding Prospero in a large circle and she knew exactly what was going on in the horse's head. Ever since she was a child she had been told that the only dangerous horses are the clever ones. She had learned that most horses have no idea of their own strength, otherwise humans would never have been able to tame wild horses in the first place. Prospero, most decidedly, was clever and potentially deadly to anyone he did not like. He was the one in charge and was only letting Angelica have her way, and Angelica understood this.

The great horse had his head down, blowing heavily from quivering nostrils, his ears well back, every muscle ridged with building tension. Angelica was trying to coax him to bring his head up because she knew what could happen when a horse drops his head. Gently but deliberately she moved the reins to work the bit in his mouth but he was determined to keep his head low. Then came the explosion everyone, including Angelica, had been waiting for. With his head tucked into his powerful chest, the horse leaped into the air with three quick bucks.

Angelica astonished herself by staying with him and she thanked Providence for the adhesive qualities of a side-saddle, which she counted as the sole advantage that ladies held over gentlemen. A lesser rider might have panicked; the bucks, although rough, were not vicious and were not intended to part company with a capable passenger. Angelica just laughed and patted Prospero on the neck, saying, 'Full of the joys of spring, old fellow? You're glad to be out for a change!' With that, an understanding was well and truly established and the pair—the huge horse and his slight mistress—happily trotted off towards open pasture.

While the stable lads scratched their heads in disbelief, the delighted Binstead was busy collecting his substantial winnings.

SIX

That evening, during a lull in the dinner conversation, the Earl caught Angelica's eye and said, 'I was sorry I had to desert you at the stables this morning. Did you manage to go riding?'

'Yes, thank you, Lord Greystone, I had a lovely outing. I rode Prospero.'

An almost imperceptible shadow of anger flashed across the Earl's face. Angelica caught it but she was sure it escaped everyone else because he immediately covered it in a broad smile.

96

Hearing her words, Park, the seasoned and usually implacable butler, dropped a silver serving fork which twanged loudly as it ricocheted off the stave of Lord Avery's chair. Lord Avery, who was taking a drink of wine at the time, started at the noise and almost choked, but the Earl was too preoccupied to notice this uncustomary lapse in Park's demeanour or his guest's discomfort.

'That is wonderful news!' said the Earl in his most sincere manner and then turned towards the others. 'I can't tell you, Lord and Lady Avery, what a great favour Lady Angelica has done me! She has been exercising the most difficult horse in the stables.' Then, his face fully composed and friendly, he said, 'Lady Angelica, I owe you an enormous debt of thanks.'

'The pleasure is mine, but I really cannot take any of the credit for getting Prospero under saddle again. He is far too strong-minded to do anything but follow his own whim.' Afraid she had offended her host in some way she did not understand by riding Prospero, and hoping to smooth things over, Angelica began telling a story which, although true, never failed to entertain. 'In fact Prospero was treating me in the same way as a pony that I used to ride as a child. The pony belonged to my father and by the time I was permitted to ride him I was three years old, but the pony was very ancient and cantankerous. He was called Cracker—short for firecracker.

'Cracker was very wilful and would not permit large children on his back. If they climbed on board, he would immediately gallop away and then dig in his "toes" and stop suddenly. The rider, of course, would go flying. But Cracker was kind to me and so in charge that he would not permit me to fall off. My parents got a great surprise one day when they were having tea in the garden, and as I trotted by on Cracker, I started to slip dangerously sideways, he stopped, turned round and, with his nose, pushed me back into the saddle.'

As she finished her story, the Earl, who had been listening entranced, gave a great hoot of appreciative laughter. 'No, Lady Angelica, you are trying to dupe me! I refuse to believe a word of your charming story—marvellous as it may be! Tell me, Avery, that I am being made fun of!'

'Not in the least!' Lord Avery confirmed in jovial protest. 'The phenomenon is absolutely true, and I witnessed it myself on at least one occasion!'

'I have to say, I have not heard a story that has entertained me more, Lady Angelica,' said the Earl, still shaking with laughter, 'and in return I hope you will ride Prospero whenever you like. He is yours while you are at Cranleigh.'

After dinner the Earl pressed Angelica to play the piano. 'This instrument has a lovely tone, and I do hope you will favour us with a piece, Lady Angelica,' and bestowing a fetching smile upon Lady Avery he said, 'I ordered that the piano should be tuned in honour of your visit, Lady Avery, as I know how you enjoy being surrounded by music.' Angelica played well and it was obvious that the Earl was impressed. Even if she had not played with great ability, she looked stunning and it would have been entertainment enough for the Earl just to gaze at her. Dressed in her simple, beige grosgrain, her only jewellery a small gold locket at her throat, she sat at the rosewood piano. Her face, fresh and slightly flushed from the day out of doors, was illuminated by the candelabrum and she had never looked lovelier. He admired her beauty and grace and it intrigued him how her natural elegance enhanced the rich surroundings of Cranleigh Castle.

The Earl was standing beside her turning the pages of music as her delicate fingers glided across the mellow ivory keys. When Angelica had finished, he warmly congratulated her on her musical ability.

'You flatter me, sir, but I really only play a little. It is quite fortunate for me that fashion frowns upon young ladies who play so well that they might be mistaken for professional pianists. My playing falls well short enough for that to never happen to me.'

The Earl laughed. 'Well, I would not dream of insulting you, Lady Angelica, by insisting that you play brilliantly!'

They both laughed at this and Lady Avery, who was busy with her tatting, looked up approvingly. She was glad that Angelica seemed to be getting on well with the Earl. He was very eligible and when he inherited Cranleigh he would be one of the best-placed men in England. She silently congratulated Lord Avery for this detour to Cranleigh as something fruitful might come of it. Lady Avery was very fond of Angelica with the same absentminded affection she had for the plants in her garden. Like one of her rarest botanical specimens, Angelica had developed beautifully, and Lady Avery was prepared to accept the credit for what she knew would be Angelica's great success at Court and, eventually, a brilliant marriage. On this point Lady Avery was determined.

She often and loudly, voiced the opinion that too many parents listened to romantic notions and nonsense from their marriageable daughters and it always ended in disaster. Witness Angelica's parents. But *her* marriage to Lord Avery had been arranged by her father and they had always been quite content. Everyone said so. She was only eighteen when she married, the same age as Angelica. Although Lady Avery did not love her husband when they married, she had grown to respect him and they lived very amicably.

With all this in mind, her ladyship was closely monitoring every word, gesture, and nuance of every moment Angelica spent in the Earl's company. By now, they had abandoned the piano and were chatting agreeably as they wandered back to rejoin the others by the fire. Lady Avery cocked an ear as she strained to catch the Earl's words, and he was saying:

'Tell me, Lady Angelica, do you enjoy dancing?'

'In truth, sir, I have not done it often enough to know, but I am sure I shall. Although, I enjoy

100

the music so tremendously I am very likely to be listening too intently to it and forget what the steps are.'

'I hope you will save a dance for me on your card at Lord Revelstoke's ball next week.'

'It is extremely good of you to save me from being a total wallflower, as I am sure it will be the only dance I don't find myself sitting out,' confided Angelica with sincerity.

The Earl found Angelica's conversation refreshing. From her, this sort of comment was not the false modesty or the coquettish fishing for compliments that most young ladies indulged in. She was remarkably frank—perhaps a bit too frank—but, he speculated, she was still young and her personality has not been properly moulded.

'You could never be a wallflower, Lady Angelica, I will take it upon myself personally to see to that.' Then indicating a large folio resting on a heavy mahogany table near the fire, he asked, 'May I show you some watercolours by Turner from my late cousin's collection?' Leading her to the large table where the folio lay, he added, 'I had them brought through before dinner as I was hoping you would enjoy seeing them.'

'Oh, yes,' said Angelica enthusiastically, 'I cannot think of anything I'd rather do. I adore Mr Turner's oil paintings, but I have never seen any of his watercolours.'

Seating themselves, they began viewing the two dozen pictures. Angelica looked at the scenes in wonder: castles teetering over the

Rhine, mist-filled Alpine valleys, sunlit views of Piazza San Marco, all rendered by the hand of a genius capable of conveying wit and delicacy. 'I have never seen such beautiful colours. Look at the red in that sky. It is almost as blinding to look at as a real sunset.'

'One wonders if he hasn't gone too far with the colours,' suggested the Earl blandly. 'Surely they cannot be natural.'

'But I want to believe they are real—it allows me to hope that I will see a sunset like that someday. I would love to go to Venice and see for myself—' Angelica tilted the picture this way and that to see it at its best in the lamp light, '—I would love to see these pictures again sometime in daylight, as that is how Turner would have painted them, I presume.'

Taking the next picture from the folio the Earl smiled warmly at her and said, 'I am delighted you are fond of these pictures, and I can assure you that I am at your command to produce them at any moment it is your desire to see them again. I wish it was also in my power to assure you that you will go to Venice someday, but I am sure you will have everything you could possibly wish for in life.'

The Earl and Angelica continued turning over the pictures one at a time commenting on details and technique. On more than one occasion the Earl's hand brushed Angelica's fingers as she reached out to lift a picture. The first time it happened Angelica thought it was an accident. The second and third time she was not so sure.

Before they all retired for the night, Angelica went to select a book from the library for her bedside reading. While scanning the titles of the leather-bound books, her eye fell upon a Spanish dictionary and, almost involuntarily, her hand reached out for it. Then she realized what was at the back of her mind. She took the book to the light of the table lamp and opened the pages until she found what she was looking for. There it was—*Gitano*—that was why it seemed familiar to her; it was the Spanish word for gypsy. Curiosity satisfied, she returned the dictionary to the shelves, selected a novel for light reading, and went up to her room.

She had selected the first of a three volume novel, and unable to sleep, stirred by the excitement and newness of the last twenty-four hours, she sat reading it by lamp light in her room long after the household was asleep. Angelica came to the end of the slim volume and could not make herself go to bed without knowing what was the fate of the hero who had just gone off to the Crusades. Over her bedgown she put on a heavy silk dressing gown and tied it tightly around her, knowing the house would be chill and dark as the downstairs fires would be out at this late hour. Putting another log on the fire to insure her room would be warm on her return, she lit a candle and slipped out of her room into the cool, silent corridor which, after a dozen yards, opened out onto the great marble stairs.

Down the stairs, across the wide icy marble

floor of the vast hallway, she came to the door of the library. The curtains were not drawn here and the moonlight plashed across the thick ornate carpet and wood panelling. Looking up at the bookshelves, trying to recall the exact place where the next volume lay, the toe of her slipper struck something on the floor near the hearth. *It was alive!*—an animal that cried out startled and afraid and scrambled wildly, trying to hide. Angelica, terrified and alarmed, jumped back and dropped her candle, which thudded onto the carpet in a shower of wax, and went out. Both she and the animal let out a squeal of fright, and Angelica found herself standing up on the seat of an upholstered chair where she had somehow, to her own amazement, managed to scramble to safety. If it was a mouse she did not want to be on the floor where it might confuse her sweeping dressing gown skirt for a window drape and think it a hiding place. Her body was prickled with shocks; she pulled the dressing gown around her tightly to try and dispel the chill tremble of fright that shook her, and she sat down on the arm of the chair, her feet still safely off the floor, deep in the seat cushion.

She looked around. *A mouse?* Impossible. It had been too large to be a mouse. Had a squirrel somehow fallen down the chimney, or a fat, waddly badger got in by some wrong turning in a subterranean burrow? The room was again silent and Angelica peered hard into the dark recesses beyond the moonlight trying to see if the creature had gone—*whatever* it was.

From behind another over-stuffed chair, came the face of the creature as he peered cautiously around the upholstery to look at her to see if she was something dangerous. It was the grubby face of a small, thatch-haired boy! He blinked at her and she blinked back, then relieved it had not been a toothy rodent after all, she almost laughed. 'Good heavens...a boy...you gave me such a fright!'

She could see that the frightened look remained in his eyes, which were only made bright by the welling-up of tears. He said in a hoarse whisper, 'I'm sorry, ma'am! I fell asleep polishing the hearth! Please don't tell on me!' Running the sleeve of his thin, tattered jacket across his face he wiped the unmanly tide away, before it spilled out onto his freckled cheeks, he came out from behind the chair and stood limp and round shouldered before her.

'Who are you?' she asked.

'Boots, ma'am.'

Angelica puzzled at the name, smiled to show she meant him no harm and asked, 'Boots? What kind of name is that?'

'I'm the boot-boy here, you see, ma'am—that's why they call me Boots.'

'But you must have a real name?'

He brightened a little and whisked back the fringe of straw-coloured hair with his hand. 'Yes, ma'am—Titus, ma'am.'

'Titus. I like that. It's a wonderful name.'

'Thank you, ma'am.' He allowed himself a cautious smile.

'How old are you?'

'I'm nine, ma'am.'

Now that he stood before her, she could see he was a sturdy, freckle-faced boy, pale and a little too thin for his age.

'Well, Titus, now that we've frightened each other half to death, come and sit down and tell me why you are so naughty as not to be in bed at this hour.'

Titus did not move but stared blankly at her for a second as he wondered at her ignorance. 'I-I was just working, ma'am and I fell asleep. You see—' he knelt by the grate and picked up an oily rag he had been using and gave a fire dog a quick rub with it to demonstrate, '—you see I was polishing the grate and I must'a fell asleep—and my candle went out.' He picked up a crude pewter candle holder from the hearth and looked forlornly at the cold wax puddle that had recently been a candle.

'But why are you working this late? You should have been asleep hours ago?'

'Well, I have to work late, ma'am, 'cause all my jobs are night work like polishing the boots and shoes and polishing the grates and things that can't be done by day.'

'But that's terrible—I shall have a word with Lord Greystone about this.'

Titus's whole body jerked in a spasm of fear and he raised a hand as if fending off a blow. 'No! No—please, ma'am—don't do that! Please don't say nothing to his lordship!'

'But why not?' Angelica was staring at him frightened by his reaction.

' 'Cause his lordship might be angry—think I

was complaining or the like. Please, please don't say nothing, please ma'am!'

His pleading twisted her heart and she slid from her perch to sit on the edge of the chair seat and took one of his oil-stained hands in hers. 'Hush—not another word about it—I'll say nothing—nothing, I promise. A solemn promise! All right?'

'Thank you, ma'am...' Titus looked down, a little embarrassed to have his hand held by a great and beautiful lady who glistened before him in shining silks, and who smiled at him so prettily and kindly.

'Now, Titus, come and sit down and tell me about yourself.' She led him to a small sofa where she sat and urged him to join her.

He was hesitant to sit on the opulent damask fabric. 'I'm afraid I'll get the furniture dirty with my clothes being dirty and all,' and he sank to the floor to sit beside her feet.

'You can't sit there, Titus. You must sit beside me.' And she patted the sofa beside her. He reluctantly and carefully perched on the very edge, careful not to besmirch the fine fabric with his work clothes.

'You told me your name, but I never told you mine—my name is Angelica.'

'I know who you are—I saw you arrive in the big carriage with those plump stiff old people.'

Angelica let out a delighted laugh. 'You mean my aunt and uncle, Lord and Lady Avery!'

'Yes, ma'am.' Titus looked down apologetically. 'Sorry.'

'Don't apologize! You obviously have a talent for summation.'

Titus, not sure if this was good or bad, gave her an apprehensive sideways glance and asked, 'What's that?'

'It means you understand exactly what you see.'

Titus was sure this was a very ordinary thing and said, 'Oh...'

'Have you always lived at Cranleigh?'

'No, ma'am. I was born at Crowood, Lord Greystone's estate, but when his lordship came to live here at Cranleigh he brought some of us servants with him.'

'Do you like Cranleigh?'

His face lit up for the first time and was covered by a large cheeky grin. 'Oh, yes, ma'am. All the servants here are jolly nice and kind—not like Crowood where everyone is mean and ill-tempered. I especially like Cook, and Mrs Banks, the housekeeper. They sometimes let me sleep in in the mornings if I've been very late to bed the night before from working.'

'And what about your parents? They must be here, too?'

The boyish glee gave way to a weary, aged look and he said, 'No, ma'am...my mother died when I was born...' his expression was empty, but then a light came into his eyes, '...they say she was very beautiful and her hair was the colour of strawberries and she was the sweetest person in the whole world—they say she was like a saint.'

Angelica smiled at this, thinking of her own mother. 'And, what about your father?'

Titus's small face became dark and he turned away to face the shadows. 'I don't know who my father was...nobody seems to know...'

'Oh, dear Titus, you're all alone just like me—' She put her arms around him and rested her warm cheek against his sooty face. He was startled at first and then overwhelmed by the warmth and the fragrance of rosewater in her hair, and almost swooned with the headiness of it all. 'We'll be friends always!' Angelica held him tight for a moment.

Titus flushed hot with embarrassed delight and came to his feet. 'Oh, thank you, ma'am! You are the kindest, most beautiful lady in the whole world!'

'Thank you for the lovely compliment—but friends don't have to say pretty things to each other.'

'Oh, but I mean it!'

Angelica cocked her head to one side and smiled at him for a moment. 'It's very late. I suppose I had better go up and you had better go to bed. Let's find my candle.' They searched around the rug for a moment and found it near the hearth. Angelica broke her long candle in two and put half in each candle holder. Titus took down the box of red-phosphorus safety matches from the mantel piece and lit both candles.

He gave her a hesitant look. 'If it's not a cheek to ask, ma'am, why are you down here this late?'

'First of all—as we are friends—you must call me Angelica.'

Titus looked shocked and then amazed as he tried the word on his silent lips. He said shyly. 'I'm a servant—I couldn't go calling you by your name!'

She smiled. 'I'll answer to no other.'

He laughed and tried her name in a small whisper. 'Angelica.'

She smiled, stricken that such a small civility could give him so much pleasure. 'And to answer your question—I came down to find a book.'

Titus became excited and scanned the towering bookshelves in awe. 'Can you really read all these books?'

'Well...most of them I suppose...but not the Latin—my Latin is terrible.'

'What do these books say?'

'Well...many different things. Some are novels —stories...and histories...philosophies...science... some written in different languages like French and Latin...many, many different things...'

Titus looked up at her, listening wide-eyed and enthralled, then he looked down trying to hide a little sheepish grin. 'Can I tell you a secret?'

Angelica sat on a footstool next to him to hear the confidence. 'Of course, friends can share secrets.'

'I'd like to learn to read proper someday—to be able to read about all the things that happened in history. I know my alphabet now and a lot of words and Mr Park, the butler, he's teaching me to read from the Bible.'

'That's wonderful—can I give you some lessons too while I'm here?'

Titus gave a surprised flinch. 'Oh, no, ma'am,—I mean—' again the tiny whisper '—Angelica—that wouldn't do at all—that would get me into awful trouble if anyone thought I was pestering a fine lady to teach me to read!'

'I see what you mean...and I suppose my aunt would scold me as well for forgetting my place...' Angelica's face was troubled. The world was full of so many injustices. 'I don't want to get you into trouble, but when you can read well enough I will send you some books. Would that be all right?'

Titus gasped with such a jolt his freckles almost shook loose. *'Oh, yes!* Thank you! I would treasure them forever!' His face was alight with the thrill of expectation.

Angelica could see by the moonlight that the clock over the mantel said 1.30 a.m. 'Now promise me you will go straight to bed?'

'Yes—' He tried her name again in a tiny voice, afraid to say it boldly, '—Angelica. I promise.'

'Good night then, Titus. I'm glad we're friends.'

Angelica gave him a peck on the cheek, took her candle, and went out the heavy library door, and smiling at him over her shoulder, she said, 'Straight to bed now...promise?'

'I promise!' said Titus watching her go, but he had lied. He had much work to do before he could rest and could not be bound by such a promise, even a promise made to his greatest friend. He went about finishing his chores with a warm throb in his thin chest where his young heart felt childish and hopeful for the first time.

SEVEN

From daybreak the next morning, rain spattered against the windows in waves and the wind whipped across the open parkland. Looking out, Angelica could see only the blurred, distorted image of the garden through the dripping pane. Returning to her chair next to the fire in the library, she continued, in solitude, with her book. She had hoped to go riding, but the rain was too fierce.

After another interval, a faint streak of sunlight falling across the page of her book made her look up. The rain had stopped and the sun had slipped out between the heavy, dark clouds that dominated the sky; it was only a pause in the storm. She was feeling restless after a morning of imposed inactivity and the lull in the rain drew her into the garden. Gratefully she inhaled the fragrance of the wet herbs and juniper that rose up in the fine wisps of curling mist which floated about her as the sun warmed the cool, damp earth. The sunlight bathed the trees in gold against an uncompromising charcoal sky that told Angelica she would not have long before the next shower. As her footsteps crunched softly along the pebble path, water dripped from every leaf and the blackbirds all round her rejoiced loudly at the interlude in the downpour.

She wandered through the beautiful and elaborate gardens where, because it was too early in the year for flowers, the colours were created by ivy, bay, holly, and endless evergreens of every hue and texture. Following an old yew hedge, she found herself at the mouth of the large convoluted maze she had seen from her bedroom window. She glanced about her in response to a sudden feeling that she was being watched; she saw no one but a stooped old gardener in the distance who was filling a wheelbarrow and quite oblivious to her existence. Out of idle curiosity she walked a few feet into the maze, never intending to embark on its tangled pathways. Turning to walk back out of the entrance, she was startled to see the Earl standing before her.

He was dressed in an elegant coat and muted, plaid trousers more suited to town wear. His ensemble was completed by an ebony, silver-topped cane. Smiling and coming towards her, he said, 'Admiring our little puzzle, I see. It was designed by the fifth Duke upon returning from the Grand Tour. He was very taken by the gardens he had seen in northern Italy, with their little tricks, and he immediately ordered this to be planted. It is far larger than the one at Hampton Court. Let me show you the way round it, Lady Angelica.'

'Thank you, Lord Greystone,' she replied lightly, 'but I was not really attempting to go into the maze. I was just taking advantage of the break in the storm to get a little air...'

He raised his eyebrows in twin imploring arches. 'Do let me show you the maze while you are here. It is really very simple and it can be rather entertaining.'

Although she smiled she said more firmly, 'Really, I don't wish to see the maze. Mine was only a momentary show of interest. I know from viewing it from the upstairs windows that it is extremely complicated. I'd much rather stroll by the lake,' she demurred wishing she had never left the path as she could now feel the damp grass soaking through her light calf pumps.

'You will find it extremely witty,' he insisted with an unrelenting smile.

After a few more polite refusals, Angelica's disinclination was overruled by the Earl's equally strong insistence. She finally had to consent, as continued refusal would have been rude. The Earl offered her his arm, and good manners demanded she take it. He led her into the dark corridors of yew and, as they went deeper and deeper into the maze, Angelica lost her bearings. Despite the Earl's bright chatter, she started to experience a nagging, disquieting feeling; the towering, dark, green walls blocked out the sun's hopeful rays and cast the rain-damp passages into an unhappy gloom. An insidious fear began to seize Angelica and she soon felt lost and completely out of control, like an amnesiac awakening into an unknown world, unable to see anything familiar or reassuring. 'Please, Lord Greystone, may we return now? I feel I have seen enough. One path looks quite like another.'

'That's what's so clever about the place, it's confounded confusing. We lost the head gardener in here for three days once, and had to send in a search party with a ball of string.' He laughed loudly at his own joke and then, feigning confusion, he looked about and asked, 'Now...let me see, which way...?'

Angelica tried another, more urgent appeal: 'I would really like to leave now. I find I don't like this place. There is something frightening about it.'

'No need to be frightened, you are in safe hands.' He laughed. 'Look, I shall protect you with this!' and the Earl gave a small twist to the shaft of his cane and drew out a long, menacing silver sword blade which he instantly thrust back into its sheath with the ringing sound of tempered steel. 'Nothing could harm you here.'

Less than reassured, Angelica felt she was being suffocated by an unknown threat; the damp air was oppressive and the high dark walls seemed to close in on her. There were no landmarks, just featureless strips of glowering grey sky above the walls of the impenetrable evergreen prison. The Earl's company was now weighing heavily upon her. Stopping to talk, he insisted upon standing far nearer to her than was absolutely necessary. His advance was slow and sure and they were so close she could feel the chill pouring from his presence. Angelica found herself having to step backwards as casually as she could to create a distance between them. But immediately, damp branches prodding her in the back prevented further retreat.

She felt an icy shiver cross her shoulders as the Earl continued his banter: 'What would happen if we were lost here all night, do you think? We should have the servants lower us a bottle of champagne from a ladder. It would be extremely diverting.'

Angelica's face was now reflecting her mounting alarm, but she did not know that the Earl found irresistible the look of fear pouring from her blue eyes; she had the terrified look of a small, cornered animal. He edged forward again and as she turned to slip away, he playfully raised his cane to cut off her one escape route. She could feel his fusty breath cascading down on her and she hated it. The more her fear and anger rose the more he was drawn by the blush of her lips; his arm encircled her small waist with the touch of some scaly creature and she recoiled at the audacity of his clammy hand pulling her towards him. Suddenly he held her roughly and brought his face close to hers, fully intending to force her into an intimate and unwelcome embrace. To her horror she was suddenly aware that his other hand was probing, exploring the folds of her skirt. She wanted to strike out at him in rage at his presumption. Instead, she twisted free, pushed his cane to one side and darted out of the way. She instantly chose to make a show of ignoring his boorishness, for to

116

remonstrate with him would keep the subject alive and might cause him to make further advances. It would be useless for her to dash away deeper into the maze where she would be equally lost, perhaps with him in pursuit and thinking she was leading him on. She stood her ground. Breathlessly, she said with a strained mask of cheerfulness, 'Perhaps if we go this way—' She did not dare turn round and let him see her face, which she knew must be colouring in her confusion and disdain.

Just at that moment, as if by a miracle, a bent old gardener appeared round a corner. He was very stooped and his battered old hat and jacket were damp with the rain and enveloped his face and twisted form. He was carrying hedge clipping shears and a ladder. Upon seeing the Earl he apologized abjectly, 'Oh, beggin' yer pardon, yer lordship. I didn't know there be anybody about. I'll be off then,' and he turned to go.

Before the Earl could angrily send the servant away, Angelica called hurriedly to the gardener, 'How splendid! A guide! We are quite lost. Do please show us the way out.' The situation was irredeemable. Not only had she refused the Earl's advances, she was now implying that he too was lost, and therefore making him look foolish in front of a servant. The old gardener grunted stoically and, leaning his ladder against the hedge, said, 'This way, ma'am,' and he scuttled before her like a giant spider through the web of green. He was so bent and old that Angelica could not imagine how he could see where he was going, much less find the way, but a few twists and turns later she was relieved to find herself stepping back through the entrance into the safety of the open garden. She had not dared look at the Earl since she had slipped away from him. As they emerged from the maze in silence she imagined she could feel the frost of his anger as he followed her at a distance.

Angelica thanked the old gardener who, without raising his bowed head, touched the brim of his hat and disappeared back into the maze. She did not know what would have happened if he had not come.

The Earl was silent until the gardener had vanished; his face was scarlet with the rage of assassinated passion. Finally he spoke with chilled formality, 'I have some matters to attend to, Lady Angelica, but first may I walk you back to the house?' He spoke through clenched teeth.

'Thank you, sir,' she responded, hoping some naturalness had returned to her tone, 'but I think I will walk in the Italian garden until the rain starts again.'

'As you wish,' he said, and delivering a stiff little bow, he strode away.

Angelica was relieved, an hour later, when the Earl sent apologies to his guests that he would not be taking luncheon with them as some estate business required his urgent attention.

'Did you say you had been in the garden this morning, Angelica?' asked her aunt, who was helping herself to the artichoke bottoms.

'Yes, only briefly,' said Angelica not elaborating,

'and there is something I wanted to ask you, Aunt Clarissa.'

'Yes, my dear, what is it?'

'Would you clip a yew hedge when it was wet?' The question had been on Angelica's mind for some time.

With a slightly mocking laugh, Lady Avery said, 'Of course not, you silly child. Why do you ask? You haven't suddenly taken an interest in gardening, have you?'

Angelica politely waved away a footman who was offering her a dish of assorted relishes, and said, 'No...it's only that I thought I saw an old gardener preparing to clip a hedge during the pause in the storm today.'

'You must have imagined it! You would have to know nothing of gardening to attempt it,' explained Lady Avery. 'It is quite impossible in the wet. First you'd get soaked, as hedges hold water like a giant sponge, and secondly, the shears cannot get a good clean cut in the damp, and you would end up with endless jagged bits. You must have been mistaken,' she concluded as she selected a plump roast quail, larded with bacon, from the silver serving dish held at her elbow by Park, the butler.

'Yes, I must have been mistaken,' repeated Angelica, thinking how odd but fortuitous the old gardener's timely appearance had been.

'I am much relieved, Angelica, to hear that your knowledge of gardening is still nonexistent,' chuckled Lord Avery with the light sarcasm of a man who has been listening to his wife's gardening and landscaping chatter for the last thirty years. 'I do not think I could bear up under the weight of *both* of you discussing greenery. And by the way, dear ladies, if I may be permitted to raise a topic which is not of horticultural nature...I received a reply to my letter, of a few days ago, to the Chief Constable of Kent. I have an excellent letter from Captain Ruxton. He says that *whoever* or *whatever* those men were, who invaded the Royal Oak the night we were there, they were *not* constables. He expresses his thanks in very gracious terms for my extensive report, and promises to look into the matter further. He sounds a capital fellow to have responded this quickly to my letter.' His lordship nodded emphatically, feeling well pleased with himself and seeing no other implications.

'*G-g-good g-g-gracious above!*' stammered and wailed Lady Avery, slamming down her fork with a resounding *twang!* 'That means they were *robbers*, or *smugglers*, or...I cannot bring myself to speculate what else!' Her ladyship's voice trembled. 'A-and to think I hit one of them with your cane, Avery! I could have been murdered! I-I've q-q-quite lost my appetite!' and she fell back in her chair stunned.

Seeing the colour drain from his wife's face, his lordship jumped to his feet and cried, 'Park! Bring her ladyship a brandy, at once!'

'I'll run and get the salts!' offered Angelica, pushing back her chair.

'N-no, just the brandy, I shall be all right in a moment,' gasped her ladyship. '*Really*, Avery! You could have chosen a better moment to

120

tell me I was so close to a violent death!' she groaned, snatching the brandy snifter from Park's silver salver before he could put it before her. She downed it in one gulp.

After a few moments, Lady Avery regained her composure and was able to replenish her drained strength with the help of a few slices of roast beef, some glacé potatoes, broccoli, a Welsh rarebit, a portion of suet pudding with clotted cream, and the tiniest morsel of Stilton cheese.

The rain returned and it persisted into the afternoon. After luncheon Lady Avery went to her room to write letters; and Lord Avery settled comfortably into a chair by the hearth, surrounded by the scaly, fire-emitting nostrils and startling pink eyes of the fantastic serpentine creatures that slithered around the walls as decoration in the Chinese room.

Angelica went to the library and picked up a book which she had left on a side table; turning to the page where she had left off, she settled into a chair and began to read, but her mind would not let her eyes draw in the words. There were thoughts stirring which she was trying to ignore because they were rather unpleasant...on the other hand, her honesty made her admit that perhaps the reason she did not wish to think in this vein was because some of her thoughts were disturbingly pleasant.

The disagreeable side of her musings was how horrid the Earl had been to her in the maze. No man had ever insulted her so rudely before. Indeed, no man had ever tried to kiss her. Her French cousins had stolen kisses, but they were boys and did not count. The Earl had acted in the vilest way, and she dared not think what might have happened, or how far the Earl would have pushed his advances, if that old gardener had not arrived just at that moment. But the pleasant side of her thoughts was taking her back to that old coaching inn, that night at the Royal Oak, when the man called Gitano had entered her room and had stood so closely and intimately with her while she willingly shared his danger. In that space in the dark where they had waited together, feeling the pounding of a conjoined pulse, holding fast to a secret and exchanging soft whispers, Gitano had made no move to take advantage of her complete vulnerability. Instead he had done everything to reassure her and to preserve her trust, and she had found that and everything else about him irresistible...

She shut her eyes for a moment and without even willing it, she was sure she could feel his warm breath on her cheek again as he whispered gently into her ear, and then the recollection was so strong that her fingers tingled where he had kissed them; a delicious shiver passed through her. Startled by the vividness of her imaginings, her eyes blinked open and she scolded herself for letting an encounter with a charming rascal have such a strong effect on her. But, all the same, even if the Earl had not been so beastly towards her, the thoughts of Gitano had been lurking softly somewhere inside her, and now

122

that the contrast between the two men was so immediate, those brief moments in that moonlit room surged up and wrapped her in a delicious warmth. Then, through the closed door behind her, which led to the Earl's study, she could hear his voice as he spoke to his servant. The spell cast by Gitano was broken, and Angelica, wishing to distance herself from the Earl, put down the book and left by the door leading to the hall.

Angelica made her way to the wide, marble staircase that led up to the long gallery. It was here, on the gracefully winding stairs, that a strong sensation visited her. She felt that Cranleigh had a happy aura about it. She was convinced she could feel that the house had once been a joyous place. Even her dislike of the Earl could not diminish Cranleigh's mood of contentment. She looked at the steps of the curving marble stairs and noticed their once-sharp edges worn smooth with years of footsteps. Or, more likely, she thought from her own experience, they had been worn down prematurely by children using large wooden kitchen trays (stolen from the butler's pantry) to sit upon and descend the stairs as if it was a fantastic toboggan run.

Near the top of the stairway was the entrance to the long gallery and she was pleased to find it deserted. She had only briefly glanced in at the gallery before and was glad to have time to study the paintings properly. The Dukes of Stanforth had all been avid art collectors from the earliest times, and the paintings and *objets d'art* amassed at Cranleigh were numerous and varied. As she stepped into the gallery, Angelica immediately saw what she thought were a van Dyck and a Rembrandt. She was pleased, when she approached the pictures, to find that she was correct. Her family had owned a large collection of paintings and these had been the first things to be sold when her parents tried to pay off the family debts.

She remembered that her father had kept, for as long as possible, the less valuable collection of engravings. They showed many famous pictures so, even as a child, her interest in art had been developed as she sat on her father's knee and he turned the pages of the large engravings for her. He would tell her the stories in the pictures and the artists' names. Sadly the engravings eventually had to be sold along with everything else.

Even her own name had artistic connections. After a good deal of family protest, on the basis that it was not suitable for a duke's daughter to have as a namesake a 'mere' artisan, Angelica's parents had named her after Angelica Kauffmann, one of the original Royal Academicians and one of Robert Adam's favourite painters. Kauffmann's own beauty had been captured twice by another great painter, Reynolds. Two of her best pictures had been in Angelica's family home. Both were small circular panels high on a wall in her mother's sitting-room, designed by Adam. Angelica recalled that when she was about three or four, she had often been lifted up by her mother to see the two classical scenes of beautiful, stately women in Roman dress against an Arcadian landscape.

The picture gallery at Cranleigh was very peaceful. The only sounds were Angelica's soft footsteps on the parquet floor and the persistent rain lashing against the windows. She moved slowly from picture to picture, in various moods of excitement stirred by the painted scenes, and she found them totally absorbing.

Eventually she came to a large canvas showing an idyllic scene of a family group. The mother, beautiful with dark eyes, was wearing a rich blue satin dress. She was seated with her chin resting lightly on her hand as she gazed fondly upon her two sons. Angelica decided they had to be her children because they had her lovely eyes. The setting was a fantasy garden bower where perfect roses and garlands of flowers clung to what the artist suggested might be a ruined temple. The elder of the two boys stood resting against a marble column reading a small book. The younger boy was admiring a goldfinch perched on his finger; his other arm was reaching up to the back of a lanky Irish wolfhound that posed with saintly patience.

It was a very attractive picture and Angelica looked to see who the subjects were and who had painted it, but the small plaque that had once been part of the gilt frame was missing, leaving a small patch of bare wood. She tried to judge when the picture had been painted, but, as the figures were wearing Italian costumes, it was impossible to guess. As she studied the picture, she felt that there was something familiar about the little family in the romantic bower, but she could not understand what it was. She was sure she had never seen an etching of the picture before. Angelica was drawn to it; it had a warmth she liked, but she felt there was another element which appealed to her; however, after much thought she could not fathom what it was.

Angelica was still contemplating the picture when a disturbing feeling made her turn round. She gave a startled little cry to find the Earl's servant, Hibbard, standing only a few feet from her.

'Really, Hibbard!' she protested, trying to catch her breath, 'How long have you been standing there? You startled me!'

'I beg your pardon, m'lady,' he murmured, without a trace of apology in his voice, 'but Lord Greystone desired me to find your ladyship and ask if you would join his lordship and Lady Avery in the green drawing-room for tea.' It was quite obvious from his manner that Hibbard felt no repentance for his habit of silently sliding up behind anyone who came within his realm in hopes of giving his victim a good fright.

'Thank you, Hibbard, you may tell his lordship that I will be joining them directly.' Angelica did not try to disguise the chill in her voice. Hibbard smiled his unfriendly, crooked little smile while his eyelids lowered in their irritating way. He made a curt little bow and departed as silently as he had come.

In the green drawing-room, the Earl and Lady Avery were embroiled in an intense conversation, sitting in an almost conspiratorial manner side by side in low chairs near the fire. As Angelica entered their voices died away. The Earl rose and, drawing up a little spoon-back chair, invited her to join them. His bearing betrayed no hint of the events in the maze. Addressing her in the friendliest of manners, he said, 'I have been trying, with very little success, I may tell you, Lady Angelica, to win Lady Avery's support in a little project I have devised. I am hoping, Lady Angelica, that you will be a greater ally to me than your venerable aunt.'

'I shall do my best to assist you, Lord Greystone, but if my aunt is not enthusiastic I would presume she has some solid reason,' Angelica replied affably, trying to keep the dislike she felt out of her voice. 'Lady Avery has very good judgment in all matters and I would trust her taste on any subject.'

'You have already started to side with Lady Avery, and you have not even heard my plea!' chided the Earl in jest. 'I will tell you what I have told Lady Avery, and hope you will receive it better than she. I have been imploring Lady Avery to let me present you with this—' and he held out a small box to her, '—so that you might have something to amuse you, and to wear to Revelstoke's ball next week if it appeals to your taste.'

Angelica's face registered surprise as she hesitantly took the box and opened it. Inside was a dazzling diamond brooch. She was taken aback by the total lack of warning and by the extravagance of the obviously priceless jewels.

'I-I—' she stammered, 'I truly don't know what to say, except...it is very generous of you, Lord Greystone, but I cannot accept it.'

'Of course you cannot, my dear!' announced Lady Avery emphatically, as she presided over the tea pot and poured out a steaming cup for Angelica. 'That is precisely what I have been telling my dear Lord Greystone for the last half hour. It is totally inappropriate for a young lady to receive an expensive gift from a gentleman. The most a young lady can accept would be a posy of flowers or a very trifling little book. And you are very naughty indeed, Lord Greystone, because you know that as well as anyone,' and she playfully cuffed the back of his hand to soften the effect of her words.

Closing the box, Angelica placed it meekly on the arm of the Earl's chair. Her cheeks were burning; feeling badly used by being catapulted against her will into the centre of attention and left completely at a loss to understand what was happening, Angelica chose to retreat into the safety of silence and fixed her eyes on the dizzy arabesque pattern of the oriental carpet which seemed to spin before her.

'Don't scold me, Lady Avery,' cried the Earl in feigned horror, 'I know I am a bad-mannered clod, and I hope Lady Angelica will forgive me, but this little bauble has been languishing for years at my house, Crowood, and it seems such a shame for it not to get an airing.'

Even in her wretchedness, Angelica could not help but admire the Earl's performance. He was acting the injured party with complete confidence. Was it his rather ghastly way of apologizing to her for his behaviour in the maze? Whatever his motive for entrapping her in a second unbearably embarrassing situation in one day, one thing seemed certain: he was confident that she had not mentioned the incident in the maze to Lady Avery. *Or even worse*—thought Angelica with a sinking heart—he presumed that, even if Lady Avery did know, her ladyship was so taken in by his charm that she would let it pass thinking that Angelica—an inexperienced girl—was exaggerating matters.

'What conspiracy is this?' laughed Lord Avery, entering the room and viewing the seemingly tight-knit, little group around the tea table.

Having composed herself, Angelica was attempting to make light of the proceedings. 'It is a conspiracy to stay warm on a very chill afternoon. Come and sit down, Uncle, and we will conspire to give you a cup of tea.' She was hoping that his lordship's arrival would divert the conversation on to other things, but it was not to be.

'Help me, Lord Avery!' pleaded the Earl. 'These heartless ladies are trying to ruin all my enjoyment! They are treating me very badly and not letting me have my own way.'

'What? Are these ladies being bad guests and not joining in on the planned entertainments?' offered Lord Avery, immediately entering into what he took for harmless banter.

The Earl feigned triumph. 'Exactly! What a sagacious fellow you are, dear Avery! I had hoped to give a little gift to Lady Angelica, as to do so would brighten a dull afternoon for me, but Lady Avery has thrown all manner of obstacles in my way!' He popped a sugar wafer into his mouth.

'Surely there can be no harm in this, ladies?' queried Lord Avery in a jocular mood, pulling up a chair to join them.

'Well, if it was a small gift it would not be a matter for discussion, but our dear friend Lord Greystone has asked me if he can present...this brooch...to Angelica, and of course I have said "No," as I know you will.' Lady Avery, with a stubborn expression, passed the box to her husband.

As Lord Avery opened the box, his face became a tumbling kaleidoscope of emotions. At first a look of surprised shock passed over his features, followed by an expression more difficult to define. Lord Avery could see in an instant that the brooch was no mere trinket. It was fabulously valuable and it was not in his nature to turn his back on riches when they beckoned. The inappropriate nature of this proposed gift was an enormous hurdle, but leaping impossible chasms where money was concerned was what Lord Avery loved best in life.

'Charming...charming, I'm sure...' he murmured, casually closing the box as he handed it back to the Earl, '...but of course, *quite* impossible.'

'That is what I have been saying all along, Avery, but dear Lord Greystone has been very persistent,' confirmed her ladyship.

The Earl groaned, 'Don't tell me, Avery, my old friend, you are going to side with the ladies against me!' He pouted a little in Lady Avery's direction. 'I haven't a friend in the world,' and he played at giving her ladyship a stricken look which made her utter a silly little titter: *'Tee-tee-tee!'*

After a moment of calculation, Lord Avery said, 'Naturally I have no choice. As Angelica's guardian I cannot permit her to accept it, for all the reasons you already know. It is the place only of a young lady's father to bestow such gifts or, as in Lady Angelica's case, me, her guardian.' Rising and ambling to the fireplace, Lord Avery went on, 'There you have it, my dear Greystone. It is a most generous gesture for which I am sure we are all grateful, but society dictates that it is not to be.'

'Oh, but it is!' cried the Earl, gingerly leaping from his chair and snatching up the box. 'You, my old friend, Lord Avery, would not be offended if I presented *you* with this small token of our long friendship?'

Lord Avery was delighted but not surprised that the Earl had picked up his lead, and he gave the Earl a little bow. 'How could I be offended by such a thoughtful symbol of our many years of good fellowship?'

'Splendid! Please accept this little *cadeau!*' said the Earl, handing the box to Lord Avery with an extravagant, play-actor's bow.

Almost unable to conceal his delight, Lord Avery returned the Earl's deep bow and, stepping up to Angelica's chair, he handed her the box.

'My dear niece, I hope you will accept this brooch as a gift from your affectionate old uncle, and that you will wear it in good health and happiness.'

Angelica watched this virtuoso performance in dazed disbelief. All she was able to say was a weak little, 'Thank you, Uncle.'

'There! It is done!' exclaimed Lady Avery, clapping her hands together in glee. 'Everyone has had their way and everyone is happy!'

Angelica was far from happy. Her gaze was again fixed firmly on the carpet as she nervously fingered the now repugnant little box; with a great effort of will, and partly compelled by grim fascination, she raised her eyes and looked around the room. Their faces all smiled back at her with a glowing intensity that made her feel as if their eyes—crinkled up with delight—were somehow draining the strength from her body. In a vague and uncomfortable way she felt she had been betrayed by her aunt and uncle.

EIGHT

After carrying the brooch to her room, Angelica opened the box and looked at it again. It was just as large as she had first thought; it was rectangular in shape and the stones seemed to peer back at her in their multitude like the magnified eye of a fly. How can I possibly wear this to the ball? she asked herself. It is far too large and garish. But how can I *not* wear it without giving offence to my uncle? Angelica was confused by Lord and Lady Avery's actions and did not even try to find the answers to her own nagging questions. She sighed and put the jewel in a bureau drawer under layers of thick, heavy blankets as if she was trying to suffocate it and damp out its tainted light. Even after the drawer was shut, she unconsciously avoided looking at the bureau as though she feared it contained something nightmarish and alive with sinister power.

Just then, Lady Avery came in followed by Sarah who was carrying a large parcel wrapped in brown paper. 'Angelica, I have a little surprise for you,' announced her aunt. 'When Lord Greystone told us about the Revelstokes' ball I sent a messenger immediately to your Cousin Beatrix and asked her to dispatch these with all haste. Quickly, Sarah, run and get a scissors!'

'What is it, Aunt Clarissa?' asked Angelica, trying not to show that she had suffered enough surprises for one day.

Sarah was wrestling with the heavy brown wrapping paper, string and sealing wax as she fought her way into the bundle.

'As you have absolutely not a thread to wear to the Revelstokes' ball—you cannot possibly wear your old muslin—dreadfully out-dated—' continued her aunt, '—I remembered that Cousin Beatrix had preserved a few of your mother's dresses with the intention of giving them to you when you were older. So I have sent for these and here they are in good time for

133

the ball. I am hoping that there will be something here we can have cut down to fit you and make fashionable. We will trust Sarah to be at her cleverest with her needle and thimble.'

Three dresses spilled out onto the bed when Sarah had finished her battle with the wrappings. One was yellow satin, one a shimmering Indian silk, and the third was a sea of ivory lace covered with tiny sparkling crystal beads and pearls that winked softly in the lamp light. All three women looked in awe at the fabulous lace dress.

'I had no idea,' said Lady Avery, lifting the dress. 'It is your mother's wedding dress. I have often wondered what had become of it and I had no idea Beatrice had it. How wonderful it still is...and how beautiful your mother looked on her wedding day.'

'My mother's wedding dress...' Angelica repeated the words in a hushed tone and, approaching the bed, she touched the dress in disbelief. 'I have so few reminders of my mother that this seems too good to be real.' As Angelica took the dress from Lady Avery, a gossamer veil slipped from its folds onto the bed. 'It is beautiful,' said Angelica, having difficulty speaking through the rush of memories that poured over her. She raised the sleeve of the dress to her cheek in a faint hope of recapturing the longed-for sensation of her mother's cool, reassuring hand on her face. Then, as she caught sight of the Indian silk dress on the bed, a long forgotten memory of her mother rose up before her mind's eye with such clarity that her mother could have been in the room. She seemed to

134

be standing before her, beautiful, delicate, her golden hair piled high beneath a sparkling tiara, and she was dressed for a ball in the Indian silk, swirling and laughing, and showing off her new dress to four-year-old Angelica who was about to be put to bed. Angelica could see candlelight shining in her mother's eyes as she scooped up the little girl into her arms and spun her around, humming a waltz in a cloud of lavender scent. The child was laughing and clinging tightly to her mother's soft neck. The image was so strong, Angelica could feel what it was like to be that child again, laughing in that uncontrollable, childish way that always ended with aching tummy muscles. This was always followed by being tucked into bed with consoling warm kisses. The sudden recollection was over-powering and, at first, Angelica didn't hear her aunt speaking to her.

'Angelica!' Lady Avery repeated for the third time.

Angelica started out of her trancelike state. 'I'm sorry, Aunt Clarissa. I have just remembered something!' and, rushing up to her bemused aunt, Angelica excitedly grasped her ladyship's hands. 'Oh, Aunt Clarissa, it is wonderful...I know I have seen that silk dress before. Seeing it now after all these years made me realize I saw my mother wearing it! She must have been going to a ball. Isn't it wonderful!' Then she let out a sigh and her shoulders dropped in dismay. 'Oh, why can't I remember more about my mother?'

'Well, you were only just turned seven when

135

your mother died, and most people don't remember much of anything before the age of four or five—all in all you remember a great deal,' Lady Avery said in a real attempt to comfort her niece.

'Oh, dear—my mother has become almost like a dream to me. Sometimes I wonder if I confuse what I really remember with some of what you have told me about her...but what I recalled this instant was utterly real—I know I truly remember it. It's just that I feel so close to her and miss her so that it seems terribly unfair that I don't remember her better.' Still clinging to her aunt's hands, Angelica suddenly wondered if she was being selfish to her hardworking aunt. 'Aunt Clarissa, I am sorry to go on about my mother. You have always been such a dear—no one could ask for a better aunt than you!' and she gave her ladyship a fond hug.

Lady Avery, who was never very good with displays of affection, gave an embarrassed little titter and pretended to spank Angelica's arm, saying, 'Now, enough of that, we absolutely must get on! Here, hold the wedding dress up to yourself and let's see how it looks,' and she arranged the dress against her niece.

Sarah, whose own sturdy parents were still flourishing, and whose mother had just produced a tenth child, watched this little scene feeling a twinge of pity for Angelica in her isolation. In Sarah's vast, unruly family, in spite of spankings and punishments for the sometimes impossible, half-wild children, there were plenty of hugs and cuddles to go round for everyone. Not completely lacking in tact, Sarah pretended not to have witnessed Lady Avery's discomfort at Angelica's spontaneous show of affection, nor her ladyship's inability to absorb it. Sarah busied herself by pulling the full-length standing mirror across the floor until it faced Angelica.

As Angelica held the wedding dress up to herself in the mirror, Lady Avery exclaimed. 'You are the picture of your mother on her wedding day!'

Angelica looked at her reflection in the mirror and tried to imagine what her mother must have looked like in the dress. She was absorbed by this for a few moments and then, as she inspected her likeness in the mirror, something less pleasant occurred to her. She began to realize for the first time the real implications of marriage. She understood fully at that instant that she had not really given any thought to the role that lay ahead of her as some nobleman's wife, if she was fortunate enough to attract the proposal of a high-born suitor. She had always vowed that she would never marry for love after the disastrous poverty she and her parents had suffered; she was quite prepared to be practical about accepting a marriage that would be financially secure. But she had been carried along, partly by the muted excitement of the prospect of a year as a debutante and partly by the understanding of her duty to Lord and Lady Avery. They had brought her this far in life and now it was up to her to do her best to make her own way—and that meant making a good match.

The thought that entered her mind at this moment was something she had overlooked. It had never occurred to her that she might be bound in a marriage to someone whom she detested. It was too terrible a thought and Angelica put it instantly out of her mind. Bringing her attention back to her reflection in the looking-glass, she watched Sarah arranging the veil. After a moment of silently looking in amazement at her own reflection she said, 'It is just like the portrait of my mother in my locket.'

'It is *exactly*, my dear,' agreed Lady Avery, almost breathless with sentiment. 'You are the exact picture of your mother on her wedding day and every bit as beautiful. You will wear that dress on your own wedding day—which I cannot believe is too far off.'

This last remark made Angelica hastily fold up the dress and carry it to the bed. 'Really, Aunt Clarissa, please don't say such things. In any case, I haven't any suitors.'

'It is a wise young lady who knows who her admirers are,' replied Lady Avery obliquely. Angelica said nothing to this but felt a sharp stab of uneasiness.

'Now we must find you something to wear to the ball and I think it will have to be the yellow as the Indian silk is quite out of the question. Slip into the yellow for me quickly, my dear, and let's see what we can do with it.'

Sarah helped Angelica into the dress and Lady Avery clucked and 'tut-tutted' around the room as she looked at Angelica and the yellow satin from all sides. 'Thank goodness it has its own cape,' she said at last. 'It will be the extra material we need to extend the skirt. And Sarah, don't even *think* about cutting the bodice until you have it completely pinned and ready for me to see at a fitting. The sleeves will have to be reduced to almost nothing and the dress must not actually come off the shoulders. There may be just a hint of the shoulders but they must still be covered, do you understand? We might consider tiny self-bows at the sleeves, but that can wait until the last minute.'

Her ladyship continued with increasing enthusiasm, 'And the neckline must not be too low, just a gentle curve. We haven't enough material for a *single* mistake. It will be such a squeak—be very careful! Three flounces in the skirt, I think...humm...and not too full! It makes it too difficult to dance or to take a gentleman's arm if you are standing miles away stranded in the middle of a sea of skirt.' Then, rattling off a long list of orders for Sarah about the transformation, her ladyship concluded by asking, 'Sarah, there is an immense amount of work here. Do you really think you can do it all by yourself?'

'Oh, yes, m'lady! It's simple really, but lots of stitching. My new friend Jane—she's a parlourmaid downstairs—she does lovely needlework and she'll help me if I get behind. I'm sure we can do it in time for the ball!' Sarah was fired with the momentum of someone keen to show off her prowess with a needle to her new friends below-stairs.

'Well, if you're sure—but you must tell me *the minute* it is getting too much for you, and I'll send for a seamstress from the village if necessary. Now you had better hurry and finish pinning and help us both dress for dinner. I shall be in my room.' Lady Avery turned and glided from the room on a sea of silk over crinoline and called behind her as she floated out, 'Come through as soon as you finish here, Sarah!'

Sarah set about the dress with silk pins while Angelica stood motionless for the process. Sarah had never stayed in any place as grand as Cranleigh Castle and she was in a permanent state of thrall with all she had seen and experienced. Although Ickworth, Lord Avery's estate, was large and the house well-appointed, there were few houses in England to compare with the opulence of Cranleigh. As soon as Lady Avery left the room, Sarah confided in Angelica. 'Isn't it grand here, m'lady! There are such a lot of rooms and such a lot of servants! And it's that crowded at meal times below-stairs, they have to have *two* sittings in the servants' hall! When the old Duke was alive and there were house parties, there was over three hundred servants in the house and gardens! That's what Mr Park, the butler, says!' Sarah nattered through the fence of pins in her mouth while pinning the dress and snatching a glance, now and again, up at Angelica who was giving Sarah her full attention. Sarah chatted on:

'They are *ever* so nice downstairs. Even Mr Park is quite jolly—if a butler can ever be *jolly*, if you know what I mean, m'lady.' Sarah rambled on regardless of a mouthful of ironmongery. 'Mr Park and his family has been at Cranleigh Castle for almost forever, m'lady, and he was 'ere when the *Queen* came and visited—and you'll never guess! The Queen wanted Park to work for her! But Park and the old Duke put off the Queen! Can you imagine saying "No" to the Queen?! Leastwise, that is what my friend Jane tells me.' Sarah was now gabbling at high speed. Angelica knew there was no slowing the flow of her chatter and she just let her ramble on.

'And do you know what, m'lady,' demanded Sarah, not waiting for or expecting an answer, 'it was Mr Park what found the murdered young Duke—and his brother standing over him with a pistol just a second after he killed him! That's what Jane tells me! He's usually quite nice, Mr Park. Oh, a bit stuffy sometimes, if you know what I mean, but he heard Jane and me talking about the murder, and did he read us a lesson! He was that cross I thought he'd bust his buttons!'

Angelica's tone was quiet but firm. 'I am sure he was, Sarah. You must not talk of such things. What if Lord Greystone should overhear your chatter?'

'There ain't much likelihood of *that,* m'lady. His lordship won't tolerate the sight of female servants in the reception rooms. Jane tells me that the parlourmaids have to be all done with their work by *noon sharp* including cleaning all the lamps! If his lordship walks in and sees one of the maids above-stairs anytime after twelve noon, he dismisses 'em on the spot!

141

It's downright shocking! It happened to a poor girl what was new 'ere about three months ago and she was still sweeping the grate in the blue reception rooms, and in walks his lordship and he sees her—and he looks at the clock on the mantel piece which said five minutes past noon—and *out she goes* without so much as a by-or-leave thank-you-very-much!—and *no* reference!' Sarah quaked at the terror of the thought. 'She'd have starved to death if Mr Park hadn't found her work at the vicarage,' Sarah narrowed her eyes a little. 'Yes, he's a right Tartar that one—that Lord Greystone.' Sarah shook her head slowly and philosophically.

'That is quite enough, Sarah. You must not speak in such a way about Lord Greystone. It is improper and does you no credit.' Angelica hated reprimanding Sarah but if Lady Avery should hear her talking along these lines she would give Sarah a very abrasive tongue-lashing. Hoping she had not sounded too severe, Angelica added gently, 'There are some opinions we have to keep to ourselves.' Sarah stiffened a little and pursed up her face into an injured look; she did not consider herself a gossip.

Angelica caught the look in the full-length mirror and was truly sorry she had upset Sarah. And from a more practical standpoint, she also knew that Sarah was quite capable of pricking her with one of the silk pins in retaliation, so she ventured a safer topic. 'Please, tell me about the old gardener.' Angelica could see by Sarah's expression that the question had not registered so she said, 'The bent old one—he's *ancient*—I've seen him wearing a big hat. Have you come across him?'

Sarah's forehead was a crisscross of baffled wrinkles as she tried to think whom Angelica could mean. Finally she said slowly, 'No, m'lady...I can't place who you might mean...'

Angelica wondered if Sarah was being evasive as revenge; after all, Angelica reasoned, she had all but called Sarah a chatterbox, so the maid might well be cross. Angelica said, 'Oh, do please tell me, Sarah!'

Sarah had meant to be unhelpful to get back at her mistress, but she was rather intrigued about this old gardener and she forgot to hold back, so she thought hard for a moment and said, 'Jane is walking out with one of the gardeners and I thought I'd seen 'em all...there ain't anyone *very* old. There's Scrimmage, of course; he's the oldest gardener, but he ain't that old neither. And he's as thin as a post and just as straight—he's six-foot-tall if he's an inch! The others joke that Scrimmage's got a built-in ladder for trimming the hedges.' Sarah's expression continued to float on a sea of perplexed musings as she silently did a head count of the gardening staff, wondering how anyone with her practised powers of observation could be so careless as to overlook any member of the estate staff (she would never admit that she was nosy). She was disconcerted to think she had missed anyone in her relentless personal quest to know the business of everyone at Cranleigh as the busy estate offered her a vast new crop of servants, *all* with large storehouses

143

full of wonderful new tales which could be reported by her to the other servants back at Ickworth when she got home. Leave someone out?—unthinkable! Sarah wondered if she was slipping.

Angelica was watching her, hoping she would suddenly recall the stooped old gardener—or maybe Sarah was holding out on her just to tweak her ladyship—but as Sarah fell silent and slowly rotated her head back and forth in a long drawn-out negative motion, like a clockwork toy winding down, Angelica could see that Sarah was really concentrating hard on the subject of the phantom gardener. Angelica crimped her eyebrows together and said, 'Well...how very curious...too curious...I know I wasn't dreaming...' and she let a soft tide of confusion flow over her as she tried to remember more about the old gardener, but those moments in the maze had been frantic and the gardener was now just a blur of hat and crumpled coat; she trembled a little, as recalling the gardener brought back the distasteful memory of the Earl as he had forced his attentions on her, and she shut the recollection out. Then she was suddenly distracted by another, clearer thought that darted into her head, and she asked, very curious now, 'But do please tell me about the young boy, Titus.'

Sarah, caught off guard by the unfamiliar name, looked up keenly interested. *'Titus,* m'lady? I don't know anyone called Titus.' Sarah then remembered to crank her eyelids down halfway over her eyes and stiffly elevate her chin—again the picture of the dejected, scolded maid.

'Yes, you do, Sarah. The little boy who does the boots!' Angelica was watching Sarah's face to see if her memory loss was genuine or if she was still smarting from the rebuke.

'Oh, you mean *Boots,* m'lady!—the boot-boy! I didn't know his name was Titus!' Sarah blurted this out enthusiastically and then remembered she was cross, wove a few more pins into the shiny silk and retreated back into her pout.

'Yes, *Titus.* Such a nice, bright little boy—tell me about him.'

'Well, I'm no gossip, m'lady.' Sarah was now sitting on the floor, edging slowly around the hem of the skirt, her face still shuttered. It was a look Angelica knew to mean Sarah had something very ripe to relate, but because she had been put in her place she was only going to tell if coaxed very prettily.

'Oh, please, Sarah, please tell!'

Sarah said nothing and went on pinning.

'Well, anyway, what on earth could be of interest about a little boy.' Angelica did not really mean it, but she thought it might get Sarah to speak.

'*Hurrmph!*' Sarah was indignant and said, 'That goes to show how much *you* know, m'lady—but I can't tell you. It isn't the sort of *in-fo-mation* a young lady should know.' Sarah was determined not to call her *in-fo-mation* gossip.

Angelica stamped her foot—something she almost never did. 'Oh, Sarah, you are maddening!

145

Do *please, please* tell me what you know about little Titus—otherwise I shall worry so!'

Sarah was still sitting on the floor putting the last pins in the skirt's hem and she ignored Angelica's plea, as she was waiting for *The Grand Apology*.

The Grand Apology came. Angelica put her hands on her waist, elbows akimbo, lifted her chin and tried to look in command, but she knew it was hopeless; she could only play-act when it came to running the servants because she liked them all too well. 'All right, Sarah, I am very sorry I even hinted that you might engage in gossip and for that I am really immensely sorry.' She dropped the pose and looked down at Sarah and said sincerely, 'Please forgive me.'

Sarah was on her feet as if propelled there by an explosion of dynamite, her face flushed with eagerness as she came close to Angelica to whisper. 'There is the most *a-maz-zing* story about Boots—I mean Titus—my friend Jane told me and she made me promise not to tell—but I know it's all right telling you m'lady—' Sarah drew breath. 'Well, it seems that Titus's mother was the beautiful daughter of one of the Crowood estate workers—a shepherd, I think—and she had strawberry-coloured hair and was very pious—read from the Bible all the time—but some people thought she was putting on airs and graces. *Well,*' Sarah glanced around at the empty bedroom as if to make sure no stray ears were listening, 'the story goes that Lord Greystone seduced her by tricking her into a bogus wedding ceremony performed by an itinerant clerk dressed up to look like a vicar! He then made her take an oath on the Bible to keep the marriage secret—which she did—but then when she found out that she had been tricked, and that she was *not* married at all, she tried to drown herself and the baby boy she had just borne him. She was drowned dead—but a water bailiff found the baby tangled up in some watercress in the river and rushed him home for his wife to look after.' Sarah was watching Angelica's horrified expression, which was very satisfactory indeed, as it was the picture of shock. Angelica's mouth was dropped open in an astonished oval and her hands were folded in an anguished knot as if at prayer.

Angelica finally spoke, 'Sarah—are you saying that—that the baby was Titus—and that he is the child of Lord Greystone, born out of wedlock?! That Lord Greystone tricked a poor girl into thinking she was married?'

Sarah was nodding enthusiastically and composing her face with finely practised gravity. 'That is *exactly* as how it was told to me, m'lady!'

'Good gracious! Do you think poor little Titus has ever heard this terrible story?'

'Oh, no, m'lady, he don't know nothin' of this. Nobody would have the heart to tell him.'

'Well, I certainly hope not! What a horrid story to be going round, and it is hateful to think the little lad might hear it anytime!'

147

Angelica's face had an expression Sarah had never seen before: she was very angry. 'Sarah, you must *never* repeat that story again—*ever!* It is too vicious and horrid! Just think how dreadful it would be for Titus if he ever heard it. *Secret weddings indeed! Such nonsense!* It's all the fabrication of evil-minded gossips and cannot possibly be true! All it can achieve is to torture the mind of a little boy who adores a mother he never knew. I won't hear another word about it!'

Sarah was so stunned seeing her mild mistress raging—face flushed pink, eyes sparking with fury—that she knew not to speak; she picked up her pin cushion and quickly finished her pinning with nervously shaking fingers, and without uttering another word.

The first dinner gong, which alerted guests that it was time to dress, sounded just as Sarah finished with her pinning. Angelica tried to dispel the angry silence by trying to be cheerful to show Sarah that the fury had passed, but not so gay as to erase the sternness of her words. Angelica chose to wear her drab, blue moiré which she was wrongly convinced did not flatter her. Sarah quickly helped her dress and then slipped away to Lady Avery's dressing room to assist her ladyship with her evening dress. Then, when Sarah returned to Angelica's room, she was surprised to find that Angelica had dressed her own hair, and to rather severe effect. But, as Sarah secured a few renegade locks of her mistress's hair, she commented, 'I didn't think that style suited you at all, m'lady, but now that I look at it I think it shows off your neck rather nice.'

Sarah's innocent comment was only meant as an olive branch, but it succeeded mainly in compounding Angelica's glowering feeling of self-consciousness that had haunted her all day; never before had she felt this awkward and aware of her own body, as if vast seas of eyes were ogling her even in solitude. When the second dinner gong sounded, Angelica slowly descended the marble stairs feeling exposed and naked. The undercurrent of vulnerability was so strong that, although she tried to resist the ludicrous temptation, she glanced down at herself to make sure she actually did have on a dress! How wildly ridiculous I'm being! she chided herself, amused at her own absurdity. You are no longer a gauche school girl. You must expect people to pay attention to you. If this is the way you are going to react whenever someone odious presses you with unwanted attentions then you may as well retreat from the London Season now. She mastered her courage and decided that being in Lord Greystone's company would serve as an acid test to prepare her for going into Society. She told herself: It is all together a good thing really because it has prepared me for meeting disagreeable people—something I've been too naive to think would occur—and surely no one could be quite as disagreeable as Lord Greystone.

Angelica found Lord Avery and the Earl in sombre conversation in the green drawing-room as they waited for the ladies. As she entered, the

Earl's eyes locked upon her and she resolutely met his steely gaze with feigned courage. She knew as she looked at him, his well-made features set in serious but convivial attitude that, unpleasant as he was, it was impossible that he was capable of doing such a thing as Sarah described. In any case, if such a story was going around and had any credence at all, Lord and Lady Avery would not be associating with him. Angelica did not care one speck that people were making up stories about the Earl, but it was dreadful to think that some innocent like young Titus might be hurt by such falsehoods. Angelica marvelled and despaired at the malicious nature of people who could dream up such tales.

Lord Avery was standing near the Earl as they had been speaking in hushed tones. He turned to her and said with gravity, 'Good evening, Angelica, my dear. Lord Greystone has had some serious news. It seems that Lord Anthony—of whom I know you have heard—is dead. This means that Lord Greystone will now become the Duke of Stanforth and inherit Cranleigh Castle and estate.'

'Yes, it is true,' began the Earl, struggling to hide his delight. 'When I had to leave you at the stables the other day, I had word from America that Lord Anthony has been executed as a common criminal, and I have just had the confirmation of this a few minutes ago. It is a very bizarre story and I hope you will not find it too unsettling, but I was about to relate the details to Lord Avery.'

Angelica nodded her assent and the Earl continued:

'It seems that after he murdered his brother, Lord Anthony fled first to France and then to America. He fell in, quite naturally I gather, with a group of ruffians, in the state of Virginia, who were armed and hiding out in the wild and thickly wooded hills preparing for a general uprising that would attempt to free the slaves. There are thousands of African slaves in the Americas, as you know, and it is becoming a more and more contentious issue daily, with feelings divided between the northern and southern states. These people Lord Anthony joined up with were paid by perhaps well-meaning abolitionists to mount a raid on a federal arsenal at a place called Harper's Ferry. It was an attempt to start a slave insurrection. The entire plot was a disaster. Their leader, a fellow called John Brown, and his little gang were finally overcome after two days of siege by the American marines, under the command of a Robert E Lee. Brown and his followers, including Lord Anthony, were all tried and hanged for their crime.' As he concluded, the Earl brought his glass of sherry to his mouth in time to cover the sardonic smile that had begun to contort his lips.

Lord Avery listened in fascination, hands clasped behind his back, rocking gently on his heels: 'Ah yes, I recall this business now—an attempt to incite a slave insurrection! It comes back to me.' Lord Avery continued. 'I remember reading something about the Harper's Ferry

151

incident in *The Times* at the end of last year, but naturally this is the first anyone has heard that Lord Anthony had any part in it. It is truly strange. He was presumably living there under an assumed name. Matters are very torn up over there—it would be easy for someone to disappear and reappear in another guise. There will be civil war in America soon,' he said gravely. 'But back to the matter of the minute! It certainly clarifies *your* position, Greystone, or should I say,' he inclined his head in a show of deference, 'my dear Duke of Stanforth?'

'No—please!' demurred the Earl, a bit too humbly, 'Please continue to call me Greystone for the moment. I am not rushing into my new title and all the weighty responsibility that goes with it.'

'All the same,' insisted Lord Avery, 'you will now be one of the richest and most powerful men in England, and I know you are more than worthy of the position.'

'You do me honour with your confidence, Avery. I shall always endeavour to uphold the title of the Duke of Stanforth, and do my best to blot out the memory of the terrible murder which has shaken this noble old family and propelled me into this position. In any case, there will be no one who will mourn the death of that foul murderer, Lord Anthony.'

Upon hearing the Earl's words, Angelica remembered how sad Binstead had become talking of the late Lord Anthony. Perhaps not everyone would be as pleased as Lord Greystone, she reflected silently.

NINE

Prospero was tossing his head to show his enthusiasm for the day which was bright and warm. Angelica was reining him along hedgerows that were bursting into bud in the unseasonably mild weather. She had decided that, as she found the Earl's company so unwanted and unnerving, she would spend every possible remaining minute of her visit at Cranleigh away from the castle, riding. That would prevent accidental meetings with the Earl. He had said himself that he had no time to ride; they would meet only at dinner, when Lord and Lady Avery would be there as well.

After the Revelstokes' ball she and Lady Avery would finally go up to London as planned to arrange for her wardrobe, and all would be well.

Angelica had been up at daybreak and, after a quick breakfast in her room, she rode off before anyone else was stirring. She had sent a request to the kitchen for some small repast to take with her and Cook had responded splendidly with: a slice of her best game pie; a plump, blushing pear; a small wedge of mature cheddar cheese; and a few sugar biscuits, baked golden brown. Angelica found all this tied up in a heavy, blue tartan napkin, waiting for her on the heavy hall table near the front door. Beside this compact feast lay, to Angelica's surprise, a large well-scrubbed carrot. She looked at it in amusement for a moment and then realized that Cook had kindly sent a snack along for Prospero. This horse is not as unpopular as I have been led to believe, thought Angelica and she heard herself laugh out loud as she put the carrot into her riding habit coat pocket.

That lowly vegetable had more subtle significance than Angelica realized. Cook might have understood it if she had taken the time to think about her own actions, but she was far too busy ruling her kitchen-kingdom and had only sent the scullery maid to the cold-larder to find 'the best carrot you can lay hands on!' Cook remembered how Prospero's previous owner had charmed her into parting with her best carrots to spoil the big horse, but it was more than just that memory that prompted her gift. Great houses need people and, since the Duke's murder, there had been no one in the castle, apart from the Earl; no visitors, apart from a few of his lordship's business acquaintances; no parties, until now, and the Averys and Angelica could hardly be said to make up a party. Since the tragedy, the house had lacked soul, life, and especially, promise. And then Angelica arrived. She had youth, spirit, hope, and a future; her mere presence encouraged the faintest recollection of what life had been like before everything had been shattered in that awful instant heralded by a pistol shot. It was as if Cranleigh was coming to the end of a period of mourning; as if the curtains, long closed, were opening to let in a ray of hope-giving sunlight. The gloom that had descended upon them all after the Duke's death had lay undisturbed until now. Without it being put into words, or even put into ordered thought, there was a sense, a hazy awareness amongst the servants that Cranleigh was awakening, cautiously, to the possibility of better things.

Her picnic slipped easily into the leather sandwich box Binstead had attached to the saddle and Angelica felt wonderfully free and self-reliant as she rode off to explore the thousands of acres of Cranleigh.

This routine came as no surprise to Lord and Lady Avery who reassured the Earl when he enquired about Angelica's whereabouts on several occasions. To disappear for whole days on horseback, was her greatest pleasure and long-established habit at Ickworth. 'Lady Angelica always returns in time for dinner,' assured Lord Avery.

'But, don't you *worry* about Lady Angelica?' asked the Earl, somewhat puzzled.

Lord Avery displayed consummate disinterest. 'Not in the least, sir. Lady Angelica is more at home on horseback than on a Chippendale chair. She is not foolish and has yet to come to grief. You must not give it a thought.'

'Of course, my guests must do exactly as they please. I would have it no other way,' responded the Earl with great amiability.

For all the Earl's supposed lack of concern, Lord Avery thought he detected a note in his voice that showed he was somewhat put out. In private, his lordship chuckled to Lady Avery, 'I wonder if Lord Greystone is smitten with our Angelica. If that is the case, the more the lady is absent from Cranleigh the warmer his ardour will become. Angelica is artless and will have no idea what effect her absence will have on this admirer. But it matters not, as the result will be the same.'

Angelica had Prospero trotting nicely along a dry dirt lane when he came to an abrupt halt which tossed her a little forward in the saddle. He looked about frantically, raised his head and sniffed the warm humid day with a fanatical air; he pricked his ears and began to prance excitedly well before Angelica even heard hounds baying in the distance. The potent associations of vocalizing hounds and thrumming hooves was driving Prospero mad with the desire to join in the unseen hunt. He pranced and crab-stepped, dancing in small circles, flicking his head and letting out a series of tight little bucks trying to convince her that they should bound across the muddy fields to join in the giddy chase.

'Whoa, Prospero—steady.' She only pulled gently on the reins to discourage him, knowing if he decided to take off she would have no power to stop him. She turned him away from the direction of the hunt, but he would not budge; he stood like a rock in the lane, his ears flicking about like the wings of a captive bird. Seeing that he would not go away from the hunt, she turned him and let him prance and cavort slowly down the lane in the direction of the noisy hounds. A moment later, the countryside was silent again. The fox had given the hounds the slip. Without the barking to whip him up, Prospero became calmer and walked on more sedately. That moment of calm was short-lived as the sound of clopping hooves preceded the arrival of six members of the hunt who had become detached from the field and left behind. A woman's voice, shrill enough to skin a peach, jarred the air:

'I tell you, Freddie, the hunt went the *other* way!'

Angelica could see them now. A half dozen riders, the men in hunting pink, the ladies in trim black habits, clattering towards her in a steamy cloud of sweating horses.

'Nonsense—*this* is the right way!' cried a thin man in a silk topper whom Angelica supposed to be the aforementioned Freddie.

'It's all Dodo's fault!' cried the woman with the razor voice, whom Angelica could now make out to be a very fat woman, of a certain age, atop a watermelon-shaped horse.

There was a good-natured laugh from one of the young women. 'It's not my fault you all decided to follow me instead of the Master! I only came this way as it used to be a short cut. How was I to know they'd built a lake!' This rider was young—about two years older than Angelica—and she was riding a colossal, dappled grey with a chest as broad as a marble fireplace and feet the size of tea trays. She was a tall, plain, big-boned girl with a long nose, but, even under her top hat and hunting veil, Angelica could see that her expression was so open and full of fun and energy that she looked tremendously attractive. The riders were deep in chiding one another and they were almost on top of Angelica before they noticed her and came to a halt. Prospero darted about happily in the confined space of the lane giving Angelica everything she could cope with.

'Heavens above!' cried the young woman they had called Dodo, 'I don't believe my eyes! Is that really Prospero?!' She had a vast grin on her face and nudged her horse forward towards Prospero.

'It is!' cried Angelica between bucks, 'But perhaps it is better not to get too near—I don't know what he is like with other horses!'

'It's all right! My horse, Cally, and Prospero are old friends.' Dodo came close enough to extend her gloved hand for Angelica to shake. 'Hello! I'm Dorothea Revelstoke.' Angelica stretched out and shook hands quickly not wanting to take a hand off Prospero's reins for longer than absolutely necessary. As soon as the big grey was next to him, Prospero settled down a little.

'Call me Dodo—everyone does—and you must be Angelica! Don't look surprised—Lord Greystone sent a note across asking if he could bring his visitors to the ball, and naturally you and your aunt and uncle are most welcome!' Dodo took a long look at Prospero and gave her head a disbelieving shake. 'And forgive me for blinking, for I *can't* trust my own eyes! Is

158

that *really* the same Prospero? I never thought I'd see this. How'd you tame him? Did you slip some brandy into his corn? It's the only answer!' and she laughed loudly.

Angelica laughed and immediately took to Dodo and her brusque sense of humour.

Dodo suddenly turned and waved her whip hand at the others, whose impatient horses waited in an agitated cluster a few dozen yards away, 'You go on ahead. I want to talk to my new friend! Anyhow, you can all get just as lost, just as well without my help!' The other riders laughed, shrugged, and released their restless horses into a trot to squeeze single file past Prospero and Cally who were blocking most of the lane. As the five riders whizzed past, all friendly smiles, the men lifted their toppers to Angelica and the women nodded as Dodo rattled off lightning-fast introductions of the speeding parade. With the men posting up and down in their stirrups, and the ladies rocking in their side saddles, it was like being introduced to people glimpsed passing on a racing carousel, and Dodo cried out their names like a fairground barker, turning the whole thing into a heady carnival atmosphere. Dodo laughed, pointed with her whip, and sang out over the clacking sound of the hooves as they passed: *'All right, you lot; this is Lady Angelica Winsford and that's—Tubby Coffer* [he rode with his stirrups so short his bony knees seemed to flank his ears] *Mrs Manwaring Puckett* [this the big lady on the watermelon horse] *Jimbo Jasper Bultrap-Guph* [a man with a head

159

like a muscat grape] *Caroline Culpeper-Squill* [immensely beautiful and knowing it] *and my own dear Freddie Bigelow!'* This last was aimed at the thin young man who raised his topper high and flashed past in a streak of hunting pink, a big smile and a longing look of love for Dodo. Dodo laughed at her own exuberance, turned back to Angelica and said:

'There you have it! You've met the neighbours! Rather rushed I'm afraid! Next time not quite this frantic!' Dodo gave a quick glance down the lane at the disappearing horses. 'I hope they find the others, otherwise they shall all blame me for weeks for leading them astray!' Dodo laughed again and drew breath. 'I'm very glad you're coming to my ball. Papa is giving it for me to announce my engagement. I had not much reckoned on getting married, but Mama said that if I was to be a spinster it would ruin her life. She said she would not be able to hold her head up in society, as people would say that she had failed to find a suitable husband for her eldest. In any case, she says my little sister Annabel cannot marry until I do and there is a nice young officer of good family she has taken a shine to, and Mama said I could not put it off any longer so they found me Freddie. That's Freddie there!' cried Dodo, pointing enthusiastically with her whip at the backs of the riders as they trotted away down the lane. 'That's him! *There* in the scarlet coat and topper and the sticking-out ears!' Angelica could see exactly to whom Dodo was pointing, and from the previous angle—when the riders

160

had trotted past—she had not noticed the acute set of Freddie's ears. Under the circumstances, Angelica could think of nothing to say, but it hardly mattered as Prospero's continual antics were occupying her attention; he was prancing and crab stepping keen to follow the other horses. Angelica and Dodo turned their horses to walk slowly down the lane in the same direction the others had gone, and that seemed to calm Prospero a little.

'Freddie's a lamb really,' Dodo confided. 'He says he loves me but I really can't imagine why. I'm enormously fond of him, of course. Mama likes him as he is *frightfully* rich, or at least his father is. His papa made a fortune with spinning machines or bottle tops or something like that and he wanted to make sure his son would be a gentleman so he sent Freddie to Eton and Oxford—and for all *that* he's actually turned out all right! His father sends Mama into a decline when he visits as he never knows which fork to use, but I don't care. I think he's *jolly nice* and he always makes me laugh with his stories and I guess he's pleased his son is marrying someone with a title, but I shan't use it. I'll just call myself plain old Mrs Frederick Alphonse Bigelow. We'll live in the dower house and have lots of Jack Russells. And Freddie says I can do as I like when we are married.'

Angelica was listening to Dodo and snatching a glance at how the two horses walked contentedly side by side and, after a moment, asked, 'How is it these two horses get on so well together?'

161

'Of course, you can't know—these two horses have been friends for years. Prospero belonged to Anthony Stanforth—Lord Anthony—but naturally you never knew Anthony. He hunted Prospero all the time. Anthony and I were great chums as children, and when he named his horse Prospero I was very jealous that he had found such a clever name. So old Cally here is really Caliban,' she giggled. 'I called him that just to show Anthony how smart and daring *I* was. Mama would have a swoon if she ever knew that my horse is named after a Shakespearean character who was unwashed, lived in a cave, and had amorous tendencies!' Dodo laughed with satisfaction. 'Mummy doesn't even know I've read Shakespeare. She thinks I've only read *Lamb's Tales!* Aren't there strange conventions about what daughters are permitted to read? Papa knows about Caliban and he thinks it's very funny! But he would *never* admit it!' Dodo studied Prospero for a moment and then looked inquiringly into Angelica's face. 'But—seriously—tell me how you managed to tame Prospero. He was *never* very tame, but since Anthony disappeared that horse has been completely crazed. How did you calm him down?'

'I didn't do a thing—Prospero did it all. He's the master and he's in charge. I'm only here as a passenger!' But then Angelica suddenly remembered that her uncle and the Earl had said that Lord Anthony was dead and she frowned, wondering if Dodo knew.

'That's exactly what Anthony used to say!'

Dodo's voice softened at the memory, 'Oh, by the way,' she added with her usual openness, as she could see a look of concern clouding Angelica's face, 'it's all right—I know...about Anthony...I know...he's...dead... Greystone sent across a note last night to Papa telling what happened.' Her voice became thin. 'It's a terrible business and we are all desperately sad about it...' With forced brightness, she added, 'In any case, Anthony would have been glad Prospero isn't being deprived of his gallops.'

'Some people have said it is hard to believe he could murder his brother,' offered Angelica, restraining Prospero from breaking into a trot.

'*Murder!* Whoever mentioned murder to you?' demanded Dodo with ironic resignation. 'His brother's death *had* to have been an accident! We all refer to it as *the accident*. It's the *only* explanation. Now we will never know exactly how it happened, but I can only guess that Anthony, realizing circumstances would be impossible to explain, must have fled knowing that no matter what he said in his defence it looked too much like murder and he would hang for it. He stood next in line for the succession and Papa says any jury would have convicted him in a second. Anthony was very quick witted and, in many ways, far better suited to be the Duke than his brother, who would have been happier in an academic life. And perhaps Anthony *did* take the jewels—*I'd* say good luck to him—and I thought it at the time. He was no fool. His brain always worked as quick as lightning and he must have known he would spend the rest of his life going from pillar to post, always running or in exile. To survive that, you must have money, so he must have snatched up the jewels as he fled.'

As Dodo continued, her eyelashes flicked away tiny, tell-tale drops of moisture which caught in her veil. 'I was besotted by him when I was a girl. No one deserved to be as good-looking as he.' Then she laughed as she recalled, 'But he broke my heart and threw me over when I was eleven, when he schooled Missy Stuart's pony over jumps for her! I never really forgave him.' Dodo laughed at her own foolishness. 'And when we were older he had a string of society beauties in London throwing themselves at his head, so I cast aside all hope and here I am settling for Freddie! And there is poor Anthony being executed in the end anyway. It's too awful to think about.' She was pressing the back of her gloved hand to the corners of her eyes. 'In any case it's typical that he met his end trying to help other people—trying to help the slaves in America is what Papa said. For all his sporting style of life, Anthony always had time for someone in trouble.' Dodo gave an embarrassed little laugh. 'Anyway, I must stop with this endless dissertation about someone you've never even met! It must be the most frightful bore for you!'

Before Angelica could comment, Dodo started off on another tack in an attempt to distract herself from the painful subject she had thought she could talk about freely. But finding the memories too painful, she was in danger of dissolving into unthinkable, uncontrollable tears; she took a deep breath and said with forced gaiety, 'Please tell Lady Avery that Mama and I hope to call upon her before the ball, maybe tomorrow, but not the end of the week as we have to go up to London for me to have a fitting. Don't you find all that fussing with clothes tiresome when we could be out doing *this?* And do you know that the dresses at the French court have become so wide that it takes *two* seamstresses *standing on chairs* to dress you! Well, you *must* believe me in this because I have seen it with *my very own eyes!* Last year in Paris I went with a great friend of mine, Kitty Lawrence, to a fitting. Kitty is married to a French count. I almost died of laughter, but to save Kitty's blushes I tried to control myself for her sake. She had to stand in the fitting-room, which has to be vast to hold all the acres of dress. Two assistants had to stand on high stools with these things in their hands that look like pairs of very long broomsticks. They lifted the dress up with these broomstick contraptions—up over Kitty's head. Kitty got underneath the gown and then they *lowered* the gown on top of her! I promise you the skirt was twenty-five feet round if it was an inch! I know you think I'm mad or making it up, but it is quite true! I watched it myself! When you know me better, Angelica, you will know that I *never* exaggerate!'

Angelica laughed and was captivated by Dodo's enthusiastic energy. Angelica said,

'Well, I can assure you I am not going to come to your ball in anything as extravagant as that. Aunt Clarissa is having a dress made over for me and I have high hopes for it.'

'How fortunate you are to have such a clever aunt! Mama could never be organized enough to have a dress made at home. That's why I am having to trek back and forth to London. I tried to persuade her to have Mrs Adler in Tunbridge to do me a gown but Mama insisted that it be designed in London. "One must be fashionable!" she is very fond of saying,' laughed Dodo with affectionate contempt. 'As a consequence I have become a slave to the train. I do hate it as all that rhythmic swaying back and forth makes me rather giddy and I am sure Mama feels the same way but she won't admit it. She leans back in her seat and shuts her eyes tight and says, "I'm just resting," and she stays like that until the train rolls into London Bridge Station!

'Quite frankly, I'm terrified of the train—it's all a bit *modern* for me—and we were going up once in the winter and the carriage behind us caught fire! Some sparks from the funnel, or chimney or stack or whatever it's called, started it. The train's speed was apparently fanning the flames!' Dodo then began imitating the locomotive action with her arms and making a *'choo-choo!'* noise which made her horse turn his head and stare back at her for a moment. Caliban fixed his passenger with a baleful eye, snorted, and turned away as if disgusted, or questioning his passenger's sanity. The horse's

166

expression seemed so sagacious that it made both Angelica and Dodo laugh, and then Dodo continued. 'I think Cally is trying to tell me he's heard this story before.'

Undaunted, Dodo continued. 'Anyway, the fire could have ended in disaster. Fortunately we knew nothing of it until the train made an unscheduled stop and they put out the blaze with buckets of water. We had to get off the train as they were afraid the fire would spread. We didn't see the smoke as it was blowing back away from us, and apparently the passengers behind, in the burning coach, just assumed that all the smoke that was seeping in was from the engine—you know how smoky it can be—and trains are so new, how does anyone know *what* to expect!—and of course the passengers just thought it was *quite normal!* We could have all been cinders if someone along the line hadn't spotted it and signalled the guard! We were in a state of collapse by the time we arrived. I had hoped that it would put Mama off trains forever but no! She is determined to travel on that dragon! Every time I say to Papa that I would rather go by the road coach or carriage he says, "But we must be modern." ' At this moment Caliban let out a huge, protracted yawn as if by way of critical comment on his rider's conversation. Angelica and Dodo stared at the gaping, toothy horse-yawn for a moment. Angelica tried not to laugh but Dodo caught her eye and they turned to one another and burst into amazed laughter. 'How I do run on!' cried Dodo through her laughter,

'Even Cally is getting bored. Forgive me! I'm keeping you—and Cally will make my life a misery if he does not get the rest of his day's hunting!'

'Dodo, it has been wonderful meeting you! And thank you for keeping me company. It's lovely to have someone my own age to talk to!'

Dodo laughed. 'You mean someone to listen to! How I do blather on! I must be off now. Must find the rest of the field or Freddie will be furious with me. He hates having to listen to Mr Bultrap-Guph complain about his chilblains! We'll meet soon! Very soon!' Dodo gave Angelica a vast smile and a little wave with her whip hand, and Caliban broke into a brisk trot. Angelica watched as they sprinted away down the tree-lined lane and over a small rise, and then they were suddenly out of sight. Prospero was desperate to follow—to join the galloping horses and baying hounds flying and scrambling over fences and ditches. He cavorted and bucked and Angelica could barely hold him.

'Whoa, Prospero!' She was having trouble keeping him from bolting, and was trying to turn him in the opposite direction to the way the horses had just gone. When she did manage to turn him, he would not go forward but pranced backward before flying around again, pirouetting on his hindquarters, to prance after the others. 'Please, Prospero, not that way!' Angelica spoke to him gently through the reins, knowing strength was not the answer. She got him turned around again in the direction of a beechwood, from which came the nervous reedy squawk of a startled pheasant which, perhaps fleeing a fox, must have bolted into a napping tawny owl, which cried out from its disturbed sleep. Prospero pricked his ears and suddenly began to trot along the lane towards the wood—the direction Angelica had been urging him. 'Good fellow!' She reached forward and patted his neck as he stepped gingerly along the lane away from the hunt, going faster than she really wanted, but she was so pleased that he was going the right direction she did not want to hector him any more with the reins and gave him his head. The sun was cloud-filtered; the air, scented with ploughed fields and still-dewy pine trees, was pushed by a gentle breeze as Prospero's hooves thudded with excited beats on the firm dirt track which was overhung with tall bare elm trees. A flock of Long-tailed Tits flitted and fussed overhead in the branches and fluttered after horse and rider as if drawn along by Prospero's magnetic energy.

After two hundred yards, the lane turned left and swept up a slow hill, but Prospero ignored the turn and surprised Angelica by leaving the lane and jumping a ditch and a small fallen tree that lay across the entrance to the wood. 'Prospero,' she laughed, 'where are we going?!' She let him have his head and he came down to a walk.

Angelica had gone only a short distance into the wood when she thought she heard the trill of a skylark but discounted it, knowing them to be meadow birds and that it was unlikely to hear one in a thick wood. Just as she was puzzling over the skylark song, Prospero seemed to go lame and favour his right foreleg. 'What's the matter, old fellow?' Angelica said aloud, pulling him to a halt. She slid from the saddle and walked round to inspect the injured leg. 'Have you hurt your leg or picked up a stone?' she chatted as if half expecting the clever horse to answer.

As a child at Ickworth, Angelica ran the stable staff quite ragged with her constant questions about all aspects of horse husbandry, so a bone spavin or a cannon splint were equine mysteries well known to her. As a result, a small stone trapped in a horse's hoof held no terrors for her. She encouraged Prospero to lift his right fore by lightly grasping his ankle joint and resting her insubstantial weight against his right shoulder, and he readily lifted his hoof. She could see nothing amiss and let it down to the ground. Walking round to his left fore she carried out the same inspection and again there was nothing to see. Returning to his right fore, she lifted it again and started cleaning it out with the only tool to hand, a strong hairpin that helped hold her veil and silk topper in place.

In deep concentration, she busied herself with the hoof, which Prospero was patiently holding up for her to grasp, and she was startled when a man's voice behind her asked, 'Has your horse cast a shoe?'

The unexpected voice took her off guard.

But as the speaker—as yet unseen—sounded educated and was surely one of the hunting gentlemen to whom she had just been introduced by Dodo, she did not bother to turn round. Angelica carried on with her work, saying, 'I think he has picked up a stone, but I really can't find it. It must be well lodged.'

'Perhaps I will have better luck. Would you like me to look at it for you?' the voice asked politely.

As Prospero was now bored with having his feet tampered with, he was no longer bearing most of the weight of his leg and it had become a great burden in Angelica's slight hands. Putting his hoof down with a puff of exhaustion, she said, as she straightened up and turned round, 'That would be very helpful—' Her words evaporated. Standing before her was not a scarlet-clad rider, as she had expected, but a tall powerfully-built Gypsy who stood holding the reins of a sleek bay horse. His clothes were almost conventional, but they had the instantly recognizable Spanish influences that gypsies favoured. Instead of a cravat he wore a cotton bandanna, and his face was shaded by a wide-brimmed hat.

Angelica stammered, 'I—I—well, yes thank you...' and before she could study his features, hidden by the shadow of the hat, he said, 'I believe we have met before,' and removing the hat he swept it in a generous arch in front of him and gave a theatrical bow. 'I hope my guardian angel is well today.'

It was Gitano—the stranger she had met at

the inn; Angelica's astonishment was complete. She was stunned by his sudden appearance and his jovial mood. She could not speak, but hid her face for a moment behind her gloved hand as her laughter was uncontrollable. Finally through her surprised laughter, she said, 'It's you! I can hardly believe it! I have wondered many times if you had got away from those terrible men at the inn, and I am glad to see that you did! But what are you doing here? Are you still in danger?'

'So many questions! Hadn't we better see to your horse?' he smiled evasively and, tethering his own horse to a branch, walked towards Prospero.

'No. Please wait!' said Angelica, remembering Prospero's high-strung nature. 'Perhaps it would be better if you did not come near this horse after all. He is not very sociable and he can be dangerous.'

'Gypsies can work all sorts of magic with horses,' he said, and with that he produced a small lump of a hard white substance from his pocket and offered it to Prospero at arm's length. Prospero sniffed, snatched at it and then, with an excited neigh, strode forward and started to inspect Gitano's pockets for another sample. Offering Prospero another few helpings, he stroked the big horse's sleek neck, saying, 'You're not such a monster.'

Seeing the usually skittish Prospero instantly tamed, Angelica asked in amazement, 'That's remarkable. What are you giving him? Is it sugar?' She watched incredulous as Prospero, like a family pet, nuzzled Gitano.

Gitano gave her a dark-eyed, wily look and said, 'It is something the gypsies make. It is partly sugar that is melted into a syrup and then certain herbs are added just as the sugar is cooling—the herbs are not cooked but preserved in the sugar to keep their fragrance.' Handing her a piece, he said, 'You'll find it has a strong mint fragrance, although the real appeal comes from the magical incantations murmured over the cooking pot to give it its special powers.'

Anglelica looked at his face to see if she should believe all this, and she could see a playful smile hovering on his lips.

He continued, 'The formula is a closely guarded secret, but horses find it irresistible—as you can see,' and they both laughed as Prospero barged into him in friendly pursuit of another treat, and then the big horse nuzzled and bullied Angelica until she parted with her sample.

Fearing Angelica was going to be knocked over by the horse, Gitano grabbed Prospero's bridle and restrained him. As he held the bridle fast, Angelica noticed his hands; the skin looked soft and slightly freckled by a foreign sun. They were hands that had done manual work; they looked strong and capable, but at the same time they were not the hands of a labourer. What an appealing puzzle this man is, she thought, and she turned to look at his face; his eyes held her for a moment and she felt as if he was reading her mind. She was sure she should look away or at least speak, but she found something restful there in his soft eyes,

173

and the need for conventional niceties fell away. Somehow she felt she had known him a long time—perhaps a lifetime. Theirs was an easy silence as their eyes met without awkwardness for a long moment and then he broke the spell, 'Maybe we should have a look at this lame horse of yours.'

Like someone awakened from a trance, Angelica started at the sound of his voice. 'Oh...yes...thank you,' she mumbled feeling foolish, and she stood to one side while he took charge of Prospero.

After inspecting Prospero's right fore, he led him up the wooded path a few paces and back again, all the time concentrating on the movement of the horse's legs. Angelica stood back and took in the scene with fascination because she had not seen anyone with as much rapport with the difficult horse apart from herself. Bringing Prospero back to her, Gitano said, 'I think you must have cured whatever was ailing him. He seems to be going sound now.' Gathering up the reins of both horses, he began to lead them as he and Angelica strolled on through the wood.

Still surprised by his sudden appearance, she said, 'Thank you for your help. But now please do tell me, are you still pursued by those terrible men?'

'Not in the least,' he said lightly, 'it was really a small misunderstanding and it has all been worked out quite amicably.'

Angelica shot him a glance of disbelief. She knew so little about him but she did know from

174

their previous meeting that he displayed only a casual interest in his own safety, and it troubled her. 'Well, I hope you are right, but please don't take any...any unnecessary chances. It concerns me that you have such a small regard for your own preservation.'

With an appealing grin, he said, 'How could I ever be in danger? I am convinced I have a guardian angel to look after me.'

Angelica just shook her head and laughed at his continual prevarication. 'You refuse to be serious. But please—you still haven't told me your other name?'

'My gypsy friends call me Ursari.'

'What an exotic name—what does it mean?'

'Oh, it's a very ancient name for gypsy bear drivers—who travel with half-wild bears that are sometimes tame and tractable enough to perform tricks, but are capable, at any moment, of becoming vicious and attacking their owners. My friends say I am like a man who shares his life with an angry bear.' He stopped walking and laughed a little as he looked away and shook his head. 'It isn't really anything worth explaining.'

'Do they mean that you are travelling with a dangerous, unpredictable burden?' She was looking at him with wide expectant eyes, unaware that she had gone straight to the heart of his existence.

His eyes shot to hers and he was silent for a moment, then he looked away from her innocent face for fear he might say too much. She was watching him all the time trying to read his sombre expression. He distractedly snatched a dried leaf from a sapling next to his hand and crumbled it to dust in his fingers before letting it sprinkle from his grasp. After a few seconds he laughed sullenly at himself and then smiled at her. 'Angelica, I do believe you have angel's wings hung up at home in your wardrobe.'

She laughed at the thought of it, and protested, 'What an idea!' Her expression became serious again. 'But tell me one thing—how is it you have come to be *here* of all places?'

They strolled on again as he explained: 'The gypsies I am travelling with always come this way every year on their way to and from the horse fairs in Cumbria. All of this is familiar country to them.'

Angelica clasped her hands together excitedly. 'Oh, how thrilling to travel so! But how do you know the gypsies? I have always heard that they live in a secret society.'

'It's quite a long story, but...when I was a boy, I came across a gypsy lad who had broken his leg when his horse fell and became trapped in a bog. He had been thrown clear but the horse was in danger of drowning. We helped the horse swim free—it was a smart horse and didn't panic. And finally, I was able to help the gypsy back to his people who doctored his leg. I often visited the gypsy camp to see how his leg was mending and we became like brothers.

'They live in a very closed circle and it is very hard to gain their trust, but once you have, you are blessed with friends for life. They have a very strong code of honour, and often it is much stricter than the laws of many of the countries through which they travel. I chose the gypsy life when I wearied of the outside world, or when it wearied of me. The life of "getting and spending" has nothing to attract a man like myself who has no fortune. I find the gypsies more honest and trustworthy than *honourable* men.' He said the word *honourable* with a sharp edge of irony.

As they walked, Angelica realized that she had only seen him before in near darkness. When his features were in repose his strong jaw and faintly scarred cheek made him look arrogant, but when his dark eyes came into play they radiated a kindness that gave the recipient of his gaze a sense of well-being. He still retained that same relaxed manner that had made Angelica feel so unafraid the night of their unconventional first meeting. 'How long have you travelled with the gypsies?' she asked.

'About a year. Before that I would see my gypsy friends only occasionally whenever they were passing...in the North where I lived.'

'How I envy you!' she said, spotting a large flat boulder and sitting down to rest, and her eyes sparked with excitement as she imagined the gypsy life. 'It must be wonderful being able to travel anywhere you please *whenever* you please and not be beholden to anyone.'

'Y-Yes,' he hesitated slightly, 'it does have many advantages, but there is much to be said for a home and a hearth, and a hat-stand always in the same place so you can pitch your hat at it at the end of every day without thinking.'

Tethering both horses loosely to low branches, he sat down beside her.

'I can certainly understand that, as I can hardly remember having a home in which I really belonged,' Angelica said. 'My parents died when I was very young, and although I have some memories of home, I was too young to understand or appreciate how wonderful it is to be in a house where you really belong. I have spent most of my life living in other people's houses. It would be nice to have a place to call one's own. But going about in one of those beautiful, little, gypsy caravans would be quite like having a home. And if you tired of the view from the windows, or if you had a disagreeable neighbour, you could just roll away to something nicer.' And she smiled softly to herself at the thought.

'You have only thought of the advantages of gypsy life,' he said lightly, and then more sternly he added, 'The women, most especially, have a very hard existence. They work terribly hard and they never really know if their men will come back at the end of the day because the life is unpredictable and sometimes violent.' Not wanting to overrule her thoughts completely, he added, 'But I admit, there are attractions.'

Angelica sighed philosophically and said, 'And now, I have to go to London for the Season and spend my time lining up in the draughty corridors of the Palace to be presented to the Queen,' here her tone became whimsical, 'and I shall have to smile at gentlemen who dance on my feet and spill lemonade on my gloves, and I shall perish from hunger because the chaperons will be so devoted to their rubber of whist that the supper rooms will never be visited.' She gave a light laugh and added, 'At least that is what people tell me the Season is like. I must say, travelling with the gypsies has a great appeal compared to that.' Her gay laughter drifted up through the quiet wood.

He laughed with her and smiled to himself for a moment: 'I have to confess that I have done both—lived in London and lived with the gypsies—and your understanding of the Season is very accurate. I'm inclined to agree with you that the gypsy life must be better,' he said, not totally in jest, and then they both laughed in sympathy. Suddenly his tone became moody. 'In any case, you mentioned chaperons a moment ago...' he looked round him to make sure they were not being observed, 'it would do you no good if you were seen alone—particularly with a stranger...you had better go.'

'I suppose you are right,' said Angelica a little sadly. 'I think it is sometimes a silly convention, .but, as well as living in their house, I live in my aunt and uncle's shadow and I must follow their wishes. It would upset my aunt if any tittle-tattle reached her ears. I suppose if my parents were still alive I might be as superficially defiant as other girls seem to be. But leading a life like mine—feeling gratitude for everything that I am given—makes me feel bound to do exactly as my aunt and uncle tell me. It really is the least I can do not to make extra problems for them. I do try to make myself obliging.

179

Although I am very fond of my aunt and uncle I have always had the feeling that they are only tolerating me from a sense of family responsibility.' She frowned. 'I am sure that would sound terribly disloyal to anyone who knew all that they have done for me—but this is awful!' she gasped suddenly and laughed at herself. 'How can I bore you with all this? If this is any example of my drawing-room small talk I shall be drummed out of London society instantly! Please, excuse me for being tedious!' But secretly she wondered in amazement at her own openness as these long-concealed thoughts spilled forth for the first time in her life. He was smiling at her so she added, 'Goodness, I have never spoken to anyone like this before,' and quite sure she should feel embarrassed, she was puzzled to find that she did not. Then the memory of her vivid dream flashed before her. She coloured a little and turned away to hide it, saying: 'I hope you will not think me foolish.'

'I am honoured that you feel you can speak to me with frankness. It may mean we are friends,' he said warmly. Angelica smiled approvingly at this notion. 'But you must go,' he said, without much conviction. He stood up, offered his hand and brought her to her feet. He untied Prospero's reins from the branches and brought him to her saying, 'You have a fine horse here.'

'Oh, he's not mine—he belonged to someone who, sadly, has died. Someone called Lord Anthony.'

'Yes—of Cranleigh Castle? I have heard his

strange story. Everyone who passes this way hears that odd tale. People here seem to speak of nothing else.'

'It is very sad.'

'Well—from what I am told—he deserved whatever punishment he got.'

Angelica looked at him startled. He did not strike her as someone quick to condemn others. 'Why do you say that?'

'He must have been guilty of a great deal, including stupidity. They say he was very irresponsible and a wastrel.'

Angelica felt strangely defensive. She studied his face and his expression was still kind, but she detected a hint of something else there that she could not fathom. She surprised herself by saying with sudden heat, 'I don't know how you can speak ill of the dead and condemn a man you never met! All I know is that this wise and big-hearted horse was his, and from that connection alone I am convinced he must have had many redeeming qualities.'

'You are too kind-hearted and trusting. It will get you into trouble some day.' He was looking down at her with a half smile—almost rueful—and then before she knew it, he had placed his hands on her waist and lifted her onto Prospero's saddle.

Angelica gathered up the reins feeling rather cross and flustered, but then she could not help but laugh. 'What a curious enigma you are! You have put me in a temper and made me feel I should defend a poor dead man I never knew.'

He stroked Prospero's neck for a moment and then looked up at her. 'I am sorry I angered you. It is only that life is so precious, I have very little time or patience with anyone who does not see the value of it.'

'And you believe, like many, that this Lord Anthony was a wastrel?'

'Everyone says so.'

'Well—perhaps.' Her voice softened and she too stroked Prospero's neck. 'But I still cannot help having a fondness for someone who could have tamed this half-wild horse.'

He smiled up at her and said quietly, 'No, neither could I.'

Angelica nodded in agreement and only realized later, on reflection, that his words could have had a double meaning. She said: 'There—you see—you are not so condemning as you think you are.'

'I stand corrected.' He played at giving her a humble bow watching her mischievously out of the corner of his eyes and it made her laugh.

'You can never be serious, can you?'

'No, my lady—life is too short. Every day and every hour is too short.'

'They are—and that is why I must go.' She held out a gloved hand to him and he took her small fingers in his strong hand for an instant. Angelica could feel the warmth of his grasp through the soft leather. 'Goodbye,' she said and reluctantly nudged Prospero onward through the wood. She glanced over her shoulder to catch another glimpse of him, but he was gone.

TEN

When Angelica returned to the castle just before dark, lamps were lit in the stable against the encroaching gloom. Binstead, the head groom, helped her stable the horse for the night and she would not leave until she had seen that Prospero was fitted with a blanket and given a full measure of corn.

As she was leaving the stables, she happened to pass the open door of the tack room. The room, with saddles and bridles hung floor to ceiling, was illuminated by an oil lamp in a wall bracket. Huddled close under the lamp, curled up on a pile of empty flour sacks used for polishing the saddles, was young Titus labouring hard, trying to read a section of a ragged old copy of *Whitaker's Almanac*. The room was pungent with the fresh smell of saddle soap and the saddles glowed on their racks with a warm patina that told her they had all just been polished by the grooms. Angelica paused in the doorway and watched him for a moment. His blond hair drooped over his eyes as he sat cross-legged, peering intensely down at the limp book in his lap; his lips were moving silently as he tried various words. He was just trying to sound out the word *eclipse* when he looked up; seeing her smiling at him from the doorway, Titus sprang to his feet delighted and confused.

'Oh! M'lady! I didn't know you was 'ere!' He looked shyly from her to the sawdusted floor and back again, bashful and thrilled to see her.

'Hello, Titus! How are you?'

'Well, ma'am. Thank you.'

'I see you've forgotten my name already.' She smiled at him, came into the room and sat down on a low bench.

Titus smiled nervously at her. 'No, m'lady, it's just that—well—someone might hear and think I'm giving cheek.'

'I understand. I don't want to get you into trouble. We'll be very formal in public, shall we, Mr Titus?'

He laughed at hearing his name so grandly used.

Angelica was charmed by seeing his serious, fretful expression banished by crinkles of childish laughter. 'Mr Titus, come and sit by me and let me hear you read.'

Titus sprang to the bench and sat beside her; he opened the dog-eared book with great purpose, rolled back the limp pages to get a firm grip on them, and cleared his throat. He read haltingly from a short essay on sowing crops by the phases on the moon, and stumbled on the words *patrimony* and *circumspection,* but Angelica helped him through them and explained their meaning. When he was done, she said, 'Titus, you read extremely well for a beginner. You read almost as well as any boy your age.'

His face was ablaze with triumph. 'Oh, thank you m'lady! I've been working very hard on my reading and there just isn't time enough for it!'

'I am sure there isn't. But Mr Park has taught you very well. Will you read something else for me?'

Titus avidly thumbed through the pages until he found a couple of paragraphs on pig ailments which had a lot of impressive words in it that he could pronounce but could not understand, and he was just about to start when a dark chill invaded the room and made him look up.

Towering in the doorway was Hibbard. He was wearing a long black frock-coat that almost went to his ankles and made him look ten times taller than he really was. Seeing Hibbard, Titus gasped, screwed up the book, stuffed it into his hip pocket and came to his feet in an alarmed scramble of arms and legs. He did not look anywhere except at his feet, and Angelica could see his small hands clenching and unclenching in nervous jerks. Hibbard gave Angelica a simpering smile. 'Good evening, your ladyship.' His lidded eyes then rotated towards Titus like a hawk following the movement of its prey. 'Off you go, *boy!* You know house servants have no business here in the stable—get off to where you belong!' Hibbard was blocking the doorway completely and moved aside just enough for Titus to bolt past him like a fleeing mouse squeezing through an impossibly small escape hatch. Titus had vanished without another glance or word for Angelica—gone in a fit of panic. She wondered what Hibbard had done in the past to instil such fear in the boy, and scowled at him as she came to her feet. What a disdainful creature, she was thinking, as he filled the doorway, leaning on the door jamb in an arrogant, very unservantlike way. She wondered if he had been drinking.

'That boy has ideas above his station, he's lazy and fanciful. Learning to read indeed! His lordship, Lord Greystone, would not thank your ladyship for encouraging him.'

Angelica was pleased that she went pale with anger rather than pink, which can be terribly unconvincing when trying to put a bad-mannered lout in his place. Her tone was as brittle as an icicle. 'I am sure there is only one servant here who has ideas about his station. And as far as I am aware, his lordship is quite capable of expressing his own opinions, and if his lordship wishes me to know something, I am sure he will manage quite well enough to speak for himself. Now, Hibbard, I would be obliged if you removed yourself from the doorway and let me pass.'

Without a word he slid back from the doorway and stood aside, but only a little; he had his head tipped slightly to one side, and as he watched her, the same simpering smile curved his thin lips. Angelica swept past him and out of the stables.

Angelica was pleased with her timing; she had returned too late for tea, but in good time to dress for dinner. That meant she only had to be in the company of the Earl during dinner. She had spent such an exhilarating day, had met such amusing and interesting people—Dodo, Gitano, little Titus—who had befriended her and to whom she found she could talk. After such a near-perfect day, blotted only by the dreadful Hibbard, it seemed small penance to have to be polite to the Earl over dinner while heavily chaperoned by her aunt and uncle.

The rising sun sent a thin pink line up to run across the treetops that swept away into the distance beyond Cranleigh's open parkland, which was dotted with dappled cows. Angelica was already in the stables and a sleepy Binstead, his shirt tails still adrift, had only just surfaced from his bed and was stoically saddling Prospero for her.

Riding across the wide acreage of Cranleigh Estate, Angelica was struck by the beauty of the well-managed farmland and forests. She found herself riding through the estate village, which consisted of one wide, unpaved street flanked by pristine little clapboard and brick cottages with six-over-six Georgian windows, or latticed windows, where flower pots rested on the sills and were filled with herbs or occasionally a carefully nurtured burst of early daffodils.

The tiny village was loved and tidy and the sound roofs, which sealed the cottages tight from the elements, were the hallmark of an estate that had been governed and maintained with generosity and kindness for generations. Only here and there were the occasional broken tiles or stucco which looked like recent wear and tear during the period of upheaval at Cranleigh caused by the transition between the Duke's death and the Earl's arrival. Estate workers, busily sweeping doorsteps and mending gates, tipped their hats as she passed; some stared and marvelled when they recognized Prospero.

Angelica had already discovered just how clever Prospero was, as no matter how far they went from the castle, if given his head, he would always find his way back to the stable. She had come across an old, Roman road, enclosed on either side by hedgerows; the road was now paved with a soft cushion of grass and ran on for miles. She could tell that Prospero recognized it immediately as a familiar place for an unfettered gallop and she let him kick his heels and fly. She had to laugh aloud at the exhilaration of his speed and spirit as they cut through the fresh morning air, crisp and clean, promising a new and burgeoning day. Prospero was scarcely winded for his gallop, but Angelica found herself breathing a little harder. This was magic! And as Dodo had said, who wanted to be fussing with dresses and crinolines when there was all this freedom to be found racing with the wind. She had been riding a couple of hours when she was surprised to come upon a public road where a granite milestone stood with *Ashford 10 Miles* carved upon it.

'How we've travelled!' she said aloud to Prospero, patting him on the neck. 'It's because you gallop so fast!' Turning him homeward at a walk, she could see from the sun's position that it was still early in the morning. Lord and Lady Avery would still be at breakfast. Not long after, she came to a lane and followed it, knowing that she was lost but that Prospero was not. The sun was becoming warm and the sky was filled with birds. Swans were flying north; floods of starlings, in one huge, malleable, changeful black cloud, moved from place to place in the distant landscape; Chaffinches scolded Coal Tits in the branches over Angelica's head; and the hedgerows were alive with winged darts flashing in and out—a busy metropolis of birds. It was a morning feeding period for the birds, and all was alive with *cheeps, squawks, peeps, pips, hoots, whirs,* and *clucks!* A feathered orchestra without a leader.

Rested and refreshed from walking, Prospero broke into a fast trot and Angelica did not restrain him. He knew the territory better than she, and she was happy to let him ramble. The lane divided; to the left, a narrow lane crossing the fields; to the right, a wide lane passing through a small wood. Prospero took the wooded lane. Huge, leafless, gnarled old trees, with vast trunks and branches, stood guard over the lane and the floor of the wood was carpeted in a soft mulch of leaves from the previous autumn; dotted here and there were unfolding ferns, awakening after a winter beneath the leafy blanket. The sun infiltrated the bare branches and the wood was silent except for the hum of the birds and the distant, insistent drilling of a woodpecker. Suddenly a friendly voice came from somewhere near Angelica's right ear:

'The angels are awake early this morning.'

She turned her head quickly in the direction of the voice, and she could only laugh: there, right up at eye level, fifteen feet away, lounging along a massive, accommodating branch of an ancient tree, was Gitano, reclining on his back with his hands resting behind his head, like a man at home, deep in the comfort of a favourite old sofa. He was gazing up into the sunlight that streamed across his handsome, amused face.

'I hope I didn't startle you,' he said, raising himself onto one elbow to look at her. 'Isn't it a wonderful morning?' He spoke casually as if he found nothing unusual in carrying on a conversation from that elevated position.

Angelica was still laughing, and Prospero was snorting, confused and excited, raising his head trying to get a better look at the tree dweller. Through her laughter Angelica said, 'I was surprised more than startled.' She was stroking Prospero's neck to reassure him that all was well.

'It is mornings like this that make it all worth while, don't you think?' As he spoke he lazily fingered and inspected a plump leaf bud that dangled near his face.

'Yes, it's my favourite time of day. It's selfish, I know, but I love getting up early so I don't have to share it.'

His face clouded a little and he made a move to depart (convinced he would not have to go). 'Shall I leave and let you be on your own?'

'*Please* don't go!' Angelica raised a hand in a gesture to stop him. 'I didn't mean it the way it sounded. It's only that there are so few people who really appreciate this time of day. Most people are rushing about too much to notice it.'

'Yes, the thing to do is to stay in one place

and watch the day awaken.'

She glanced contentedly around at the soft grey-green woods, speckled with sunlight and given music by the birds. 'I always think the birds are especially wonderful at this time of day, bustling and free to do as they like.'

He smiled at her. Her low silk topper was perched on the twisted knot of golden hair and her blue eyes were shining through the wide lattice of her veil as she looked openly and frankly straight into his face. He wished there was not such a distance between them; and she—although she could see a frown in his eyes—she thought it was the same sadness she had seen with that first glimpse of him on the ship.

He spoke quietly: 'Do you ever think of the birds as in these lines:

The birds, great nature's happy commoners,
That haunt in woods, in meands, and flow'ry
    gardens,
Rifle the sweets and taste the choicest fruits,
Yet scorn to ask the lordly owner's leave.'

Angelica was silent for a moment, watched his stern expression, and wondered if he was thinking that the gypsies were like the birds who came and went as they pleased and lived off the land—anyone's land—without permission. She asked a little meekly, 'That is by Rowe, isn't it?'

Surprised that she knew, he laughed and almost lost his balance. Angelica's heart leapt

191

with sudden terror that he would fall, but when she saw him clinging firmly to the branch and laughing, she could not help but join in, even though she did not know the source of his mirth. Finally wiping tears of pleasure from his eyes he said, 'My dear lady, there is *nothing* you do not know! All my suspicions that you come from somewhere in the heavens are now completely confirmed.'

'I am sure that every school girl knows Rowe!' she insisted.

'Well, perhaps. But do you think Rowe was correct about the birds? Are they nature's commoners?'

Angelica was emphatic. 'Oh, not at all! They are the most uncommon of all creatures. They can fly, build their homes, sing and soar! What could be more *uncommon* than that?'

This made him smile and he asked, 'Then you think that perhaps the birds are nature's aristocracy?'

'Least of all that! The aristocrats of this world are very much earth bound—in absolute reality tied to the land, and bound by duty with little time to set aside to truly sing or soar... I suspect that the birds are more like the gypsies.'

He had a thoughtful gaze trained on her. 'Indeed the birds and the gypsies are much alike—but you must remember that the birds are the frailest of creatures. They are only strong when they band together—like sparrows chasing a crow.' His face showed that he was intrigued. 'But—I hear you decrying the aristocracy...' and he smiled as he joked, '...am I to believe you are an anarchist?' It had the desired effect and she laughed.

'Well, perhaps not, but I do often think there is so much injustice in the world and that those born into positions of power and responsibility should not abuse their privileges by thinking only of their own happiness. So often the aristocracy does not know what it has until it is lost.' Angelica suddenly found it difficult to speak as the thought of her parents' fall into destitution made her throat contract hard. She found it difficult not to be honest with this man, and she said, 'I suppose I am thinking of the experience of my own family who lost everything.' He could see her eyes darken with a private memory and he wanted to reach out to her, to somehow lift her sadness.

He said, 'So perhaps all aristocrats should change places with their butlers for a month a year to remind them of how lucky they are?'

Angelica burst into bright laughter as she imagined Lord Avery waiting table for his butler and servants as they growled at him for more sauce. 'What a notion! I think that might be a little *too* cruel!'

'Ah, so the lady is not an anarchist! Well then, I will not expect to see Cranleigh Castle blown up by anarchist bombs.'

Her face was suddenly serious. 'Oh, you would not even joke in that way if you knew that house. It is the most perfect house! Nothing bad should ever happen to it—it has been so lovingly looked after for so long.'

His mouth turned down into a faint frown.

'It is odd to hear you say that. I have heard that although it is large and rather grand, it is still very ordinary for its type of house.'

'Well—I know you will laugh when I ask this—but have you ever been in a house which you felt had a heart—a house with a spirit of its own that transcended everyone and everything in it?' Angelica could see that he was smiling warmly at her and she tried to read his expression. 'You see, I knew you would laugh!'

'I am not laughing at all. I am only thinking back to just such a place as you describe, a very special house where I suppose I must have felt exactly what you are describing now. But I was too preoccupied by other things to recognize it at the time and to put it into words. I will never again let another place slip by me unappreciated.'

'Then you do understand?'

'More than you could ever imagine.'

Angelica was now in a gay mood and asked prettily, 'Ah, and if it isn't an impertinent question, sir, may I ask *why* you are sitting in a tree?'

'Can you think of anywhere nicer to sit? It is off the cold ground and nearer the sun. But to give a plain answer to your question—' he gave her an enigmatic smile, '—I was waiting for someone.'

Prospero had been contentedly cropping the grass beside the lane all this time and suddenly brought his head up and cocked his ears to listen. After a few seconds they too heard the sound of hooves ahead in the lane and it made them both turn and look towards the noise. In the distance, coming into view through the trees and around a bend in the lane, was an open landau drawn by a slick pair of high-stepping bays. Behind the horses, high at the front of the landau, was perched a liveried driver. Over the rim of the carriage, Angelica could just make out the tops of two fashionable bonnets with ribbons and flowers swaying with the movement of the carriage; above and behind the bonnets were the twin suns of brightly coloured silk parasols. Prospero became excited at the sight of the horses and pranced in place for a moment and Angelica concentrated on keeping him to the side of the road to avoid a collision.

'Driver! Do stop!' cried a woman's voice from the carriage as it was almost alongside, and Angelica knew the voice to be Dodo's. Angelica hardly recognized her. The previous day, Dodo had been dressed in a trim, sensible wool riding habit, but today her face was framed by a flowery bonnet and she was engulfed by a crinoline and several hectares of rich jasper silk. 'Dear Angelica!' she cried, 'What a lucky chance! We are just on our way to call upon Lady Avery!—*And you,* too!—if you were *at home!* But sensibly you are not!' Dodo was laughing and shouting as if she was still out hunting.

'Not so loudly, Dodo, dear!' said her companion, an older woman with a face that was delicate and still pretty. Angelica knew it had to be Dodo's mother, and she also knew at once that plain Dodo must have taken after her father. Lady Revelstoke shot her daughter a mild, scolding look. 'And *do* introduce me to your friend!' Lady Revelstoke gave a little laugh, flicked open her fan and waved it at herself as she smiled up at Angelica.

'Mama, this is my newest, greatest friend, Lady Angelica Winsford—Angelica, my mother, Lady Revelstoke.'

After they exchanged greetings, Angelica raised her hand towards the tree and turned to look at Gitano to make introductions. 'May I present...' Angelica looked full round behind her with a start. The branch was empty. She twisted round in the saddle and scanned the woods—he was gone.

Dodo and Lady Revelstoke were looking at her puzzled. 'What's that you said, Angelica dear?' asked her ladyship eyeing Angelica curiously and wondering if she was some sort of eccentric, which was her view of so many of Dodo's modern young friends.

'Oh—nothing. I—I just wondered if you had—ah—noticed the very pretty flock of—ah—chaffinches—but they seem to have gone.'

'So that's what you were doing when we arrived!' cried Dodo enthusiastically. 'You were *talking* to the birds! For the life of me I couldn't figure *who* you could be talking to in a tree! Isn't that sweet, Mama? Angelica is more of a country lass than even I! She can talk to the birds!'

Angelica smiled nervously at Lady Revelstoke, whose little bow lips were compressed into a showcase smile, but Angelica was thinking, oh, dear, her ladyship is going to think me quite mad.

'Well, for myself, I think it's charming that you talk to the birds!' declared Lady Revelstoke. 'And perfectly *harmless!* I know that Angelica and I shall get on very well, very well indeed!' Lady Revelstoke tweaked her prim little bow lips in Angelica's direction and said, 'Do ride alongside for a little ways, won't you, Angelica dear, and we can talk. Drive on, Brent!' The driver flicked the reins and the horses moved off slowly with Angelica walking Prospero alongside. Angelica was hoping, now that they were on the move, the whole bizarre topic of her talking to the birds would be dropped, but Lady Revelstoke chatted on and chewed it over like a beagle with a bone.

'Yes!' she trilled as she inspected one of her wrist-length kid gloves before removing an invisible speck from the index finger. *'Talking* to the chaffinches—I *like* that! Very *harmless* indeed! Unlike the habits of some of Dodo's modern young friends.' Lady Revelstoke's eyes narrowed as she looked at her daughter. 'Dodo once brought a friend down from London—Lady Flitwell's daughter—who was a fanatic for archery and she had everyone out, every waking hour of the day, firing arrows into a target in the garden and firing arrows in all directions for that matter, until Lord Revelstoke had to put a stop to it when our rare ornamental duck population was all but massacred! We ended up eating duck for weeks! I do bemoan all these *fads* you young

people seem to get up to these days!'

Angelica looked at Dodo to see if her face would confirm or deny the duck story, and Angelica gathered from the suppressed laughter shaking Dodo's shoulders that the story was quite true. After an amiable, gossipy ramble alongside Lady Revelstoke's carriage, Angelica began to find Prospero restless and difficult; he was bored with all the inactivity, so Angelica excused herself, thanked Lady Revelstoke for the invitation to the ball and expressed how much she was looking forward to it. She then turned Prospero down a track and let him canter to his heart's content.

Angelica recalled that, earlier, she had seen a little spring flowing from the base of a rock cliff and she decided to stop there for a short rest. The spring tumbled into a little pool that flowed away to form a narrow stream. Dismounting, she knelt and drank from the spring by cupping the cold water in her hand. Prospero, wading into the pool for his share, playfully pawed the water and created a tremendous shower that nearly drenched them both. Laughing, Angelica tried to haul him out of the water, but knowing he would come only when he was ready, she left him to amuse himself after securing the reins over the saddle to prevent them from falling into the water and tangling in his legs.

Seating herself on a mossy bank, she ate her sparse lunch. The air was filled with the scent of grass and earth warmed by the faint sun. A few early crocuses nudged their way out of the ground. For the first time in days, she felt at peace. So many events had intruded on her sense of well-being that she knew she had been in a state of mental confusion. The unwanted attentions of Lord Greystone, his frightful servant, Hibbard, all the talk of murder and death, the diamond brooch, Lord and Lady Avery's behaviour—it had all become too much for her. She lay back on the cushion of moss and looked up at the cloud-dappled sky where a kestrel hovered. All was tranquil.

Another thought took shape in her mind. It had been floating slightly submerged for some time and in the peace of the moment it was finally allowed to surface. She was now acutely aware of how secure and serene she felt in the company of this man, Gitano, who kept crossing her path. He was charming, of course, and could make her laugh, but there was something more than just that. The Earl had also been charming at first, and was very witty, but that incident at the stables, when he lashed out at Prospero, had exposed his darker side. With Gitano, it was different. Perhaps he *was* living a low life with the gypsies, but she was convinced of the goodness of his heart.

She recalled with clarity again how she had felt during the chance meeting with him a few days before at the inn, and it added to her confusion. How could she feel so trusting of a man who might even be a fugitive? He had vanished at the arrival of Lady Revelstoke's carriage. He must be living a dubious existence not to want to come across strangers. And what added to her mental turmoil was that the people she should be able to trust—her aunt and uncle—were behaving in ways that made her feel insecure. Everything in her world had been turned upside down.

Drowsily following the progress of the kestrel with her eyes, she decided it was all too difficult to fathom and she would just put it all out of her mind. She relaxed for the first time since she could remember. Her thoughts soon felt uncluttered and ordered in these surroundings. She was determined to remember how quiet she felt at this moment and to use it as a touchstone whenever events became too tangled. It is much easier being a child, she thought; the adult world is like being at sea without beacons or charts to follow.

Not wishing to be late for dinner, but not wishing to be early enough for tea, which could mean a lone encounter with the Earl if Lord and Lady Avery were otherwise occupied, Angelica decided to meander in the direction of the church tower she could see in the distance amongst the trees on a ridge not far from the castle. Prospero was still fresh after a long day, but Angelica was beginning to feel a little weary. The church was stone and the tidy and trim churchyard was surrounded by a stone wall. Only the old grey gravestones defied its orderliness by leaning this way and that as they had been let down a little by Mother Earth who had supported them for a couple of centuries. As she rode slowly along the perimeter of the churchyard, admiring its peacefulness, Angelica could see the back of a hunched figure skulking about in a furtive manner by a half-sunken door at the base of the church. All she could make out was that he was dressed in black and wore a battered old beaver top hat. She reined Prospero to a stop and watched as the figure hoisted a sack to his shoulder—a burglar with his swag? The figure turned around and Angelica could see it was a vicar. What curious behaviour for a vicar, she was thinking, and she watched as he made his way along the stone path towards the carved oak arch of the churchyard gate. He was elderly, with a fine head of white hair; slightly stooped, he supported himself on a gnarled blackthorn walking-stick. He turned suddenly and caught sight of her; she could see that his eyes twinkled with an elfin spark. He stopped and called out to her, 'Good day! You're just in time!'

Angelica turned Prospero and came round the wall towards the gate, puzzled to know what the vicar meant. As she approached, he repeated, 'Just in time you are! Just in time! Come with me! Come with me!' He shifted the heavy sack on his shoulder, braced his walking stick and bustled quickly away down the lane. After a few yards he looked round at Angelica, who, although baffled, had just slipped from the saddle and, leading Prospero, was walking quickly to catch up with him. He called, gesturing for her to hurry, 'Well, *come along*, dear girl—you'll have tea, won't you?' He turned away and scuttled on.

Tea? A nice hot cup of tea on a chilly day? She would indeed have a cup of tea. 'Oh! Yes!

Thank you, Vicar!' Angelica had finally caught up with him. 'I should introduce myself—' and before she could, he said:

'I know who you are, dear girl—the lady who talks to the chaffinches!' His eyes sparked playfully, and it made her laugh. He went on, 'And I am Mr Compton, the vicar round here. Cranleigh Estate is my parish—but you can see that for yourself.' And Angelica *could* see, for he wore a white ecclesiastical collar and a very threadbare suit of rough woollen cloth. They walked quickly down the little lane leading to the vicarage and Mr Compton chatted on. 'I know about you talking to birds because I called on Lady Avery this morning and Lady Revelstoke and her daughter were there.'

Good heavens, Angelica was thinking, everyone must think I'm mad—they all think I talk to the birds. She blurted out, 'But, Vicar, I'm not really in the habit of talking to—'

He interrupted her. 'You don't have to explain, child. It is very commendable, very commendable indeed to try and get along with all of God's creatures!' A gleam in his eye made Angelica wonder if he was completely serious, but still, she could feel her face beginning to flush. A second later she forgot her own embarrassment because she could see the vicar was struggling a little under the weight of his load. 'Can I help you carry your bag, Vicar? Or at least let me tie it to Prospero's saddle.'

The vicar stopped and turned round to look at Prospero, letting the sack slide to the ground. 'That really is Prospero, is it? It's been such a long time since I've seen him I hardly recognized him. A fine animal he is.' The vicar absently handed Angelica his walking-stick to hold while he leaned down to open the sack. He pulled out a bright orange carrot, snapped it into three pieces and held out a piece on the palm of his hand. The horse sniffed at it suspiciously before taking it and chomping it, and then the rest of the carrot with greedy bad manners. As he fed Prospero, Mr Compton turned to Angelica and said, very matter of fact, 'I store the vicarage garden vegetables in the church crypt because it is much cooler there than the vicarage cellar. Keeps them firm all winter.' He closed the sack, hauled it back onto his shoulder, took his walking stick back from her, and walked on.

Angelica smiled to herself. The vicar was obviously an unconventional fellow who did what was practical even if it was a little odd. She liked him instantly. As they walked towards the tidy little Georgian vicarage, a thought struck her, 'Oh, Vicar, I don't think I can come in for tea after all. I can't leave Prospero unattended.'

'Don't give it a thought. My stable is empty. We can put him in there with a blanket over him. The vicarage used to have a horse, but I cannot afford to keep one now...not since the young Duke died.'

Shortly after they had settled Prospero in the minute stable behind the vicarage, they arranged themselves before the coal fire in Mr Compton's cosy little sitting room, surrounded by copious piles of papers, sermons in progress, and stacks and stacks of books. He had to move a pile of books to find a place for Angelica to sit down and she was revelling in the homey informality of it all. His housekeeper, Mrs Keswick, brought in a steaming pot of tea and a plate of maids of honour, warmed and lightly dusted with powdered sugar. Mr Compton chatted about every topic under the sun; and Angelica found herself laughing a great deal, not her previous experience in the reserved company of scions of the church. One minute they were discussing art, and the next the history of Cranleigh Estate and the Stanforth family, and the next, the best way to trap moles in the garden. Mrs Keswick brought more hot water for the teapot and a plate of shortbread, and Angelica thought it was the gayest tea party she had ever attended.

When the conversation turned to the flora and fauna around Cranleigh, Mr Compton gave her a mischievous look and said:

'And *as to chaffinches!* (with which we are blessed with a great many) and commendable as it is, I suspect you weren't really talking to the birds at all—no aspirations to be a St Francis, I suspect? My guess is that you were talking to a young swain who had perched himself in a tree—' Mr Compton gave her a quizzical smile, '—for some reason they often do, you know—' Mr Compton was grinning at her and Angelica, who was trying to sip her tea at the time, almost spilled it because she caught the glint in his eye and it made her laugh. He went on, 'But I can't imagine who it would be around here—unless it is one of the young gentlemen staying at Doddington Hall—one of Lord Revelstoke's guests staying for the hunting and the ball. Ah! But never mind! We shall *all* know exactly *who* it was when we see who claims you for the most dances at the ball!'

Angelica rested her teacup back into its translucent little saucer and smiled at him. 'You are very clever, Mr Compton, but you are only partially right.' Her face then became faintly serious. 'I was talking with—' she paused, as she was not really sure how to describe Gitano. 'I was talking with a gentleman who travels with the gypsies—someone who I know to be of an extremely noble nature as I witnessed him saving a drowning child when we were on the Channel ship—' and she added hastily, '—but please don't mention it to my aunt. It would only put her out of countenance to know I was speaking with a stranger.'

Mr Compton was cocking a grey eyebrow at her and giving her a fond look that said, what a curious child you are, and then he smiled and commented, 'I had heard the gypsies were passing by this way again. One often never sees them at all as they are rather shy about advertising their presence. As to Lady Avery—' he did not finish but gave her a twinkle and gravely raised his right index finger to his lips to signal *silence*. They both laughed at this; then Mr Compton was sure Angelica would want to hear about the greenfly which had almost annihilated his roses the previous summer and the conversation sped off in that direction.

Two hours later, Angelica rode back towards

the castle warmed by a hearty vicarage tea and Mr Compton's jolly conversation. She could tell that Prospero was already familiar with the path to the castle which Mr Compton had instructed her to take. The big horse strode along with his head held a little lower than usual, not quite tired, but less high-strung and more relaxed from a day of good gallops. She smiled to herself and was thinking, if anyone saw Prospero looking like this—the image of a lady's gentle back—they would not believe he was the same half-crazed horse that the Earl had threatened to have destroyed. The Earl would now not have the nerve to have Prospero put down—she could barely get her mind to form the horrid thought—*no one* would dare to do such a thing now that everyone around for miles had seen the massive horse ridden by no one stronger than a slim lady—and ridden, for that matter, *sidesaddle.* No responsible lord of the manor would dare waste such a useful horse and risk being censured by every horseman in the county. With a feeling of relief, she reached out and patted Prospero's neck and he responded by flicking his ears attentively as if waiting for her to speak, but she just patted his neck again and he pricked his ears and turned his attention back to the path which would soon lead to the stable and a large pail of corn. They meandered alongside the high, serpentine, brick wall surrounding the estate fruit garden, and which enclosed orchards and a hothouse.

The sun was vanishing behind the trunks of the high elms that lined the path, and

Angelica turned up her coat collar. Just as she glanced up she saw a figure in the path ahead. It was fleeting—gone in an instant—but she immediately recognized the wide hat, and the old coat that seemed to drag on the ground. It was *that hat,* worn by the old gardener who had rescued her in the maze. Before the figure vanished she could see he looked small under the hat and coat which swamped him. So, she had not been dreaming after all, he really did exist even if Sarah did not know who he was. Angelica lifted the reins which clicked Prospero into a smart trot, but by the time Angelica got to the spot, the flash of old hat and waxed-cotton coat was gone. She reined Prospero to a stop and found herself by a solid wooden door in the brick wall. Dismounting, she grasped the iron ring on the door, turned it and pushed. The door creaked open with a sorrowful moan. She was sure this was the direction the gardener had disappeared and she peered inside the walled garden. In the failing light she could see rows and rows of budding apple and pear trees running away in diagonal lines to the distant boundary of brick wall that enclosed the little orchards, safe from the deer. Quickly tethering Prospero outside the gate, she stepped inside. A few dozen yards away on her right she could see the tall, wide expanse of glass walls of the hothouse which was two-stories high and built along one wall of the garden; the setting sun glinted crazily on the glass and almost blinded her for an instant—but there he was again, carrying a basket, vanishing through a door into the hothouse. Angelica ran after him and called out, 'Hello! Please wait!' The low, hatted figure did not seem to hear, and the door that he had pushed open swung shut behind him before she could get to it.

Pushing the wooden door wide, a blanket of warmth spilled out over her, dispelling the evening chill. She stepped inside and the door, hauled by a counterweight, slowly closed behind her. It was suddenly summer inside the hothouse; the fragrances of warm earth and sweet fruit swirled about her in the humid air. The glass wall enclosed a wild tangle of fully-grown orange and lemon trees, their roots bulging from deep oak troughs, their fruit shining in the rosy light. The brick wall was covered with tall wooden lattices on which passion flowers and fruit dangled amongst the twisted tendrils of the thick vine. And there, just sliding away into the jungle, was the bent figure scuttling under a low branch. Angelica called out again, 'Please wait!' and ran across the brick floor after him. At her voice the figure turned, this time coming back towards her. He hurriedly stooped under the branch again, the wide-brimmed hat and coat swamping him, and as he straightened up, he pulled off the hat with a wide cheeky smile for her—it was Titus.

'*Titus?*' She stood looking at him in disbelief.

He was surprised and delighted to see her and clung to the basket and hat in his arms unaware that he was crushing them both in his excitement at seeing her. 'Hello, m'lady!' He was all grins and freckles. 'What a treat seeing you here!' Then he dropped the hat and basket with a puff of exhaustion in the sodden heat and started to peel off the coat, which was ten sizes too big for him. He puffed again, 'Phew—it's something hot in here, isn't it, m'lady!'

Angelica was still looking down at Titus, her face a combination of amusement and confusion. 'Titus—' she dropped her voice, '—was that *you* in the maze?'

'What, m'lady?'

'In the maze? Was that *you* who showed me the way out of the maze the other day?'

Titus was not following any of this and just stared at her for a moment. 'The maze, m'lady? I don't go near the maze. I'd get a good whipping if I went there, m'lady. That's not for the likes of me, m'lady.'

'You mean you didn't go near the maze—the day it was raining?!'

'Oh, no, m'lady! I was never near it, never!' Titus answered like someone being accused of a crime and Angelica laughed a little at his answer.

Giving him a warm smile to reassure him, she said, 'It's all right, Titus, you haven't done anything wrong. It's just that I'm confused about something.' She eyed the heap of hat and coat on the floor at his feet, and smiled, now more amused than perplexed. 'Tell me—where did you get that hat and coat?'

'Oh—them's just old things that hang up in the potting shed at the end of the garden. They belong to the gardeners, but nobody in particular. Everybody uses them and the gardeners don't mind as long as they get put back in their proper place. You see, Cook just sent me down here to get some fruit from Mr Scrimmage, the gardener, and as it was so cold out I just grabbed this old hat and coat on the way.'

Angelica was now thoroughly confounded by the mystery of the bent old gardener, but before she could give it some hard thought, Titus scooped up the coat, hat, and basket, grabbed her hand and was leading her excitedly through the tropics. 'Come and meet Mr Scrimmage—you'll like him!' She could only laugh and follow her guide through the dripping rain forest of exotica. 'Look there!' Titus was pointing proudly up into the fronds of a tall palmetto which had a heavy green burden hanging from it. 'Them's bananas! You can eat them when they get yellow—so Mr Scrimmage says!' Titus looked a little sceptical and then began tugging her forward again on their safari. As they scrambled out of the twisted branches, Angelica could see a tall man, thin as a feather seen side on, standing quietly in the steamy atmosphere slowly filling small clay pots with spongy earth. 'This is Mr Scrimmage!' announced Titus.

Seeing Angelica, the reedy gardener slowly doffed his straw hat, which Angelica noted was out of season—but not inside the sweltering hothouse. He moved like any man who had become used to life in a hot climate: very slowly. 'Good evening, your ladyship.' He smiled, pleased to have a chance to introduce his jungle kingdom to a visitor. And then he sneezed, '*Atchoo!*' He quickly whipped out a tartan handkerchief and wiped his nose before snatching it back into his pocket. 'Beggin' yer pardon, m'lady, but workin' in 'ere always gives me a cold—it's the goin' in and out of the chilly air. It's like the Carrabee Islands in 'ere—or so I'm told.'

'Cook said I'm to bring her six of your best oranges,' said Titus with more than a shade of bossy in his tone as he was showing off for Angelica, but when Scrimmage cocked a glinting eye and peered down his long, thin nose at him, the boy added quickly, '*If you please*, Mr Scrimmage.' The old gardener smiled at this and took the basket from him. Angelica and Titus followed him to watch as he very slowly picked his way through the fruit trees to carefully select and pick the precious oranges that dangled above his narrow shoulders.

They stepped carefully over the hot-water pipes that crossed the floor; the dripping heat was melting Angelica and she slipped out of her riding habit coat as she went. Scrimmage hummed softly to himself and scarcely seemed to notice his camp followers and Angelica spoke. 'You keep a wonderful greenhouse here, Mr Scrimmage.' Although etiquette did not require a lady to call a servant *Mr*, Angelica felt it was somehow appropriate here in this strange green snarl, as if she was an accidental visitor to a tropical island and Scrimmage was her host and sole resident.

'Thank you, m'lady, I does my best with it.'

He was concentrating on a bright orange that he was weighing in his hand before picking it.

'Can you tell me, Mr Scrimmage, is there a very old gardener who works on the estate? He must be very old as he walks quite bent and doubled up.'

Scrimmage was studying another orange, and said without looking at her, 'Don't know who you mean, m'lady. Can you tell me more about what he looks like?'

'Well, actually I can't. I never saw his face. He had on a big hat like that—' and she pointed to the now squashed felt hat Titus was clutching.

Scrimmage plucked the orange. 'Now fancy you asking me that question, m'lady. You're the second person to ask me that very same question in the last couple of days.'

Angelica was taken aback. 'I am?'

'Yes, m'lady. That fellow, Hibbard—' Scrimmage turned and gave her a forlorn look, '—does yer ladyship know the fellow I mean? Hibbard—the Earl's servant? He asked me that very same question yesterday. And I told 'im same as I'm tellin' yer ladyship: there ain't no such gardener.' Scrimmage turned back to his orange harvesting.

'Oh...' was all that Angelica could say, and neither Scrimmage nor Titus noticed her heavy frown as she turned over the implications in her mind. She was thinking, Lord Greystone was furious after that old gardener led me out of the maze—but had he been furious enough to send Hibbard to find the old servant and perhaps dole out some punishment or reprimand to him for interfering with the Earl's callus entertainment? How horrid to think that Greystone could take his anger out on an old servant—but would he really do such a thing? Angelica kept thinking it over and could find no other explanation for Hibbard seeking out the old gardener—or *whoever* he was. She was glad that Scrimmage had told Hibbard as little as he had told her—and perhaps that was really all he knew—but in any case it would mean that Hibbard had not found the mystery gardener either.

The little basket was now full of oranges and Scrimmage handed it to Titus, saying, 'Now don't you go dropping them, my lad! There isn't another orange this side of Kew Gardens this time of year and I won't have 'em spoiled!'

'Yes, sir!' said Titus, carefully taking possession of the basket.

Angelica jumped with a start. 'Oh my goodness. I forgot Prospero—I left him standing in the cold. I must run! Goodbye, Mr Scrimmage—and thank you!' With that she fled through the herbage towards the door, closely followed by Titus who shouted his goodbyes to Mr Scrimmage over his shoulder. Once outside in the cold, Angelica and Titus scrambled into their coats again, their warmed breath now visible in the frosty air. Prospero was patiently cropping grass beside the path; Angelica gathered up the reins, gave him a few apologetic pats on the neck and decided to lead him the few hundred yards back to the stable. After a few yards she looked round for Titus; he was a few paces behind her cradling his cargo of fruit in front of him securely in both hands. Angelica stopped and said, 'Titus, aren't you going to walk with me?'

He looked surprised. 'Well—no, m'lady—' He sounded a tich insulted, 'I know how to behave.'

She smiled at him. 'Oh, Titus—do walk beside me—otherwise I'll get a crick in the neck trying to look back to talk to you.'

He hesitated. 'I don't think I ought.'

'Well maybe I ought not ask you—' she stopped Prospero and walked back a few paces until she was alongside Titus, '—so I'll walk beside you.' It made Titus laugh with shy delight, and they strolled along the deserted path.

Titus said, 'You know you was asking Mr Scrimmage about some old gardener? Well, I heard Hibbard asking Mr Binstead the same question yesterday in the stables.'

'You did? And what did Binstead say?'

'He said there's never been anybody like that round 'ere for ten or fifteen years. He said there was a lame old gardener like that a long time ago, when the old Duke was alive, but that gardener has long since died.'

'How very, very curious!' Angelica was stumped. 'Tell me, Titus,' she asked half in jest, 'do you have ghosts here at Cranleigh?'

Eyes and mouth popping with surprise, he said, 'Oh! Yes! m'lady—*lots and lots!*—least wise that's what Mr Binstead and the stable lads tell me.'

Angelica laughed, 'Titus, you mustn't let them fill your head with such nonsense. Ghosts don't really exist.' Then she said, as if to convince herself, 'Truly—I am sure they do *not.*'

They were just coming to the end of the path where it opened out into the stable yard and up ahead, through the trees, they could see some of the stable servants milling about. Titus decided that this was the moment he had better make a dash for the kitchen with the oranges so that no one could report him to Cook for dawdling. 'I'd better run. Bye, m'lady—and *thank you!*'

As he took to his heels and sped away, she called after him, 'Goodbye, Titus!' and she wondered what he could be thanking her for, and then she realized that he was thanking her for being his friend.

ELEVEN

Angelica's plan to absent herself daily from the Earl's company worked admirably. She always returned to the castle in time to dress for dinner. To her satisfaction, she detected a slight coolness in the Earl's manner during these evenings and that made her feel more at ease. Lord and Lady Avery were always there, insuring that it was impossible for her to be left

215

alone with him.

The dinners at Cranleigh were splendid formal affairs with an endless array of beautiful and priceless plates that the Dukes of Stanforth had acquired over the generations. Fresh flowers—lilies, roses, narcissus—and bowls of exotic fruits—mangos, pineapples, oranges—from the heated greenhouses at Cranleigh, decorated the massive damask-covered table. Candles were everywhere, reflecting in the gold mirrors lining the walls, the cut glass wine goblets, the gold fruit bowls, the lustrous porcelain, and the towering epergne with its frolicking cherubs frozen in gold.

Behind each diner's chair was a liveried footman standing sentry, attending to every need or whim, (their stiff patent leather shoes squeaking with every step) and the able Park was in control of the entire culinary spectacle. The Earl seemed to bask in these lavish dinners, surrounded by so many riches. He was the perfect, generous host, talking with wit and intelligence on every subject, putting everyone at ease and creating a gay atmosphere. Angelica wondered if this could really be the same man who had behaved so odiously in the maze. Sometimes she had to stop herself from staring at him in astonishment because the contrast between his two characters was startling.

Lord Avery, a practised trencherman, was enjoying his stay at Cranleigh as the food was very much to his liking. After that 'complicated French mess' he felt he had been forced to eat for the previous few weeks, he was in heaven. Cranleigh's cook was an unseen enchantress who wooed him with her delights; for dinner there were two soups, one clear, and a practiced gourmand like Lord Avery usually managed to have both. There might follow fresh potted lobster; grilled mackerel in a fennel and gooseberry sauce; a saddle of lamb; roast pigeons; quail stuffed with pâté de foie gras surrounded by oysters, truffles, prawns, mushrooms, tomatoes and croquettes; stuffed artichoke; asparagus in a white sauce; fruit *macedoine* in champagne; and orange trifle.

At these dinners, the conversation was light and entertaining and Lord Avery never slackened in his duties as a model guest, bursting with excellent food and good humour. 'Did I ever tell you, Greystone, about the time Lady Avery was caught by the Queen raiding the Royal Garden at Windsor?' The Earl, who was sucking the meat from a lobster leg, shook his head, which encouraged Lord Avery to continue his story with enthusiasm. 'The whole court had gathered, and it was a fine day. It was autumn, and an official state visit for someone or other...I can't recall who. In any case, there was Her Majesty,' and to emphasize his story he gravely listed the Queen's titles, 'Queen Victoria, Queen of Great Britain and Ireland, Empress of India, Defender of the Faith, who had just presided over an excellent luncheon! Ah, yes! A truly memorable luncheon! We had baron of lamb...ah...yes...' he sighed at the memory of that plump, tender, pink roast. '*Anyway,* Her Majesty was strolling about with a few of her courtiers and the

Belgian Ambassador, enjoying the air in the garden. They came to a parapet where the Queen wanted to show off the view of the Thames below, and as the whole assembly looked expectantly over the edge there was my *own*, dear Lady Avery in *full view* on the terrace directly below, busily removing seeds from some of the Queen's miniature sunflowers!'

Lady Avery was now immune to this once-mortifying but much-told story; she hid her face behind her fan, shamming embarrassment, while shaking with laughter like the others and pleading, 'Avery, you *must* stop telling that story! I am sure I wish to forget it!'

'And what is it the Queen says to you every time you see Her Majesty...?' prompted his lordship, tossing down an oyster.

'Her Majesty always fixes me with a stern look and wickedly says, "Ah! *Lady Avery*, and how does *our* garden grow?" ' They all happily rocked with laughter, including Angelica who had heard the story countless times before.

So the evenings progressed with digestion much aided by Lord Avery's vast fund of entertaining anecdotes. On this occasion, when pudding was served—*creme brulée* made with white seedless grapes, brown sugar, and soured cream—the Earl turned to Angelica. 'Do you enjoy hunting, Lady Angelica?'

'I hunted a great deal as a child. I was very fortunate, as Lord Avery very kindly gave me for my twelfth birthday a wonderful little grey that was a very bold jumper. I think my addiction to fast gallops must have developed then. Now I hunt whenever the opportunity presents itself.'

'I ask because Lord Revelstoke has sent a note inviting us all to go out with his hunt tomorrow morning. He is a very avid huntsman and hunts his pack himself. Unfortunately, I cannot go,' and he looked towards Lord and Lady Avery with an expectant expression. In reply Lady Avery comically threw up her hands and rolled her eyes heavenward at the mere thought of hours spent shivering with cold in the hunt followers' carriage with nothing to see but a few, distant dots—horses and riders; smaller dots—hounds; and an almost invisible dot—the fox; all the dots constantly retreating into the landscape and vanishing over the furthest hill. And Lord Avery did not seem to hear the invitation as he was locked in armed combat with a vast lobster claw.

Not really expecting the Averys to be interested in anything as strenuous as a day in the open, the Earl turned again to Angelica. 'It might be entertaining. I recall that Prospero was hunted often,' he said dryly, 'although it would be perfectly reasonable if you wished to take out a less spirited animal.'

Angelica said, 'Thank you, Lord Greystone, it sounds excellent sport. As to hunting Prospero, the point you make is very sensible. He would certainly be quite a handful with other horses about.' After a reflective pause, Angelica continued, 'I suppose if I kept him well away from the rest of the field at the meet, it might work well enough. I would like to try hunting him, as the opportunity to hunt such a horse shouldn't be missed. I fear I should have to decline the hunt breakfast, as I would not like to let Prospero out of my sight in unfamiliar surroundings. That might end in disaster!'

'Splendid! What could be better! In the morning I'll send orders for a groom to escort you and to show you the way,' said the Earl.

Angelica was up early the next morning, dressed in her best riding habit and ready to go to the meet long before the rest of the house was up and about—or so she thought. She dashed silently down the wide marble stairs to collect whatever portable snack Cook had laid out on the hall table for her—something small and simple to fit into the leather sandwich box attached to the saddle, and just enough to see Angelica through a long day's hunting. But the heavy mahogany table was empty apart from a few letters waiting to be posted that morning.

A voice made her start. 'Are you looking for this, Lady Angelica?' She turned round and there was the Earl who had been concealed by the vast baroque coat stand. He wore a heavy tweed Norfolk jacket which made his wide shoulders look even broader. Angelica could see that he had been out early shooting—a double-barrelled shotgun, smelling faintly of cordite, lay broken on the stand's wide, wooden bench. The barrels were flanked by his recently discarded hat and fingerless shooting gloves. He held in his hand the little brown-paper parcel tied up with a string that Cook had prepared for her. As if weighing it in his hand for a moment, he said, 'Not a very big luncheon to look forward to while out hunting.'

'Perhaps not.' She offered him the vaguest hint of a smile as her fund of civility for the Earl was almost exhausted. Meeting his cold eyes and holding out her hand, she said, 'But all the same, I will be glad of it, sir.'

He smiled at her, and if she did not know better, she would have mistaken it for the smile of a friend. 'You are welcome to it, Lady Angelica, but surely you will let me have the kitchen prepare you something more substantial.'

'Truly, no, but thank you, sir.'

He still held on to the parcel. 'I hate to let you go with so meagre a repast.'

Angelica was losing patience with what was clearly his little game. She said coldly, 'Thank you, sir, that will be more than sufficient.' Now unsmiling, she continued to hold out her hand for her parcel. As he only smiled at her and made no move to hand over the little bundle, she said, 'Very well—I shall do without it. Good morning, sir.' As she stepped away and turned to open the front door he blocked her way and turned the key in the latch to lock it. Under her veil he could see her face colour to the desired effect. She said, 'Sir—do you intend that I shall not pass?' Angelica's voice trembled a little with anger and the Earl responded with a low, mocking laugh that was edged with delight, like the cat that has goaded the mouse into snapping back.

'Why do I get the distinct impression, Lady

221

Angelica, that you do not like me?' He said it as he would to Lady Avery, all coaxing and boyish.

Angelica almost gave an angry laugh at the absurdity of it and at finding herself yet again compelled into an impossible situation by the Earl. 'Really, sir, if it is *only* an impression you have, then I have failed to communicate it properly to you.'

'I am afraid I have been a bad host if you have taken against me.'

'Sir, how can you stand there blocking my way and then wonder if you have failed in your hospitality? I was willing to ignore your insulting behaviour in the maze to the extent of remaining civil to you, but now you will not let me pass and you play word games about your measure of hospitality.' She could see him smiling patronizingly at her; she flushed angrily and said, 'But, this amuses you too much and I refuse to engage in your games another moment.'

'I think you must be very interesting, Lady Angelica, when you are in a fury—even a hint of anger makes your complexion soar a little—and it's very charming indeed.' He moved towards her, holding out the parcel like a peace offering. But she recognized it for what it was, a piece of bait, and did not take it. He went on. 'Few ladies can rise to much at this early hour. I think you must have quite a talent.' He poured every possible insulting innuendo and invitation into his voice and Angelica turned away to leave the house by the French windows to the terrace. As she turned, he tossed the parcel to one side onto the bench and grabbed her wrist; he snatched her waist with his arm, laughing as he did so. Partly amazed that this was happening in broad daylight, in full view of anyone who might happen to step into the huge open hall, Angelica slapped him hard with her gloved hand which made a loud, but nearly harmless, *thwack!* as it crossed his cheek.

'How dare you behave in such a manner!' She pulled away from him, tears of fury pricking her eyes.

'I dare very easily, thank you,' he said through an amused laugh. 'As host I am concerned that all my guests are properly served!'

Her voice rose in a fury. 'You are disgusting and impudent, and if you do not stop at once I will be forced to consult Lord and Lady Avery!'

This made him roar and he threw back his head in laughter to relish it. 'To tell them what? That I was a little too attentive to a most attractive lady guest? You are very naive, Lady Angelica. Chaperons are supposed to be blind—or certainly at least myopic—at the right moments.'

'That may be your experience, sir, but I can assure you that is not what I am accustomed to.' Angelica was not really sure what she was accustomed to, as Lord and Lady Avery had been behaving very strangely as of late, and she looked round the vast deserted marble hall desperately wondering how long the rest of the house was going to sleep. *Where* was everybody?

She decided the safest retreat was back up the stairs in the direction of Lady Avery's room and she turned towards the stairs, but before she could get to the first step, he blocked her way again. His violet eyes seemed solid and penetrating as his hands roughly pulled her towards him; Angelica struggled furiously in his grasp. What happened next was a complete fluke, as he was twenty times her strength, but because the steps were immediately behind his heels, when she pushed hard to repel him, he lost his balance slightly, stumbled backwards and fell, lightly catching himself before sitting down on the stairs to laugh at her anger. Not waiting a second, Angelica seized the opportunity and raced across the hall towards the open door of the white drawing-room knowing that there were French doors in the rooms beyond.

Angelica's anger had turned to fear. He had shown no contrition and had even found it amusing to misuse her. He seemed to think he had perfect immunity to do anything he wished, and she was afraid to even contemplate how far he would dare go in making free with her. As she ran she glanced behind her and could see the Earl focused hard on her as he came to his feet. On the far side of the white drawing-room was a closed white and gilt door, and she threw herself at it and it opened; she slammed it shut behind her as she fled through the next interconnecting room where she frantically tried the row of French doors but they were locked. The floors were paved with thick carpet so she could not tell if he was behind her and then she heard his footsteps coming quickly as he crossed a section of parquet floor. As she ran, she found herself in the ballroom, a gigantic chamber with heavy, two-storey windows overlooking parkland. The wall opposite the windows was painted entirely with a vast *trompe l'oeil* mural depicting a fantasy town; temples, towers, and castles, all with amazing and amusing architecture, seemed to grow out of the vast expanse of polished-wood floor and assemble themselves on a high, fictional hillside.

As Angelica ran into the ballroom, she almost slipped on the slick floor in her leather-soled riding boots. The door she had just come through slammed shut behind her with a loud, echoing *boom!* and she spun round breathless and alarmed thinking the Earl had caught up with her. But it was Titus who had slammed the door—he had just finished polishing the ballroom grates and, as he was about to leave, he saw her run out of the white drawing-room and frantically try to unlock a row of French windows in the adjacent room before giving that up and running on towards the ballroom. He also glimpsed the Earl chasing behind her. Titus's sharp young brain put it all together in an instant. She was thrilled to see an ally but speechless with confusion as she glanced around in a panic at the wide open spaces of the ballroom—nowhere to hide, nowhere to run—not a door in sight except at the very far end of the room—and it was so far—but before she could start off in that direction, Titus grabbed her hand and she ran in blind faith with him towards what looked like a solid wall on which the towering mural was painted floor to ceiling. Titus ran up to the realistic-looking *trompe l'oeil* and came to the image of a life-sized Tuscan house; he pushed at what appeared to be only a painted door—but the door miraculously swung inward and they scrambled in behind it and pushed it shut with a soft thud. There was a faint light coming from behind them as Angelica found herself and Titus standing on the top landing of a stone spiral staircase, and a window, out of sight around the corner, was affording them its light. They stood silently, breathing heavily and Titus peeked through a crack in the door as the Earl came into the ballroom expectantly glancing round and, seeing the room empty, he immediately made for the door at the far end of the room which he opened and went through.

'He's gone!' Titus whispered and his shoulders dropped with the release of tension; he was looking up at her wondering if she was all right.

Angelica gave a little involuntary shudder and stood breathing heavily while looking down at the toes of her boots trying to compose herself. She could not quite believe what had just taken place and as her fear subsided her anger returned, but she controlled it and after a moment she rested a hand on Titus's shoulder and said quietly, 'Thank you, Titus, I really don't know what I would have done without you.'

Titus's young face was drawn down in an angry frown. 'I wish I was bigger! There's no telling what I'd do to his lordship if I was grown.'

'Hush, Titus,' she gave him a quick hug, 'you mustn't say such things.' Then Angelica started to get a fit of the giggles. She suddenly realized they were like a couple of school children hiding out from the adults; she gave Titus a sidelong look and he giggled quietly with her. Looking round at the stone stairs that fell away behind them, she asked, 'Where in the world are we?'

'These steps go below-stairs,' he explained. 'The servants use this door all the time—I suppose the door's always been here but whoever painted that big picture on the wall must'a had to just leave the door where it was and paint it into the picture. I was praying his lordship didn't know about it as only the servants use it.'

There was a faint noise behind them and they fell silent. Titus put his finger to his lips to signal *quiet* and started down the stairs on tiptoe to look around the curve in the stairwell. What he saw there made him gasp silently. Standing a half dozen steps down was Hibbard, who rested nonchalantly against the stone wall with his arms folded over his chest. Hibbard looked up at him with a curious twisted smile on his face, and his eyelids slowly lowered over his unfriendly eyes. It was an expression Titus knew. Hibbard had heard everything.

Angelica's soft whisper drifted down the stairwell over Titus's shoulder: 'Is everything all right?' she asked. As if held by Hibbard's piercing eyes, Titus answered in a raspy whisper. 'Yes, everything's all right.' Titus backed slowly up the stairs until he was again beside her. He gave her no sign that anything was amiss, but Angelica noticed he was a little pale and asked, 'Is something wrong Titus? You're not ill?'

'No, m'lady—I—ah—I just ain't had breakfast yet.'

'Well, you must go now and have something. And I must go out hunting. Thank you again for saving me from his lordship—I'll always be grateful.'

Titus turned out a brave smile for her and pulled open the door to let her back into the ballroom. She gave him a wave and an appreciative smile over her shoulder, and then, unaware that she was leaving him to his fate, she hurried to the stables.

Binstead had wisely decided to escort Angelica to the meet himself. Prospero, hearing hounds barking even when they were a mile off, excitedly started an impromptu display of dressage movements. 'Prospero has started hunting already and we haven't even arrived at the meet yet,' observed Angelica nervously, seeing that he was definitely going to be as much as she could manage.

'I'm hoping he'll be all right, m'lady, after he's had a bit of a run,' offered Binstead trying to prevent the bay hack he was riding from being pushed off the road and into a ditch by Prospero's capering.

'I'm sure you're right. But I hope the

huntsman doesn't keep us standing about forever at the meet. Prospero is very excitable—the sooner we go off the better.' She was starting to feel a little apprehensive about Prospero's energetic and erratic show of enthusiasm.

The meet was at Lord Revelstoke's hunting lodge. The enchanting, Palladian-style building was set high on a grassy terrace, about five miles from his house, Doddington Hall. Servants, offering the riders glasses of port and hot, miniature pasties, stepped warily with their silver trays amongst the horses' restless heels. Angelica stopped Prospero some distance away to let him continue his dancing-about in harmless isolation.

Dodo saw Angelica arrive, trotted up on her big grey, Cally, and called out, 'Hello! Have you given Prospero the dose of brandy as I recommended to calm him down?'

'I wish I *had!*' laughed Angelica. 'With all his larking about, I daren't get any closer than this to the other horses as I'm not sure what would happen. Do you think Prospero would eat the whipper-in?' she joked.

'Very likely! Whip, twenty-five couple of hounds and all! Never mind! I'll stay at the back with you and we can have a good gossip. In any case, I think Papa's taking hounds off now. We should be on the move in a minute. Ah, listen to that!' Dodo said, directing her attention to the hunt. 'It sounds as if hounds have picked up a scent. We'll be away in a moment.'

In a nearby spinney, hounds and huntsman—

broad and muscular Lord Revelstoke—were hidden from view until the hounds yelped in hopeful chorus and dashed out across open country, followed by Lord Revelstoke, mounted on an implacable liver chestnut. The Whipper-in emerged on his quick-footed bay to chase after a brainless hound going in the wrong direction, and calling crossly after it by name in a gravelly chant, *'Ey Uup Dozzie! Dozzie! Ey Uup!'* The errant hound, hearing its name, suddenly looked up from its manic sniffing and, seeing the pack racing in a line in the opposite direction, snorted with such embarrassed surprise that its floppy ears shot straight up into the air, and it fled after the others. As Angelica and Dodo watched, the field—forty or more horses—suddenly bounded off, the scurry of hooves throwing up a shower of grass and sod. Angelica and Dodo laughed; delighted, they galloped off, both pulling hard to keep their horses in check. After a few moments of battling with their excited horses, and trying to get them down to a collected canter, Dodo called across to Angelica, who was flying alongside, 'It's no good! I can't hold Cally any longer! He wants to go and he's pulling my arms out of the sockets! What about you? Shall we give them a run?'

'I'm willing to give it a try, Dodo, but if I commit the ultimate crime of overtaking the Master, I'll just keep galloping until I get back to Cranleigh!' Angelica called this gaily over the roar of the drumming hooves. She gave Prospero his head and the horses flew forward as if in a race.

The pair galloped in unison up to the back of the field which was galloping across the pasture land towards a hedge and a ditch. Overtaking the entire field in a dozen strides, Prospero sailed over the hedge, and Angelica, holding her breath, stayed with him. Thudding hooves pounded up spirals of dust; flocks of startled wood pigeons burst into the sky; the cutting wind snapped at the riders' faces. It would have been impossible for anyone to guess that, although she seemed to ride at every obstacle with complete ease and assurance, often Angelica's excitement was tempered with fear. She possessed a strong sense of pride which she inherited from her father and this pride would never allow her to reveal her lack of confidence to anyone. It took great courage to match Prospero's boldness as he hurled himself at every jump.

Even as a child, Angelica had experienced a combination of pleasure and pain out hunting. Her fingers would become so frozen that she could not grip the reins for the terrible burning sensation caused by the cold. Often her feet were in agony and she would have to force herself to wriggle her toes inside her boots to return the feeling to them. The pain was sometimes unbearable and it felt as if her toes would crack. If she was exhausted, she would not let herself retire early from the field, but push herself on, knowing that the more tired she became the more the risk she would take a fall.

But to Angelica's mind, the excitement and

the freedom of riding was far greater than the hardships. To be part of a galloping storm of powerful horses was thrilling. She loved being in the front line of several waves of horses racing towards the next stone wall. Even at a flat gallop, when she should have been concentrating on the next jump, she could not resist glancing left and then right to see the other horses straining at the bit as they fought to go faster and faster. As they lunged forward she could see their heated breath pouring from their foaming nostrils, exploding into whirling clouds in the icy air.

She loved these wonderful gallops and never felt that she had made the best of the day unless she was exhausted, rain-soaked, and trembling with the cold and exhilaration on the long ride back to the stables. She always refused to take a carriage home, snuggled under warm rugs, with the rest of the ladies who left their hard-worked horses to be ridden home by the grooms. Angelica always made her own way home no matter how dark it was getting and she would never leave the stables until the grooms had cleaned and rewarded her horse with an extra helping of corn.

Hunting on Prospero was a thrilling new experience. He knew his job, had courage enough for both of them, and Angelica had never felt so confident. After an exhilarating run, the hounds lost the cunning old fox and the field was slowing to a walk. As Dodo caught up with her, Angelica confessed, 'I've never known anything like this! Prospero understands what he is doing far better than I. He took that five-bar gate as if it was a little stick in the road. His timing is perfection and he needs no hints from me!'

The huntsman guided hounds to a new cover. The tan-and-white hounds, tails waving like a forest of metronomes and their dun-coloured noses burrowing into the damp grass, ran crisscrossing an invisible trail left by the fox. Snuffling and sneezing with tremendous concentration, they finally raised their droopy eyes skyward and bayed joyously.

'I usually hope the fox gets away,' said Dodo, gathering up her reins preparing to gallop, 'but the farmers round here haven't a hen left because of this fox! Papa won't be able to face the farmers if he lets them down today and gets out-witted by this greedy old thief that's stealing the food right off the farmers' tables! And I don't want Papa in a foul mood because Mama is about to tell him how much my wedding is going to cost—' Dodo's fine arched eyebrows shot up like exclamation marks, '—it's going to cost a bundle because we have to have it in London! Daddy will be furious, but it isn't Mama's fault. I was quite happy to have the wedding here and let the Reverend Mr Quince perform the ceremony at Doddington, but Mr Quince has been ill. You don't know him, of course, but he's the vicar of our parish. While Cranleigh is such a large estate it has to have its own vicar—dear Mr Compton—Doddington and Crowood estates are smaller and have always shared a vicar—Mr

Quince—who is very old and Mama says he's gone a bit dotty. Says he keeps ranting on about this and that and all kinds of nonsense that doesn't mean two pins to anyone else and he just isn't himself at all, poor man—' Dodo shot Angelica a rueful glance, '—such a dear man, always very timid, not like Mr Compton who always speaks his mind. But Papa says Mr Quince's illness has to do with him having been a missionary in South America early in his career when he got a touch of malaria. So of course it isn't Mr Quince's fault that we have to have the wedding in London, but Papa is going to go all red in the face and boil like a tea kettle when Mama tells him about the cost and on top of all that, Papa is already cross because the gypsies are back.'

Angelica became suddenly interested and asked, 'Doesn't Lord Revelstoke like the gypsies?'

'Not a bit of it, though in truth they've never really done him any harm. He's rather biased really as years ago some wily old gypsy won one of Papa's favourite horses from him in a racing bet and Papa has been furious with them ever since. It was all fair and square but Papa got a bit too big for his boots and thought he had the horse to beat them all and let himself get talked into putting his horse up as the stake.' Dodo lowered her voice which was usually on high volume like a frantic auctioneer. 'Papa would be furious if he knew I was telling this story!' She laughed wickedly as she went on, 'Anyway, it wasn't so much losing his favourite horse as the way his friend the old Duke of Stanforth would ride over from Cranleigh Castle just for the pleasure of laughing and calling him a silly beggar for trying to beat the gypsies at their own game—that was what really scalded his pride.' Dodo's laughter at her father's expense was infectious and Angelica couldn't help laughing a little.

Angelica asked, 'But how do you know the gypsies are about? Do you ever *see* them?'

'Not often, but Papa says he knows they are in the county because whenever they are about he always gets a terrible pain in his purse!' Dodo allowed herself a little whoop of enjoyment at this. 'But they are very private and were always permitted to camp on Cranleigh estate land by the old Duke, so I suppose that is where they make themselves to home when they travel this way.'

Angelica asked, 'How often are they here?'

Dodo gave her a probing look. 'Why are you so interested in the gypsies?'

'Oh, no reason really—' and before Angelica could think of an answer, Dodo interrupted her:

'Ha! I know *why* you're asking!'

'You do?' Angelica was startled and not at all sure she wanted Dodo to know that she was hoping to find out more about the intriguing stranger, Gitano.

Dodo had Angelica fixed with a knowing look. 'I understand *precisely* why you're interested in the gypsies—you want to have your fortune read by one of those gypsy fortune-tellers!'

'I hadn't really thought—'

Dodo leaned towards Angelica and interrupted in a sharp whisper, 'Don't tell Mama, of course, but I had a gypsy woman read my fortune last year at the Derby!'

Angelica was fascinated and leaned in Dodo's direction to listen. Prospero and Caliban seem to sense a secret was being shared; they stood quite still and pricked their ears as if eavesdropping. Dodo whispered, 'She told me I had the longest lifeline she had ever seen,' Dodo peeled back a kid glove to display her palm to Angelica and point to what Angelica thought was an all but invisible crease in her hand. Dodo went on, full of enthusiasm, 'And—look at *this!*' she was pointing to another supposed crease in her smooth white palm. 'This is the line she saw Freddie in. She actually *knew* I'd meet Freddie! Well, naturally she didn't know his name or his hat size or anything as specific as that. But of course I did meet him—I met him a few weeks later at Pippa Truscott-Tiverton's ball!' Dodo set her jaw with the firmness of a true believer. 'The gypsy fortune-tellers really *do* know!'

Angelica was looking a little doubtfully at Dodo. 'But Dodo—you strike me as being so...'

'*Sensible?*' Dodo supplied the word.

'Well...yes.'

'I know I am—I can be *painfully* sensible sometimes! But that still doesn't mean I'm completely devoid of imagination.' Dodo was talking louder now. 'I was sceptical at first, too, but this fortune-teller knew all about me—it was truly uncanny! But just you wait 'til you've had your fortune read—you'll be humming quite another tune!'

'I'm not at all sure I want to know what the future holds.' Angelica laughed, but she meant it.

'Oh! Nonsense! You'll be just like me, sceptical one day and making wedding plans the next!'

Then Dodo rattled on about her wedding gown—the Honiton lace veil, the brocaded silk, and the chemisette of the finest silk, and the orange buds and white roses—now and again interrupting her dissertation as they galloped after fox and hounds, pounding turf and track in earnest pursuit.

The field came to a momentary rest in a dip in the rolling pasture land; the horses' sides heaved slowly as they caught breath and all was engulfed in a soft billow of their warm breath turned cloudy in the cold air. Dodo plucked a late lunch from her sandwich box and began to eat hungrily. 'I forgot to eat! Always do!' She rolled up her veil to feed in the doorstep slabs of bread which held a sliver of beef between, none of which diverted the flood of her talk. Her tone was offhand as she asked, 'So—do tell me—what sort of host is Lord Greystone?'

Trying to be diplomatic, Angelica said, 'Have you spent much time with Lord Greystone?'

'Hardly a minute!' said Dodo, still cranking in the bread and beef. 'But Papa has. Says he's a good enough sort of fellow—but Greystone has never spent much time down here in the country. Even when he lived at Crowood he spent most of his time in London. He's never done much socializing round here so we don't know him awfully well.'

'I see...' Angelica tried to compose her face into a noncommittal expression, but Dodo read the look aright and said:

'*Ha!* I know that look! I bet he's been chasing you round the billiards table! A bit of an old roué is he?'

Angelica laughed in spite of herself. 'Dodo! I never thought I could laugh about this. He's been *awful!* I'm really quite terrified of him.'

Dodo, who had only been chased around a billiards table by the love of her life, Freddie, thought it all sounded rather like a joke; she laughed and then swallowed the rest of her sandwich. 'I thought I'd heard that he was quite something for the ladies, but there's never been anyone around this part of the world worth chasing, so I suppose he's been entertaining himself in London Society for the last few years. And then, of course, there've been stories...' Dodo gave her an oblique look that said stories too vague to be repeated.

Angelica said, 'Well, to be perfectly frank, I'm amazed by his behaviour. One minute he is quite civil and the next—well, let us just say, he has been rather...*direct*—odiously so. I must be terribly naive as I just didn't think a gentleman could behave like that.'

Dodo's tone was brusque and world-weary. 'Oh, you know what men are like! They can get away with most anything as long as they don't actually ravish their neighbour's wife on the croquet lawn!'

Angelica was a little scandalized. 'No, I don't think I do know!' She looked admiringly at Dodo. 'You know you really are quite remarkable. You've made me laugh about something quite horrid. I feel better for it—thank you, dear Dodo.' She became very serious. 'But all the same, I wouldn't leave a little sister alone with his lordship.'

'*Ho! What a thought!*' said Dodo so loudly that several riders turned and looked at her. 'If anybody laid a paw on my little sister, Papa would have his hide nailed to the stable door!'

A little flash of truth almost blinded Angelica, and she said, almost to herself, 'Yes...I suppose that's the great advantage in having a father—he's someone who truly wants to protect you.'

Hounds started baying loudly again and Dodo just had time to secure her veil before they were off at a gallop. The men who had been taking a warming nip from their hip flasks scarcely had time to stuff them back into their pockets before the field scrambled after the pack down a long slope and across a stretch of pasture which was crossed by a narrow stream and, a few hundred yards further on, a high yew hedge. Prospero was almost on the heels of the Master's horse as they took the hedge and Angelica was too preoccupied trying to hold him back to notice which way Dodo had gone. Dodo knew that Caliban was beginning to tire a little after the long day, so she kept him near the back and rode wide to the far end of the hedge where it had already been crushed down a little by Squire Futtock's steamroller of a horse, a colossally big heavy-hunter that was part plough horse and did not so much jump as demolish the fences. As Caliban popped up through the gap in the hedge, Dodo's attention was caught by something in the distance. It was only the quickest blur of an impression, but she saw something in the shadow of a distant hedgerow that was almost invisible, but, at the same time, once recognized, was unmistakable.

Dodo pushed Caliban on into a canter, and peering between the horse's ears, as if using them as a sight, alternately pulling the reins, aiming him this way and that, scanning the field of clamouring horses and riders—men in scarlet, ladies in black, toppers bobbing and swaying maniacally, and mysteriously staying put—and then she saw Angelica, who had finally got Prospero to slow a little. Whipping up Caliban, Dodo galloped him until she was racing alongside Angelica, who saw her out of the corner of her eye and turned to give her a questioning look. 'Are you all right?' Angelica called to her over the blare of the roaring wind.

Dodo shouted back, *'Follow me!'*

'What?'

'I said, follow me!' Dodo shouted and sounded a little exasperated. *'Come along then!'* She smiled and gestured for Angelica to follow as she turned Caliban on the left rein and peeled off away from the field. Angelica turned

Prospero, followed, and the two horses galloped away from the others until they came to a three-bar gate leading to a lane. Dodo, who was now trotting Caliban, put him over the low gate and Angelica steered Prospero over. Once in the lane Dodo brought Caliban down to a walk. The noise of the hunt faded as it disappeared over a distant hill.

Angelica brought Prospero alongside and, intrigued and laughing, she asked, 'Dodo, where are we going?'

'I have a little surprise for you.'

'Whatever can you mean?'

'If my eyes are not playing tricks on me, and I am sure they are not, I am taking you to see someone.' Dodo was wearing a self-satisfied smile and gave Angelica a little wink.

Angelica laughed, 'What are you about? I suspect it must be something rather interesting for you to sacrifice a moment's hunting for it.'

'Oh, I am sure it will be interesting.'

Just then Dodo reined Caliban to a halt and began peering over the hedgerow that edged the lane. 'Ah! Just as I thought!' She trotted on and when she saw Angelica sitting mystified and inert, she called over her shoulder, *Well—come along!*

Angelica put Prospero into a trot and obediently followed. After a few dozen yards, Dodo turned her horse through an opening in the hedgerow and as Angelica followed she too could see it; there was a gypsy caravan, exactly like the ones Lord Avery's coach had overtaken a few days before. The caravan had been drawn tight alongside the hedgerow which was overhung by a cluster of bare trees. Its green bow-shaped roof was the same pale colour as its woody backdrop. Tethered nearby was an old chestnut horse rhythmically cropping grass, and beside the caravan was a small fire where a black iron cooking pot dangled from an iron trivet. Sitting next to the fire was an old woman with white hair which was partly covered in a tartan wool shawl. She had her back to Angelica and Dodo, and showed no sign of hearing their approach as she continued stringing bright glass beads onto a needle and thread.

Casually reclining on the seat of the caravan was a younger woman whose looks had begun to be overcome by the hardness of the travelling life. She had one small, booted foot resting up on the seat beside her which drew out the fullness of her Spanish skirt into a wide slice of rainbow colours. Her tangle of dark hair framed her cinder eyes as she gave the approaching ladies a few desultory glances between taking draws on a small cheroot which she held deftly between the middle and ring fingers of her left hand.

Dodo was the first to speak, and dismounting near the fire, she said, 'Good afternoon, I hope you will forgive this intrusion, but my friend wishes to have her fortune told.'

Angelica looked aghast at Dodo. 'No—really—truly, nothing could be further from my mind!' She gave Dodo a pleading look.

Dodo shot her a mischievous look. 'Don't cavil!' Then ignoring Angelica, Dodo smiled at the gypsy women, 'Do not be confused by my friend's protests. She suffers from a nervous disposition, that is all.'

'Dodo, please, no!' whispered Angelica, but Dodo gave her an insistent look and waved for her to dismount. Angelica slid to the ground and, unable to take her eyes off the two women, was consumed by the entwined confusion of fascination and dread. 'Please, Dodo, I'm not at all sure that this is what I want.'

'Of course you are!' said Dodo bluffly.

Now watching them intently, the woman on the caravan stubbed out the cheroot on the underside of the seat and came to her feet. Standing tall and erect she rested her knotted fists on her slim hips and said, 'I'll tell the fine lady's fortune—you got money?'

'No!' cried Angelica, relieved.

'Yes!' jumped in Dodo, and she took a silver coin from a tiny slit pocket at the waist of her melton cloth riding coat. The gypsy woman looked mildly interested, stepped down from the caravan and approached; she held her hand out a little arrogantly and Dodo placed the coin in her upturned palm. The woman barely glanced at it before slipping it into the bodice of her heavy, embroidered jacket; then turning towards the fire, she gave an almost imperceptible gesture for Angelica to follow her. Seeing how offhand the woman was, Angelica thought that she must be humouring them and it made her relax a little. Angelica handed Prospero's reins to Dodo and followed the woman to a wooden trunk where the woman indicated that she wanted Angelica to sit next to her.

The old woman had not looked up from her work for even an instant since their arrival, and for her they did not seem to exist.

Angelica sat beside the woman who held out her slim dark ring-covered hand with an impatient gesture. The woman's whole demeanour was so blasé, verging on boredom that Angelica was beginning to think it was all rather a lark and not at all to be taken seriously. She slipped off her right glove, but the woman frowned, shook her head and indicated Angelica's left hand. Angelica pulled off the other tissue-thin kid glove and held out her left hand. The gypsy woman took it and inspected it, turning it over a few times with a professional air like a physician looking for signs of injury. She then held Angelica's hand palm upward for a moment and peered closely at it before roughly pushing it away and standing up. 'No,' she said sharply, 'I see nothing there!'

Retrieving the coin from her bodice she held it out to Angelica. Something in the woman's face frightened her, as if she herself had been frightened by something she had seen in Angelica's hand.

'Why—what is it?' asked Angelica softly as if in confidence.

'There is nothing there, I tell you. Take your money and go!' she said and pushed the coin again in Angelica's direction.

For the first time the old woman looked up; she came to her feet and, in one smooth movement, crossed the small space and slipped the coin from the younger woman's fingers. 'I must be the one to tell your fortune,' said the old woman, sitting down beside Angelica; and with an impatient gesture she waved the younger woman away. The old woman's stringy grey hair was dragged back tightly into a bun under the shawl and her thin round face was crosshatched by a network of fine dry wrinkles. Her colourless lips moved in silent exclamation as she took Angelica's small hand in her knotted old fingers and regarded it closely. After a moment the woman turned up her damp, red-rimmed eyes to look into Angelica's young face.

'I see much sorrow here—many tears,' the old woman's voice came out in a rasping, private whisper as she glanced to one side at the others to make sure they were out of earshot. 'I see tears: a mother's tears, a child's tears. But those tears are past.' Angelica was not expecting anything that would even remotely touch a nerve, and certainly nothing that would cut so deeply. The old woman had instantly found Angelica's deepest hurt; she was shocked at the mention of her mother and tried to pull her hand away, but, as if by telepathy, the old woman tightened her grip before Angelica could free her hand. The old gypsy went on, 'I see more tears...and there is a young man...no, I see more than one...I see two men...and I see a great house where one man is rich and happy. The other man...the other man is poor, he has nothing, and he is alone...alone and soon to die...' Angelica went rigid. Who could she be

245

seeing there? The only poor man she knew was Gitano, but *alone* and *soon to die?* The thought was unbearable. And could the great house be Cranleigh and the rich man be the Earl? The old woman now had a tight grip on Angelica's hand, holding it with surprising strength, straining to hold it as Angelica again tried to pull away. The old woman said, 'No, wait! I see more—I see a wedding! You are to wed, and very soon.'

Angelica trembled suddenly as all resistance drained from her, and she stopped straining against the old gypsy's hold on her. Angelica had to know. 'Will...will the man I marry be...rich?'

Angelica saw the surprised and sorrowful look the old woman gave her—the look of someone who has misjudged another—and she answered, *'Yes!'* The old woman almost spat out the word and she virtually batted Angelica's hand to one side before coming to her feet. The old woman stood over Angelica and fixed her with a piercing eye. 'You must go now—your friend will need you.' Angelica was shaken and could not take it all in. It all touched too near too many buried thoughts and instincts. Was there any truth in what the old woman had said? Her legs felt weak as she came to her feet and walked back to Dodo, half suffocating in a smothering cloud of fright and confusion.

Dodo had heard none of this and said brightly, 'What did she say?'

Angelica took Prospero's reins from her and whispered so quietly that Dodo could barely hear her, 'N-nothing—nothing at all. Just some

246

nonsense.' Angelica then turned abruptly and, leading Prospero, walked back to the lane as Dodo followed. Dodo did not notice how strained Angelica looked until they were remounted and riding back in the direction of the hunt.

'Angelica, you look a bit off-colour—are you quite all right?' Dodo was concerned and said it quietly instead of in her usual booming voice.

'I—I'm quite all right.' Angelica could see Dodo's worried expression. 'Truly I am—'

A quickly trotting horse with rider came into view ahead in the lane, coming towards them. On top was a scarlet-clad man in a topper with decidedly sticking-out ears. Freddie. *'Ho!* Dodo, old thing! I was just wondering where you gels had got to!' Freddie rode up to them, raised his topper, slowed his horse and swung alongside Dodo so the three horses were walking abreast. 'Nobody's got "a muddy shirt" I trust?' yucked Freddie.

'No, my darling,' said Dodo patiently, 'neither of us fell off. One simply cannot fall off sidesaddle as I've told you a thousand times, my sweet. And if you must know, we've been visiting.'

Freddie looked around at the seemingly empty landscape. 'Oh? I say—out here?'

Dodo ignored the question as she could see how grey Angelica was looking. Dodo turned to Freddie and demanded, 'Give me your flask at once, old fruit.' Freddie obediently fished out his slim, engraved, silver hip flask and handed it to his heart's desire. Dodo deftly unscrewed the

247

thimble-sized cap, poured in a little of the amber brandy and handed it to Angelica. 'Here, drink this—you look absolutely dire!' Angelica stopped Prospero, accepted the tiny draught, put it to her lips and drank. The warm fragrant dram seemed to calm the rising tide of sickness and she handed the drained cap back to Dodo.

'Thank you,' said Angelica, 'I'm feeling a little better—' she tried a smile, '—but somewhat ridiculous.'

'Whatever did that woman say to you?' Dodo asked while replacing the cap and handing the flask back to Freddie in such an offhanded manner he might not have even been there.

Angelica gave Dodo an embarrassed look which encompassed Freddie; it made Dodo turn to her dearest one and demand loudly, 'Trot on, Freddie, my dear—there's a love!' Freddie, who could take a hint especially when it smacked him in the ear, tipped his hat again to the ladies and obligingly trotted on ahead.

'All right, now *what* did she say?!' Dodo asked, exasperated.

'Well...she said I would marry soon...and...'

'*And?*' Dodo's eyes were drilling her full of inquisitive holes.

'...and that he would be rich.'

'*And?*'

'And that is all...'

Dodo looked vastly disappointed. 'For heaven's sake!—why on earth did *that* give you the vapours?'

Angelica wanted to escape from this conversation; she wanted to forget all about the gypsy woman and her predictions, but she did not want to upset or offend Dodo who had thought it was all going to be such a jolly diversion. Angelica said finally, 'I suppose because—because she told me what I wanted to hear.' She gave Dodo the best smile she could muster. 'Now, shouldn't we catch up with Freddie and the hunt?'

After they found the rest of the field, they had a few more good runs, but the fox kept giving the hounds the slip. By the time the sun was getting low, the fox was still toying with his pursuers; there had also been much standing about waiting for hounds to find a scent. And, as Prospero was tiring a little, he was less skittish with the other horses, allowing other riders to get close enough to chat in a friendly horse-gossipy way with Angelica and she had managed to put the old gypsy woman out of her mind. The huntsman was planning to try one more covert before darkness closed in, and the horses and riders had followed the pack across a meadow to a spinney where they waited for hounds to find a scent.

Angelica looked at the angle of the sun and turned to Dodo. 'I must go. It is getting late and I promised my aunt I would be back in time to have another fitting of my dress. I had better not be late as she has put so much planning into it.'

'Good heavens! I had no idea of the time.' Dodo scanned the sky quickly and could see how the sun was disappearing behind the silhouette of spindly bare trees.

Angelica glanced round at the other riders whose restless horses champed waiting for a run. 'I had better make a start, but I wonder what has happened to the groom?' She was looking around for Binstead, but she could see only the inert horses and riders, chilled by inactivity and waiting impatiently for the huntsman and hounds to find the fox. 'I can't see the groom anywhere,' Angelica said at last.

'We are very close to Cranleigh here as we've been circling round all day. All you need to do is ride straight through that beech wood and you will see a wide path.' Dodo pointed with her whip to the stand of pale trees. 'Just follow the path to the other side of the wood and you will see Cranleigh Castle on a rise directly across from you. You'll know the way from there—or at least Prospero will. You go on ahead and I'll tell the groom you've returned to the castle. It's Binstead, isn't it? I'll tell him he can make his own way back in his own time. Anyway, it will save you ages if you take my advice and go through the wood.'

'That's wonderful, Dodo, I'll follow your directions,' said Angelica and she added, 'I am so looking forward to your ball. I have to confess that I was terrified at the idea of meeting so many new people all at once, but everyone has been so kind that I know it is going to be such fun.'

Leaning across and squeezing Angelica's hand, Dodo said, 'I'm so pleased you'll be coming to the ball—and promise me now you'll come to the wedding, too!'

Angelica assured her that she would, but as she said good night to Dodo, she realized that the mention of a wedding had brought back to mind the old gypsy woman's prophecy and she brooded on it again. It had been filled with so much sorrow she wished she could just brush it away, but it pressed down on her and darkened her thoughts. She turned Prospero at a walk towards the wood. She felt an urge to gallop off, as fast as he could carry her, to leave the fortune-teller far behind, but she knew it was futile to try to escape; no amount of speed could separate her from the words that now pursued her. The words hung in the air everywhere, and they were now part of her, 'A poor man, alone and soon to die...'

TWELVE

Angelica found the path almost instantly. The leafless wood was very still, apart from the flight of a pair of bullfinches, diving in and out of some holly trees, and a wren earnestly scratching about in some dried leaves. A pair of eyes watched Angelica as she rode along. Behind a black mask, stony eyes, stared relentlessly. Angelica suddenly saw him—the big dog fox; he sat curled up on an old oak stump regarding her unafraid and panting softly as if he had just been indulging in some light exercise. In the distance could be heard the faint sound of hounds as their cries became more and more remote as they moved farther away. The fox stood up and gave horse and rider a look that was neither accusatory nor smug; he jumped down from his perch, boldly trotted along the path in front of Prospero for a few yards and, with a defiant flick of his brush, shot into the undergrowth to go in pursuit of his chicken dinner.

Angelica watched the fox's vanishing act somewhat amused. Then she looked around the quiet emptiness of the wood and a pang of disappointment prodded her until she realized what it was she was looking for. She had to admit to herself that she had half expected to see Gitano, who had previously slid in and out of view like the bright moon in a cloud-scattered night sky. Gitano was like that, she thought, someone whose light was smothered in a troubled darkness, and no matter how much he smiled and made her laugh, there was a deeply turbulent spirit that dwelled behind his dark eyes. And now, after what the gypsy woman had said, she was disconcerted further. And—he was there!—in front of her, beside the path, leaning lazily against a tree with his arms folded casually across his chest; he was bareheaded and seemed to be waiting for her—and the gloom was dispelled.

'Well...good afternoon, Lady Angelica.'

She could not help wondering at the way he would suddenly appear, and she reined Prospero to a halt. 'Good day, sir. I hope I find you well.'

'Not as well as I find you, madam.'

Angelica smiled at this easy repartee. Their paths had indeed again crossed as if he had found her intentionally, and as her eye strayed into the surrounding wood, she noticed on a log a brace of plump pheasants hanging from a snare wire next to his hat and a poacher's bag. 'I see you have also found a feast.'

He laughed. 'A poacher's haven this—I understand the gamekeeper is laid up with gout. And did you have any sport today?'

'Only the fox had sport. Old Renard ran us ragged all day.'

'Yes, I saw him just now—going off to do his round of poultry houses.' His smile dimmed. 'But you have to sympathize with the fox—it cannot be much fun being on the run like that.' He came forward until he stood beside Prospero's head and reached out to stroke the big horse's neck. He looked up into her face for a moment, studying the drawn expression behind her smile. He said, 'Forgive me for speaking so, but I cannot help but notice that you look troubled.'

'I am, I must confess. I've had rather a shock, and there is something I should like to ask you.'

'I will answer if I can.'

Angelica slid from the saddle as Gitano tethered the reins to a sapling. Trying to clear her thoughts, Angelica walked to the log and sat down. He sat a little ways away from her and waited for her to speak, and she began, 'You will think me frightfully silly...and you may laugh if you wish, because if what has happened is amusing then I should surely like to know it.'

His attentive silence bid her go on.

'I ask you this for two reasons: firstly, because you are the only person who knows gypsy ways, and secondly, because it may concern you in another sense. Today an old gypsy woman read my fortune and what she saw there frightened me—and I don't know if I should believe anything she told me, and I would not but for her seeming ability to read my past. What worries me most is that she told me that a man I know...' she lowered her eyes, '...a poor man, was soon to die...' Angelica looked back up at him, '...and...and well...'

He was watching her with a sombre expression which was slowly intersected by a soft smile. 'And *I*—I presume—am the only *poor* man you know?'

Ashamed, she looked down again, 'Yes.'

'Tell me everything the gypsy told you.' His expression was solemn and kind and Angelica could read nothing else in his face. She went on:

'Well...there were two women, and the first said she could see nothing in my hand and tried to give back the money. She had the strangest expression on her face, as if she was afraid of something. And then the second woman came forward and said that she must be the one to tell my fortune and...'

As he listened a dread descended upon Gitano's heart. He had once witnessed just such a scene as Angelica was describing now—an incident in which a gypsy fortune-teller had seen a hand that contained portents of so much sorrow that she had refused to read it. A second gypsy, almost against her will, had been compelled by some force to relate the woeful fortune and, soon after, all of the sad prophecy had been fulfilled. Gitano knew the gypsy fortune-tellers were never wrong and frantically searched his mind for anything but the truth to tell Angelica. He startled her with a little laugh, and said, 'My dear Angelica, you have been teased very badly by the oldest gypsy trick in the world. I have been present many times at the miniature drama you have just described. The last victim I saw subjected to this wicked gypsy theatrical was a Spanish countess who was frightened half out of her wits by two gypsy women who pretended to fight over the privilege of not being the bearer of bad tidings. It is a little piece of play-acting that the gypsies reserve for fine ladies who arrive in grand carriages. You can rest assured that the gypsy fortune-tellers see nothing more than the coins they are given.'

Angelica gave a joyous gasp and put her hands together as if about to deliver a prayer of thanks; but in her happiness, she was restraining the impulse to fling her arms around his neck. 'Oh! I am so happy! I was so afraid that terrible things were going to happen! How foolish I was to believe it all!' Then she gave him a perplexed look. 'But—she seemed to know so much—it was absolutely uncanny.'

'They know nothing. They are well practised

in saying things that can relate to anyone. I am sure if you think about what she said to you, it might apply to any lady you know.'

She was smiling at him, an outpouring of happiness. 'I really don't know how to thank you. I wouldn't have had a moment's rest for worrying about what was going to happen!'

'And what did she say about your future?'

Angelica was a little tentative. 'Oh, all sorts of wonderful lavish things.'

He smiled. 'So it is only this *poor man* that the Fates will supposedly dispense with.'

Angelica thought back. 'Well—I suppose—yes, that is what the gypsy said.'

The dark shadow lifted from his heart; the gypsy prophecy was that Angelica would be safe. It was only 'the poor man' whom the gypsy predicted would be ill fated—and that prediction held no particular surprise for Gitano. He said gently, 'I am sorry that the gypsies tormented you, but I'm grateful that you wanted to warn me about my impending doom.' He gave her a smile to convince her that the prophecy was harmless.

'Now you're making fun of me!'

'Not at all.'

'Well, it is worth feeling a little foolish just to be reassured that it was all hocus-pocus. Thank you so much for putting my mind at ease.' His face was momentarily pensive and his eyes drifted to look at nothing in particular as faint highlights outlined the high angles of his cheekbones and his solid chin. Suddenly aware that she was looking at him, he smiled at her;

his eyes crinkled slightly, and one corner of his mouth drifted up into a slow smile. Angelica thought she might like to sit there all day, just tangled up like that, ensnared by his gaze, but then she remembered she would be late at the castle and said, 'Gracious—I must go!' He rose reluctantly and offered her his hand to bring her to her feet, and she was fully aware that, for a second after he released her fingers, she involuntarily clung to his and made herself let go. Aware of this, he looked at her with slightly troubled and profoundly interested eyes; but her face was closed and she was making herself look anywhere but at him; she pretended her attention was full on the sight of Prospero idly nibbling at a few sapling buds.

Gitano broke the silence. 'You do not seem to mind that you no longer believe in all those *wonderful lavish things* the gypsy promised you.'

An instinctive smile came to her lips and she was again looking him full in the face as she said, 'I would much rather believe nothing than be haunted with worry about a friend—' Angelica stopped abruptly and said, 'That's odd. The last thing she said to me was, "You must go now, your friend will need you." Now what do you suppose she—' Angelica burst out laughing. 'Oh no! I almost forgot! It's *only* nonsense! But terribly infectious nonsense all the same. I was completely taken in!'

He stepped nearer to lift her onto the saddle, as he had on a previous occasion. And as before, he encircled her waist with his hands; her face was turned up and their eyes lingered together

257

as he waited for her to rest her hands on his shoulders for balance, which she did very slowly, delaying the moment, and they were held like two people in a prelude to a kiss. Angelica's heart was racing. All he had to do was to close those few inches between them and bring his mouth down onto hers and, for a second, he thought he might, and every honest particle of her hoped he would, but, for reasons even beyond the gypsy prophecy, he did not. Instead, breaking the spell, he lifted her onto the saddle, and as he lifted her up and away from him, she felt a pang of...? she was not sure what. Rejection? Sorrow? Disappointment? For her this was all new and unexplored territory with a million unlabelled sensations.

He handed her the reins and smiled up at her, she thought a little sadly, as he said, 'Don't let thoughts of the gypsy prophecy trouble you again.' He was stroking Prospero's neck and she reached down and ran her gloved hand along the silky mane; their hands were so close to touching, and as she watched his bare hand she felt a compulsion to slide her hand into his to more fully feel the warm strength of the bond that seemed to charge the very air around them.

Or was this all just a trick that her nerves were playing on her, heightened by the contrasts between Gitano and the Earl? They were vast oceans apart: the Earl pressing his attentions on her, and Gitano making her feel that she was the one who wanted to reach out to him to capture, over and over again, that sense of security his very presence gave her—that secure sense she had even felt at that first impossibly improper meeting in her room at the inn. Gitano had never, as Dodo would have put it, 'chased her round the billiards table.' And, she thought, maybe that was why she wanted to reach out to him—to fully experience this feeling of trust. But to what end? To no end but momentary hope followed by endless sadness. She was thinking, perhaps it was just a trick of reversals and the more the Earl pressed her the more she felt driven to Gitano. The whole emotional atmosphere had become distorted, she assured herself as she tried to be convinced that nothing more was needed to restore her emotional balance than to escape Cranleigh and Gitano, and to let herself be ruled again by common sense.

Gitano stood looking up at her, his smiling eyes softly penetrating every layer of her defensive armour and, at first Angelica smiled a little sadly at him, but something, somewhere, deep down and unexplored within her, ached. It startled her and then she became angry with herself. Now she knew what was happening and she feared it; she was becoming hopelessly infatuated—the word *love* never entered her head—infatuated with a man who was no better than a vagabond, a charming gentleman who had fallen upon penniless, hard times. And she resisted the infatuation. Her parents had suffered misery and death by allowing romantic ideas to blind their good sense and it terrified her to think that she could ever teeter on the sheer ledge of that very same precipice. She felt dizzy as if reeling with vertigo on the edge and she was going to fall, fall right into the same dark sorrowful cavern that had swallowed up the young lives of her parents.

He watched, puzzled and concerned, as the colour drained from her face; her soft cheeks, one minute bright with the cold air, went white and her pink lips were suddenly pale. He thought she was going to fall from the saddle as she wavered there for a moment, and he reached out a hand to steady her, but she recoiled—her shoulders tightened and her whole body stiffened as her fingers scrambled frantically at the reins, gathering control and hauling up Prospero's head, ready to bolt. She could not bring herself to look again into those warm eyes and she yanked the reins to one side as she said with sudden cold formality, 'I must go. Goodbye, sir, I am most grateful to you for your time!'

He was mystified and troubled by her stricken expression and her sudden, inexplicable change towards him. Angelica gave a sharp flick of the whip which sent Prospero cantering off, away into the blur of trees, leaving Gitano alone to wonder.

Lady Avery saw her return and swooped down on her as she was just about to gain the refuge of her room, but her aunt had come out of her en suite drawing-room and caught sight of Angelica turning down the corridor towards her own room. Her ladyship came close to Angelica to examine her face, which was still pale. 'Angelica, I think you are getting far too much exercise. You look rather tired.'

Angelica tried to laugh. 'Nonsense, Aunt Clarissa, I-I am just out of breath—rushing because I knew you want me to have another fitting of my dress!' Somehow plastering on a false smile for her aunt made Angelica feel stronger, perhaps because it convinced her that she could wrestle her armour back into place at will.

'All right, dear. Well, *do* hurry and get out of those muddy riding things and I'll send Sarah to you.' Lady Avery sailed off in pursuit of Sarah, and Angelica fled into her room for a moment's peace to collect herself. A few moments later Sarah came in with the yellow dress which was now in two separate pieces, the bodice and the skirt. With unusually awkward fingers, Sarah adjusted them on Angelica, tweaking the fabric here and there and finally piercing her mistress with a pin.

'Ouch!' Angelica cried out and then she noticed for the first time the deep, troubled furrows on Sarah's brow, half concealed by her lopsided cap and tangle of wiry hair. 'Sarah, what are you *doing?* I've never seen you in such a fit of nerves!'

'Oh! I'm sorry, m'lady. It's been a terrible day! Everyone below stairs has been in a temper—bothered as bats they've been, and it's made me a heap of nerves. It's his lordship what's done it. They say Lord Greystone's been in a foul temper all day. *Nothing* pleases him—'

'Oh well, never mind about his lordship, Sarah, at least *you* don't have anything to do with him.'

'And a blessing that is, too, I'd say!'

Angelica swiftly dressed for dinner and was surprised to find that she had arrived in the green drawing-room before the Earl. Lord and Lady Avery were there, a little surprised by their host's tardiness, but they pretended not to notice and chatted brightly about the events of their day as Angelica, face composed to suggest that she was listening, smiled sweetly at them while trying to dispel the impossible tangle of feelings she had been left to unravel after the encounter with Gitano.

A moment later, the Earl came in rather abruptly; his face was a black rage which, catching sight of his guests, he instantly readjusted into an apologetic smile. His hands gripped a silk handkerchief which he worked around hastily, rubbing at his hands like someone trying to remove an invisible spot; almost instantly he stuffed it away into a pocket. 'My dear friends, forgive me!' He plied Lady Avery with his most penitent smile and hung his head a little, like a naughty boy, while looking at her from under his eyebrows to see if she would be charmed by the sincerity of his apology, and she was. Her ladyship said:

'Oh, dear Lord Greystone! How winningly you put your case! We've only just arrived this very second ourselves, so there is no need to apologize.'

The Earl took Lady Avery into dinner; Lord

Avery offered Angelica his arm; she took it gladly and they paraded into the gleam of the mirrored dining-room. The Earl seemed in good form; he was his usual good-host self, thought Angelica, notwithstanding his habit of mauling any attractive female guest he might catch alone. Angelica was appalled that he could sit there and smile at her in his charming, almost innocent manner and make her feel quite churlish for scowling back at him. However, Angelica did think she detected something strained in his manner—perhaps his gestures were a little too broad, and his laugh a little too jovial. And Park, the estimable butler, seemed somehow out of countenance; she was sure she could see the butler's folded hands tremble as he stood near her chair to supervise a footman offering her the serving dish of squab. Concerned, she glanced up at Park's implacable, grey face, but she could detect nothing. And later, over pudding, she just happened to glance up and could see some tiny, almost invisible little drama going on over the Earl's shoulder, by the sideboard, where Park seemed to be dismissing a footman from the room, not crossly, but in a paternal manner. But, as no words were spoken by the servants, she had only her instincts to rely upon. Angelica glanced in Lady Avery's direction to see if her ladyship had detected something as being a bit *off*, but her aunt was spooning in a large mound of *mousse au chocolate* while simultaneously trying to laugh at one of the Earl's jokes.

After a day spent hunting, it was easy for

Angelica to make the excuse, early in the evening, that she was tired, and after only one rubber of whist she bid everyone good night. She felt more mentally and emotionally drained than physically tired; she wanted to be by herself to chide herself for behaving so uncivilly to Gitano in the wood. And—what did it matter? She worked hard at convincing herself that it did not matter to her one way or another. It was all swimming around in her head in a whirlpool of confusion.

Angelica made her way slowly up the marble staircase, lost in thought. She opened the door to her room and as she entered Sarah came out of the dressing room, through the door on the far wall, beyond the four-poster bed. 'Oh, good, Sarah, you're here. Help me undress. I'm so exhausted, I'm going straight to bed.' Angelica paused and looked at Sarah. Something was wrong. It was not that Sarah's cap was almost completely adrift, and that her hair stood in fuzzy peaks, darting this way and that as if all her hairpins had been extracted by some gigantic magnet, but Angelica could see clearly that Sarah had been crying. The maid's face was red and her nose looked raw from frequent blowing. Angelica went over to her immediately. 'Why, Sarah, whatever is the matter?' Angelica said kindly, and the effect was for the flood gates to open and Sarah's hands, which had been pawing distractedly at her starched white apron, brought the apron up to her face and she wept into it in heaving sobs.

'Good heavens, Sarah, please don't cry so!'

said Angelica and she led the maid to the day-bed at the end of the bed and made her sit down. Angelica plucked a silk handkerchief from a drawer and made Sarah blow. Then she sat down and put her arms around Sarah until the weeping fit had almost been exhausted. When Sarah seemed to be coming to the end of the torrent, Angelica encouraged her to unburden herself.

'Sarah, please try and calm yourself and tell me what has happened.'

'Oh, m'lady! It's the cruellest thing I've ever known.'

'But, what is, Sarah? *Tell me.*'

Unable to speak through another rush of sobs, Sarah got up and, taking Angelica by the arm, led her to the door of the small, windowless dressing room. She pushed open the door for Angelica to see for herself. There, laying on his side on the floor, was Titus, his thin limbs limp and motionless. His head of blond thatch, matted with fevered sweat, was propped up at an awkward angle on a rolled bed quilt. His left eye was swollen black and blue; his bottom lip was split, and blood had been spattered on his torn shirt. Angelica stood horrified in the doorway for a moment and then went down on her knees beside the boy whose eyes were half shut and vague. 'Dear God! What's happened?' Angelica gave Sarah a pleading look and demanded, 'Tell me *immediately* what has happened to him!'

By way of answer, Sarah, who was now on her knees on the other side of Titus, lifted the tatters of his shirt to reveal to Angelica a lattice pattern of deep red welts which crisscrossed his back. Angelica put her hands to her mouth to muffle a horrified cry. 'Oh, mercy! What—what does this mean?'

Sarah nodded her head towards the door to indicate that she thought it better to speak in private, so they slipped back into the bedroom where Sarah said in a sharp whisper, 'It's that Lord Greystone!' Sarah spat out the words, hard and cold. *His lordship* lost his temper and beat the poor boy with his whip, beat him for nothin' at all! Beat him for gracious knows what?! For maybe being a bit tardy that's all! And then he gave an order to have the boy thrown out of the house, and said that if any servant or even an estate worker was caught helping him, then all the servants would suffer.' Sarah could see the look of contempt on Angelica's face, and said quickly, 'Don't be hard on the servants, m'lady. They all got families to feed and any servant helping this 'ere lad would be thrown out as well, to starve to death for all his lordship cares! You know for a servant dismissed without a reference is like getting a sentence to the workhouse! Some of 'em would have no where's else to go. And that horrid man servant of his—Hibbard has been slippin' and slidin' round half the night to make sure the boy is out of the house and that nobody's gone out to help him find shelter! So me, not bein' Lord Greystone's servant—I was the only one what could help young Titus because his lordship can't give *me* the sack. So I sneaked him up here to your dressing-room with the help of Mr Park, but Mr Park can't do another thing or he'll be out, and there ain't nothin' else I can do. Will you help, m'lady?'

Angelica could hardly get the words out as anger had set her fine jaw tight. 'I shall see Lord Greystone about this at once and make him send for a doctor!' Angelica started for the door to the corridor in a fury.

'No! Wait, m'lady!' Sarah sprang after her and imploringly grabbed her mistress's hand. 'Don't you see—if you tell Lord Greystone that you know about this—and that I meddled—it could get *all* the servants in trouble as it would be horrid embarrassing for his lordship if this comes out. Who's to say which of his other servants he'd take it out on!'

'Oh, it's too evil!' Angelica buried her face in her hands for a second and then she forced herself to be calm. 'I know you are right, Sarah!' Angelica thought for a moment. 'I will go to Lady Avery and ask her to help. She will be coming up for the night soon and I will go and see her. In the meantime, get some hot water and carbolic and bring it here and you and I will look after Titus as best we can. And, Sarah, wash your face before anyone sees you. We don't want anyone to guess anything is amiss and discover Titus here. We *must* hide him.'

'Oh, *thank you,* m'lady! I knew you'd help!' Sarah brought her apron up to her face to give it a final wipe and then started off in pursuit of doctoring materials.

Angelica called after her in an urgent whisper, 'And put on a fresh apron, and pin your hair!

267

Otherwise questions will be asked!'

Angelica went back and knelt beside Titus whose eyes were shut and whose lashes were wet with tears of pain, but not of self-pity. She gently slipped her hand around one of his and he opened his eyes a little. She whispered, 'Dear, Titus, I would not have had this happen to you for all the world. No one will harm you now—you have my solemn promise.' Angelica would not realize until much later that Titus was the friend spoken of by the gypsy.

He tried to smile but his bloodied lip pained him and he could only squeeze her fingers a little as he shut his eyes again. Angelica's tears fell on his hand and startled him into opening his eyes again, but she whipped her hand across her eyes before he could see that she was crying, and she smiled down at him. He seemed to be sleeping by the time Sarah came back. They dressed his wounds and made him as comfortable as they could in the safety of the dressing room. It was a safer hiding place than Angelica's bedroom which Lady Avery might decide to visit at any time.

When they had Titus settled for the night on a miniature bed they fashioned from layers of counterpane and pillows, Angelica set off to speak to Lady Avery and she went out into the corridor in the direction of her ladyship's room. As Angelica neared the wide marble staircase, the Earl came into view as he walked up the stairs. As he ascended he appeared gradually, first his head and then his shoulders and his trunk; he seemed, smiling up at her in the candlelight, to rise from the floor like some satanic embodiment. Angelica's first instinct was to fall back in fright and then to fly at him and berate him for his monstrous treatment of Titus, but she fought to compose herself and behave as if she knew nothing.

'Good night, Lady Angelica,' he murmured, his eyes and lips drawn thin by a solicitous expression arranged superbly to convey the refined civility of five hundred years of good breeding. 'I hope you enjoy a peaceful night.'

Angelica's heart roared with rage, and a hard knot in her throat almost deprived her of breath and speech. She forced the corners of her mouth to turn upwards in the semblance of a smile which, if the Earl could have seen her face more clearly in the shadows, he might have been able to read as actually commending him to the devil: 'Good night, Lord Greystone. I wish you the deepest of all possible sleeps.'

With a little nod of the head in his direction, she could see that he was well pleased by her fulsome greeting and gave her a slight bow. Angelica then hurried on down the picture-hung corridor and dashed into Lady Avery's drawing-room. That brief meeting with the Earl had left her fighting drowning anger, but she knew she did not have time to indulge her lacerated nerves. Across the room, Lady Avery was sitting at a little Sheraton desk writing a letter. Her ladyship looked up and smiled at Angelica. 'Why, Angelica dear, I thought you had gone to bed. You must be tired after a long day in the fresh air. You don't have a headache do you?'

Angelica stood before her in the middle of the Persian rug, her hands folded in front of her, and she spoke a little nervously, not knowing what her aunt would say about the news that she was about to impart. 'I am quite well, thank you, Aunt Clarissa, but...there is something I wish to speak to you about.'

Lady Avery looked interested and laid her pen down on the desk to give Angelica her full attention, knowing that young ladies of marriageable age sometimes had very interesting news. 'Yes, what is it, my dear?'

Angelica hesitated a little and glanced down at the carpet. 'It is a rather delicate matter...'

'Yes? You know you can always confide in me. You know you can say *anything* in the world to me—*anything* at all.' Smiling sweetly, her eyebrows raised in supreme attention, Lady Avery leaned a little in Angelica's direction to encourage her to speak.

'Well...Aunt Clarissa, it is about Lord Greystone—that is to say, Lord Greystone has...' Angelica faltered.

Expecting anything but what was coming, Lady Avery, by sheer dint of will, pushed her niece to speak. '*Do* go on, my dear. Say *whatever* is on your mind!'

'What troubles me is that I believe Lord Greystone is guilty of mistreating a servant and—'

Lady Avery's face snapped shut and she raised her right hand in the air to show Angelica that the interview was at an end. '*Stop!* Not another word!'

Angelica pleaded: *'But—'*

Lady Avery's hand was still in the air raised like an orchestra conductor's, demanding silence. 'Not another syllable on that subject—not now or ever!'

Angelica was dazzled by her aunt's abruptness. *'But—'*

Lady Avery's eyes were closed as if that would block out an unacceptable subject, and without opening her eyes, Lady Avery said, 'There is one rule you must know and abide by *always.* And that is *never, never, NEVER* interfere between master and servant.' Lady Avery opened her eyes and drilled Angelica with a look. 'One may lure a servant away from his master with the promise of higher wages, but one must never interfere with a master's right to rule his servants as he sees fit! It is a cardinal rule by which civilized people must abide, and it is a rule which must *never* be broken. Just remember that!'

Tears of frustration pricked Angelica's eyes. 'But, dear aunt, if you only knew the circumstances! If you will only listen—you can't possibly imagine—'

Lady Avery scalded Angelica with an angry look. 'Do not press me on this! Not *another* word! Now—*good night!'* Lady Avery dismissed Angelica with a final angry flash of her eyes, turned back to her letter writing and scratched distractedly at the thick vellum with the pen. Angelica moved towards her aunt and was about to go on her knees to plead if necessary, but she could see by the tightness of her aunt's lips, that it was useless. Lady Avery could be the most stubborn person in the whole world. Angelica wondered if she should be defiant and just blurt it all out so that her aunt would have to listen, but she decided that it might only incur Lady Avery's worst anger and make things bad for Sarah if her part in the whole business was ever found out. Sarah's interference would be, at least in Lady Avery's eyes, seen as brazen defiance of the Earl's order forbidding the other servants from offering aid to the boy.

When Angelica returned to her own room a moment later, Sarah was hovering nervously, and when she saw Angelica's strained expression she hardly needed to ask, 'What did her ladyship say?'

Angelica sat down on the narrow day-bed and her slim shoulders drooped in defeat. 'Her ladyship wouldn't even let me tell her about it. She wouldn't even discuss it.'

'But—if she only *knew*—' Sarah let herself wearily down onto the seat beside Angelica and drooped as well.

Angelica wrung her hands a little. 'No, it's no good. You know what Lady Avery is like when she is defending a principle that she is sure is right—nothing will budge her.'

Sarah nodded, let out a heavy sigh and stared off into space having already spent all her resources and imagination on smuggling Titus into Angelica's dressing room.

Angelica suddenly sat up straight, took Sarah's hand and gave it an affectionate squeeze. 'You did absolutely the right thing bringing him here,

Sarah, and I am so proud of you for risking it. Now I must do my part!' Angelica stood up and started to slowly pace the room, her wide hooped silk skirts swinging slowly as she turned, pacing and repacing the rug. After a moment, she spoke in a low whisper, partly not to wake Titus who was sleeping, and partly not wanting their conversation overheard outside the room. So that Sarah would stop worrying, Angelica made herself sound very decisive:

'This is what we shall do. I will write a letter to Lady Avery's cook at Ickworth and tell her to expect a young servant boy who has had an accident and needs rest and proper looking after to recuperate. I will write the letter tonight and you can make sure it gets into the post in the morning. And tomorrow morning I will ride over to the vicarage and see Mr Compton. He is a dear man and by far the nicest, cleverest vicar I have ever met. I just *know* he can keep a secret and that he will want to help and I will ask him to find a way to get Titus transportation up to Ickworth. By the time we get back to Ickworth, I will find a way of talking Lady Avery round to giving Titus a position and she need never know that he was ever one of Lord Greystone's servants.'

Sarah's face glowed, full of hope. 'Oh, m'lady! That sounds wonderful!'

Angelica sent Sarah off with the promise that she would come back early in the morning with a breakfast tray of porridge, milk, weak tea, and anything else that an invalid might be able to eat, and of course pretending all the while to the other servants that the tray was for her mistress. As Sarah went, Angelica whispered the warning, 'Make sure you bring the tray *yourself.* We don't want anyone else coming into my room and getting a clue that we are hiding Titus. Even if it was a servant who meant well, they might let it slip to someone dangerous.'

Sarah nodded and slipped out. Angelica closed the door silently behind her and stood for a moment listening to the word she had just spoken as it echoed in a whisper around inside her head. *Dangerous*—she had said *dangerous*, and now that her anger and shock were more controlled, she realized that *dangerous* was the only way to describe a man who could beat a small boy like that. And then she remembered how Titus had run away from Hibbard that evening in the stable. Was Hibbard dangerous, too?

After she wrote the letter to the cook at Ickworth, Angelica took a downy coverlet from the bed and tiptoed into the dressing room where a single candle in a wall sconce illuminated Titus's battered young face. He was asleep. She rested her hand lightly on his brow, brushing back the blond fringe to feel for fever. He was cooler now. Angelica put the coverlet down on the rug near him and lay down to watch over his troubled sleep; her anger and silent tears would keep her awake until dawn.

THIRTEEN

In the morning, Sarah came early as planned with a breakfast tray. She was dismayed to see that Angelica had sat up all night and looked wan and desperately in need of sleep. When Titus stirred a little, Angelica helped him up into as near a sitting position as he could manage and encouraged him to eat a little porridge which he did silently, twitching now and again at the pain that racked his bloodied back. When she had him settled again and he was asleep, it was nearing noon. Angelica quickly changed into her riding habit, and drank half a cup of tea at Sarah's insistence that she must at least have something. Angelica then hurried off to the stables and was soon cantering Prospero the short distance to the vicarage.

The vicarage housekeeper, Mrs Keswick, opened the door and dropped Angelica a delighted curtsy. 'Oh, your ladyship! Mr Compton will be disappointed he's missed your visit, but he's gone to Crowood for a couple of days to the Reverend Mr Quince's funeral.' She smiled up at Angelica and then said, stepping aside as she held the door wide, 'Would your ladyship like to come in and get warm by the fire?'

Angelica stood in the doorway and was now barely listening to Mrs Keswick as she had already established that Mr Compton was away and could not help Titus. She was biting her lower lip a little in concentration, trying to decide what to do next. She thanked Mrs Keswick in such a vague manner that the housekeeper stared after her and watched her wander back to where Prospero stood lightly tethered to the garden gate. *What to do? What to do?* Angelica asked herself, tapping her whip against her leg. What about Dodo? Could Dodo help, or would Dodo's parents put a block on it—or worse, tell the Earl what was afoot? Oh *tish-tosh!* she said to herself in dismay as she remembered that Dodo was away too, in London for a fitting at the dressmakers! *Tish-tosh indeed!* She stamped her foot. Worst luck! What to do? Who could help? Who *would* help? She remembered Gitano—but he had been the cause of such disquiet and confusion that she was quite sure she never wanted to see him again. But this was an emergency and her own preferences could not be taken into account. She had to do what she must to help Titus. But would he help? Of course he would. Hadn't he saved that boy from drowning? *Of course he would help,* she hardly needed to tell herself that. But then she remembered how ill-mannered she had been to him the day before. Well, *tish-tosh and double tish-tosh!* she would just have to eat humble pie and apologize to him for her dreadfully bad behaviour. That was all there was to it. But how to find him? He said he was travelling with the gypsies. Was he still anywhere to be found? And in any case, she was thinking, even if the gypsies were still camped nearby, the question was *where?* In the last few days she had ridden over the countryside for miles round and never come across a trace of them, except for the fortune-tellers, and she had no idea of how to find them again. Oh, dear—where to begin. She led Prospero to the mounting block just beside the vicarage gate and climbed into the saddle. Where to begin looking for the gypsy stranger who appeared and disappeared like a will-o'-the-wisp?

Her mind in a turmoil of indecision, Angelica tried to decide where best to start looking for him. She paid very little attention to the direction Prospero took and just let him have his head, thinking that he could do no worse than herself in picking a direction. She was too deep in concentration to notice the sunlight streaming into the bright wood, or the sooty cotton balls that bounced around the undergrowth and turned out to be early spring rabbits; and she never even heard the cacophony of bird calls; tweeting, twittering, hooting, all making a joyous racket that buffeted the warm spring air. Prospero broke into a slow steady canter along the lane in the wood, and suddenly ahead Angelica could see, disappearing around a bend, what looked to be the bow shape of a gypsy caravan. She wanted to catch up with it and stirred Prospero into a fast gallop and, as she rounded the bend, which was thick on either side with holly trees, she almost collided with the back of the slow-moving caravan. The caravan had a little door at the back with steps that could be folded up or down; the bow-shaped roof was covered in green canvas and every inch of wood trim was painted in shades of burgundy and emerald, decorated with flowers and birds. As Prospero, now at a quick walk, came alongside the caravan, Angelica could see a grey horse plugging along contentedly pulling the mobile home. She rode forward with the intention of coming alongside the driver and asking for any clues as to how she might find Gitano.

The driver was a tall, powerfully built man, dressed in black, and he reclined with his feet outstretched, propped up before him on the wooden dashboard; he was leaning back on the seat, his hands behind his head and his broad-brimmed hat pulled down covering his face; he had the relaxed posture of a man asleep. The horse's reins were looped carelessly over the toe of one of his riding boots. Angelica recognized him at once, even though she could not see his face. She didn't know whether to be pleased or angry. There he was again—he just kept turning up wherever she was. It was somehow maddening, but it was definitely wonderful to have found him so easily when she needed him so badly.

If he knew she was there riding alongside him, he made no sign, and appeared to sleep on. Angelica cleared her throat, *'Ah-hem.'* He didn't move. She tried a little louder. *'Ah-hem. Good morning.'*

After a moment he slowly moved his right hand and raised his hat a little—just enough to peer at her with one eye. 'Shuuush,' he said quietly with a scolding face, 'You'll wake the horse.' With that he replaced the hat over his face and continued to ignore her as the horses plodded on.

'Oh, *please!*' Angelica pleaded, 'I can understand you being angry with me after I behaved so—so appallingly badly yesterday—but—but it isn't something I can explain—and I'm sorry—truly sorry that I was so rude. But—but now something awful has happened and you're the only one who can help me.' The little sob in her voice made him instantly remove the hat, sit up, and halt the horse. His face was taut with concern as he fished into one of his pockets and produced a handkerchief which he handed to her. Angelica took it and dabbed at the corners of her eyes before handing it back to him, and she tried to smile at him to show her thanks.

He jumped down from the caravan and lifted her down from the saddle, and as he did so, bringing her gently down to earth, his strong hands encircling her small waist, she wanted to bury her face in his shoulder and cry indulgent tears of relief, but she maintained her composure and set her face in a resolute expression. As she explained to him what had happened, they strolled down the lane a short distance and back again—followed by Prospero, who made a nuisance of himself nuzzling Gitano's pockets until he was given a helping of sugar. Prospero's antics were overshadowed by Angelica's description of the injuries sustained by Titus during the beating at the hands of the Earl. Gitano's face was set hard with anger as he listened, and she could see from his tight jaw and the sparks of fury in his eyes that he must have been contemplating seeking out this Lord Greystone and giving him the thrashing of a lifetime. She anticipated his thoughts and said, laying her hand lightly on his arm, 'But no one can confront Lord Greystone with this matter because it would only make it worse for the other servants—' and she added hastily, hoping to dispel his thoughts of justice, '—and it would fall especially hard on my maid who has acted so bravely.'

'All the same, someday—someday soon—this cowardly aristocrat will be well served by a good whipping.'

She said softly, 'I have to say, it would be better than he deserves. You see, there is a rumour that the lad—Titus—is the Earl's own son by a serving girl...and it makes it all the more cruel if it is true. It was a rumour I discounted, but now I see that Greystone is capable of anything...so you see why I want to get the boy away from here.' She was watching his face and could see he was trying to master his anger and she wished she had not mentioned this last detail, but she had wanted him to know just how wicked a man they were dealing with. Then, her eyes wide with expectation, she asked, 'Will you help?'

'Of course! My gypsy friends will see him safely aboard a caravan travelling north and take him to your friends in Essex. He will be there in a few days.'

Angelica let out a breath of delight, her face transformed by a smile. 'Oh, thank you!'

Gitano said, 'Now this is what you must do. Bring the boy to me tomorrow morning, just after daybreak—that will give you a chance to get him away from the castle in the dark—and meet me by the large live oak that stands along the lane to the castle. Do you know the tree I mean?'

'Yes, it's the oak that keeps its leaves in winter—the one above the lake.'

He nodded gravely.

Angelica gathered up Prospero's reins thinking she should race back to the castle and tell Sarah the good news, and to see to Titus's welfare, but she hesitated; she was thinking that if she went back now she might endanger the whole plan as she did not trust herself to be courteous to the Earl, and he might guess that she knew something; and if she returned now she would certainly be compelled to take tea with him because if she confined herself to her room it would cause Lady Avery to think she was ill and her ladyship would flit and fuss about Angelica's room and make it impossible to hide Titus. In any case, Titus was in good hands as Sarah was looking after him, and, being Angelica's maid, she could move in and out of Angelica's room without causing suspicion.

Angelica paused and turned back to Gitano. He had stepped a little towards her to lift her into the saddle, but before he could do so, she looked up at him with a fretful expression. 'I was going to rush away, but I realize I've nowhere to rush away to. I can't go back yet.' She looked down at the ground a little confused and feeling very weary for the sleepless night.

He watched her for a moment and then said, 'You look tired. Won't you rest awhile? And I'll wager you've been too worried to eat.'

She shot him a surprised smile, 'How did you know that?'

'I am sure you're starving.' He was smiling down at her, studying her face.

'Absolutely starving!' Angelica laughed and then looked a little sheepish. 'I usually ride out with something to eat in a sandwich box, but I left it behind so that my maid could give Titus something...and...' She wrung the ends of the reins in her gloved hands, 'well, the truth is—now that I know everything will be all right for Titus, I realize I am a bit peckish.' She looked up at his face to see if he would think her silly, but he was laughing softly, smiling warmly down at her and shaking his head a little. He said, 'That is not a very taxing problem. I am sure we can do something to remedy it. I know an excellent hostelry near here.'

Angelica glanced around her at the vast wood and laughed at the impossibility that there could be any sort of refreshments nearby.

He stepped to the back door of the caravan, lowered the steps, opened the door and produced two little wooden ladder-back chairs and placed them on a grassy patch next to the lane. He

282

indicated one chair and said, imitating a well-starched host, 'If m'lady will be good enough to sit, tea will be ready in a moment.' Angelica laughed and arranged herself on the chair like any lady in a drawing-room in St James's Palace. He mounted the steps and inside the caravan began stoking the fire in a tiny cast-iron stove. Angelica could not resist seeing inside the caravan and dashed from her chair to peer entranced through the open doorway as he made tea and arranged a scrubbed-wood tray with cups and saucers, and heated some scones in the little oven. He busied himself, taking a sidelong glance now and then to enjoy the sight of her delighted fascination as her eyes roamed around inside the spruce little caravan with its carved wooden furniture, walls and fixtures all decorated in a shower of finely painted flora. Then they sat themselves on the chairs, in nature's sunlit drawing-room, and partook of their feast.

Time flew for Angelica. They had spent the whole afternoon chatting about this and that with such open, effortless ease that she looked up shocked to see how the sun had slipped down and almost vanished.

'I must go!' she cried getting up. 'I had no idea of the time!'

He replaced Prospero's saddle, which he had earlier removed and replaced with a horse blanket, and Angelica had found his consideration for both horses rather refreshing. He lifted her up onto the saddle, her hands resting lightly on his shoulders for balance;

once in place on the saddle her hands stayed on his shoulders and she remained leaning on him for a moment, as if in a trance which would not permit her to let go. She realized that her face was inches from his, looking into those dark, kind eyes; she could feel his warm breath on her cheek, and she suddenly flushed slightly and pulled herself upright. Angelica felt mildly embarrassed and gathered up the reins hurriedly while he, looking amused and a little pleased, arranged the toe of her boot in the stirrup iron. Angelica realized that she had lost her former anger with herself for her mounting infatuation with him; she now knew that it would be unnatural not to be drawn to such a kind and charming man—albeit his poverty made anything but mere infatuation impossible so, resigned to that, she was quickly able to regain her composure and extended to him her hand. 'Thank you for the most enjoyable afternoon I've ever spent. You have proved to be the kindest and most valued of friends and I hope to be able to repay you someday.'

He was looking up at her as she said this, and she could see a slight change in his expression—some of the pleasure in his face stalked darkly away as he heard her words. He took her hand in his for a moment and she could feel the warmth of his hand through the fine kid of her glove. He said: 'Tomorrow morning, then—the angel will deliver her charge just after daybreak, by the live oak.'

Angelica turned Prospero and rode quickly back towards the castle. It was much further than she thought, and she would have been about halfway back at the moment when Lady Avery took it into her mind that she wanted to redress one of her bonnets. Her ladyship rang for Sarah, who appeared, looking haggard after a day of nerves worrying that Titus might be discovered. She tried to reposition her cap at a less hazardous angle.

'Ah! Sarah, there you are,' began her ladyship, who sat with her work-basket resting on her lap in the billows of her skirt. She was surrounded by ribbons, bows, silk flowers, spools of silk thread, and pincushions full of needles and pins. In her hands was a white chip bonnet stripped of all decoration. 'I've taken a fancy to dress this bonnet after one I saw in *Goody's*. Just step along to Lady Angelica's room and bring me that length of ribbon—you know, the French stuff we bought in Tours.'

Sarah curtsied her way out of the room, her eyebrows jabbing together in the middle like knitting needles, as she was absolutely baffled as to what ribbon her ladyship meant, but she flew down the corridor and around the corner to Angelica's room. Once there she began to ransack all the drawers and trunks trying to find the ribbon. Whatever happened, she wanted to get back quickly; otherwise Lady Avery would become impatient and come to find out what was delaying her. Titus, his black eye very much blacker, sat bemused in his makeshift bed on the floor of the dressing room as he watched Sarah's hands fly through the endless drawers searching for the ribbon. Titus was much recovered and had eaten everything Sarah could smuggle to him and, although he was still weak, he had managed to sit up to practise his reading with one of Angelica's books.

Sarah was beginning to get into a panic about the ribbon as she looked everywhere without finding it; she began searching again, this time methodically, starting at the top of the dressing room wall which was fitted, floor to almost ceiling, with drawers. She stood on a small footstool to reach the top drawers which were as narrow as slits and, as she worked her way down, the drawers became deeper until she was hauling out the heavy bottom drawer which held the bed linen. Sarah was completely rattled and, without a word of explanation to Titus, kept muttering under her breath: *'Where is that ribbon?—Oh, where, oh, where?! Her ladyship will be the death of me, she will!'* She was now on the other side of the dressing room, on tiptoe on the stool opening hat boxes on a high shelf, and Titus could only watch in amazement as a cascade of bonnets and hats tumbled from the boxes onto the floor around him. *'Here it is!'* Sarah finally shouted and fled from the dressing room with the long ribbon held aloft triumphantly trailing behind her.

She dashed into Lady Avery's room with such suddenness that it made her ladyship jump with surprise and flick Sarah a warning look. Sarah was almost too breathless to speak but managed to get out the words: 'H-here it is, m'lady!' and she smiled broadly while almost lunging at her ladyship with the streamer of ribbon.

Lady Avery looked at her crossly. 'Oh, Sarah! *That's* not the ribbon! I don't know why on earth you've brought me that awful thing!'

Sarah's jaw dropped. 'But—m'lady—it's the only ribbon—I've searched *everywhere!*'

'Did you look in Lady Angelica's dressing room?'

Sarah gaped at her in horror. *'Oh, yes m'lady—I looked everywhere!'*

'Nonsense, Sarah. It's there somewhere.' Lady Avery let out a weary sigh and laid aside the bonnet. 'You've been skimpy as usual—I'll just have to go and look myself!' Putting the basket aside, she got heavily to her feet and started slowly for the door.

Sarah began to bounce around as if on springs; she dodged and darted about blocking Lady Avery's path. *'Oh, please, m'lady!* Let me go back and look! I'm sure your ladyship shouldn't trouble yourself! I'll just go and look again!'

'Sarah! Have you gone quite mad?! Get out of my way! And stop popping up and down—you're making me seasick!'

Still bouncing. 'Oh—please, m'lady, don't trouble yourself.'

'I shall do it myself! Otherwise I shall be all day at this bonnet if I leave it to you and your nonsense! Now, Sarah! Out of my way!'

Defeated and horrified, Sarah found herself brushed aside as Lady Avery whisked from the room and down the corridor towards Angelica's room. There wasn't even time to warn Titus—disaster was at hand. Lady Avery impatiently burst into Angelica's bedroom and flicked open drawers and cupboards for a moment. The door to the dressing room was ajar and Lady Avery, finding no ribbon in the bedroom, advanced upon the dressing room as Sarah stood watching helplessly. Lady Avery pulled the door wide and went into the dressing room. Sarah shut her eyes—it was too late. Titus was about to be discovered! Sarah waited for Lady Avery's glass-shattering voice to exclaim when she saw Titus—but there was no sound coming from the dressing room...then there were a few complaining grunts as Lady Avery struggled to open drawers. Silence. A moment later, her ladyship appeared with a ribbon in her hand and said with a sarcastic edge. 'Really, Sarah, you do make hard work of it sometimes! And *do* tidy up that dressing room! What an unholy mess!' Lady Avery flicked the ribbon in the air to punctuate her words and sallied from the room.

Sarah sank down on the bed, weak and floppy like a tired petticoat in need of starch. Why hadn't Lady Avery *seen* Titus? She moved cautiously towards the dressing room as if fearing some dark sorcery. She peered around the door of the dressing room and, apart from the small wooden stool and the tumble of hats on the floor—the room was empty. Titus and his bed had vanished.

'Titus?' she called quietly. There was no answer. *'Titus?'* she called a little louder. There was a soft thudding noise from somewhere in the room. Sarah flinched and looked around expecting spoors or spooks. *'Titus?'* She was now alarmed. There was another thud and this time there was a muffled voice. Sarah scrambled for the bottom drawer and hauled at it. It was terribly heavy—much heavier than before. She strained at it and as she got it part way open she could see Titus's eyes glaring up at her through the slit.

'Please get me out of here! I can't breathe!'

Sarah hauled again and he was able to scramble free. It was an exhausted, nerve-racked pair who were still sitting on the dressing room floor when Angelica returned a moment later. She knew something frightening had passed when she saw them both sitting crumpled and stunned on the dressing room rug, still shocked and dazed by how close they had come to being discovered. They recounted to Angelica how Lady Avery had come within seconds of ruining their plan, and how all had been saved because Titus, hearing her ladyship enter the bedroom, made a dive with his bedding into the open bottom drawer and managed to close it by bracing his already painful back against the bottom of the drawer and pushing with all his might against the cross pieces with his feet. Hearing of their close call, Angelica's knees went wobbly and she sank down and sat in the dark pool of her riding habit skirt.

After a moment of silence, Angelica said, 'I hate myself for not being here to help. You have both been tremendously brave. But we only have a few more hours to go...' and she whispered out the plan for the following morning. She

289

then dressed the raw, painful wounds on Titus's back, broken open again by his scramble into the drawer. He sat unflinching as she cleaned the wounds again, not wanting to appear cowardly in her eyes.

Sarah went to the kitchen pretending that Angelica was hungry after a long day riding and wishing a little something to tide her over until dinner, a half hour hence. She procured a tray of cold meats, soda bread, some fruit, cheddar cheese, and a large piece of apple tart with clotted cream. All the while Cook was laying out the tray, she kept pursing her lips into the shape of a trumpet and giving Sarah curious looks before saying suspiciously, 'Your mistress has a healthy appetite—hope this lot won't spoil her dinner!'

By the time Sarah managed to carry up the tray for Titus, Angelica was almost dressed for dinner; Sarah helped her with her stays and fastened the legion of buttons which closed the bodice of the simple white cambric, a dress Lady Avery almost forbade her to wear as it was very plain. Titus was securely tucked up for the night in his makeshift bed in the dressing room, and Sarah was sent down to her supper in the servant's hall. Then Angelica descended the stairs. She shook with a chill rage in anticipation of seeing the Earl; she knew she would have to be civil to him no matter how much she wanted to confront and berate him for his cruelty to Titus. As she walked slowly towards the yellow drawing-room, a figure made her start as he came into her peripheral vision from a shadow behind the stairs. Hibbard, his hands folded behind his back, moving so smoothly across the shining floor that he might have been an ice skater. Sliding into another shadow, he disappeared. She came to the drawing-room door, forced her lips into a smile, and she could feel it frost her face as she entered the room. The Earl was standing by the fireplace with a glass of wine raised to his lips.

She was too early—he was alone.

She did not want to be alone with him, even for a second. She hesitated on the threshold. His glass was still raised to his lips and he had not seen her; she might have time to slip away. She started to turn back to the stairs where she could see Lady Avery just beginning to descend, and thought it safe to go in. What Angelica did not see was that her ladyship then turned back up the stairs because she had forgotten her fan.

The Earl brought down the glass and caught sight of her. 'Ah, Lady Angelica, good evening,' he smiled and advanced across the deep dark carpet towards her. His face was handsome and composed into a generous smile as he said, 'You have almost become a stranger these last few days—I hope you do not feel I have been neglecting you.'

'N-not at all, sir.' Her brave smile caved in and she struggled to get it back. She turned and walked towards the fire to prevent him from seeing the anger on her face and she went on, 'There is a great deal to divert one here at Cranleigh as it is almost impossible to find time to avail oneself of all the—*amusements.*' She could hear how hard and sarcastic her tone was becoming and fought to control it.

He followed her to the fire, depositing his glass on a spindly 'pie crust' table as he passed; he moved as near to her as the protective hoops of her crinoline would allow. Thank heaven for frivolous fashion Angelica was thinking! She moved away from the fire towards the piano and ran her hand briefly along the keys as she passed to dispel some of the tension in her fingertips. Again he followed her and came nearer than she could bear.

'What a charming dress, Lady Angelica, and how charmingly you flatter it.' His mouth was drawn out into a hard little smile as his violet eyes darted like clammy fingers over her glistening hair and bare neck, and when she could feel his eyes descend to invade every fold of the soft fabric, she felt sickened and abruptly turned away. One hand snatched her wrist and held it behind her back as the other hand pulled her hard into him and held her in a long invasive kiss as she struggled furiously to be free. When he let her go she was shaking with humiliation and disgust. How dare he have the nerve to do such a thing—and how dare he do it with such insolent bravado when at any second her aunt and uncle might walk through the door. In a fury Angelica's right hand flew up and she was about to strike him across the face with the sharp edge of her carved ivory fan, but he was too quick for her and snatched her wrist, twisting it hard and throwing her a little off balance so that she could suddenly see past his shoulder. To her horror, Lady Avery stood in the distant doorway trying not to look in their direction, one hand fussing with her hair, and she was smiling a little to herself. Angelica was appalled—her aunt had obviously just witnessed the Earl's outrageous behaviour and was pretending not to have seen it. Her ladyship flicked open her fan and fluttered it around as she called towards them in a tinkle of surprise, as if she had only just spotted them. 'Ah! There you are, children!' and she glided into the room. While Lady Avery chatted animatedly with the Earl, Angelica moved away towards the fire in a flush of misery and revulsion, desperately fighting tears. She was determined not to give him that satisfaction.

It was small comfort for Angelica that she could see the irony: the Earl had at least done her one favour—she was now free to sit across from him at dinner and let her eyes ply with him as much hate as she felt, and he would just assume it was because of the forced kiss; he would never guess that her eyes were serving him with flagons of poison because of his treatment of Titus. But the more her eyes fed him arsenic the more he seemed to relish it, until she could not suffer to look at him again and diverted her gaze. Her dinner untouched, she excused herself early complaining of a slight headache as she escaped to the refuge of her room.

Angelica looked in on Titus who was asleep, lying on his side, his head cradled on a stack of broderie Anglaise cushions and his yellow

293

hair falling over his eyes. His face looked untroubled in sleep, unlike the haunted look that dogged him by day. Angelica watched him for a moment and was thinking, even if I never do another worthwhile thing again in my life, I will not fail to get that child safely away from Greystone.

It was still dark the next morning when, dazed with slumber, Titus was gently roused by Angelica who was already dressed in her riding habit. She helped him into a man's warm coat—far too big for him—which Sarah had resourcefully and unabashedly purloined from a dusty cupboard where it had been left forgotten in the maze of narrow, slanting corridors on the upper floors where the female servants slept.

Kneeling beside him, Angelica slipped two apples into his pockets and, as she rolled up the sleeves until his hands were visible, she asked very gently, 'Titus, please tell me something—why did Lord Greystone beat you?'

Titus looked down and his small face betrayed nothing. She said, 'Please, Titus, you must tell me. Was it because Lord Greystone somehow found out that you helped me hide from him in the ballroom? That is it, isn't it?'

He slowly looked up. 'Yes, I didn't want you to know.'

'But, why not?'

'Because I didn't want you to think...' His voice trailed off.

'What?' She was smiling kindly at him. 'You didn't want me to know I was the cause?'

Titus gave a huge sigh and nodded yes.

'Dear friend, you must tell me everything.' She gave him a coaxing look which made him smile. 'Please tell me anything you think I should know.'

'It was Hibbard what found out I helped you. He told his lordship. That Hibbard—he has a black heart.'

'Yes, they are quite a pair to find their fun in tormenting a small boy.'

Titus squared his chin manfully and said, 'I'd do it again, you know. I wouldn't care how many beatings I got!'

'I know you would, Titus. I am deeply touched. You are such a true friend—thank you.'

Then Angelica repeated to him the plan to get him to Ickworth. 'And remember I will be coming to Ickworth soon, and all will be well. They will look after you there. Now you must slip out of the house while it is still dark so no one will see you, and you must hide and wait for me just beyond the stables, by the rhododendrons, and I will come for you just after dawn and take you to my friend.' Titus nodded gravely. She then slipped a small book of poems into his pocket saying, 'Take this so you can practise your reading.' At this Titus was overcome and threw his arms around her neck, held her fast and cried, 'Dear Angelica! I can never repay you!'

She hugged him back, then pushed him away to tidy his hair and see his face better, and he cuffed his eyes with his sleeves to dry them. 'Titus, what you must do is get safely away so we can spend times at Ickworth reading.' She smiled at him and he grinned shyly. Angelica stood up and expected him to follow her to the door to the hall and slip out, but instead he went to one of the windows, raised the sash, and peered around into the darkness. Angelica's room was on a corner; one set of windows overlooking the cobbled courtyard, the other overlooking the Italian knot gardens and the open countryside beyond. Titus had chosen a window over the gardens.

'Titus! What are you thinking of?! We are far too high up!'

'It's all right, m'lady—it will be quieter if I go down the waterspout.'

'No! You mustn't!' she whispered sharply, but he was already scrambling over the sill and sliding softly downward. She flew terrified to the window and watched his blond head disappearing slowly as he slid down the fluted iron pipe making only a soft hush of a noise like the rustle of satin. She leaned out the window and watched, filled with a combination of concern and admiration. A moment later he was safely on the ground; he stepped back from the house wall a few steps, stumbling a little on the sloping grassy turf and, turning up his grinning face, he waved up at her before padding silently away into the darkness.

An hour and a half later, when the sky in the east had a pale grey streak across it which lit the misty countryside with a damp light, Angelica walked quickly across the courtyard as she had at this hour on many previous mornings during her stay at Cranleigh, the cobblers' nails in the heels of her black riding boots clicking quietly on the stone paving. She had never noticed the sound before, and this morning when she wanted to be inconspicuous it sounded loud enough to wake the entire household. She thought about tiptoeing but realized she must not do anything that would be construed as out of the ordinary in case the eyes of the house were watching her, so she continued, clicking her way through the small gate to the right of the vast black and gold iron entrance gate, and then on to the stables.

The morning mist draped the world in a soft haze. Titus was waiting for her as planned and, as she rode up to their meeting place, his head popped out from under a giant old rhododendron bush where the gnarled thick branches formed a hollow as accommodating and as dry as a cave. Angelica dismounted and led Prospero to a fallen tree and instructed Titus to climb up and behind the saddle, and to hold onto the back of the saddle. Titus, who had never been on a horse before, was tentative and nervous. Prospero turned his head and watched this unusual cargo with a guarded eye as if wondering if he should object, but he flicked his tail, stamped his near hind once, and tolerated it; and Angelica then climbed up onto the fallen tree and slipped back into the saddle. All the while, Angelica was looking round to make sure no one was about; they were on a remote section of the drive that led up to Cranleigh Castle; here she could now direct Prospero to a parallel path that was screened from the drive by trees, but to make the rendezvous with Gitano at the live oak, she would have to ride a ways along the exposed section of the drive where the vast old tree was located. Twenty minutes later Angelica reined Prospero out onto the drive again and she could see the live oak ahead clearly in the mist. It was thick with leaves and spread wide over the lane like a heavy green umbrella supported by a massive trunk. The tree—an easy landmark—stood beside the drive in open parkland which then rolled down to the lake. As she neared the tree she looked around and was disappointed that Gitano was not there to meet them.

Just as she came within a few dozen yards of the tree, she was alarmed by the sound of galloping horses. She looked around and could see nothing as yet, but she could tell by the noise and speed that it had to be a landau or small coach coming down the drive from the direction of the castle. She looked about in a panic, but there was nowhere to conceal a horse with two riders without galloping flat out for a wood three hundred yards away, and if she did that, Titus would be sure to fall off and be injured. She had to do something; the galloping horses would burst into view in a second from out of the mist. Angelica said, 'Titus, hold fast!' and she trotted Prospero quickly the few feet to the base of the tree and around behind it just as the Earl's landau burst out of the mist; the Earl was the sole passenger, and the driver was liberally giving the pair of bays the whip.

She had been hoping the tree trunk would at least screen Titus from the view of the passing carriage, but it was no good; even though the Earl saw only her at that moment, as the tree blocked his view of Titus, he had signalled the driver to stop. The Earl was going to speak to her and he would then certainly see the boy. Titus, still holding onto the back of the saddle, cowered behind her and made himself as small as possible; his heart was juddering with fright, but he did not cry out as the pair of strong hands reached down for him and plucked him out of sight, up into the thick foliage and onto the safety of a heavy bough just a split second before the Earl's carriage passed to that side of the tree. Titus found himself perched on the wide limb looking into Gitano's reassuring face. Titus stopped breathing as they listened to the Earl, whose speeding carriage had come to a halt a few feet away. Angelica had been watching the Earl's advance in horror and she was unaware that Titus was no longer sitting behind the saddle.

The Earl seemed pleased to see her and smiled at her in a manner to suggest they were the best of friends. 'Good morning, Lady Angelica. What brings you out on such a misty morning?'

Assuming that Titus was still sitting behind the saddle, she glared at the Earl angrily, thinking he had seen the boy and was now proceeding to torment her. She answered coldly, her tone heavy-laden with sarcasm and disdain, 'Good morning, sir. As you can see I am simply engaged in one of the pastimes so graciously afforded by your lordship's hospitality.'

The Earl laughed at her hauteur, thinking that she was still angry about his advances the previous evening, and said, 'We do our best to find amusements for all our guests, Lady Angelica,' to which Angelica just returned him a cold stare. He continued, 'It promises to be a fine day when the mist blows off!' Then he gave the driver a prod in the back with his cane which indicated that he wanted to drive on. As if charged with amusement by her chill towards him, the Earl laughed, tipped his topper to her, and the landau whisked him away again into the mist. Angelica was mystified. Why had he made no reference to her passenger? She was convinced that the Earl had just been toying with her by pretending not to notice the boy. What would the Earl do? Get Hibbard to find out to where she had helped the boy flee? It was intolerable! Angelica let out a little whimper and turned to look behind her at Titus, saying, 'Oh, Titus, I am sorry—' Discovering that he was no longer behind the saddle, she did a colossal double take and looked all around her, behind and below, and called out, *'Titus?* Where are you?'

'Here I am!' came his cheery voice, and the rustling over her head made her look up. The branches parted and the smiling faces of Titus and Gitano were laughing down at her.

Still amazed, she stared at them. 'But-but do you mean to tell me Greystone never saw you?'

'No, m'lady—this gentleman saw to that!'

Angelica burst into laughter with the others, and Titus had never had so much to laugh about or laughed so hard in his young life, and in spite of the pain of his lacerated back and battered face, he hooted and crinkled up his freckled face in delight at seeing the Earl outwitted. And as Titus laughed, he looked at the faces of Angelica and the man who had just saved him—they were laughing uncontrollably too—and he relished their delight. Then their eyes met and their laughter faltered a little and slowly died and they were looking at one another in penetrating silence, their faces unlike anything Titus knew—somewhere between happy and sad—and being only nine, Titus did not recognize that look. He fell into silence, too, and wondered if he had erred in some way which had caused their mood to change from gay to sombre. As the lowliest member of a vast household, and general scapegoat, Titus was well used to more than his fair portion of blame for just about anything. He asked meekly as he watched their solemn faces, 'Did I do something wrong?'

At the sound of Titus's voice, Angelica looked flustered as she drew herself away from the refuge of the kind eyes. 'No, of course not, Titus! You've been very good and clever.'

Gitano swung down from the tree and brought Titus down safely before saying to her, 'We must go now to be in time to get the boy on the road north.'

Angelica slid from the saddle and said, 'Titus,

this is Gitano. He is a friend of the gypsies and they are going to take you to Ickworth.' Titus nodded to show he understood.

Taking Titus by the hand, Angelica led the way down the slope towards the lake as Gitano directed, and he followed leading Prospero. Once on the lake shore, they turned left, followed the shoreline round a short way and entered a wood. They were only a little distance into the seemingly empty wood when Angelica realized that she was walking towards the back of a little gypsy caravan only a few yards away from them. It blended so well into the soft greens and browns of the budding wood that it was almost invisible at first. A sleek chestnut stood patiently in harness while exploring the inside of a feed bag.

Gitano said, 'This is how we will travel so that the boy will not be seen and recognized by anyone on the estate. We must meet a caravan going north, this side of the Ashford Road.' Titus's face had lit up at the thought of riding in a gypsy caravan and he looked up at Angelica and could see her smiling, too, at the prospect. So stashing Prospero's saddle inside the caravan and replacing it with a horse blanket, Gitano lashed Prospero's reins to a ring at the back. He then helped his passengers settle on the seat at the front, showing them how to open the door behind them in case they needed to slip inside the little rolling house if anyone should approach. So horses and passengers made ready, they set off through the shining mist which swirled softly through the wood as a warming sun worked hard to dispel it. The caravan creaked and rattled as the fine chestnut trotted smartly along the mossy lane. Titus was seated between Gitano and Angelica and, looking from one to the other, excitedly asked, 'Does this mean I'm going to live with the gypsies?'

Angelica laughed. 'I'm afraid not, Titus. That's something you'll have to think about when you are older. For the moment you'll have to be content with living at Ickworth which is rather large, very ordinary, and not on wheels I am sorry to say, but very pleasant all the same.'

Gitano gave Titus an amused sideways glance. 'Well, Titus, what makes you think you would want to live with the gypsies?'

He looked up brightly at Gitano. 'Because they're clever and know almost everything about everything and they sometimes play tricks on people.' He giggled, again thinking about the trick Gitano had just played on the Earl by snatching him out of sight.

Gitano laughed a little as he watched Titus. 'Who told you that gypsies could do all those things?'

Titus became a little shy and said, 'Ah...Lady Angelica did.'

Gitano smiled across at Angelica whose eyes were sparkling with amusement. 'So our guardian angel said that, did she?' He looked down at Titus again. 'You know that to be a gypsy you have to know all about horses?'

Titus gave his head an emphatic shake to say

no, he didn't know, and then he said with some awe, 'I'd never even been on a horse before this morning. I was frightened somethin' dreadful!'

'You just have to remember that horses are a little like people—if you are nice to them, on the whole they are nice to you.' He was looking down at Titus again and said, 'In that case I don't suppose you've ever driven a horse either?' Titus shook his head no. Slowing the horse to a walk, and handing Titus the reins, Gitano said, 'Well, I think you had better take these.' Titus took them with as much surprise and delight as a child handed his first Christmas present.

Angelica watched as Gitano patiently arranged Titus's small eager hands on the wide leather reins. Gitano's strong firm hands gently guiding the boy's small inexpert fingers until they were gripping the reins confidently. Titus listened intently to Gitano's instructions and was keen to learn, and then Titus smiled up at Angelica proudly as if to say, look at me!

Gitano left Titus to it as the horse plodded on happily unaware that a novice was in control. Gitano put his feet up on the wooden dashboard, leaned back and folded his arms to show Titus that it was entirely his show. Gitano and Angelica could see that this made Titus sit up straighter and concentrate all the harder on his new responsibilities. They watched Titus for a moment, enjoying his pleasure, and then Angelica turned to Gitano and said lightly, with mock formality,

'I believe, sir, there is a little quarrel between us.'

He was unworried as she was still smiling happily, so he said, 'I am not aware of it, madam.'

'You may recall the other day when you were in that tree, sir, and disappeared when the carriage arrived?'

'Ah, yes?' He was now looking slightly wary; his amused eyes narrowed a little as he tried to read her face and guess at what was coming next.

'It may interest you to know, sir, that you are solely responsible for me now having a reputation as someone who *talks* to birds.' Angelica let out a little giggle at the memory. 'Their ladyships could see me talking to someone or something in the tree and could only conclude I was conversing with the birds!'

Gitano started to laugh. 'They now all think, madam, you are an ornithologist with curious ways?'

'Indeed!' Angelica was spilling over with laughter, 'They all think me most terribly eccentric! And it's all down to you, sir!'

Titus was carefully holding the reins just so, and he was concentrating too hard to listen to their conversation, and was only aware that they were both now laughing uncontrollably about something; he saw none of the electric sparks dashing over his tousled head as his passengers held one another in the intimate embrace of a private joke.

The caravan rumbled quietly along the lane through the wood as the day unfolded and the mist slipped away revealing an encouraging sun that quickly dispelled the wintry chill that still intruded upon the early spring mornings. They came to the end of the wood where it opened out into a narrow tree-lined lane, rutted and bumpy, and soon turned onto a wider lane bordered either side by hedgerows, where Gitano let Titus bring the horse up to a trot. Titus was elated when the horse momentarily broke into a canter, but Gitano added his hands to the reins and slowed the horse back down to a safer speed, saying, 'You don't want to tire your horse by asking too much. You know the story of the tortoise and the hare?'

Taking his eyes off the horse for only a second, Titus gave Gitano a pleased look and said, 'Yes, I read it in a book—*Aesop's Fables.*'

Gitano gave Titus a look to show he was impressed and then glanced at Angelica for confirmation. 'Titus is keen to read all the books ever written,' she said, smiling.

'Oh, well, in that case, Titus, I don't think you'll want to be a gypsy. Gypsies don't have very much time to read—too busy with other things.'

Titus looked disappointedly from one to the other. 'Oh, does that mean I can't drive anymore?' to which Gitano and Angelica laughed. Gitano said, 'Of course you can—even scholars should know how to drive a horse.'

After another two miles they were nearing the estate village and would have to pass down its one and only street, so Gitano took the reins and Angelica and Titus slipped inside so as not to call attention to the caravan by their presence.

Gitano put on his wide-brimmed hat, slipped a black cape over his shoulders and slowed the horse's pace as they passed between the tidy little cottages; he did not want anyone to remark on a gypsy caravan in a hurry if the Earl later tried to piece together the method and route used to smuggle Titus off the estate. One lone gypsy with a plodding horse seen passing through the village would not even be worth a mention. There was scarcely anyone about at that early hour. The blacksmith's chimney already had a long column of smoke reaching high into the still air, and Gitano glimpsed the butcher, still in his nightcap, pushing open his shutters, his plump pink face eclipsed by a cavernous yawn, but otherwise the village was barely stirring.

Inside the swaying caravan, Angelica and Titus looked around in fascination at the intricately engineered fixtures and fittings, the table and chairs and bed all made of carved and inlaid wood, with little panels of bevelled glass and mirror fitted into the doors of the miniature cupboards. Angelica studied the interior, at first enchanted and curious, and then somewhat saddened as she realized there was nothing to make the little abode seem lived in. There was nothing personal—no mementos, books or letters scattered about—nothing to give it the earmarks of a home or to reflect an owner's personality.

Through the side windows she could see that they had passed through the village as pastures were beginning to appear on either side, so she and Titus opened the little door at the front of the caravan and were about to take their places on the seat beside Gitano again, when he held up his hand to signal them to wait, and they could then hear the sound of a fast trotting horse. Without having to speak, Angelica and Gitano both recognized the free and fast clicking noise as that of a fast trotting hackney pulling a light trap coming towards them in the lane. Angelica and Titus retreated back into the caravan and shut the door to wait for it to pass.

The horse and trap came into view in the distance in the lane ahead. A man wearing a fine beaver topper was whipping the willing horse into a lather and showed no indication that he was going to render any of the road to the gypsy caravan—rather foolishly, as Gitano knew that in a collision the light trap would come off worse than the heavy caravan. Gitano reined his horse to the side so that it plodded on the grassy verge and left the majority of the road to the oncoming traffic. The trap kept up its speed, and as the horse and driver flashed past the side window, Angelica and Titus, who were looking out, mostly in idle curiosity, fell back in amazement to see that, of all people, the driver was Hibbard. They exchanged a stunned look and threw themselves at the back window and looked out past Prospero, hitched to the back and still contentedly following, as Hibbard flew by, seemingly without so much as a glance at the caravan. They let out a duet of sighs of relief as they watched the trap moving off into the distance. They were just watching for it to finally fade into the distance, when they could see Hibbard's whole demeanour change as he looked over his shoulder back towards the caravan, and at the same time, started hauling on the reins with all his strength trying to slow his horse. They were still watching, now in horror, as Hibbard halted his horse and executed a complete turn in the middle of the lane and cracking his whip, drove the hackney into a flat-out gallop back after them until he was alongside the caravan where he slowed his horse again to a walk so that he could speak to Gitano. Again Angelica and Titus raced back to the side window and tried to peek out and listen.

Hibbard gave Gitano a quick look up and down, and what he saw was a bent old Gypsy in a big hat and cape; Hibbard couldn't see the Gypsy's face, but he was sure he was old by the way he sat all folded over. 'I say—you there!' shouted Hibbard trying to get the Gypsy's attention.

'G'day to yer, sir!' said Gitano in his antique-Gypsy persona.

'Look here, you miserable old scallawag—how in the name of blazes did you steal that black horse?!'

Inside the caravan Angelica and Titus were dying a thousand deaths; unable to see or hear Gitano, they were only catching Hibbard's side of the conversation.

'Steal it, Your Grace? Not I, your eminence.'

Hibbard's usually sallow complexion had gone quite puce and his head started to resemble

309

an inflatable radish somewhat constricted by his precisely folded cravat. 'Well I know you certainly didn't *buy* that valuable beast as it is the property of my master, the Earl of Greystone!'

'Ah, that's as mebby, your honour, but I never stole this 'ere horse. I done found this 'ere horse.'

'Ha!' Hibbard barked out a sceptical laugh, 'And I suppose you are taking this valuable horse, which you have just so conveniently *found,* to hand it over to the Chief Constable?!'

'Aye! That I woz, m'lord—that I woz indeed!' growled Gitano in a gravelly dialect from his Gypsy repertoire, and his ancient Gypsy was nodding his head vigorously under the hat.

Hibbard glared in righteous indignation and spat out, 'A likely story as any I've ever heard! This is outrageous! I'll see that the Chief Constable hears about this—you can be sure of that! Pull over this instant and turn that stolen horse over to me!'

'As you like, your worship.' Gitano halted the caravan and the play continued as he clambered down from his perch and moving like a frail old man, scuttling along close to the ground, moving slightly sideways like a crab, until he was at the back of the caravan where he untied Prospero. As Gitano, in the guise of an old man, scooted past the window where Angelica and Titus were watching, Titus whispered to her, 'Why is Gitano acting like that?'

Angelica knew at once. 'Because if there is trouble later with the constabulary, they will be

310

looking for an old gypsy who does not even exist.' And then it was like a champagne cork going *pop!* in her head, and she whispered, more to herself, *'Just* like an old gardener who doesn't exist!' Titus was trembling too hard with fright to hear.

Hibbard had turned the trap around again to continue his journey and pulled alongside the back of the caravan where Gitano handed up the ends of Prospero's reins and watched as Hibbard wrapped them around his left wrist. Hibbard continued his fusillade of insults, 'The damnedest insolence I've ever heard of! And in broad daylight! What will you gypsy tricksters get up to next, I wonder?! The very idea—stealing a fine animal like this! His lordship will take a very dim view of this and you can be sure the constabulary will hear of it!' All the while, Gitano's hat was bobbing up and down as if in agreement until Hibbard finally whipped his horse up and clattered off down the road with Prospero in tow, cantering alongside, still with the gypsy blanket draped over his back. Smiling to himself, Gitano took his seat at the front of the caravan and they started off again. Angelica and Titus watched out the back window as Prospero was led away, back towards Cranleigh and she wondered for a moment how she would get back without a horse and how she was going to explain how Prospero had been lost or stolen right from under her while out riding. Oh, well—she would think of something. She and Titus continued to watch out of the caravan's back window as Hibbard, horse and trap and Prospero receded into the distance away from them in the lane.

And then it happened.

From inside the caravan, with all the creaking and squeaking of the wooden structure, Angelica and Titus could not hear a thing. But they could see, as they watched Hibbard's trap becoming smaller in the distance, Prospero suddenly dig in his heels and come to a complete stop. As the trap and Hibbard had been flying forward at the time, and as Prospero's reins were still entwined around Hibbard's wrist, something had to give and the thing that gave was Hibbard. He was abruptly launched into an aerial somersault over the back of the trap where he landed in a heap in the lane. His horse, with trap, continued to vanish into the horizon, grateful for the lighter load; Prospero, his reins now no longer wrapped around Hibbard's wrist, galloped at full tilt, kicking his heels, relishing the joke, tail arched and flying, to catch up with the caravan, leaving Hibbard alone and in the middle of the lane with nothing for company but his bruises and his flattened top hat.

It happened so quickly that Angelica and Titus could only gasp at first; they did not dare believe their eyes for many long seconds afterwards when Prospero was fast gaining on them. With jaws dropped, they exchanged disbelieving glances and then opened the back door so that Titus could lean out and retrieve Prospero's reins. It was only then that they dissolved into a pool of laughter. Tears of joy rolled down their cheeks as they stumbled out to join Gitano at the front again, where the three of them rocked with merriment until their sides ached.

Exhausted with laughing, they were silent for a while, and Titus was again in charge of the reins and the plodding horse. Angelica was letting a few puzzling thoughts tumble around in her mind before turning to Gitano to ask, 'Why on earth would a horse do what Prospero did? Why would he stop so suddenly and then come back to us?'

Gitano gave her a slow smile. 'It is impossible to say. You have a very smart horse there—and very witty.'

'Yes,' Angelica laughed, but was further puzzled. 'For some days I've been wondering who the old gardener was who came to my aid when...when...' Angelica coloured a little at the memory.

'When you were in the maze with Greystone.'

'Yes. And now after your brilliant charade with Hibbard, I know it was you—but how was it that you came to be there?' Her blue eyes watched him closely.

'Perhaps I was just returning the compliment —or have you forgotten how you came to my rescue at the Royal Oak?'

Angelica smiled to herself a little, feeling that he was hiding a great deal. 'But how did you *know* to come into the maze as you did?'

'Very simply—the gypsies know everything about the country they travel through, and Greystone has a grim reputation where ladies are concerned.'

An icy thought made her shudder. 'He deserves a far worse reputation than he has.

I really don't know how far he will stoop and I dare not think—' she gave him a worried look, '—and you will not know it, but that was a sword cane he had with him in the maze. It frightens me to even think...really I don't know what he is capable of.'

In an angry gesture, Gitano swept his dark hair back from his forehead where it stayed for a second before tumbling back. 'We know what cowardice Greystone is capable of—' and he glanced at Titus to clarify his meaning, but then he forced his tone to become lighter and he lapsed into the voice he had used when he had disguised himself as the old gardener, 'In any case, m'lady, no sword cane could be any match for my trusty hedge clippers.'

Angelica gave him a grateful little laugh and thought how true to form for Gitano to make light of his own safety. First he saved the child from drowning, then he helped her, and here he was again risking who could possibly guess how much to help Titus. There were a few moments of dreamy peace as they were lulled by the rhythmic beating of the horses' hooves as Titus sat, hands poised, like an experienced driver tending the reins. He did not take his eyes off the road and his tone was so unremarkable that they had no warning of what he was about to say.

'You know—some people say Lord Greystone is my father.' Angelica and Gitano's eyes met in an uneasy glance as Titus went on in the most matter of fact tone. 'I don't know if it's true or not, but if it was true I would have to work

314

very hard trying to make up for the bad way he treats people.' He was then silent. The thought having been expressed was no longer of interest to him, and his attention was again fully on driving the caravan. Gitano and Angelica were left soundly winded by his expression of youthful charity, and the subject of Lord Greystone was at an end.

Gitano again took the reins as he turned the caravan down a wooded track and after a few moments they came upon another gypsy caravan drawn up to the side of the lane. Gitano stopped the horse and they all climbed down from the seat and walked towards the new caravan.

As they came up to the front of the caravan, they could see a massive skewbald horse, almost as large as the caravan, standing patiently in harness. The caravan seemed to be uninhabited, until a huge man's face suddenly shot up from behind the horses and towered over it. His sudden appearance and his startling size made Angelica and Titus jump. He wore a blue bandanna over his black hair and a gold hoop in one earlobe. His fierce, swarthy face was cracked open by a sudden wide smile which revealed that one of his front teeth was missing. 'Ah! Good day, friends!' he cried. Then, just as quickly, his head vanished behind the horse again and he was out of sight tinkering about with the harness.

Titus took Angelica's hand and she could tell, by the tightening of his fingers on hers, that he was afraid of the gypsy. 'It's all right, Titus, don't be alarmed.' She smiled reassuringly down at him, but his eyes were riveted on the giant as the huge man appeared again and strode round the horse to meet them. Under his open coat he wore a cummerbund where the carved hilt of a dagger glinted. He was so tall Angelica had to look up as if addressing a tree. Gitano introduced him as Oren Pozzo, and when Angelica offered him her hand, it was swallowed up by the huge slab of his hand, but he handled hers carefully as if it was a bird's egg. When Titus was introduced, the boy backed away a little. Pozzo saw this, put his hands on his hips and let out a huge guffaw of laughter that shook the surrounding trees.

Angelica watched as Gitano gently put a hand on Titus's shoulder and went down to his level so that he could talk quietly to him. 'Titus, you are right to think that Oren Pozzo is a dangerous man—he is, but only to his enemies—and your enemies. He is your friend and will protect you with his life if he must. If *you* are frightened of him, just think how frightened of him your enemies would be because they are not half as brave as you.' Titus smiled at this and looked up at Angelica for confirmation; she was smiling warmly watching them both, and she nodded to reassure him.

Pozzo boomed with a laugh, 'Ha! We are friends now, are we, lad?!' to which Titus shyly nodded yes. 'Good! Then we must be off!' With that Pozzo picked up Titus, tucked him under his arm like a small parcel, mounted the caravan seat with him, and set him down beside him.

Angelica ran forward and gave Titus a last

hug and slipped a letter into his pocket saying, 'This is addressed to Mr Compton, the vicar. When you get to Ickworth, ask Cook to post it for you and that way I will know you have arrived safely.' She thanked Pozzo again and again and stood watching as the caravan squeaked and rattled its way through the woods and finally went out of sight. When she turned around, Gitano was watching her with a faint smile.

'Am I so terribly silly?' she asked, a little amused.

'Not in the least; only kind. There are very few in your position who would trouble yourself with the fate of a boot-boy.'

'Maybe it is only because people like myself are helpless to do anything. We are raised to be rather useless. You have done it all.'

As Gitano removed the horse blanket and saddled Prospero, they were both revisited by the memory of Hibbard's tumble and tried not to laugh too wickedly. Then Gitano and Angelica strolled through the woods for a short distance to where Gitano showed her a path that would take her back in the direction of the castle. As they talked, Angelica found a fallen tree on which to rest; she realized the difficulty of the last few days, and sleepless nights, had made her weary. Letting out a little sigh, she said, 'When I saw that caravan going just now, I somehow wished I was on it, going away to some other, less complicated life.'

'The nomadic life is not all it seems,' he

replied, tethering Prospero before sitting down beside her.

'Perhaps not. But at least there is the freedom to go.'

His tone was flat. 'That particular freedom will have very little appeal to me when I leave tonight.'

Angelica looked up suddenly. Somehow it had never occurred to her that he would ever leave. 'But—but why should you go?'

'Why should I not? There is nothing for me here.' He said it frankly and quietly and held her eyes with his for a moment before letting his gaze roam across the peaceful wood.

'Where will you go?'

His eyes darkened. 'That is undecided as yet, but it could be Spain or the Balkans.'

'Oh...I shall miss you...' she said softly, quickly turning away to hide her look of disappointment. When she glanced at him a moment later, he leaned towards her; sunlight struck the side of his face, lit his faintly scarred left cheek and the tips of his dark lashes, and Angelica felt somehow blinded by the gentle light as it filled her eyes and her mouth with warmth and it seemed to enfold her and suspend her. She made no move to retreat, looking into his dark eyes with hypnotic fascination. Her veil, like gossamer armour, crisscrossed her slightly parted lips, and she watched spellbound, swept along by the surge of her heart as he raised his hands and lifted her veil which separated them.

He touched his lips lightly to hers at first,

318

and as she was drawn into the kiss he pulled her firmly into his arms and held her with a kiss more loving, tender, and at the same time more alive with passion than any dream kiss she had ever imagined. She was made dizzy by the sensation of the heat of his body as he held her into him, her every nerve colliding in delicious confusion. Everything in her cried out for him and she slid her arms around his neck hoping never to let go. For the first time ever, she let her emotions run free and they soared; the fear of the love she had been denying was overpowered by the force of that love, and she felt a wave of defiant hope that somehow the strength of this newly released emotion could master all barriers.

An overwhelming sensation of wholeness swept through them both and Gitano, too, felt the promise of the strengthening force their love was yielding, but he could also feel this trusting young creature rendering herself to him completely and his shame was scalding; he recognized himself fully as a scoundrel and a fraud.

She suddenly felt his shoulders tense and to her amazement, he drew back from the kiss and released her; his handsome features were transformed and hard with torment. He stood up and walked away a few yards; not looking at her while angrily decapitating a few low saplings with a stroke of his whip.

Frozen with astonishment, she watched him pacing restlessly about, his face cold with fury. He was suddenly speaking in a challenging tone she had not heard him use before. 'So—you want to run away and live with the gypsies, do you? Why don't you come away with me then? Come and be my gypsy bride? How's that for a fine proposal?' He said it bitterly. 'I have much to offer you—a life of hardship in the lonely wilderness of the world. How could any fine lady resist such an offer?!'

Bewildered, Angelica stared at him, not knowing what to make of this sudden outburst. They looked at one another in anguished silence and, as Angelica was about to speak, he raised a hand to stop her and cried out urgently, but less severely, '*No*—no, please don't say a word! I could not bear to have that question answered. Please show you forgive my loutish behaviour by saying *nothing*.' Striding towards her, he took her firmly but gently by the arm and drew her up to her feet. In one swift movement he lifted her onto Prospero's saddle and, snatching up the reins which startled Prospero out of his grazing daydream, he handed them to her. Turning Prospero towards Cranleigh, he stood looking up at her like someone trying to memorize her face, and he whispered unhappily, 'Goodbye, Guardian Angel.'

She was about to speak, but he kept her silent with the most heartbreaking look; she would have done anything to ease the pain she could see in his eyes. Helplessly, in silent farewell, she offered her hand and, taking it, he held it lightly in his fingers for a brief moment. Angelica was in utter turmoil because of his abrupt change towards her and she frantically searched his face for an explanation.

'Go now!' he said, roughly cracking his whip in the air behind Prospero's heels. Prospero bounded forward carrying her away and, as she parted from Gitano, she felt an unbearable pain pierce her heart. She had been carried only a dozen paces when an overpowering feeling of loss gripped her and she tugged wildly at the reins and wheeled Prospero round. Her eyes raced to the place where Gitano had been standing. He was gone. The woods were empty. A muffled cry caught in her throat and burning tears of grief blinded her eyes.

It was a long time before she realized that Prospero was wandering aimlessly. She was haunted by misery and confusion, her mind swamped and drowning in unanswered questions, and she was exhausted from the strain and lack of sleep, but she could not make herself go back to the castle and chance an encounter with the Earl. She let Prospero meander on, and he eventually came to the spring to drink and she rested for a while on the sun-warmed mossy bank while her head agonized with a darting tangle of thoughts. When the sun was low, she finally rode back towards the castle. She was riding along a lane that ran between patchwork fields and led to the back of the castle. A rider suddenly appeared in front of her in the near distance. He was on a dark horse and the horse was turned across the lane, blocking it. It was the Earl. He was watching her with impassive, predatory eyes, but he made no move. She halted Prospero for a moment wondering what to do—she would go anywhere as long as it was away from the Earl—then she turned and rode Prospero at a low gate beside the lane and galloped away across the pasture land towards the castle. To her relief the Earl made no move to follow.

Lady Avery, who was already dressed for dinner, was waiting impatiently in Angelica's room and insisting that she try on the yellow gown for a fitting, which gave Angelica no time to concentrate on her own thoughts. 'Quickly please, Angelica! Into the dress for a fitting, and then you must rush and dress for dinner as you are very late. There isn't a minute to lose!' Helped by Sarah, Angelica slipped hastily into the yellow creation. 'It is going to work wonderfully well!' said Lady Avery with satisfaction. 'One more fitting and it will be finished!'

With her ladyship in the room, it was almost impossible for Angelica to tell Sarah that Titus had made a safe departure. Only when Sarah came close, to adjust a pin at the shoulder, could Angelica whisper the news. Sarah almost went limp with the welcome news and dropped her pincushion. As Angelica stood still for Sarah to make fine adjustments, she was facing one of the windows with the view of the Italian garden and the distant landscape beyond. It was almost dark and beginning to rain. Through the rain-spattered window, she thought she could see, in the far distance, crossing the horizon, the silhouette of a line of gypsy caravans moving slowly south—or was it just the wind blowing the trees? She was not sure. She was only sure of the sharp longing that rose in her. Lady Avery's voice cut through her thoughts. 'Now, dress for dinner with all speed and come down! There will be another guest at the table tonight!'

As Angelica and Lady Avery descended the marble stairs a few moments later, they witnessed Hibbard crossing the hall and limping painfully; the liberal quantity of bandages on his head resembled a turban.

'Gracious me!' hissed Lady Avery to Angelica in a booming whisper, 'I wonder what happened to him?!'

'I cannot imagine!' said Angelica, surprised to find herself smiling.

FOURTEEN

The additional guest at dinner was Mr Compton, the vicar, and he was plainly thrilled to be included in the Earl's hospitality. Angelica was delighted to see the vicar again. And his presence would also swell their numbers, lessening the demand upon her to make polite and painful conversation with the Earl. Angelica got the distinct impression that this was the first time Mr Compton had been invited to dine since the Earl had taken over the running of Cranleigh. She found this odd, as country vicars traditionally had their tiny stipends supplemented by frequent and substantial meals at the manor house to which they administered their spiritual guidance, especially, as in this case, where the church was on the estate and contained the Stanforth family chapel.

Mr Compton was deboning his trout with the alacrity of a cat while trying to convince the Earl of the merits of financing an expensive stained glass memorial window for the church. 'It would carry on the Stanforth tradition; a memorial window has been erected by every Duke. The old Duke had the south transept window made in France, and it is one of the finest examples of leaded glass in all of England.'

The Earl said blandly, 'I am sure you are right, Vicar. I have to confess matters have got away from me with trying to administer Cranleigh and my own estate, Crowood, at the same time. But, although there is no denying that all your arguments are persuasive, my inclination is to hold off for the moment. It would be a pity to have the church full of builder's rubble if it is needed for anything important this year.'

'Of course, of course, I understand perfectly that you do not wish the church to be in an uproar just as you succeed to the title. I am sure it is my fault that I did not mention the stained glass window to you before. I have been wishing to speak to you on this matter for some time, but the weight of your work has made you elusive,' said Mr Compton, charitably offering the Earl an excuse for his total inaccessibility. 'Now that the second son, Lord Anthony, has also departed this world—may God have mercy on his soul—I feel some sort of monument in the church would be appropriate. I will naturally offer prayers for Lord Anthony tomorrow, but that is not really enough to mark the passing of a whole generation.'

'The Vicar is right,' chimed in Lady Avery. 'You will feel such a sense of relief that the whole sad episode has finished if you have a really proper memorial in hand for the last Duke as you take the title.' Looking puzzled, her ladyship asked, 'But tell me, Vicar, is it *truly* appropriate to wish to remember in prayers someone who has left this world having performed as much evil as Lord Anthony?'

Mr Compton smiled at her and said quietly, 'We are all God's children and He alone is capable of judging us. It would be uncharitable if we ignored the poor sinners of the world. In any case, there are many people on the estate who knew and had great affection for Lord Anthony before his...' Hesitating for a moment and looking thoughtfully at his fellow diners, Mr Compton said, 'As many people believe, as I must confess I do myself, that he did not intentionally kill his brother, but that it was an accident, it would be a terrible oversight not to remember the late Lord Anthony in prayers.'

'You are a good man with a generous nature, Vicar,' said the Earl without conviction, 'but, as a man of the world, I am inclined to believe that there are sensible limits to charity, both secular and spiritual. However, it does you credit, as a man of the cloth, to take as lenient a view as you obviously do on this matter. But I must say, had Lord Anthony been tried in an earthly court, even by his peers, he would not have escaped his just desert.' His voice was rising in irritation. He glanced at the silent Lady Avery and Angelica, and his delivery returned to its more usual silky texture. 'Forgive us, ladies, we have ventured onto a topic which is distasteful to your ears, and we will quit it at once.' Smiling at Lady Avery and picking up the thread of their previous conversation, he continued, 'Yes, Lady Avery, your advice about the memorial window is most excellent. To know that a memorial window for my predecessor was even in the planning process would help me adjust to my new and unsought-after position. I can always rely upon you to guide me on the correct course, regardless of how delicate the matter might be. The vicar and I *must* discuss it fully very soon.'

Changing the subject, the Earl locked his eyes on Angelica before rotating his gaze round the table to include the others. 'I believe Lady Angelica has had a rather adventurous day which we must press her to tell us about.'

Angelica's heart jumped; she thought that somehow the Earl was privy to Titus's departure and destination. Then she realized she had forgotten she would have to explain how it came to be that day for Prospero to be towed behind a gypsy caravan; and then she also realized she could declaim any knowledge of it if she was clever.

Giving the Earl a stony smile she said, 'Yes!

What a goose I was—and how embarrassing to be found out!' To this she added what she hoped sounded like an embarrassed laugh. 'When I was out riding today, I stopped to rest and removed Prospero's saddle to let him graze for a few moments—and I am so ashamed to say that he slipped away from me! I was heartsick with fear that he should come to any harm and I hunted for him desperately for what seemed like hours. Thankfully I found him again, grazing as if nothing had happened. The naughty creature! He gave me the fright of my life. What a grave responsibility it is riding a valuable horse which belongs to another. I am so utterly apologetic, Lord Greystone, and I hope you will not think me careless or cavalier in my use of your fine horse.' She smiled around the little circle of popping eyes that were glued upon her.

Lady Avery was not pleased. 'Angelica, *dear*, you must be careful! It is one thing to ride about the countryside—but *walking*—that is quite a different thing and could be dangerous! Promise me you will be more careful in future.'

'Oh, it will never happen again, dear aunt, I promise,' said Angelica, and her ladyship seemed reassured and returned to inhaling spoonfuls of hot *potage Chamonix*.

'Then you do not know the rest of the story, Lady Angelica?' said the Earl, smiling at her.

'The rest, sir?'

'Yes, Lady Angelica, your horse had an even greater adventure than yourself—it was stolen by the gypsies!'

Angelica hoped she looked surprised enough at this piece of news, and tried to copy Lady Avery's genuine open-mouthed astonishment. 'Truly, sir!' Angelica said, 'I am horrified to hear that!'

'Yes—it is quite true—my man, Hibbard, was en route back to the castle after transacting some business for me and he came upon four unscrupulous gypsies who had obviously found the horse wandering, and they had tried to disguise it with one of their blankets, but Hibbard recognized the horse and claimed it. Naturally the gypsies did not want to give up their booty and fell on Hibbard and beat him as he valiantly liberated the horse and, in the ensuing fight, the horse ran off. And fortunately, as we now know, the troublesome horse was found by your ladyship.'

As she listened to the Earl relate Hibbard's fanciful report of his encounter, the image of Hibbard's flying somersault flashed through her mind, and Angelica knew she should be fighting an uncontrollable explosion of laughter, but none came; it was the funniest set of events she had ever encountered, but her laughter stuck in her throat and all she could think of was how much she would have loved to share this delicious story with Gitano, but now he was gone, and she never would.

After a burst of excited chatter, from everyone except Angelica, as they examined the courageous Hibbard's selfless bravery from all sides and angles, the Earl turned to Mr Compton and said:

'But tell me, Vicar, what of the late Mr Quince's affairs?'

Mr Compton said, 'Ah—Mr Quince.' He smiled apologetically at Lady Avery. 'Please excuse us for speaking of business which will hold no interest for your ladyship.' Lady Avery smiled over a chicken thigh and nodded in a bid for him to continue; Lady Avery was interested in anyone's business. Mr Compton went on, still addressing Lady Avery. 'Mr Quince was the vicar at Crowood, a very ancient and troubled man who died recently and left me to tidy up his papers—an enormous task, I must say.' He looked again at the Earl. 'As to Mr Quince's affairs, they are in rather a state and will take me some time to sort through them. His papers are in something of a mess—' then he let out a laugh and said, '—rather like my own, I'm afraid!'

Angelica liked Mr Compton enormously. He was full of fun, unlike other country parsons of her acquaintance who felt they had to parade a stuffy, pious face. He partnered her at whist and made a great show of their triumph over Lord and Lady Avery by congratulating Angelica heartily on her excellent play and giving her all their winnings—six pence—to which she responded as gaily as she could, 'I will put it all in the plate tomorrow at church.' By the time Park brought in the tea urn, the little gathering had scattered itself about the room in various pursuits. Mr Compton and Angelica were talking again about the proposed stained glass windows.

Mr Compton produced a ragged little sketch-book from his pocket and showed it proudly to Angelica, saying, 'I am a bit of an amateur painter—most of us country vicars are you know—and these are some preliminary drawings I have done in hopes that Lord Greystone will consent to a memorial window, but I'm afraid my opinions carry little weight with his lordship.'

Looking at Mr Compton's drawings with interest, Angelica observed, after a few moments' reflection, 'The composition of this sketch is very like a picture upstairs in the long gallery. I wonder if you had it in mind when you did your drawing?' and she turned the book for him to see his own sketch and be reminded. 'I am sure you must know the picture I mean. I think it is by Francis Hayman, but of course his subject is not religious.'

'No, I can't say I recollect it,' Mr Compton said, rippling his brow in thought. 'It has been so long since I've seen the pictures here...will you show me the painting you have in mind?'

'I should be delighted,' said Angelica, getting up and crossing to the Earl and Lady Avery, who were poring over a set of large botanical prints. She said coolly to the Earl, 'May I take the vicar up to the long gallery? There is a picture I should like to show him.'

'Of course, Lady Angelica. I am delighted you take such an interest in the pictures here at Cranleigh.' Snapping his fingers in Park's direction, the Earl said loftily, 'Have the lamps in the long gallery lit immediately, Park.'

'Very good, m'lud,' intoned the old retainer who shuffled from the room more slowly than usual as his lumbago always acted up when the Earl lapsed into the vulgar habit of snapping his fingers at the servants.

Mr Compton, rising to join Angelica, said, 'And then, after our little expedition to the picture gallery, I must go. I have work to do on my sermon for tomorrow.'

'I insist you let me send you back to the vicarage in a carriage,' said the Earl obligingly, 'I understand it is raining.'

A servant, with a long, smoking taper, was just finishing lighting the lamps in the long gallery when Angelica and Mr Compton entered. They passed along the room to the picture they had been discussing. 'Ah! Yes! Yes! I know this picture! I just could not remember it for an instant. Now I realize I know it well,' he said, enthusiastically inspecting the small canvas of a group of people in theatrical dress. 'It is one of the best Haymans I've ever seen. I recall the old Duke telling me that it once hung in the infamous Vauxhall Gardens in London in the last century. It would have decorated the interior of some fashionable person's box, where they would have dined and observed the festivities in comfort and privacy. I don't suppose it would be considered a popular style now, but the old Duke never leaned on fashion when buying pictures. He always relied upon his own likes and dislikes. You are correct, Lady Angelica, it is very like my little daub—but, of course, only in composition,' he added humbly.

They discussed the picture for a few more minutes before starting to retrace their steps out of the gallery. As they were passing the large canvas of the family group with the mother in the blue dress and the two small boys, Angelica stopped and said, 'I am terribly fond of this picture, but as you can see the little plaque has come away from the frame, so I know nothing about its history. I feel I have seen it somewhere before, but I am sure that is not possible. Do you know who painted it, Vicar, or who the people are?'

'I cannot recall who the artist was, but I know who the subjects are. It is a painting of the last Duchess of Stanforth and her two sons. The studious-looking one became the last Duke, and the younger one was Lord Anthony,' Mr Compton said fondly.

Stepping up to the picture and looking hard for a few moments at the image of the younger boy, Angelica realized at last what it was about the picture that appealed to her so much. It was the eyes—dark, kind and gentle. Suddenly she reeled back from the picture as if struck by lightning.

Seeing her start at something invisible to him, Mr Compton was concerned. 'Are you all right, Lady Angelica?' he asked urgently.

She did not seem to hear the question, and without turning round she asked in a shaky voice, 'Mr Compton...how old was Lord Anthony when he got the small scar on the left side of his face?'

'Much older than in that picture...I think he must have been about fourteen. He and his brother were at fencing practice without protective masks and he was cut by his brother's foil. The injury was small, but I remember the incident well because the old Duke was very angry that his sons had disobeyed his order that they should always wear masks.' Mr Compton was warming to his subject and at first did not notice how the colour was draining from Angelica's face. Suddenly curious, Mr Compton asked, 'But I thought you had never *met* Lord Anthony?'

'I-I did not know I had until this minute.'

Mr Compton joined her near the picture and could now see how wan she looked, but before he could say anything, Angelica demanded weakly, 'When was Lord Anthony supposed to have died in America?'

'Well, let me see...by my reckoning it had to have been last December or November at the earliest. But why do say, "*supposed* to have died?" '

Taking Mr Compton's arm for support, she said quietly, 'May we sit down a moment, Vicar? I have something to tell you.'

'Are you feeling ill, Lady Angelica? You look very pale—'

She said faintly, 'No, it's just that...for a moment, I thought I had seen a ghost.'

'What on earth are you saying?' he asked, leading her to the nearby chairs that lined the wall.

When they were seated, Angelica looked at

333

Mr Compton earnestly and whispered, 'He—he isn't dead!'

'Who isn't dead? Child, you are not making any sense,' he protested in mild frustration, patting her hand to give her assurance as she was looking so faint.

'Lord Anthony is not dead! I have seen him frequently—I saw him today—we have spoken many times.' She was breathless and watched Mr Compton's face for a reaction.

As Mr Compton could only look at her in bewilderment, she related the story of how she had first seen him on the ship when he saved the drowning child, and later, at the inn, and finally, that very day, helping Titus get away. Seeing that Mr Compton's face was already a jumble of shocks and starts, which showed that he was having difficulty enough grasping what she was already telling him about Lord Anthony, she explained Titus's predicament briefly and without detail.

She was now speaking slowly so that the befuddled Mr Compton could take it in. 'Lord Anthony said he was leaving with the gypsies tonight. I am sure there can be no mistake about his identity. Even if I had not noticed the scar, I should have known him from this painting. I don't know why I didn't see it before! There was something about this painting that was familiar to me, but until this instant I didn't understand what it was. It is, of course, the eyes. Anyone can see from the painting, although he is only a child there, that it is Lord Anthony...' She breathed out sharply and her eyes darted unseeing around the room as she tried to understand the implications. Smiling a little she said, 'There will be many people who will be so happy to know that he is alive!' After pausing for a moment to look at his puzzled old face, she asked doubtfully, 'Vicar, do you believe me?'

'*Yes!* Yes, of course I do,' he responded in a hushed voice and patted her hand again in a dazed fashion. 'I am soundly shaken by this news—I must collect my thoughts.'

Mr Compton's mind suddenly snapped into sharp focus. 'Angelica—dear child—you must listen to me closely! *Whatever* happens, you must *not* tell a soul about this! It may be hard on his friends to believe him dead, but it will only increase the danger for him if it is known that he is alive. His friends all believe that what happened on the day the Duke was killed was an accident, and Anthony, seeing that it looked like murder, fled. He must have realized it would be impossible to prove otherwise. He can *never* return. If he did he would be signing his own death warrant. His friends know he must be protected from the forces of the law for, in this case, I am convinced it would be impossible for justice to be done. This may sound like a *very* curious stand for someone in my position to take, but I know he must be innocent of murder. However, the law would never conclude that. He *must* remain in exile. There is no other way! He is much safer if people believe him dead.' Mr Compton looked around to make sure they were alone and then asked quietly, 'Did you say the men searching for him at the inn were definitely *not* constables?'

'Yes. As they looked so disreputable, Lord Avery wrote to the Chief Constable to ask him why his men were out of uniform while performing their duties. The reply came very recently that they were not constables at all.' As Angelica said this, she suddenly awakened to the terrifying significance and sense of Mr Compton's logic.

'This is even worse than one could possibly imagine!' he said, his voice trembling with emotion. 'Perhaps those men were hoping to collect some sort of reward if they captured him. It is really too monstrous! But people of that sort do exist in the world. I can only hope that Anthony uses his good sense and leaves the country immediately! But this must be between you and me. No one else must know. If the constabulary finds out that he is alive, it will mean twice as much danger for him. Keep your own counsel on this, Lady Angelica. I cannot stress that enough. I know it may be difficult for you if you hear his friends speaking with sadness of his death, but you must *not* breathe a word of it—*ever!*' Mr Compton concluded with such sternness that it surprised Angelica.

The parquet flooring uttered a small squeak under a silent step and it made them look up. Hibbard was limping noiselessly up to them across the shiny floor. Angelica and Mr Compton exchanged alarmed looks, fearing that their conversation had been overheard.

Hibbard's injuries had done nothing to alter

the oiliness of his tone. 'His lordship wishes me to inform you that the carriage is below. It is at the door for you, Vicar, whenever you desire it.'

'Thank you, Hibbard, I am just coming now,' replied Mr Compton, pulling himself to his feet with the aid of his cane and taking Angelica's arm for further support. They returned to the others in a worried silence, followed closely by a somewhat damaged, but nonetheless alert, Hibbard.

As Mr Compton was taking his leave of the Earl and Lord and Lady Avery, he was resolutely maintaining a relaxed facade in spite of what he had just learned. 'I look forward to seeing you all in church in the morning. However, I cannot guarantee to keep you awake with my sermon, considering how late I have kept you all this evening. It has been delightful however, and I thank you all for your amiable society!' Park arrived to escort Mr Compton to the carriage and Angelica followed the vicar to the drawing-room door. 'Good night, Lady Angelica,' he said with steely brightness, and then in a whisper, 'Remember what I told you—*silence!*' And then, with a reassuring smile, 'Don't be surprised at anything I say or do in church tomorrow.' Angelica nodded that she understood.

Lord and Lady Avery and Angelica had wanted to arrive at church early the following morning to have time before the service to view the stained glass windows of which Mr Compton had spoken so highly. They had gathered in the hall of the castle to wait for Lord Greystone when Hibbard appeared in his usual manner; he seemed to float across the marble floor, with perhaps a trifle less than his usual fluidity due to his injured leg, and he gave Lady Avery a start when he slid noiselessly up behind her and spoke into her ear. He was the bearer of the Earl's apologies, 'His lordship wishes me to convey his compliments, and regrets that he cannot accompany his esteemed guests to church this morning. He looks forward to seeing your lordship and your ladyships at luncheon.' Angelica looked searchingly at Hibbard's face to see if there was any hint there that he had overheard her conversation with Mr Compton the previous evening, but the closely shuttered eyes betrayed nothing.

When Hibbard had gone, Lady Avery confided to Angelica, 'That man gives me a very unsettled feeling the way he goes sneaking about. I really don't know why Lord Greystone keeps him on. Oh, I suppose he was very brave to fight all those terrible gypsies or whatever, but the way Hibbard dresses! All those fancy clothes. You would think he wasn't a servant at all but at least a marquis!' And she added with an indignant snort, 'All his airs and graces! It really is a wonder Lord Greystone puts up with it. He's *most* disagreeable!' Angelica saw no point in trying to enlighten her aunt further on the subject of the appalling Hibbard.

Mr Compton greeted their carriage at the churchyard gate and showed off his church with pride as he led them along the pews,

338

where a church servant was putting hot coals into the brass foot-warmers in preparation for the congregation's arrival. With a proprietary wave of his hand, Mr Compton said, 'This is the original Norman nave and tower, and the rest was built and rebuilt a little at a time over the centuries to accommodate more stained glass.' After guiding his visitors to some of the church's finer points, he said, 'Now, if you will excuse me, I must get ready for the service,' and conducting them to the Stanforth family pews, he went through a little door that led into the vestry.

After the lesson was read, Mr Compton, mounting the pulpit, began, 'Many of you will have heard the sad news of the death of the younger son of the Stanforth family.' Angelica's eyes shot up to his face to find that Mr Compton was looking straight at her and she remembered his words, 'Don't be surprised by anything I say or do...' She sat motionless, listening.

'For whatever crimes he may or may not have committed, earthly courts will now never pass sentence. However, he will be judged by a higher power and may God have mercy on his soul.' A sniffle could be heard at the back of the little congregation, and Angelica wondered if it was one of the old, family servants. Mr Compton then offered up prayers for the passing of the man she knew to be alive. She understood the vicar's reasoning: if he omitted the prayers it might create rumour and suspicion about Lord Anthony's death; his safety depended upon the world believing him dead.

Mr Compton's sermon was lively and thought-provoking. He spoke so spiritedly on the evils of covetousness, the Tenth Commandment, that even Lord Avery was able to stay awake.

Gathering up her prayer book after the service, Angelica followed Lord and Lady Avery up the aisle to the door. Shaking hands with Mr Compton, Angelica was sure he delivered her a tiny wink, but it was difficult to tell as his eyes always wore a mischievous glint. She told him how much she had enjoyed the sermon, and he responded that he wished Lord Greystone had not missed it.

'The poor man works too hard,' sighed Lady Avery, 'and on a Sunday, too. He really shouldn't. He truly is a martyr to Cranleigh. He will ruin his health, Vicar, if he goes on like this. I do wish you would have a word with him.'

Mr Compton smiled a little. 'I am sure, Lady Avery, such advice would come much better from your ladyship. And, by the by, I am glad to know we may meet again soon. Lord and Lady Revelstoke have very kindly asked me to attend their ball. I look forward to seeing you all there.'

The day was so fine that Lady Avery waved the carriage away, choosing to walk back to the castle along the pleasant, dry path that bordered the patchwork fields. A small stile caused Lady Avery some difficulty, but, with Angelica pushing and Lord Avery pulling, her ladyship managed to scale its lofty twenty inches in spite of her crinoline repeatedly trapping her by looping itself over the top of a fence post. Watching this complex procedure of extricating Lady Avery from the stile was a cluster of doe-eyed bullocks that stared rudely for a long moment and then finally took to their heels and frolicked away as if running off to giggle in private at her ladyship's predicament. When they arrived back at the castle, Lord Avery said, 'I suppose, Angelica dear, you are going to gallop off and leave us old people to pursue our indolence and our luncheon. If I were not a gouty old man I'd join you. It's a pippin of a day! Go and enjoy yourself riding.'

Angelica left them, glad to have this chance for solitude to think about the one question in particular that had been piquing her overworked curiosity. The question was: who had kissed her in the wood? Had it been Gitano or Lord Anthony? They were the same man, of course, but which one had kissed her, and which one had pushed her away?

FIFTEEN

Angelica spent a fretful few days waiting for the Revelstokes' ball—which would mark her longed-for departure from the company of the Earl, whom she had managed to avoid except when they were safely separated by an expanse of dinner table. Even her long rides on Prospero were less enjoyable since that day she had

341

seen the Earl on horseback, as she was now constantly on her guard that he might appear at any time. And since Gitano—or as she now knew him to be, Lord Anthony—had gone, there were no pleasant interludes in his company to cheer her day. The knowledge of his real identity explained so much to her and she recalled with clarity all their conversations and was able to put them into new order like arranging the pieces of a still incomplete puzzle.

Once she found herself idly speculating what it would have been like if their paths had crossed under different circumstances, but that only increased the dull ache that constantly pained her and she banished such thoughts. She was sure she now understood his brooding undercurrents—he was a man deprived of his birthright by a terrible accident, and all the more painful to have all he owned pass legally into the hands of a man like Greystone who was capable of such low acts as beating a defenceless boy. She also wanted to know if Titus had arrived safely at Ickworth. Her only real confidant, Mr Compton, who might have news of both, was away at Crowood sifting through the late Mr Quince's papers. She felt isolated and adrift.

At daybreak on the morning of the ball, dressed in her riding habit, on her way to the stables, Angelica found herself drawn almost against her will towards the long gallery. She hurried through the nearly deserted reception rooms where, at that early hour, she only encountered maids and footmen gossiping in a desultory fashion as they busied themselves with their dusters and polish. Surprised by her appearance, they paused to say 'G'd mornin', m'lady,' or simply bowed a little or dropped a sleepy curtsy. Something had compelled her to go and look at the picture of the Duchess of Stanforth and her two sons.

Standing before the picture of the enchanting family group, Angelica was tapping her whip impatiently against her leg, feeling irritated with herself because she suspected the picture had another clue in it, but she could not make out what it was. She was cross with herself that it had taken her so long to discover the first secret it held—Gitano's real identity—and now she was fretting because she was convinced there was something more for her to see, but she could not fathom it. Losing patience with her own shortcomings, she finally gave it up and continued on to the stables.

Lady Avery had asked Angelica to make sure she returned from her ride just after luncheon at the very latest to allow time for any last minute adjustments to the dress. Angelica tried on the newly finished gown. 'Look, Angelica, what a splendid job Sarah has made of your dress. It really is quite remarkable!' trilled Lady Avery while Sarah beamed with pride.

'It does look lovely, and wonderfully fashionable. I have never had a dress that was this elegant. Thank you, Sarah, you have done wonderfully well!'

Rosy with delight, Sarah was making a small alteration to the tiny bows on the shoulders. 'You will be the belle of the ball, m'lady.'

'You will indeed, my dear,' said Lady Avery, pleased at the sight of her beautiful niece in a fashionable dress and the knowledge that she could hold her own head aloft while Angelica outshone all the other young ladies at the Revelstokes' ball. 'Now, as you have missed luncheon, with all your riding about, go down to the green drawing-room and ring for Park. I left instructions for Cook to have something ready for you to eat. I don't want you swooning with hunger this evening.'

'But I will have tea later, Aunt Clarissa,' protested Angelica.

'You will indeed, my girl, but you will have something substantial now, and no arguments! You will want all your energy for dancing this evening, and I won't have you starving yourself like some fashionable young ladies. Now change into something serviceable and go down.'

'Yes, Aunt Clarissa,' said Angelica obediently, knowing it was pointless to argue with her aunt once she had taken a stand.

'Good! Off you go then! I am going to instruct Sarah in the packing of our gowns and our dressing-cases. Thank goodness we are staying overnight at the Revelstokes'. At least we will be able to change into our gowns there and have our own rooms to retire to when it all gets too much. Sleep is always what I crave when everyone is having breakfast at some *astonishing* hour in the *middle* of the night.'

Following Lady Avery's orders, Angelica went to the green drawing-room and was relieved not to find the Earl about. She rang for Park who appeared shortly afterwards. 'Good afternoon, Park. Please ask Cook to send me something to eat. Some fruit would do, or a bit of cheese and bread. Nothing very much.'

'Yes, m'lady. Very good, m'lady,' said Park as he melted away. Returning after a short absence, he arrived with a minor feast on a tray which he put on a side table. 'I hope this will be satisfactory, m'lady.'

As Park floated about the tray arranging a plate of food for Angelica, she remembered what Sarah had said about Park and the Queen. Her curiosity found it too tempting. 'Have you been at Cranleigh long?' she asked.

'Yes, m'lady. My father and my grandfather were butlers to the Dukes of Stanforth, and I am happy to say that my son is the butler at...' Park hesitated as he was not yet able to reconcile the fact that Lord Greystone was to be the new Duke. 'My son,' he continued finally, 'is butler at...His Grace's house in London.'

'Such a long time with the Dukes of Stanforth! That is quite remarkable,' said Angelica with genuine interest. 'You must come from a family in which loyalty is very important.'

'Yes, m'lady, my grandfather was batman to the ninth Duke during the siege of Bell-Isle. They are credited with saving one another's lives at one time or another, but that is a very long story.'

'Forgive me for asking this, but is it true that the Queen wanted you to run one of her houses?'

Park's face betrayed no emotion, though

the closest observer might have detected a slight tremor in his right eyebrow. 'It is true, m'lady.'

'Do please tell me the story! How is it you are here now? I thought it was *impossible* to say "No" to the Queen.'

'It is, of course, impossible not to do as the Queen commands, m'lady, and any loyal and true Englishman would be willing to lay down his life for Her Majesty, as I would myself. But in this case it was a matter of *avoiding* the command before it was given,' said Park elusively.

'What do you mean "avoiding the command"?' asked Angelica, consumed with curiosity.

'Well, m'lady, if a question is not asked, it need not be answered. If a request is not made, it need not be granted,' continued Park with maddening slipperiness. 'What I mean, m'lady, is this—our great and good Queen came to Cranleigh Castle as a guest of the old Duke. She was very young then and at the beginning of her reign. May I say, m'lady, with all due respect to our great Sovereign, she was new to dealing with affairs of state and she was—as you might say—no match for the wise old Duke.'

Angelica was intrigued and sat absorbing Park's every word.

'The Queen was travelling with a very large entourage which included six blackamoor pages in blue silk knee britches. The whole county came out to see Her Majesty, and the spectacle of so many grand carriages. Also a guest at the castle, at the same time as Her Majesty, was Mr Mendelssohn. I know you will have heard of the great composer. He had taught the Queen music and singing when she was younger. There were many gay musical evenings during the Queen's visit, and I had the great honour of hearing the Queen sing. As I recall, she sang *Pilgerspruch* and *Lass dich nur*. I remember hearing Mr Mendelssohn say that the Queen sang quite faultlessly, with charming feeling and expression.'

Warming to his subject, Park continued, 'Mr Mendelssohn was a close friend of the Duke's; he remembered me from his previous visits to Cranleigh, and he always had a kind word for me. One day, when no one else was listening, Mr Mendelssohn turned to me and said, "You had better be on your guard, Park. I hear the Queen means to spirit you away!"

'Nothing could have surprised me more, m'lady, but I did not miss the *meaning* of Mr Mendelssohn's words. The Queen intended to ask the Duke to release me into her service. I passed this on to the Duke, who was just as appalled as myself at the prospect of ending such a long family association. In the end, the Duke said, "Leave it to me Park. Our forbears have had bigger battles than this! I'll settle the matter." '

'What happened, Park? What did the Duke do? What *could* he do against a royal command?' asked Angelica, captivated by the story.

'That very day there were many important guests for tea here at Cranleigh—in this exact same room.' Park looked round as he

347

remembered the scene of the lofty guests, comfortable in the Queen's presence, languidly draped on chairs while taking tea; the Queen, still pretty but already inclined to plumpness, slightly flushed from a long walk in the country air, was relaxed and finding her stay at Cranleigh amusing. Park continued, 'Out of the blue, as it were, the Duke said to the Queen, "Your Majesty is not superstitious, I suppose?"

'Not knowing what prompted the Duke's sudden question, the Queen replied, "We are all superstitious about certain things, my dear Duke. Perhaps we are not as guided by the oracles as the Ancients, but do we not all have our little foibles?"

' "How right and wise Your Majesty is! Now—for example—take Park there," said the Duke, nodding towards me as I served tea. And I have to confess, m'lady, I was so taken off guard, I almost spilled the tea with the anxiety of wondering what the old Duke was going to say next. But, of course—I didn't,' he added with professional pride. Park would have been horrified if he had realized that his own voice had taken on a bass tone as he unconsciously and fondly mimicked the old Duke's manner of speaking. Park continued, 'And the old Duke said to the Queen, "Yes, superstitions are interesting. Take Park there. Now, his family has been in the service of the Dukes of Stanforth for four generations. My grandfather and his grandfather fought side by side in the battles of the Seven Years War. Both men were badly wounded and both recovered. I'd thought about this often—how the two families have had this long established link. I often wonder if it could be more than just chance. Well, Your Majesty, I sometimes have gypsies here camping on the estate. I permit them to set up their tents and caravans in peace, and they cause me no trouble."

' "One day an old gypsy woman approached me and asked if she could tell my fortune. Stuff and nonsense, I thought, stuff and nonsense! But I saw no harm in it. Now this old gypsy told me something that shook me to my very foundations! If I had not had witnesses, I would not have believed I had heard it myself. This old fortune-teller prattled on about this and that for a few moments—utter rubbish it sounded to me—but then she fixed me with a gimlet eye and said in her terrible croaky voice something that makes me shudder even now. She said that if the families of Stanforth and Park were ever separated, the house of the Dukes of Stanforth would fall and the Stanforth fortunes would be swept away like the autumn leaves. And, you know, Your Majesty, I do believe it, I do indeed. That is what I am superstitious about, and I live in constant terror of anything happening to Park or his family." '

Park was completely taken up by his recollection; it was as if he was reliving it. 'I watched as the Queen gave the old Duke a slight smile and Her Majesty said, *ever* so quietly, "My *dear* Duke, what an...*interesting*...story. I hope nothing will ever happen to prove the prophecy true." And then she abruptly changed the subject. It was never mentioned again, and the Queen never asked me to go into her service.' As he finished, Park exhaled with relief as if his lucky escape had just taken place moments before, instead of decades.

'Park, what a wonderful story!' cried Angelica. 'But was it true about the old gypsy woman?'

'I am inclined to doubt it, m'lady. There were often gypsies on the estate, but the old Duke never had his fortune told, to the best of my knowledge. I would guess it was something he made up on the spot. It was just his way of steering the Queen away from commanding me into her service. The old Duke knew that if a question is not asked it need not be answered, so he stopped the Queen before she could ask. It would have been impossible for the old Duke to say "No," so he made it impossible for the Queen to ask in the first place.'

'The old Duke must have been very wise,' Angelica said, deeply impressed, 'and he obviously valued you greatly.'

'Yes, m'lady, thank you, m'lady,' responded Park, regaining all his previous formality.

Angelica thought it sadly ironic that the old Duke's prophecy had in a way come true, except that Park had not been the keystone of the family's demise. She thought she could detect a downcast look clouding Park's usually implacable face. 'These terrible events must be very distressing for you,' she said, in a hushed tone. 'Will you remain here at Cranleigh now that...?' she trailed off as she wondered if the subject was too upsetting for the elderly butler.

'I must confess, m'lady, that my spirit has been all but broken by the demise of this great family. And although it was not my place, I was very fond of both the old Duke's sons. This latest piece of news about Lord Anthony's death has laid everyone very low in the servants' hall. I myself simply refuse to believe it. I suppose I am deluding myself, m'lady, but it is the only way I can go on.'

Angelica felt pangs of guilt and compassion as she witnessed the old butler's sadness. She wanted to comfort him by telling him what she knew, but even if she had not been bound by her promise to Mr Compton to keep her silence about Lord Anthony, she would do nothing that might endanger him. But then she thought, perhaps it was better for Park not to know the truth. What would it do to the old butler to know that the rightful Duke of Stanforth was doomed to travel the world in the guise of a gypsy called Gitano. She permitted herself to say only, 'In the short time I have been a guest here, I have been told by many people that they refuse to believe...' she stopped speaking as the door opened and Hibbard slid into view. The white of his head bandage made his sallow complexion seem even greyer than usual.

Hibbard remained silent for a moment with his heavy eyelids lowering and then raising. He finally said, through his cracked smile, 'His lordship wishes to speak with you at once, Park.'

'Thank you, Mr Hibbard,' responded Park, with perhaps the tiniest hint of ice in his voice.

He finished arranging Angelica's tray in an unhurried manner and after enquiring as to any further needs she might have, he joined Hibbard at the door. Bowing, they went out, closing the door behind them.

As she watched them go, Angelica thought what a contrast they made: Hibbard—dripping with malevolence; Park—so obliging and kind. While she ate, she pondered on the thought that there was a quote she had read somewhere about how a servant reflects the character of his master. She decided to look it up that afternoon as she had very little to do to get ready for the ball.

SIXTEEN

Having spent some time in the castle library, Angelica was quite familiar with the volumes. She also knew that the library had two doors, one to the hall and the other to the Earl's study. He had taken over the late Duke's study—the place where the infamous shooting accident had taken place. Angelica stepped into the library through the hall doorway. She could see that the door to the Earl's study was open and her inclination was to retreat. Feeling cowardly and foolish, she listened for a moment and was assured that no sound was coming from the study. Satisfied that the Earl was not about, she made her way to the bookshelves. The library was cosy with a faint smell of beeswax from the often-polished panelling and a warm fire crackled in the grate. Angelica easily found the volumes she wanted. Settling into a high, winged-back chair, which faced the windows, she was soon absorbed in her books.

After a while the sound of voices made her look up from her reading. 'Ah, there you are, Avery!' she could hear the Earl saying. 'I have been rather preoccupied with other matters and I haven't had an opportunity to settle that French transaction with you...' and then Angelica could hear the murmur of their voices discussing financial business in the study next door. She turned again to her book and the voices did not distract her until a little later when she was startled to hear her own name mentioned in the conversation; she put down her book and listened.

'...I wish to make an offer for Lady Angelica's hand in marriage,' the Earl was saying resolutely. The unexpected words made her flinch uncontrollably as if someone had struck her hard in the face. She felt numb at first, then flushed hot and shook with a violent chill as tides of sickness rose up in her.

'You do us a great honour, Lord Greystone, my dear old friend,' Lord Avery responded, not trying to hide his delight. 'I am sure Lady Angelica will be truly sensible of the honour, and I know Lady Avery and myself are cognizant of the esteem with which your proposal may be duly held.'

Knowing he would not be rebuffed by Lord

353

Avery, the Earl was on safe ground. Therefore there was no element of challenge to keep him entertained and, feeling a bit bored by the proceedings, he did not think it necessary to keep up the niceties for too long. He said rather sharply, 'I wish you to make my offer known to Lady Angelica as soon as we return from Revelstoke's tomorrow, for I intend to make my proposal to Lady Angelica immediately thereafter.'

Lord Avery was perplexed by the Earl's desire to declare his proposal so soon. Still maintaining his joviality, but vacillating slightly while searching for the right words, he said, 'Ah...well...don't you think you are rushing your fences a bit, Greystone? My niece is very young and has not been in Society. Perhaps it would be better to wait a bit.' Lord Avery wondered if bringing Angelica to the Earl's attention had succeeded too well—too soon.

'I am not a man to wait about, as you know. My intention is to marry your niece next week in the chapel here at Cranleigh.'

Breathless with horror, Angelica thought she was dreaming the most unimaginable nightmare as his words drifted through the open door to her ears.

'B-but—my *dear friend*,' stammered Lord Avery who, for all his smooth manners, found himself gawking in astonishment at the Earl. He was now finding the conversation seriously disturbing. For a moment he was at a loss for words, but then offered, 'My dear Lord Greystone, I can understand your impatience.

You will soon take the title of the Duke of Stanforth and wish to proceed with your life, which has been much interrupted by all this bad business at Cranleigh. You must be anxious to be settling down into a suitable marriage and a quiet existence. But Lady Angelica is very young and has no experience of the world, and it would be unfair to her to cast her into such a sudden—although, I *willingly* grant—fortunate match.' His tone became slightly patronizing as he became enamoured with the sound of his own voice. 'There are matters to be settled. A dowry, for instance. I plan to make a generous settlement upon my niece. Naturally, my heirs are my younger brother and his son, who will someday inherit my title and fortune. Therefore Lady Angelica will not come into a fortune from me, nor has she an income of her own, but I plan to give my niece a dowry when she marries which will do credit to her position as a Duke's daughter. And there are other considerations—banns to be read, guest lists, official announcements in the social papers, and Lady Avery will have a myriad of plans to execute. In any case,' Lord Avery continued, in his most conciliatory way, 'as you are stepping into the title of a royal duke, is there not an obligation to inform the Queen of your intention to marry?' Lord Avery folded his hands and gave the Earl the sort of grating little smile a schoolmaster bestows upon a promising pupil.

Sweeping all objections aside, the Earl rose irritably and paced about the room in a distracted manner. 'I don't believe in fussy society weddings! It will be a quiet ceremony conducted by that old fool of a vicar, Compton. There will be no guests—only members of the immediate families, if they *insist* upon attending!' He spat out this last as if it was the most eccentric notion for families to attend weddings.

Lord Avery was silent, partly because he was searching for something to say and partly because he wondered if the Earl had gone quite mad. He did not wish to offend such a rich and powerful ally who was proposing a very advantageous marriage, but he felt that matters were going too fast. 'Now, we must be reasonable about this,' he began cautiously. 'Although, as Lady Angelica's guardian, I consent wholeheartedly to this match, I really feel that it must be carried out according to the usual formalities. I am sure that upon a little reflection you will agree. Lady Angelica may be an orphan, but she is still the daughter of a royal duke and must be accorded the respect of that position.'

'I don't think you understand me, Lord Avery,' responded the Earl in a slow, icy manner, emphasizing his every word. 'I *will* marry your niece next week, and you will assist me.' He continued with cold assurance. 'If you do not, you will find that the loan I made to you over this French business will be recalled with remarkable suddenness. I do not believe you would be able to disperse your assets quickly enough to be able to recover from such a financial blow at this time.'

'But—this is *monstrous!*' hissed Lord Avery, shaking with rage, his colour rising.

'Call it what you will,' said the Earl, shrugging a little and sitting down at his desk. With a satisfied air, he luxuriantly arranged his outstretched, boot-clad feet up on the highly polished mahogany surface. He looked at Lord Avery and, with amusement creeping into his tone, he said, 'You have given me your blessing, and now you are just haggling over the wedding arrangements. You have *everything* to lose if you try to cross me in this. If you assist me, you have everything to gain. When I take over Cranleigh and the title, you will be connected with the richest and most powerful dukedom in England. The wedding arrangements may not be quite...*conventional,* but you will be saved a fortune in Lady Angelica being wed before you have to cover the considerable cost of launching her into Society.' He let out a sardonic little chuckle at his own tasteless wit, and a hard little smile distorted his mouth. 'I am not accustomed to waiting round for what I want—and this marriage is what I want—*now.* Do I make myself clear?'

That Lord Avery was greedy was incontestable. He did not attempt to delude himself of the fact, but the ugly and ragged edges of his avarice had always been softened by the drapery of polite social behaviour. Even the hardened Lord Avery was shocked at the Earl's determination to possess the object of his desire without even paying the slightest lip service to social conventions. What the Earl said was true, in many ways. Lord Avery was keen for this match as it might give him some access to the vast Stanforth fortune. The question of Angelica's happiness was not even an issue. Arranged marriages were the norm and, as Lord Avery reasoned, from the social and financial standpoint, to be the Duchess of Stanforth was a great prize which any sensible young lady would covet. His lordship was fond of Angelica or, in reality, rather flattered to have such a pretty creature as Angelica in his retinue and doubly flattered, as any old man would be, by a charming young lady's natural show of affection for her uncle. However, he would never allow his slight paternal feelings to get in the way of his purse. He was angered because his pride had been bruised by the Earl, who was proposing to diminish his finances—which was unthinkable. Although he would not admit it to himself, he felt completely undermined that by his greed and poor judgement he had permitted himself to get into a financial position where his fortune was in jeopardy. His lordship knew that he was powerless against the financial blackmail that the Earl threatened. He would be ruined if the Earl withdrew his loan at that moment. Lord Avery had no choice but to consent.

Lord Avery did not reply for several minutes. Walking to the fireplace, he stared at the hot coals and tried to think. He was trapped and had no way out. He wanted to say many hard words to the Earl but knew it would be pointless. He understood from experience that the Earl was a ruthless man who meant what he said. Lord

Avery looked at the Earl's face, which was set in an ugly, purposeful grin, and he had difficulty believing that he was the same man with whom he had cordially associated for many years.

Finally, after a long pause, Lord Avery responded. His lordship made a great effort to adjust his voice to a normal tone, as the last scrap of his pride would not permit him to let the Earl know how angry or contemptuous he felt, and he said, 'Matters will proceed as you ask. I will speak to Lady Angelica as soon as we return from Revelstoke's tomorrow. There will be no complications. You know I am a man of my word. You may make your plans to your satisfaction.' Then, jutting out his chin in what he hoped was a manly fashion, he added, 'I can only trust that what has passed between us in this room will remain just between ourselves.'

'Thank you, Lord Avery, I knew you would see what a simple matter it is,' said the Earl in a pleasant manner as if nothing unusual had passed between them.

Angelica's face burned as scalding tears poured down her cheeks. She could not believe what she had just heard. Not only was she to be forced to marry a man she loathed, she was to marry him in a few days' time! Her head throbbed with a pain that blinded her and the relentless cascade of hot salty tears seemed to sear her cheeks. Shutting her eyes, she blocked out the gentle evening light from the windows as if it was the source of her agony.

The voices from the next room had ceased and Angelica knew that Lord Avery had left. She sat still, not wanting to disclose her presence in the library to the Earl. She could not bear to face him—then, or at any other time.

Resting her head against the high back of the upholstered chair, she sobbed silently and then struggled to regain her composure. She could hear the Earl moving about in the next room and then, to her horror, she could hear the squeak of the oak door sill as he stepped into the library where his footsteps were muffled by the thick rug. He was somewhere in the room behind her. Not daring to breathe, and without moving an inch, she glanced round in panic to see if she was hidden from view. She was. Her slim form was completely concealed from the rest of the room as she was dwarfed by the large wing-backed chair. She was thankful that Lady Avery had suggested she put on a serviceable dress, as the skirt was of a simple, unfashionable shape that was easily encompassed by the chair. But she could not move a muscle for fear that the rustling of her taffeta petticoat would give her away. Daring only to turn her eyes, she looked about and caught sight of a mirror to the left of the windows. It was large, in a heavy carved gold frame, and it hung suspended by a chain across the corner, so from that angle almost the entire room behind her was visible in the mirror. She could see the Earl's reflection as he moved about the dimly lit room behind her; he scanned the room quickly to make sure he was alone. Terrified, Angelica watched the mirror images, knowing that if she could see the Earl reflected there, if he looked up into the mirror, he would be able to see her, too.

She stared into the mirror and watched as the Earl went to the door that led to his study, closed it, and turned the key in the lock. Then, crossing the room to the opposite side, he shut the door that led to the hall and locked it as well. In the mirror, she could see that in his hand the Earl held the yellow, pigskin document case that Lord Avery had made such a fuss about when the coach was being packed at Dover. Even in her shocked state, some things made sense and she correctly assumed that her uncle had just given the document case to the Earl when they were talking business. The Earl moved swiftly to the right side of the fireplace, which was only a few feet from her chair. Angelica, transfixed by fear, continued to watch him in the mirror. The room was darkening; the fire was low and the servants had not, as yet, lit the lamps. She could not make out where he was reaching, but suddenly a door opened where there had been none a moment before.

Angelica realized that he had opened a secret panel. Most old houses were full of them and they had delighted her as a child. The Earl disappeared from view for a moment; he then returned from the hidden room without the document case. Swinging the panelling shut, he pressed the area in several places with the palm of his hand to make sure it was secure. When he was satisfied, he unlocked both library doors and went again into his study, shutting the door behind him.

The tears tumbled freely down Angelica's

face. Even in her worst moments she had never imagined anything this dreadful. She was totally defenceless. Even if she could go to Lord Avery and protest against marrying the Earl, it would be useless. She could not ask Lord Avery to sacrifice his fortune for her happiness. Lady Avery was so enamoured of the Earl that, although she would be surprised by the sudden wedding arrangements, she would make no real protest. Even if her ladyship did object, it would do no good against Lord Avery's orders. Angelica didn't have a single ally. It all came to the same thing—she was cornered.

Trying to calm herself, she resolved not to allow anyone to see her in this state. She noticed a decanter of water on a sideboard to the left of her chair. She rose to cross the short distance and found herself weak with grief; her legs barely held her. After managing to sip from a glass of water, which shook in her trembling hand, she had to sit down again and attempted to be calm by trying to remember how peaceful she had been a few days before when she sat by the spring and watched the kestrel's flight. It seemed like years had passed since then.

Angelica stared blankly out of the window for a while, not knowing what to do next. Still feeling unable to face anyone, she knew without seeing herself in the mirror that her eyes were swollen with crying. As she rested there, breathing softly, a phrase stole into her rambling thoughts '...if a question is not asked, it need not be answered...' This rolled gently round in her mind for a short time and seemed to repeat itself over and over again like a soothing mantra, then she managed to listen to it. 'That's what Park said—' she heard herself whisper aloud, '—if a question is not asked, it need not be answered...'

If Lord Greystone does not propose to me, I need not make an answer. *That's it!* thought Angelica. To avoid ever being asked to marry him, I will run away! It is the *only* answer. Even if I tried to refuse the Earl, my uncle would keep his part of the bargain and force me into the marriage. If I run away *before* I am told anything about the proposal, they will not assume it is the reason for my disappearance. That way Lord Avery will not lose his fortune and I will not become the prisoner of that horrid man. Then a plan started to form, and she began to piece it together: it will have to be *tonight*, because tomorrow my uncle is supposed to speak to me of Lord Greystone's intentions. It is tonight or *never!* I will feign illness and not go to the ball. Angelica almost permitted herself to smile at this, for she had never felt more ill in her life than at that moment. Her whole body ached in response to her mental torment.

Formulating her plan, she remembered that everyone would be at the Revelstokes' ball, including many of the servants; that would allow her some freedom of movement. She began to reason it out: The guests will not return until midmorning tomorrow and I would not be missed until tomorrow evening at dinner. With Prospero not in the stable, everyone will just assume that I felt better in the morning and went for my customary ride. If I leave tonight, about midnight, the rest of the household will be asleep and it will give me many hours advantage. I shall ride Prospero across country and I already know the way to the Ashford road, having seen the milestone only a few days ago. I will have to ask the way to Dover unless it is signposted. Oh—why didn't I pay attention to the way the coach brought us? she berated herself. Whatever happens, I must not get lost. It will be too easy to get confused in the dark, and getting lost will ruin my plan as it would waste essential time.

She calculated: The first stage will be riding to Dover and then getting a ship to France. It will be simple getting a train from Calais to Paris and then on to Tours, and somehow a message will have to be got to Count Chénier to come and collect me in Tours. Her mind was racing. She had never travelled alone and someone else had always made the arrangements. Angelica was vague as to how to go about it and nervous and worried about the details, but she was determined to think it all out later.

Trying to imagine what Count Chénier would think of his runaway cousin, she asked herself, will he refuse to help me? He might return me to Lord Avery, my legal guardian! It is a terrible chance, but I must try it! If Count Chénier will not help me I will strike out on my own and simply vanish. I speak perfect French and could perhaps use an assumed name and work as a governess in France, or somehow get to Canada or America. My plan is so imperfect, but I cannot just do *nothing!*

Looking out of the library window, Angelica could see that it was almost dark; she knew her aunt and uncle and the Earl would be having tea somewhere in the castle. They had probably sent a footman to find her, but the servant had returned saying that he could not find her ladyship anywhere. The Earl, she speculated bitterly, had probably vouched for the fact that she was not in the library. Time was running out and she must organize her plan. Her feeling of total helplessness started to ebb slightly as she plotted her escape. She slipped out of the library, dashed silently across the marble hall to the front door and, without stopping, pulled a large paisley shawl from the vast, ornate coat stand. Walking swiftly, as she wrapped the shawl about her, she made her way towards the stables. There were details to be seen to—details that would mean the difference between success and failure.

The cold air stung her face which was still damp with tears, but she welcomed the bright clear evening which promised a frost; she knew the cloudless sky was to her advantage as she was sure there would be a waning moon later to light her way. She knew the moon would be the key to her flight; without it she would be floundering round hopelessly lost in the dark. The moon would provide her with just enough illumination for her to find important landmarks. As soon as she reached the old, Roman road, where the white chalk earth showed clearly through the close-cropped grass all along its length, she would have no trouble with her directions. With Prospero's speed and stamina, she hoped to be halfway to Dover by noon. That would give her the head start she needed before her departure was discovered.

As she approached the stables, all her thoughts were deeply absorbed in her plan, so the unexpected dark figure that hovered out from the shadow of a gnarled old tree gave her a terrible fright. It was Hibbard! *Why* was he here? Was he spying on her? Could he guess what was in her mind? How much did he know of the Earl's affairs? Was he privy to the Earl's ghastly plans for her? All these thoughts raced through her mind.

'Good evening, Lady Angelica,' he cooed in his greasy drawl. 'It's very late for a stroll.'

'G-good evening, Hibbard,' she replied, trying to control her voice, and hoping it sounded unremarkable, 'You're...you're quite right, but isn't the air refreshing?' and carrying on without slowing her pace, she slipped by him. Not daring to glance round to see if he was following her, she felt an awful chill on her back and thought it must have been Hibbard's relentless stare.

Arriving at the stables, Angelica walked to a side door knowing that, even if Hibbard was still watching, he would not be able to see her go in. She noticed with relief that there was no lock on the door. She had been in and out of the stables dozens of times, but, as it had not mattered to her until now whether or not the stables were secured at night, she had not noticed if the doors had locks.

Next she walked the length of the stable to the harness room. The lanterns were lit, but she found the stables empty. She thought the grooms would return after their evening meal to finish their chores for the night and extinguish the lamps. There would be no lanterns lit at midnight when Angelica planned to make her escape; it would be too dangerous to show a light and perhaps alert the household. The saddles hung in three rows on racks suspended from the wall. She had to climb onto a stool to reach the saddle she had been using on Prospero. Taking it down, she switched its position with one on the end of the bottom row making it possible for her to find it in the dark by feel alone. Then she found Prospero's bridle and hung it where she could find it later. She did not dare remove the tack completely as someone might notice. Without these precautions, it would be impossible for her to make her getaway in the dark.

Coming out of the harness room, she looked nervously about her to make sure she was still alone. She could see Prospero standing with his head over the stable door. He whinnied faintly as she went up to him and he nuzzled her with his velvety nose. 'You and I are going travelling out into the world,' she whispered to him before she quietly made her way to the door.

Outside it was now completely dark. She had to hurry because she could see, at the far end of the stable yard, the horses were being harnessed to the landau to take them to the ball. As she approached the glowing windows of the castle, her warm breath, hitting the cold air, spiralled back into her face; and she realized that before she had felt nothing but anguished despair, but now that she was actually creating a plan of escape, she was gaining a strength and an independence she did not know she possessed. For the first time, she felt that she might have some control over her life. She found it gave her the strength she needed to try her outrageously daring plan.

She felt slightly more composed when she went into her bedroom and found Lady Avery there. 'Angelica! *Where* have you been? I've looked everywhere for you!' her ladyship demanded sharply. Angelica had been left pale and weak by the revelations of the last hour and Lady Avery could see that she looked drained. Her tone softening, she said, 'Dear child, you look very unwell. Are you ill?'

'I-I don't think I am very well, Aunt Clarissa, I have the most awful headache. I've just been out trying to clear my head with some fresh air, but it hasn't helped. I think I just need to close my eyes for a bit.'

'I've never seen you looking this pale,' said her aunt with concern, as she placed her palm on Angelica's brow to test for fever, 'You are rather warm and certainly must not go to the ball. I will stay here with you and I shall have the doctor sent for.'

'No! No please! It isn't necessary! You must not, Aunt Clarissa!' Angelica was alarmed. She did not want her aunt in the house hovering about half the night, hindering her departure.

'I'm not ill...just a little overtired.'

'It's nerves I expect—it is a big occasion going to your first real ball and it puts many a young lady out of sorts. Sleep is definitely what you need.'

'Yes—I am sure that is all I need. But *you* must go to the ball! I won't hear of you missing it on my account. It would be such a disappointment for Dodo if neither of us appeared. Promise me that you will go, otherwise, who will tell me about every detail?'

'Are you quite sure you will be all right, Angelica? You are never ill—it's quite unlike you.' Lady Avery looked hard at her niece. She could see that Angelica was unwell and a tiny voice in her ladyship's head tried to tell her that something was seriously wrong, but Lady Avery had long since stopped listening to her small voice of intuition, and it had become very faint.

For a moment, Angelica wanted to confide in her ladyship and pour out her despair, but she realized that her aunt could do nothing to protect her from the power of the Earl. There was no one in England in whom she could confide; she was totally alone. 'Please don't worry, I will be as good as new in the morning.' Angelica promised, 'and now I really would like to lie down.'

Ringing for Sarah, Lady Avery said, as the tiny voice in her head nagged meekly again, 'I think I will not take Sarah with me to the Revelstokes' after all. You may need her here.

Lady Revelstoke will have a maid I can use.'

'I won't hear of it!' protested Angelica in pain, wishing her aunt would not create difficulties that might hamper her plans. 'Sarah will be desperately upset if she cannot go. Lord Revelstoke is allowing the servants to have an entertainment of their own—a dance or something. She is looking forward to it so much. You *must* take her! *Please* do! If I need anything I shall just ring.'

'Oh, very well, I suppose you are right. I would get no peace from Sarah for months if I didn't take her,' agreed her ladyship; and the wee, small voice, so used to being ignored by the torpid brain it inhabited, shrugged and went back to sleep.

Sarah arrived and helped Angelica to bed. She could not even tell Sarah of her plan because there was nothing Sarah could do to help, and it would ruin everything if Sarah let it slip—Angelica was completely alone.

The cool crisp bed linen felt soothing against her burning face. She told Sarah to turn out the lamp and to inform the other servants not to disturb her under any circumstances. Desperate for the refuge of sleep, Angelica wanted to close her eyes and let her troubles ebb into oblivion, but she was afraid she would oversleep and not get away until it was too late. Forcing herself to stay awake, she listened to the household noises: the footsteps in the corridor, the muted voices of servants, and finally, the sound of the landau being drawn up to the front door. The Earl's voice intruded from the courtyard below. He was asking Lady Avery if she was comfortably settled in the carriage. His voice made Angelica tremble. How could he have the audacity to behave as if nothing had happened when only that afternoon he had been threatening to ruin Lord Avery?

The landau moved off with the clatter of hooves on cobblestones and Angelica remained very still, waiting for the house to quiet before attempting to finish her preparations. When a hush eventually fell over the castle, and it sounded as if the servants had descended below-stairs for the night, she pushed back the covers. Wearily swinging her feet over the side of the bed, she sat trying to muster the strength to go on.

The throbbing in her head had been replaced by a dull pain, and her tears had dried leaving her lashes with a faint dusting of salt; she rubbed at them with a handful of bed linen. Taking a deep breath and letting it out, she thought, now I am committed to trying to form a plan which will work. Failure will mean a lifetime of misery. I *must* remain calm and, whatever happens, I must not panic. She was battling with her nerves every second, fearing that she might be discovered trying to get away.

Sliding off the bed, her bare feet touched the cold wooden floor, but she felt no chill as her mind was whirling with plans and she set to work. She lit the lamp on the bureau and turned the wick down low, hoping that the light would not be seen under the door by a passing servant who might enter to enquire as to her welfare. Seeing a better solution, she snatched a tartan rug from the day-bed and laid it along the bottom of the door to prevent any light escaping. She set out every detail in her mind: I'll put on my oldest riding habit. It is cut in such a plain way and the skirt is not extravagant—it is sure to pass for a travelling suit. I want to be as inconspicuous as possible once I reach Dover. As it is impossible to carry any baggage, I will only take what I absolutely need. This old woollen cape will cover the riding habit. But what about a bonnet? How can I possibly carry a bonnet on horseback without crushing it and making it useless? A lady would never travel without wearing a hat. My riding hat will look ridiculous once I reach Dover and call attention to me on shipboard. I must pass unnoticed. Then, spotting her large, knitted tam-o'-shanter, which she sometimes wore for country walks, she exclaimed to herself, *that* is the answer! With this hat and old cape, I can pass as a serving girl travelling alone. A lady would never travel unattended, but being dressed like a servant will explain my situation and not cause comment. It is the ideal disguise and if I am really pressed I can pose as a French servant. Everyone says my accent is perfect. If my absence is discovered too soon, they will be looking for a lady travelling alone, not a servant.

Gathering up the tam-o'-shanter, some hairpins, nets, and handkerchiefs, she rolled them up in the cape to form a tight bundle and fastened it in three places with the bits of string that had held the parcel in which her mother's wedding dress had arrived. She sighed when she thought of the wedding dress. She would never see it again. She tied on another length of string which would attach her 'wardrobe' to a metal loop at the back of the saddle.

Now for the most difficult part, Angelica agonized—what to do about *money?* I will have to buy a ticket for the Calais ship. I must have money to put Prospero into a good livery stable in Dover. He will be very unhappy staying there long and I will have to devise a way of letting Dodo know where he is without exposing my escape route. Dodo is the one person guaranteed to be concerned for his welfare and I am sure she will find a way of securing his safe return. It will be very hard leaving Prospero behind as he has been such a faithful friend.

Returning to the question of money, every purse, pocket, and drawer was ransacked in her search. A few forgotten coins that had been intended for church collections were discovered caught in a pocket lining. Some French francs her cousin had given her for her birthday and the odd shilling Lady Avery had given her to buy ribbons were all she could find. All in all it was an unimpressive little stack of coins. She had never thought about money before and she started to lose hope. Fingering the gold locket at her neck she wondered if she would have to sell the only piece of her mother's jewellery she had, but it was out of the question. Still, she simply *had* to have the money to get across the Channel; it was her only possible escape route. Then she remembered the brooch that the Earl had forced upon her.

The brooch looked even more vulgar now as she opened the box gratefully; but this time she was delighted to see it regardless of its unpleasant connections. She was thinking: If I find I do not have enough money, I will go to a jeweller's in Dover and have him remove one or two of the diamonds and pay me their value. Count Chénier said that when he was a young man he had done the same thing to have enough money to buy a neighbour's vineyard. With this, success is assured! It was ironic, she realized, that her means of escape had been delivered by her enemy.

Angelica deliberated for a moment about how to carry the brooch safely. She was frightened of putting it into her pocket as she had once heard Sarah say that steerage class on ships carried people who stole whatever they could lay their hands on. Removing her riding jacket and laying it on the bed, she very carefully pinned the brooch on the underside of the left lapel. When she was convinced that it was securely fastened and concealed, she slipped the jacket on again and put another log on the fire, as the room had become very cold. She put out the lamp. Pulling an eiderdown from the bed, and wrapping it around herself, she settled into a chair by the fire—to wait.

SEVENTEEN

Angelica awoke with the sickening fear that she had slept too long. The fire had gone out, leaving the room in chilly darkness. As she lit the candle on the mantelpiece, her hands trembled with cold and self-loathing. How *could* I have been so stupid as to fall asleep? she asked herself, choking down sobs of rage. The flickering light showed her the face of the little silver clock: eleven-thirty! I am *just* in time! She was furious with herself for nodding off—she had not intended to sleep. I must not relax for an instant until I am in France! Hurrying to the door, she stood and listened. Nothing was stirring in the house. She opened the door carefully and listened again—not a sound. Then she had to decide whether to take the candle to let herself out of the house, or chance crashing into something in the dark and creating a racket which would awaken the servants. Scooping up her gloves, her whip, and the small bundle, she blew out the candle. She decided that moving along the corridors slowly in the dark would be better than showing a light. Shutting the door softly behind her, she tiptoed along the hallway. When she came to the grand staircase, the large high windows of the hall let in enough pallid moonlight for her to see features of the stairs. Slowly and deliberately, she took a few steps, then she stopped and listened again. Silence.

The beating of her heart felt like a huge drum pounding; it was blaring in her ears; to her it seemed the noise would alert the whole house and, in panic, she looked about the vast, empty hall half expecting the dozens of doors to be thrown open followed by loud shouts raising the alarm. For what seemed like hours, she inched her way down the marble staircase and finally arrived at the solid front door. Hope lay beyond it. She turned the brass handle and pulled. Nothing happened! She tried the door again. It did not move. It had never occurred to her that it would be locked! Her hands scrambled about in the dark searching for the key but it had been removed! She almost wept with frustration. Collecting her thoughts, she moved cautiously across the marble floor to the yellow drawing-room; she found she could move quickly across its quiet, thick carpet to the next room which had French windows leading to the garden. With an unspoken prayer, she turned the French window's small, brass knob. Again—*nothing happened*. A new emotion rose in her: she felt resentment at this imprisonment. Shaking with defiant anger, she continued on through the shadowy, interconnecting rooms.

Without warning, a face suddenly appeared next to hers. His pale, bloodless features leered at her from the dark recess! Her whole body was convulsed with shock and the crashing sound of her thudding heart vibrated through her like the wild discord of a vast orchestra gone berserk. She gasped and instantly put her gloved hand to her mouth to stop herself from crying out. The blind, pupil-less eyes of the marble bust of Mozart met her stare from atop a fluted plinth. His softly smirking lips and icy features seemed to mock her. Groping blindly in the dark, she had come into the music room where this ghostly encounter made her realize how completely unstrung her nerves had become; they jangled like the wires of a harpsichord played by a maniac. Her self-confidence could stand no more and slunk away into a dark corner to cower. Angelica wanted to take refuge too but she knew she had to go on no matter how weak and utterly useless she felt.

She had no nerves left; she was drained and staggered when she tried to walk again. Driving herself forward, Angelica thought she had no energy left to be frightened by anything; then came a long dark corridor; it had no windows and was pitch dark; it gaped before her. She knew that this led down a stairs into the servants' quarters—a part of the castle, with twists and turns, completely unknown to her; there was no alternative but to attempt it in the dark. With both hands following the contours of the cold, stone wall, she slowly moved one foot forward and then the other until, with the toe of her boot, she could feel the floor falling away from her. Knowing that she had reached some stairs, and cautiously taking one step at a time, she continued on. A sudden dizziness and disorientation overcame her in the total darkness and she had to cling to the deathly cold wall to prevent herself from plunging headlong down the stairwell; she felt as if she was falling through space. To get her bearings, she clung harder to the wall and was aware of no sensation but the musty smell of the damp stone. Again, one step at a time, with painstaking slowness, she descended. When she eventually reached the bottom, there was another corridor and this one had windows, and a door with a glazed panel which let in some of the faint night light. The rest of the corridor was in pools of blackness.

This was the servants' quarters—the domain of the Earl's servant, Hibbard. Angelica froze. Had Hibbard gone with the Earl to the ball? Was he still in the castle? Was he spying on her at this very moment? She quaked with the terrifying possibility that he could silently appear from the deep shadows at any second, as he had done so often. She could feel someone's breath on her ear. *'Very late for a walk, Lady Angelica,'* the voice echoed from the dark. She peered behind her into the darkness. *No!* It was just her fevered imagination. I'm going mad! I'm losing my mind! she screamed silently in her head. No longer having faith in her gnarled tangle of thoughts, her courage almost left her and she wanted to sink down and weep cowardly tears. Trembling uncontrollably, she hated herself for being frightened. To steel herself, she tried to imagine the distance between herself and the door to the outside world to be some large, difficult stone wall she had ridden over many times. She *had* to get to that door. Gathering her tattered resolve, she moved forward a few steps and paused to listen. The only sound was the rhythmic breathing of some distant sleeper. Finally she reached the door; she put out her hand to turn the old white porcelain knob; stabs of pain raced up her arm; her tense muscles were making her arms ache, rendering them almost ridged and useless. She tried again; the pain relented. The door opened easily, but with an alarming squeak. She froze again, listened hard, slid noiselessly out. Without knowing it, in her anxiety she had been holding her breath and she found herself gasping in icy air. This detour through the castle had brought Angelica out far from the stables. She looked about to get her bearings. The moon was visible and cast enough light for her to see her way. By avoiding the pebble paths and walking on the grass verges, she discovered that the sound of her footsteps was absorbed by the dew-damp turf.

By the time she arrived at the stables, Angelica was convinced that hours had passed since she had left her room, but in reality it had been only about twenty minutes.

Her prior arrangements were a blessing. In the dark she easily found the saddle and bridle and made her way to Prospero's stall. She was sure the grooms slept above the stables, as it was the custom everywhere, and with that in mind she tiptoed on the stone floors. Prospero welcomed his nocturnal visitor with a faint murmur. He knew something unusual was happening and stood still while Angelica put the saddle on his back. She did not dare speak to him but patted him occasionally to reassure him. In the dark, she had to work out the girth and buckles by feel alone. When it came to putting on the complicated tangle of the bridle, it was a frustrating business. Prospero took the bit willingly but she just could not work out all the straps in the dark until she realized that she was trying to put it on backwards. Discovering her mistake, the unbearable tension she had been controlling broke out into an involuntary giggle and she buried her face in Prospero's warm neck to stifle it.

As she moved about Prospero's stall in the dark, she stumbled into an empty metal bucket on the floor and sent it scudding across the flagstones, making a loud grating noise. The sound struck her ears like an explosion. She stood motionless waiting for the sound of footsteps from the floor above, but there was only the sleepy stable noises as before. Daring to move again, she had difficulty, in the dark, finding her rolled-up cape which she had put down somewhere on the floor near the stall door. She finally found the bundle, but then realized she should have tied it to the saddle before putting it on Prospero. Would she *ever* get away, she wondered? Employing the bucket as a stool, by carefully and quietly turning it over, she stood on it to reach the back of the saddle to tie on her parcel. After endless trial and error, with only her fingers as her guides, she found the metal loop and threaded the string through it.

At last she was ready to depart. Pausing, she tried to define the night stable noises. Random sounds of horses changing position, snorting or munching hay, filled the warm stable with a quiet, contented hum. Frequently the noise of a hoof stepping on the stone floor was audible as the horses moved languidly about in their sleep. Leading Prospero slowly out of the stall and shutting the door, she discovered that by taking him towards the outside door a few steps at a time she could reproduce the scattered sound of the occasional footfall. It blended in with the other stable noises. To march Prospero straight out of the stable would make a half-awake groom hear the sound of a walking horse and, thinking a horse had got loose, he would come down to investigate.

Instead of guiding Prospero to the mounting block just outside the stable door, she led him along a grass strip to parkland where there was a fallen tree. Now in the open, against the sky, she could see Prospero for the first time, yet he was still almost invisible as he blended in with the black earth and sky. The big horse stood still as she scrambled onto the tree and then into the saddle. For the first time in that long and terrifying night, Angelica felt some respite for her shattered nerves.

She planned to walk Prospero until first light and follow familiar landmarks, knowing she could not afford to lose her way. When it was light enough, she could make good time at a gallop and, if all went well, she would still have hours before her disappearance was discovered. The small moon afforded very little light and Angelica picked her way cautiously along well-trod paths. She did not attempt any of the many shortcuts she knew as it was too risky in the dark. When she came to a break in the trees, Cranleigh Castle was visible behind her; without lights burning it looked as peaceful and harmless as a sleeping lion.

The further she got from the castle, the more relaxed she became and confident that her plan would work. The ride became quite pleasant. The air was cold and fragrant with the scent of newly ploughed fields. The calls of nocturnal animals broke the silence now and then. A nightingale was singing in the distance and an owl flapped past Prospero's head. The horse seemed not to notice but it made Angelica start in fright. She kept looking behind to make sure no one was following, and she occasionally stopped Prospero and listened. It was reassuring when all she could hear were the ordinary night noises.

By this time, the ball at the Revelstokes' was well underway. Dodo, in her newest gown, a lustrous green satin embroidered with ivy leaves at the bodice and hem, had been sorry to discover that her new friend was unwell and unable to attend, and she resolved to send a note in the morning with Lady Avery to tell Angelica that she would call upon her the very next day.

At midnight, about the time Angelica was saddling Prospero in the dark stable, Lord Revelstoke proudly stood at the top of the ballroom stairs, in the blazing light of the candelabrums, and announced, to the glittering assembly, his daughter's engagement. The crowd gasped with feigned surprise and genuine delight at the news; Dodo and Freddie, smiling and flushed, were toasted with champagne and showered with a barrage of good wishes.

Now it was late; the ballroom floor heaved under the weight of the young people dancing the whirling Gay Gordon. At the first skirl of the bagpipes, the old people knew what was coming and they had fled to the less exhausting supper rooms, in which Lord Avery and Lady Avery were already firmly ensconced. The vicar, Mr Compton, his toe tapping slightly with the music, watched the dancing a few moments more, and then decided it was time he walked the short distance across the gardens to where the servants were having their dance, as he had promised to have a glass of small beer with some of his parishioners amongst them. He was just making his way to the French windows, which led to the garden, when Mrs Bultrap-Guph swooped down like a fluffy pink falcon, captured him and deposited him into the chair opposite her in the card-room to partner her in a rubber of whist.

Far from the gaiety, Angelica came to the old, Roman road. It was silent and deserted; centuries before it had been a busy thoroughfare built, straight and wide, by the conquering army for the transport of troops and supplies, but when the occupation was over, it had been perversely abandoned by the citizens who somehow preferred the rutted and narrow lanes created by their Saxon and Celt forbears. Angelica was confident she would meet no one on the ancient road, which had gone to grass, and was only occasionally used by the farmers moving their livestock to market. The sheep had cropped the grass short, and even in the dark, Angelica could see the twin chalk paths stretching ahead of her like railway tracks. Normally it was a wonderful, uninterrupted eight-mile-long gallop, but, not wanting to attempt anything faster than a walk in the dark, she restrained Prospero who was pulling hard expecting his customary run.

After a few moments, Angelica was alarmed by what sounded like a horse cantering. Was she being followed? She tried to rein Prospero to a stop and listen; the creaking of the saddle, the persistent call of a tawny owl and Prospero's own hoof-beats made it impossible to hear. Tugging frantically at the reins, she tried to bring him to a halt, but he discounted her signals. He broke into a fast trot and she hauled on the reins with all her might; he suddenly lunged forward into an uncontrollable gallop. Angelica looked over her shoulder again and again trying to see if there was someone there, but she could see only darkness. Prospero had taken the bit firmly in his teeth and no matter how hard she struggled and strained on the reins it was impossible to dislodge it. Prospero suddenly veered crazily through an opening in a hedge, nearly throwing her out of the saddle, and he tore off the Roman road into open country. Panic stricken, Angelica pulled on the reins until her arms ached and became weak and useless; she knew the battle was futile against the powerful horse, half wild and driven by primeval instincts.

Prospero had never done anything like this before. She tried to console herself that, at this speed, if she was being followed no one could catch her. She leaned forward and, as a hopeless token of security, grabbed a handful of his flying mane and prayed that he would not miss his footing in the dark as they were both sure to be killed. She could do nothing but hold on. They were now on high ground and a strong wind had come up from the east. Prospero's speed and the wind combined to beat her face and roar in her ears until she was blinded and deafened. A gust of wind tore away her hat and whipped it into the night. She was being carried away by a runaway horse, hopelessly lost and weak with exhaustion.

Having given up looking behind, she was horrified when on her right a horse and rider appeared from nowhere. Not believing her eyes, and half blinded by her tangled locks blowing across her eyes, she tore at her hair trying to clear her vision. She could see the rider closing in on her, but could make out no features except the outline of a man on a dark horse galloping furiously parallel with Prospero. With her remaining strength, she tried to turn Prospero away to the left but he pounded relentlessly on, his energy unabated.

A terrifying realization shot into her mind: A highwayman! Why had this danger not occurred to her? She had been so consumed with worry that the Earl might somehow be following her that the possibility of any other hazard had escaped her. The rider was bringing his horse alongside and the two horses galloped frantically side by side for a moment in a desperate race. Angelica could see little in the darkness through her wind-tossed hair. Reaching out, the horseman pulled hard at Prospero's reins and shouted over the wind, 'Whoa, Prospero—you old devil!' Hearing this, her terror was redoubled. It *was* the Earl after all! He had followed her! Her panic turned to anger and acrid tears of rage streamed down her face. She even surprised herself as, in her desperation, she struck out at him with her whip.

'Leave me alone, can't you!' she cried in torment. 'Let me go!'

Prospero showed no signs of slowing and the horseman, to defend his face from the blows of Angelica's whip, had no other course but to let go of Prospero's reins. Catching Angelica abruptly around the waist, he hauled her roughly out of the saddle. His powerful arm held her fast and, as he pulled her to his horse, she struggled wildly and beat at him with her fists.

'Ho! Stop!' cried the horseman, pulling his horse to a halt. 'Is that any way for my guardian angel to behave!' At these words Angelica went limp. It was not the Earl, but the man she had called Gitano—the Duke of Stanforth. She was shaking with relief and exhaustion as he gently lowered her to the ground, and dismounted. Even though he was standing only a foot away, she could barely make out his face in the dark. He held her arm to steady her.

Angelica could scarcely find her voice. 'I-I'm sorry—I thought...I thought...' she stammered in her confusion, wavering and trying to hold back her tears. 'Please, help me find my horse! I must get away from here! I must get away!'

'You don't have to run away any more. No one will harm you. You are among friends now—true friends who will look after you.' These simple words and his kind, firm voice had a remarkable effect on Angelica. Her whole body shook with sobs, and tears of relief cascaded down her face. He put a comforting arm round her shoulders and she wept against the rough fabric of his jacket; childlike, the fingers of her right hand absently clung to the top button of his waistcoat. The fear and treachery she had suffered in the last few days at the hands of the Earl fell from her with her tears. Not since their last meeting had she felt safe, trusting, and at rest.

The Duke looked down at the small, weary creature that fitted so comfortably into the crook of his arm. He wanted to tell her that he had loved her ever since he first saw her that night at the inn, but even if she shared his love, and he sensed that she did, it would only increase the pain to speak his heart—the gypsy prophecy predicted that the poor man was soon to die and, even if he lived, he had nothing to give Angelica but a life of misery. He kept his silence and only wrapped her in his arms, and waited patiently for her tears to cease their flow.

Angelica tried to regain her composure. 'I'm sorry,' she whispered, searching her pockets for a handkerchief. 'I seem to have done nothing but weep like a fool since tea time.' Producing a handkerchief from his pocket, he slipped it into her trembling fingers and she took it.

Then he asked, 'Are you all right? I didn't hurt you, did I? It's just that Prospero was determined not to stop and you're a pretty cunning shot with that whip of yours. I knew I was no match for you. I'm sorry I frightened you.' Still holding her arm to support her, he looked closely into her face to assure himself of her well-being.

Flustered with shame, she said, 'I am the one who should apologize. I've never behaved that way before. It's just that I thought you were someone else.' Angelica tried to push her windswept hair away from her face and into some order, but, finding that every hairpin had deserted her, she gave it up.

'Although I can only guess, I am sure I have a general idea of why you were departing Cranleigh at such an unconventional hour.' His tone had a bitter edge, and then it abated and he said, 'I have friends very near who will protect you. May I take you there?' Angelica nodded gratefully. The Duke whistled for Prospero; the shadowy horse suddenly appeared out of the night and playfully began roughly nudging his master with his nose. Prospero was rewarded by a rain of hearty and affectionate pats and thumps. 'Hello, you old demon! I thought I was the only person you were ever sociable to!

Now I can tell you what I think of you, you fickle brute!'

As she heard his words, the clouds of confusion started to clear from Angelica's mind. 'Gitano, I know who you really are,' she said simply, 'you are Lord Anthony...or rather, the Duke of Stanforth.'

Caught a little off guard, he said, 'Ah...yes—' Then a low laugh rumbled from his chest. 'My guardian angel knows everything as usual! What gave me away? Was it my knowing Prospero?'

'No, for reasons more complicated than that, and I know you are in danger and must go away with all haste!'

'Angelica, my dear, you are generous to occupy yourself with my difficulties, but believe me, I've staunch friends who will always support me.' His tone again became tinged with amusement as he said lightly, 'Have you ever known a man of so many identities?'

Angelica found a little laugh welling up, 'No, nor anyone who could so readily make me laugh. I suppose I must now call you Anthony.'

'It is not such a terrible name?'

'An excellent name, but I had become rather fond of Gitano.'

He touched her shoulders lightly. 'I hope you can become fond of Anthony.'

'I am sure I shall...'

The Duke was very close to her, their faces softly lit by the silver light, and he could see, framed by her cascade of gold hair, how open and honest her expression was. He said quietly,

'Gitano never had a chance to say goodbye...so I'll do it for him,' and he leaned down and kissed her, lightly at first and then more deeply. Angelica reached up and touched his face with her fingertips as she abandoned herself to his embrace.

In almost a whisper, he said, 'I shouldn't have kissed you, now or in the wood...Gitano would not have done. He is the better man. I should have listened to him, but I am more selfish, and I know this is doomed.'

'Yes...utterly doomed...' she said faintly, and slid her hand into his.

They stood for a moment smiling sadly at one another, and by sharing that common sorrow, it somehow eased it.

He came close again, this time to see her face better in the moonlight. 'Shall we go? It isn't far. We can walk the rest of the way.'

The Duke led the horses as they walked in silence towards a dark wood, her hand still resting in his. As they neared the wood, Angelica said, 'I have endless questions to ask you, but first, tell me how you could possibly catch up with Prospero when we were galloping? Did your horse really match Prospero's speed?'

'You are right to wonder. Prospero is so fast. No, I didn't overtake you. *You* caught up with me. When you left the stables tonight I saw you go because I have been keeping a watch on Cranleigh. When I saw you leave, it was obvious you were in need of help. I took a shortcut to get ahead of you as I knew if you heard someone following, you would take flight, and if you galloped away on Prospero I would never catch you. Years ago, I taught Prospero to come when I gave a certain signal and that is how I got him to follow me tonight. I had to guarantee that you came this way, and the only way to do it was to get ahead of you and then signal for Prospero to follow.'

'Is the signal you use to call Prospero the cry of a tawny owl?' she asked.

'Yes—but how did you guess?' he asked with a surprised laugh.

'I heard a tawny owl that night when you escaped from the inn, and I heard it again tonight,' and she felt thankful that more of the scattered pieces of the puzzle were starting to fit together. An amused tone suddenly came into her voice. 'And I wonder if I should have heard it that day Prospero sent Hibbard flying?'

His low murmuring laughter came out of the dark to her and he said, 'Ah...there are no secrets from the angels!' and his hand pressed hers more firmly as her laughter met his.

He led her up to the wood where a wide path spread out before them. Following the path for a short distance, Angelica thought she could see a glow through the trees in front of her; she even imagined she could hear music. The forest held a secret. Soon they stepped into a large clearing where several fires were burning in a circle formed by gypsy caravans. The scene was as warm and welcoming as it was unexpected. As they came closer, Angelica could see groups of people gathered around the fires, chatting, eating, and drinking, and she wondered why she had not heard their laughing voices from a distance. A man came up to them and, shaking hands with the Duke, took the horses from him. The Duke then guided her round the perimeter of the activity.

In the firelight, musicians, with dark-blue bandannas tied around their heads, played spirited music on violins and guitars. One by one, slim gypsy women emerged from the crowd and occupied, for a brief moment, the centre stage to dance their interpretation of the *tango del merengaze*. Without a bow or recognition from the crowd, the women then returned to their places in the shadows. As Angelica and the Duke passed, a beautiful olive-skinned woman in a red fringed dress was dancing almost hypnotically in magical movements, writhing like a column of flame. She uttered a low hissing sound through her slightly bared teeth and followed the Duke with her kohl-painted eyes, trying to capture his attention. He acknowledged her with a slow smile. Watching his face, Angelica could see his proud features lose their sternness and soften a little, taking on the slight boyish quality that had become so familiar to her. They continued on past another group of gypsies; a man was weaving hemp into rope and Angelica saw a woman making what looked like counterfeit money. At last they came to an ornately painted caravan, and the most ferocious-looking man Angelica had ever seen rose up from the fireside to greet them.

The gypsy leader's hands and face were the colour and texture of antique Spanish leather and covered in scars; his small, black-button eyes shone in the shimmering light. Tall and immensely broad shouldered, he had a chest like a barrel. At his waist he wore a large knife in a plaited, woollen belt and his broad smile was crooked where a scar crossed his lip, a trophy from a knife fight years before. His teeth were like dazzling piano keys with a large gold tooth where middle D would be. His perfect manners were at first overshadowed by his remarkable appearance, but he showed polite refinement as he delivered Lady Angelica a polished bow.

'This is His Majesty, King Vaigatch, the great and wise gypsy King who, I am honoured to say, is my loyal and trusted friend and who was a friend to my father, the old Duke. Vaigatch was with me at the coaching inn the night you gave me shelter.'

'Ah ha!' cried Vaigatch. *'Ah! This* is the angel I hear about who saved this young vagabond from his enemies!' Everything he said came out in a roar. 'You are welcome to stay with us for as long as you please, Lady Angelica. Ah!—now we have the company of a *bori rani* as well as a *boro rye!'* And smiling warmly at Angelica, he translated, 'That is Gypsy for great woman and great man. Yes—what Anthony says is true! I have been friends for years with the Dukes of Stanforth,' he bellowed as he strutted about the fire. 'How else would I, *the King of Gypsies,'* and he slapped his chest for emphasis, 'consent to pose on a ship as the *servant* of this—this laddie!' He measured his words, enjoying the joke against himself, 'I would have to be a friend indeed to do that!' and he howled with laughter. After savouring this for a moment, he said, 'But you must be tired. Warm yourselves by the fire and I will make arrangements,' and he marched off, still laughing to himself.

As Angelica and the Duke settled by the fire on large logs, which served as seats, an old gypsy woman brought them steaming mugs of camomile tea. Perhaps it was the blazing fire or the hot tea, but a delicious feeling of warmth swept through Angelica; she laughed without knowing why, her face glowing with contentment. 'What made you laugh?' asked the Duke with an easy smile, delighted to see how well she was recovering from the rigours of the night.

'I'm not sure what made me laugh,' she said dreamily, 'I just suddenly felt...happier than I have in years.' She looked away for a moment hoping he would not think her foolish; turning back and seeing his soft gaze she felt encouraged to continue. 'It is rather funny—I am supposed to be at a ball at this very moment, balancing on a gilt chair and making conversation with strangers. But I feel more at home here, sitting on a log in the middle of a wood, surrounded by people who are so—kind. And I have to confess that discovering it was *you* and *not* Lord Greystone who witnessed my departure from Cranleigh has done much to reassure me. My astonishment at seeing you was doubled as I thought you had gone away. You said you were leaving when we last met.'

'Yes. I had every intention of going—I had

been convinced by my friends that there was nothing more I could do here. But something...something left unfinished made me stay.'

After a short pause, his face became serious and he asked, 'I think I can guess why you ran away tonight. I know exactly how evil Greystone is. If he has harmed you in any way—' His face became hard with the force of controlled anger.

Looking into the fire, Angelica fought tears. 'Lord Greystone wants to...marry me and he is threatening my uncle, Lord Avery, with financial ruin if the wedding does not take place next week. He has the means to do it; my uncle is completely powerless against him. I overheard them speaking about it and I had no choice but to try to escape.'

'He is capable of *anything*, that monster!' said the Duke, trying to suppress his rage. Choosing not to continue what was to him an intolerable line of conversation, he rose and put some more logs on the fire. When he had got hold of his anger, he sat down again and asked quietly, 'Who else knows I am alive?'

'Only myself—and the vicar—Mr Compton. I told him and he made me realize how dangerous it would be for you if the constabulary find out that you are alive.' Then, giving him a brief account of how she had discovered his identity with the aid of the family portrait, she added, 'I have just remembered something. It may not be important but, when the vicar and I were discussing your presence here, we may have been overheard by Hibbard, Lord Greystone's servant. Hibbard gave no indication that he had heard anything, but I do dislike the man and feel that he is untrustworthy.'

The Duke asked, 'Has Mr Compton gone to Revelstoke's ball tonight?' Angelica knew she should not find remarkable his complete knowledge of the comings and goings of the county. When she answered that the vicar had gone to the ball, the Duke stood up and without betraying any emotion said, 'Yes, that may be important. Excuse me a moment, I must speak with someone.' Striding over to a little knot of men who stood around another fire, he spoke with them briefly and then two of them broke away from the group and rode off on horseback.

When he rejoined her at the fireside, Angelica felt she had to touch the subject that had overshadowed her stay at Cranleigh. 'One thing is clear to me even having spent only a short time at Cranleigh. All your friends believe...*know*...it was an accident—your brother's death, I mean. Dodo, Mr Compton, and anyone who knew you. They all say it was an accident.'

'I see...they all think that Edward's death was an accident,' he said coldly, and then looking at her steadily, his eyes suddenly hard, he went on, 'I am afraid they are wrong. It was *not* an accident. My brother's death was planned.'

When Angelica heard his words her mind reeled and she believed them to be a hideous confession. Jumping to her feet and backing away from him, she blurted out, 'Please stop!

Don't say anything more! I don't want to hear it!'

Seeing her distress, he rose and as he moved towards her she backed away. Suddenly understanding what was in her mind, he smiled affectionately down at her; her face looked even younger and more vulnerable clouded by a stricken expression. Quietly he said, 'Forgive me, I have been very good at frightening you this evening, but you must let me finish: the murder of my brother was committed by Lord Greystone.'

'Dear God,' she breathed, sinking down onto the log again. She knew that this was the truth; he was not lying. She wondered if she had sensed all along that Greystone was even capable of murder, but her muddled thoughts had only given her half-truths; how otherwise, she wondered, could she have been able, even for an instant, to allow herself to believe that this kind man could kill his own brother.

Angelica sat feeling dazed after these shocks; the relief at his innocence was only slightly tempered by the realization that she had narrowly escaped being married to the Earl—the murderer. The danger was still there. But what preyed on her mind most, at that moment, was her own rush of emotion and her wild outburst brought on by an overwhelming terror that she had misjudged the Duke. When she found her voice she said apologetically, 'Forgive me—events have left me not quite rational. How foolish of me, I should have known. But, why has no one guessed that Lord Greystone murdered your brother?'

'He is still free because he is extremely clever. He is also the greediest man alive. He knew that if he made it look as if I had killed my brother, as I stood next in line for the succession, no court in England would find me innocent. I would be executed within months and he would succeed to the title. Only my brother and I stood between him and the dukedom—not a large stumbling block to someone as voracious as Greystone. He only had to commit one murder and the legal system would do the rest by removing me. His remarkably well-crafted plan was threatened only when I escaped. Those men who were searching the inn that night were his henchmen—his paid assassins. After my brother's murder, I first went to France where they followed me and made two attempts on my life. I then travelled to America where they tried to murder me again. All this time I have been trying to devise some way of exposing Greystone's crime, but he has covered his tracks well. There is not a scrap of evidence I can use against him. I have come back now as my friends inform me that Greystone is getting impatient to take over the title officially, and he cannot do that until he can prove I am dead. To spur things on, he paid someone in America to falsify the death certificate of an executed prisoner, replacing the dead man's name with mine. I believe it was someone at that Harper's Ferry incident—'

'Yes, that is where Lord Greystone claimed

you died! But how could he manage to create false evidence like that?' she asked, shocked by his grim story.

'I'm...not sure I should tell you any more,' replied the Duke warily. 'It may give you nightmares.'

Letting out a sombre ironic laugh, Angelica looked into his face, took a deep breath and said softly, 'Please don't try to shelter me—I need to know what I am up against.'

He thought to himself that she had remarkable courage and spirit for someone so unworldly, but he did not dare tell her so for fear his emotions would betray him. After a moment of hesitation, he said, 'Greystone would have ordered that a bribe be paid to an official in America, to say one of the condemned men was me. Or they would have offered one of the prisoners money to say he was me. All they needed was my name on the death certificate.' Although sympathetic to her insistence to know everything, he omitted to say the prisoner's corpse would have been horribly disfigured to prevent positive identification if later exhumed. He only added, 'Presumably they would have told the prisoner that they would give his family money if he co-operated with their deception—naturally his family would never have received a penny.'

'Oh! It is too horrible! Who could be evil enough to plot such things?' she asked, low and lost, and already knowing the answer.

The Duke continued, 'Now that Greystone has this falsified death certificate, he plans to deprive me of everything. I am determined to stop him and I will have to make a move soon.' His voice became hard, 'He will not live to step into the shoes of my father and my brother.'

Angelica was alarmed to hear the Duke speak in this vein. He was already condemned to death falsely for the murder of his brother, but at least he was innocent and, for the moment, free. If he escaped England undetected he might have some sort of life in exile living under an assumed name, but if he was driven to the revenge murder of the Earl there was no hope at all. 'But what will you do?' she asked unnerved.

A detached expression took hold of him as he stared into the flames. 'I cannot say yet. There isn't a tissue of evidence with which to catch him. Every path in that direction has been exhausted. There may be only one answer now...'

'You cannot mean that you are considering killing Lord Greystone?' she whispered in terror.

His eyes darted from the fire to her face and the hardness fell away from his features as he looked at her innocent beauty illuminated by the wavering light. 'Please don't concern yourself. This is an impossible matter that will not resolve itself. Greystone has shown that his evil is almost invincible, and unless he is stopped he will continue to cause misery and even death to anyone who gets in his way. But—don't think of these things. They are not for you to worry about. You must forget this conversation ever took place.'

'But I won't forget, I can't forget!' she cried, fighting back tears. 'You are free now—you have every chance of getting away from here, from England—forever—to start a new life. You are innocent of all crimes now—please don't ruin what you have left by committing *murder*. It would make you almost as bad as Lord Greystone.'

'What about you? You are here now because you are fleeing from that tyrant. Do you really believe that while he is alive you will not be hunted down? He has well-paid agents and assassins everywhere who will stop at nothing. It would be only a matter of time before he discovered where you are—and when he decides he wants to have something, he never rests until he has possessed it.'

'*I* don't matter! I will get help from my cousin in France eventually,' she argued naively, 'and you said yourself that your gypsy friends will protect me for as long as I need.'

The Duke looked sternly into her face. 'It is true that Vaigatch and his people will protect you forever if need be. It would be the only way you could live so that Greystone could not find you. But how long do you think you could exist in this way of life? It is a hard, brutal existence and you would weary of it very soon. You would be like a prisoner for the rest of your life and you deserve more than that. You should be surrounded by riches and security, not living the life of a fugitive.'

Her voice rose in desperation, 'That would be preferable to what you are contemplating! I could not bear to think that you had done such a thing as kill Lord Greystone, even though he is guilty of terrible crimes.'

'We cannot discuss this any longer, for there really is nothing to discuss,' said the Duke resolutely getting to his feet. 'There are some things which are...unavoidable.'

Driven by an uncontrollable rush of emotion, Angelica stood up and faced him squarely. Her cheeks were flushed and the firelight darted about her tumble of gold hair. 'You asked me a question the other day, but you would not allow me to answer.' His eyes turned on hers in astonishment. She continued, 'You asked me to go away with you.' Her voice was clear and steady. 'Do you really wish that? Because if you do I will come—*now*—tonight—only promise you will forget all thoughts of revenge and turn your back on all that is at Cranleigh—forever.'

He stared at her in disbelief for a moment and wondered if he was dreaming. 'You would do that...?' he asked softly. 'Give up everything—all prospect of a settled life and comfort, in exchange for a mean existence with the gypsies?'

Her eyes were shining. 'Yes...I understand now that there are more important things than all the wealth in the world.'

Stepping towards her, he slowly and tentatively raised a hand and touched her face. 'My darling, I have loved you since that first moment I saw you.' He folded her in his arms and Angelica's body was compliant and thrilled at the warmth and strength of his embrace.

Tremors of happiness welled up in her as all her defences against the love she had long feared fell away.

He held her to him for as long as he dared and then, with tremendous forbearance, laid his hands lightly on her shoulders, pushed her gently away and said, 'My darling Angelica, I cannot let you do this,' and then sitting down, he drew her down beside him. 'This is impossible. I should be the happiest man on earth, but I simply cannot let you make this sacrifice. It would be an impossible life. Perhaps love would sustain us for a few years, but I could not bear to see you suffering the hardships that the gypsy life would invariably bring; you were meant for better things. That day in the wood—when I became angry and asked you to marry me—I was angry because I know, as things are now, it is impossible. I did not want you to answer because I knew if you said 'No' I would not be able to bear it and if you said 'Yes' it would be equally unbearable because I have nothing to offer you.'

Angelica's expression showed that she was about to protest, but raising his fingers gently to her lips he said, 'This time I really must insist that you say nothing. My mind is made up. I would not be able to live with myself if I did not make some final attempt to bring Greystone to justice.' She remained silent, understanding what unstoppable forces of pride and justice were driving him, but when she heard his decision, she nodded sadly and looked down; a deathly chill made her tremble violently and she turned up the collar of her riding coat in a futile gesture to ward it off. As she did so, the diamond brooch under the lapel flashed in the remaining light of the dying fire. In spite of his astonishment at seeing the brooch, the Duke rose and fetched a carriage rug and put it around her shoulders. If he had not been so preoccupied, he might have noticed that the gypsy camp had long been asleep and wisps of low mist had silently crept in from the forest and nestled round them like lazy ghosts, too weary to raise themselves from the ground.

'What do you know about the history of that brooch?' he asked, restraining his excitement as he took his seat next to her again.

Having forgotten its existence, she raised her hand to it in surprise. 'Lord Avery gave it to me...well, in truth, Lord Greystone gave it to my uncle, who then gave it to me. I did not want to accept it—but my uncle contrived that I should. As I did not have enough money to finance my escape, I brought it with me as security. I was planning to sell it if I needed to.'

After a short pause he said, 'It belonged to my mother.' Angelica flinched with shame because she had planned to have it destroyed.

His face was pensive. 'It was among the jewels that were missing the day my brother was murdered. Greystone put the story about that my motive for killing my brother was my desire to steal the family jewels. He obviously took them and hid them somewhere.'

Angelica unpinned the brooch and handed it to him; he turned it over in his fingers several times, thinking of past associations and watching the diamonds flash. Handing it back to her he said, 'You must keep it. It is yours,' and before she could object, he slipped it into her pocket. 'You may have need of it yet.'

Blocking from her mind the meaning of his words, she asked, 'But how could Lord Greystone have the nerve to put this brooch on show? Isn't he afraid someone will recognize it and see that he has stolen the jewels?'

'That is precisely why he is dangerous; he thinks of *everything*. About six months before my brother's murder, Greystone stopped at Cranleigh for a visit. He joined my brother and me in my brother's study and saw us conducting an inventory of the family jewels. It was a task my brother had put off for years and he had finally got round to it. Naturally, being first cousins, my brother trusted Greystone and he carried on cataloguing the jewels in his presence. We talked about various things and discussed the origin of some of the more interesting pieces.

'I remember Edward telling Greystone the story of how this brooch had been given to our mother by a visiting Indian Maharajah who presented it as he departed after a particularly amusing house party. She was of course taken aback and did not want to accept it, but she knew it would offend the Maharajah if she refused it. She always thought it was too vulgar and never wore it. She kept it in the pin box on her dressing table. My father always said it should be in the strongroom locked up with the rest of the family jewels, but she never cared for it—it was just a bauble as far as she was concerned.

'When my brother and I were very small, she was fond of using it in a game.' His voice took on a vulnerable quality as he related his memories. 'She would hide it somewhere in her room and Edward and I had to find it. Hearing this story, Greystone knew that the piece was never worn and that there was no one who could identify it but me, and he assumed that his assassins would soon put me out of the way. This may mean that he has not sold the jewels yet and that they are hidden somewhere in the castle. But there are many secret hiding places—it is impossible to know where... In any case, Greystone may not even know where the secret passages are...'

'He knows about one secret cupboard,' Angelica volunteered, her face radiating excitement, and she told the story of how she had watched, unobserved, as the Earl took Lord Avery's yellow, pigskin document case into a secret cupboard in the library.

The Duke sprang to his feet and, taking both her hands in his, he said, 'That has got to be it! You are indeed an angel! I must act immediately—and you must get some rest.' Daylight was just filtering through the branches and the gypsy camp was beginning to stir.

After making arrangements for his departure, the Duke returned to Angelica's side. Her hair still fell uncombed down her back, and the early sunlight caught in her curls creating a golden halo around her face. The Duke said, 'Vaigatch's wife, Milica, will look after you while I am away. When...I come back, neither of us will be fugitives any longer. I promise you, that monster Greystone will never give you another minute's concern.'

This was the moment Angelica had been dreading. She feared for his life but knew that nothing she could say would sway him from his course. Alarmed but helpless, she asked, 'What are you going to do? Please do nothing dangerous... If you are captured they will...' she could only faintly whisper the words, '...they will hang you. I could not bear it if any harm came to you...'

She could see how hard his eyes had become with determination. The Duke, knowing if his plan failed, he would never see her again, pulled her slowly and firmly into his arms and kissed her; both finding in one another, for those brief moments, a perfect refuge from the world. Then they stood looking at one another, sharing the burdens of strength and vulnerability created by love. Without the need for another word, the Duke turned away, and as soon as he joined Vaigatch at the horses, the two of them rode away.

Vaigatch's wife, Milica, was tall and striking; her sleek black hair framed an angular face which had once been very beautiful. She wore a bright Spanish shawl over a silk dress that suggested comparative wealth, and from her pierced ears hung long, intricate gold earrings studded with precious stones. She and Angelica stood and watched their men ride off together.

'Will they be all right?' asked Angelica, not so much to Milica but to hear herself say the words.

Milica gave a small, dismissive shrug. 'They are wiser than many, and you can see from his scars that my man is an experienced fighter.' Her tone was world weary and reflected many troubled years.

'Do you think there will be a fight?' asked Angelica suddenly, as she had not been able to make herself imagine what the Duke faced. 'Do you know what they intend to do?'

'I have no idea what they plan, but there is no point in worrying. They have both come through many battles. Even your young Duke, for all his fine appearance, is a good fighter. He does not kill easily. How else would he have survived this long?'

'You mean...he has been injured? Please tell me what you mean!' demanded Angelica, panic creeping into her voice.

'Did he not tell you that Lord Greystone's men tried to kill him? There was a terrible fight, and if Anthony had not been so young and strong he would have died. He was stabbed many times but they just could not kill him. His life was in danger for a long time and my husband and I nursed him back to health. He is very strong again now.'

Angelica felt ill and weak with anxiety and she permitted herself to sink down again on the log. 'I've been utterly stupid,' she said. 'I knew there was danger, but the reality of it has only just dawned on me now. Why, oh, why didn't I try harder to prevent him from going...?'

Milica gave a shallow sigh, more akin to a little gasp. 'It would have done no good. Nothing in the world would have stopped him, not even your love. There are things that we have no control over in this world, and this is one of them. I tell you these things that he has suffered only to help you face the truth. If they do not come back, you will be ready for it.'

'I could never be ready for that,' replied Angelica faintly. She touched her lips where they were still moist from his kiss. She might never see him again.

'Come, you must sleep now,' said Milica less sternly for she could see that her words had wrought a severe effect upon Angelica.

Milica led her to a caravan where inside a small bed was built into the elaborate carved-wood fittings. When she was alone, Angelica lay down on the bed and pulled a quilt over herself. She thought sleep would never come. Tears forced themselves into her eyes. She tried not to let them spill down her face, but they evasively slipped out from under her eyelids. How is it possible, she asked herself bitterly, that I could come this close to happiness and now it is so in danger of being swept away?

She would not allow her imagination to ponder on the dangers the Duke was riding into. She thought she would go mad with worry, but finally, exhausted, sleep overcame her and she was lulled into the shelter of kindly dreams.

EIGHTEEN

The Duke and Vaigatch rode towards Cranleigh; at a crossroads they parted and the Duke continued towards the castle on his own. The sun had been up for some time and he knew that the guests would soon return from Lord Revelstoke's. He took up a position where he could watch the front of the castle unseen. Soon the landau bringing the Earl and Lord and Lady Avery back from the ball drew into the courtyard and up to the door. He watched as the occupants got out and went inside. The Averys moved with the weariness of revellers who had enjoyed too late a night. After a few minutes, the Duke rode up to the front of the castle; this was the first time he had been there in almost two years, and he felt a mixture of delight at coming home and disgust at what lay within.

As he rode into the courtyard, a lanky groom, who had been alerted by the click of hoofbeats, ran forward to take the Duke's horse. Seeing that it was the Duke, or perhaps even the ghost of the Duke, the groom was struck dumb with confusion and stood, holding the reins, gawking and snatching absently at his forelock.

The Duke walked slowly towards the massive front door; a fond old spaniel lying on the steps barked defensively, but then, cocking its ears and giving a yelp of recognition, ran forward wagging its tail wildly. A moment later the door opened and an astonished Park stood transfixed in the entrance, unable at first to believe who he was seeing. The old butler's eyes blinked furiously against a hint of gathering moisture as he tried to maintain his dignity. At first he was too shaken to speak; finally, regaining some of his usual composure, he said, 'It is wonderful to see you, m'lud!' Then, remembering that he was addressing the rightful Duke of Stanforth, he corrected himself and said with satisfaction, 'I mean... *Your Grace,*' and gave a low bow. With considerably less formality Park added quickly, 'I always knew you were not dead and that you would come back! But please! It is not safe for you here. Nothing has changed—please go while you can.'

'Hello, Park, it is splendid to see you! I am glad my friends have not given me up. But you are wrong. Things have changed and things are about to change here from this moment. Where is Lord Greystone?'

'In the study, Your Grace.'

'Will you announce me, Park.'

Park brightened, unable to guess what was afoot, and bowed with real deference. 'With the greatest of pleasure, Your Grace.' As they made their way towards the study, the Duke said, 'I am expecting some guests shortly. Will you assist them in any way you can?'

'Of course, Your Grace.'

Park had always disliked the Earl and thought him unworthy to inherit the title of the Duke of Stanforth, therefore, it was a moment of supreme triumph for the butler as he entered the study. The Earl was sitting at the desk busily writing in a ledger and, hearing Park enter, he looked up. 'Yes, what is it, Park?' he demanded, impatient at the interruption.

Trying to conceal his delight, Park announced in his usual measured tones, 'His Grace, the Duke of Stanforth.'

As the Earl assumed that he, himself, was now the Duke of Stanforth, this announcement just made him stare at Park with the suspicion that the old butler had been in the wine cellar slyly sampling the vintage port. But when, a second later, the Duke stepped into the study, the Earl started violently and jumped to his feet, his face was distorted with anger and fear. Then almost instantly the Earl's expression changed to one of satisfaction as he watched his long-hunted prey nearing capture. 'Well, well, Stanforth—it is you. But how amusing of you to have the nerve to show up here. I had heard a rumour that you were back in England.'

'Greystone, I have come to reckon with you at last. We both know who murdered my brother, and we both know it was not me.' Then addressing Park, the Duke said, 'Please ask Lord Avery to join us.'

When Park had gone, the Earl reseated himself. Putting his feet up on the desk and fingering a letter knife, he said lightly, 'This is a most entertaining situation. To show up here—you are even more foolhardy than I imagined. They *will* hang you, you know. Quite

412

an affair I should think: Duke's younger brother succeeds to the title only to be hanged for his brother's murder. Or maybe I'll save them the trouble.'

Without emotion, the Duke said, 'You have tried to kill me often enough, Greystone, as you did my brother, but you are not as clever as you would like to think. Oh, your plan was intricate, but you will not succeed in the end.'

Lord Avery entered; he was thunderstruck. *'Great heavens!* Do my eyes deceive me? You are not *dead* after all! I have not seen you since you were a lad, but I know *who* you are! It is a wonder you have the temerity to show yourself!' Then turning to the Earl, he asked nervously, 'Have you sent for the constabulary?'

'I am sure we can deal with this miscreant ourselves,' said the Earl arrogantly. However, Lord Avery, who was feeling every bit his years and suffering from a painful, gouty toe, looked at the young Duke's athletic physique and gave the Earl a doubtful glance.

'My dear sirs, I have no intention of *getting away,* as you seem to fear,' said the Duke affably. 'Please, be seated, Lord Avery, while I tell you an interesting story. You will find it particularly fascinating, Greystone.' Lord Avery looked about dubiously and retreated into the furthest chair he could find.

The Duke reached slowly across the desk towards the Earl; the Earl, on his guard, pulled back defensively and hardened his grasp on the letter knife. The Duke turned round the ledger in which the Earl had been writing, and he could see from the column of numbers, that the Earl had been totting up the wealth of Cranleigh. The Duke laughed lightly at the timely display of the Earl's avarice. Replacing the ledger and stepping away from the desk, the Duke turned to Lord Avery. 'As you know, my brother was murdered on a day of a shooting party here at the castle. Although you were not at the party, Lord Avery, you will doubtless have heard many versions for, as I understand, Society could speak of nothing else for months.' As the Duke spoke, the Earl watched him closely with a malevolent smile.

The Duke continued to address Lord Avery, 'On the day of the shooting party, Lord Greystone was not present. Although he was staying here at the castle, he had matters to attend to in London. Just before luncheon was served—it was to be in a meadow by the lake only about a mile from the castle—my brother received an urgent message that he was required back here. He returned to the castle on foot. Shortly after that I too received a message that my brother needed my assistance in some business at the castle. Both these messages were delivered by Greystone's servant, Hibbard, who had stayed behind when Greystone went to London. Now, by strange coincidence, Park, the most experienced of butlers, found that some of the champagne, which he had carefully selected and packed for the luncheon, had been left behind in the kitchens. This meant Park had to return to the castle.

'Hibbard offered to give Park a ride in a trap

and as they were coming back to the castle at the same moment as I, we all three travelled together. Upon arriving at the castle, I came straight to my brother's study and Park and Hibbard, I presume, went to the kitchens.

'When I arrived just outside this room I heard a shot. I dashed in and was horrified to find Edward slumped over his desk. He had died instantly from a pistol shot. The window was open and I ran to it but could see no one. I returned to my dead brother's side and just at that moment Hibbard burst in shouting "Murder!" and then ran off to raise the alarm.

'Hibbard was followed by Park, who, to his great credit, seeing me standing over my brother's body with the gun at my feet, did not believe for an instant that I could have done such a thing, and he encouraged me to depart.'

The Duke continued, 'Your timing was impeccable, Greystone, and you had Hibbard brilliantly rehearsed. For Lord Avery's benefit, I will explain. First, Hibbard removed half of the champagne from the luncheon preparations when Park was not watching. This necessitated Park returning to the castle to fetch it. As he is a much-respected member of the household, his qualifications as another witness were excellent. Who could possibly not *believe* the evidence when it was related by such a sensible and trusted retainer as Park? Although Park did not believe in my guilt, he was bound to tell the *truth* about what he had seen, and it was inevitably damning.' The Duke sat on the corner of the desk as he spoke, observing the Earl's remarkable lack of reaction.

'The truth is, Greystone, you never went to London that day. You only pretended to go, then you came back here and killed Edward just as you knew I was about to enter the study. You ran off through that window.' The Duke indicated the window nearest the desk.

'This is *outrageous!*' protested Lord Avery, indignantly getting to his feet. 'Greystone, we need not listen to this any longer!'

'No, let him go on. It is very entertaining,' said the Earl, gesturing languidly to Lord Avery to be reseated.

Unperturbed by the interruption, the Duke continued, 'To do credit to your cunning, Greystone, your use of Hibbard was masterful. It was under your orders that Hibbard told my brother that he was needed back here at the castle and it was also under your orders that Hibbard told me shortly afterwards that my brother required my presence in his study. Very well thought out, Greystone...and the dramatic touches were good as well. It was your instruction that Hibbard should burst in shouting "murder" and raise the alarm, immediately casting the guilt upon me. But were you not afraid to put such trust in a servant who could some day hold you to ransom with such knowledge, or were you going to see that Hibbard came to a...*premature* end? And were you not concerned that people would notice that Hibbard was always dressed in finery *far* too grand for his station, bought with the blood money you gave him? You must have paid him a princely sum for his cooperation and *silence.*'

'I have to compliment you on the inventiveness of your theory, Stanforth, but it is, of course, only supposition. *Where* is your proof?' demanded the Earl coldly.

'You know where the proof is, Greystone. You stole the Stanforth jewels, knowing that you could say I took them and *that* was my motive for killing my brother.' The Duke carried on with his cool delivery. 'If you will join me we can *show* Lord Avery where you have hidden the jewels.' With this the Duke opened the door to the library and politely beckoned the others to enter.

Lord Avery was showing signs of nerves; mopping his brow with a trembling hand he looked from one man to the other. The Duke's story was sounding remarkably plausible and, although twenty-four hours before he would have dismissed it out of hand, the Earl's outrageous threats to secure Angelica's hand in marriage had shown him capable of most anything.

In the library, the Duke spoke courteously to the Earl. 'Now, Greystone, perhaps you will oblige us by opening the secret cupboard by the fireplace.'

The Earl responded coldly. 'Very droll, Stanforth, but I know of no such compartment. Perhaps you will continue this delightful diversion by showing us what you refer to as a "secret cupboard".'

417

'As you like,' offered the Duke graciously, and stepping up to the fireplace he pressed what, even to the keenest eye, looked simply like a curl in the panelling. A tall door opened silently. 'Lord Avery, could you kindly oblige us by removing the jewels which I believe you will find there.'

Looking very wary, Lord Avery did as he was asked. Stepping beyond the panelling into the dark chamber, he presently returned struggling under the weight of a heavy iron casket. His grey, perspiring face was a picture of confusion and unease.

The Earl, still impassive, walked to a small sideboard which held decanters, and poured himself a brandy. 'May I offer you something? Avery? Stanforth?' Then after savouring his brandy for a moment he said, amused, '*Very* showy and very nicely staged, Stanforth! But finding the jewels there means *nothing*. Until this moment I knew of no secret compartment, and you prove nothing against me just because the jewels are still in the house. You obviously put them there before you fled, hoping to retrieve them at some later date.'

'Yes, that's *right!*' Lord Avery concurred, plainly relieved. 'It proves *nothing!*'

'Naturally it establishes nothing,' replied the Duke, affably agreeing, 'but, Lord Avery, will you look into the cupboard again—and I think you will find something there you recognize.'

With some hesitation, Lord Avery again went into the dark cupboard. The Earl's total self-control and seeming disinterest in

418

the proceedings did not slip, but a brief twitch caught at the corner of his mouth.

An astonished Lord Avery, his every nerve vibrating with anxiety, came back into the library. He staggered, his legs weak with the discovery that the Earl's guilt was undeniable. In his hands he held the pigskin document case that he had given to the Earl the afternoon before. 'Great heavens, Greystone! This fantastic story is true! How else could this document case get there?' Lord Avery stammered, 'Y-you told me only this morning that you had locked it up in a secure place. You can't explain *this* away!'

'Perhaps I cannot,' said the Earl deftly sliding a pistol from the sideboard drawer. 'But I hardly think that matters now.'

Terrified at the sight of the gun, Lord Avery dropped the document case and, crablike, sidestepped quickly placing himself behind a sturdy, upholstered chair, hoping foolishly that it might afford some protection against bullets.

A smile flickered across the Earl's twisted mouth as he pointed the pistol at them. 'I think *I* have the upper hand. It must be obvious to you both what happens now. When I explain *both* your deaths to the authorities, the scenario runs something like this—you, Stanforth, already wanted for the murder of your brother, have returned to collect the jewels that you stashed here. You are let into the castle by a kindly old servant who suffers from misplaced loyalties. Lord Avery and I are held at gunpoint by you as you retrieve the jewels from this secret

419

cupboard. Lord Avery valiantly tackles you, but you brutally kill him with this gun. By my good fortune, I am able to overpower you and, taking possession of your gun, I am forced to dispatch you as you attempt to escape. My word will *never* be doubted. You have saved me a lot of trouble as well, Stanforth. I *now* have the jewels to do with as I wish, whereas before I had to keep them hidden so that you would take the blame for their disappearance. Very tidy, don't you think?' and he laughed with genuine amusement.

Seeing matters come to a head more swiftly than he had anticipated, the Duke wondered what had become of his friend Vaigatch. And aware of Lord Avery's distress from being under the barrel of a pistol, an experience that was turning his lordship puce from an impending nerve storm, the Duke wandered casually between Lord Avery and the line of fire.

'Move away from there,' demanded the Earl, gesturing with the gun for the Duke to move to one side. 'I want to be able to see both of you.' With an apologetic shrug to Lord Avery, the Duke walked to the side of the fireplace where the servants' bell knob was fitted into the panelling at waist height. Although his face did not betray his thoughts, the Duke's mind was racing and he was berating himself for being so impetuous as to tackle the Earl unaided. He had been so keen for this moment of reckoning that he had rushed matters and now he was faced with certain death which would again render

Angelica the victim of the Earl. *What a fool I am!* the Duke raged silently to himself and then instantly collecting his wits he searched his mind for a plan of escape. All I need is just *one* split second distraction to occupy Greystone's attention. That is all, just a split second! And the Duke repeated to himself—and *where* is Vaigatch?

As the Duke leaned against the servants' bell knob, he reached behind his back and, unseen by the Earl, he turned the knob; in a far-distant basement corridor of the castle, the sound of a bell clanged sharply and then echoed round the deserted whitewashed labyrinth of hallways before dying away unheard—without alerting a single ear—for the usually alert Park was not at his post.

Leaning casually against the panelling the Duke said, 'There is no point in killing either of us now, Greystone. My friends are bringing the Chief Constable, Captain Ruxton, and he knows what to expect to find here when he arrives. He will have been apprised of the whole situation and your crimes. In any case, this fight is between you and me. There is no need to involve anyone else.'

An almost imperceptible bead of perspiration appeared on the Earl's forehead, but his outward manner was still controlled. 'Please don't expect me to believe that story. It's a bit flimsy for someone of your intelligence.'

The Duke tried playing for time. 'As, for the moment, you are in control, Greystone, grant me the favour of satisfying my curiosity.

Why in heaven's name did you kill my brother and formulate this fantastic scheme in the first place?'

'I would have thought it was *obvious* to you, Stanforth, but if you *insist* upon being obtuse I will explain it fully. It was quite clear to me, even when we were children, that your brother was totally unsuited to carry the title of the Duke of Stanforth. He was too soft, too concerned for the *welfare* of his servants—*his servants!*' he repeated mockingly. 'He would never have used Cranleigh as it is best suited, as the seat of an extremely powerful and rich title. And the thought of *you,* the younger brother, inheriting Cranleigh...you were never interested in anything more worthwhile than horse racing. I am the only person fit to be master of Cranleigh. I could not bear to see all this opulence wasted on the wrong owner. And I decided to do something about it instead of suffering the constant irritation of seeing Cranleigh in unworthy hands—but all this talk is a waste of time. I am now only a bullet away from becoming the Duke of Stanforth. And to think I wasted all that money on those incompetent buffoons who chased halfway round the world bungling your execution! I can now do it most satisfactorily by my own hand. Very obliging of you...' He laughed maniacally and, slowly moving forward, raised the gun and aimed it at the Duke's heart. He carefully and deliberately pulled back the hammer savouring every moment of his supreme power.

'You *rang,* Your Grace...' Park's urbane voice

intoned quietly from the study doorway where he stood, a silver salver in his hand.

The Earl's eyes darted in a flash in the direction of those timely words. In the particle of a second he looked away from his target, the Duke darted to the right and, before his movement could be followed by the gun, he struck out, felling the Earl with a colossal blow.

The loud crack of a shot sent a shock wave through the room. The two enemies grappled fiercely with the panic-stricken Earl fighting savagely like a drowning animal. The men struggled over the gun which was still in the Earl's hand, as he tried to force the barrel into the Duke's face; the Duke's fingers wrapped like a steel band around the Earl's wrist and their straining muscles locked in a stalemate until the Duke threw the Earl off balance and smashed his hand and gun against the corner of the sideboard. The Earl fell back and took the Duke with him, hammering him with his fists. They were evenly matched in strength, but the Duke slammed the Earl against the wall and, a second later, the desperate exchange of blows came to an abrupt end as the Duke's fist found the Earl's jaw with a terrible thud. As the Earl went down, the Duke pinned him to the floor and kept him there with his knee resting solidly in the Earl's back, forcing his face into the ample bosom of a nymph woven into the Aubusson carpet. The pistol had been sent flying during the conflict and landed at Lord Avery's feet. Timorously,

Lord Avery picked it up and handed it to the Duke.

Taking the gun, the Duke said, 'Thank you, Lord Avery—' and he could not resist prodding his lordship with a slight taunt about his wavering loyalties, '—I thought for a moment you were going to give it to the wrong man.' Lord Avery conjured up an injured look and then promptly backed away from the field of combat. Turning to Park, who still stood unperturbed in the doorway with his silver salver balanced on his fingertips, the Duke said, 'Thank you, Park. As ever your timing is impeccable.'

'Thank you, Your Grace. I must confess I was listening at the key hole—*not*, I *assure* you, a practise to which I subscribe, and I thought, as matters had progressed in an unhealthy direction, a slight interruption was required.'

'*What?* But I *rang* for you, Park, hoping for such a distraction!' The Duke laughed, wary and amazed.

'I'm *sorry*, Your Grace. I regret I was occupied at the keyhole and did not hear the bell.'

The Duke laughed loudly, 'The joke is on me! I'm much obliged, Park! I should have known you would not let the Stanforths down. Thank heavens the Queen didn't snatch you away all those years ago or this really would have been the end of the Stanforth line!'

A great clamour and the running of heavy feet heralded the arrival of Vaigatch, Captain Ruxton, and two of his officers. The other door to the library flew open as they burst in from the hall.

The room was filled with stunned, serious faces, apart from Vaigatch's; he grinned broadly as though it was all great sport. Vaigatch looked at the Earl in a crumpled heap on the floor, and the Duke standing over him with a pistol. The Gypsy King laughed, 'A-ha! look at *this*, my friend! Why did we bother to come! You have been *wasting* my time! It was a battle getting Captain Ruxton to come with me! *He* thought it was some gypsy plot! And for *all* my trouble you didn't need me after all! I could have spent my day doing some profitable horse trading instead of rushing all about the county on a goose chase for you!'

Releasing the Earl into the hands of Captain Ruxton's men, the Duke said lightly, 'Vaigatch, you will be the death of me! You were supposed to be here long ago! As it happens my neck was saved by Park, here,' and he nodded towards the butler.

The mighty Vaigatch took one look at the wafer-thin old servant and let out a loud hoot of raucous laughter and slapped Park heartily on the back, crying, 'Well done!' In spite of being thrown off balance, Park pretended not to notice this lapse in good behaviour.

'Captain Ruxton, I've heard Greystone confess *everything!*' cried Lord Avery, collapsing into a chair and mopping his face with a handkerchief. 'He murdered the late Duke and he was about to kill me as well! And he would have done if the young Duke here had not stopped him!

Hibbard, that servant of his, is in the villainy as well!'

It was only then that Captain Ruxton noticed the dark stain spreading across the shoulder of the Duke's coat. 'It looks as if you have caught a bullet.'

Touching his shoulder, the Duke winced slightly at the pain. 'I thought I had wrenched it in the struggle. I was too busy at the time to realize I'd been shot.'

'We had better send for a doctor,' suggested Captain Ruxton.

'It is only very slight. There is no need for a doctor. I am sure one of the servants can dress it for me,' said the Duke disinterestedly.

Grim and battered, the Earl was hauled to his feet by Captain Ruxton's men who started to manacle his wrists. 'Don't *touch* me!' he snapped arrogantly. 'Don't think you can maul me like some commoner!' Yanking himself from the constables' grasp, he made no attempt to escape, but pulled himself up haughtily and set about straightening his silk cravat and dishevelled clothing in the very mirror that had led to his downfall. Then, turning to the Duke, he said with consuming hatred, 'Tell me something, Stanforth, I would have called it a fortunate guess if you had only known about the jewels in the secret panel, but how did you know about the document case? My plan was *perfect*. You had *no* way of knowing...'

'The evening you put the document case behind the panelling...you were observed,' said the Duke guardedly.

426

The Earl watched him with sly, malevolent eyes. 'And I don't suppose you would care to tell me *who* saw me? No? And quite rightly so, because whoever it was will always be in danger—as long as I have breath in my body.'

Captain Ruxton instructed his two constables to take the Earl away. 'Keep a close watch on him and if he shows the slightest inclination to escape, you may forget he is a peer of the realm. He is still to be tried for murder.' The Earl shot a look of disdain at Captain Ruxton who, from all his years in the army and militia, was immune to abuse and returned the Earl's look with frigid disinterest.

After the Earl was escorted out, Captain Ruxton turned to the Duke and said, 'Quite frankly, this is the most bizarre case I have *ever* had to deal with. There will be an uproar when Greystone goes to trial as he is a member of the aristocracy, but there is no question—he will hang. Even if he insists on his right to be tried by his peers in the House of Lords, he is doomed. Your friend here, Mr Vaigatch, acquainted me with the details, and with Lord Avery's testimony I am sure it will be a matter of course. That servant, Hibbard, will probably sing like a sparrow to try and save his own neck.'

Vaigatch was becoming impatient and roared with delight to the Duke, 'Well, brother Anthony, I must go! I see I am certainly not needed here now!' Helping himself to an enormous glass of brandy from the sideboard, he held the cut glass decanter aloft offering it to the others as if it had all been a great party. With weary tolerance, Park stared at the unusual looking guest. Vaigatch tossed down the brandy and roared, 'Now, I must go and see a man about a horse!'

Captain Ruxton and Vaigatch departed, bundling the still-defiant Earl and the terrified Hibbard into a carriage driven by the armed constables. The Cranleigh servants, their eyes as wide as saucers, watched in awe from behind twitching drapes as the Earl was unceremoniously removed. The entire castle had been agog with excitement from the first moment of the Duke's return, but Park had insisted they continue normally with their duties. However, very little dust was shifted by half-heartedly flicked dusters, no breakfast dishes were washed, and grates were swept in a slapdash manner as the servants vibrated nervously and aimlessly about, wondering what was afoot—until the sound of the pistol shot had sent them scurrying terrified in all directions.

Mrs Banks, the rotund housekeeper, was busily cleaning and bandaging the Duke's gunshot wound. She was all a-twitter at his return and, feeling motherly towards him, she recalled to herself how she had administered occasionally to the less serious scraped knees of his youth. 'It is a good thing that the bullet went clean through, but I do wish you would let us send for the doctor, Your Grace.'

The Duke said, with a cheerfulness he had forgotten was possible, 'Perhaps tomorrow, Mrs Banks. I have far too much to do today and I

428

trust your capabilities completely.'

Park had to keep shooing away a gathering crowd of excited servants who were trying to steal a peek into the library at the newly returned Duke. Park did not want to reprimand them too roughly as his mood was benign and, were it not for the natural restraint of his position, he might even be described as verging on merry.

Although calmer, Lord Avery was still suffering the effects of the excitement and kept pacing the floor muttering, 'Thank goodness Lady Avery has slept through all this ghastly business! She was beastly tired when we returned from Revelstoke's ball and went straight to bed. We are *so* grateful, *My Lord Duke,* for all that you have done!' Lord Avery used the most deferential form of address in hopes of gaining the young Duke's approval. The Duke was well aware of Lord Avery's motives and, although he would tolerate his lordship for Angelica's sake, he had enough experience of human nature to know never to trust him totally. Lord Avery was the sort of man whose loyalties always lay with the rich and powerful. Now that the Duke had been exonerated and would duly claim his inheritance, his wealth could not be rivalled; therefore Lord Avery would always seek his society.

Observing the bandaging operation, Park was dismayed at the state of the Duke's blood-stained coat which now, because his injured arm was supported by a sling, could only be thrown over the wounded shoulder. But the Duke was in a hurry and would not wait for another jacket to be sponged and pressed.

The Duke then ordered the servants to depart, leaving him alone with Lord Avery. 'What I have to say, Avery, is for your ears alone. It was Lady Angelica who told me that Greystone put your document case in the secret cupboard.'

'Lady Angelica!' Lord Avery cried astonished, as his over-taxed brain tried to comprehend. 'But...how do you even know Lady Angelica?'

The Duke gave him a grim look. 'Because yesterday she overheard the conversation between Greystone and yourself, making arrangements for her marriage, and she was so terrified that she ran away. Fortunately she came to no harm and was discovered by friends who are looking after her.'

'R-ran away!' stammered Lord Avery in disbelief. 'But-but...isn't she out *riding?'* and then, realizing what must have happened, he said ruefully, 'Ran away...poor child,' and his head dropped forward in shame as he knew he had played his part in driving her away.

'In a moment I am going to tell Lady Angelica that it is safe for her to return. As far as anyone knows, she is simply out riding. I am not going to make Greystone's offer for her hand common knowledge, and I will certainly say nothing to Lady Avery. You may say what you please to her ladyship and I will not dispute it. When Greystone comes to trial it would be very unsavoury for Lady Angelica's name to be connected with his in any way. The gossips would devour it.' The Duke's face was stern as he spoke, and Lord

Avery, who was looking very sheepish, simply nodded his head in agreement.

The Duke sent orders that a fresh horse be saddled. Then he made his way out the front door as waves of servants poured from doors and gateways. Those of a rank that permitted them to speak offered greetings and good wishes; smiling and delighted, the Duke shook hands with some of the senior servants and acknowledged doffed hats and curtsies. The news of the Duke's return and the demise of the Earl had swept across the estate like a hurricane. Park was at first appalled by this total collapse in etiquette, but the spontaneous gathering of household servants, estate workers, gardeners, and grooms, was impossible to disperse as they crowded around the front steps. Sarah, with her parlourmaid friend, Jane, stood in the crowd and Sarah ogled the handsome Duke and congratulated herself on witnessing this remarkable episode—and as she assumed Angelica was only out riding—relished the supreme moment when she could be the first to acquaint Lady Angelica with news of this remarkable Duke. Finally Park, surveying the noisy, happy crowd which impeded the Duke's path to the waiting horse, gave up his disapproving stance and felt compelled to say a few words. Park silenced the crowd with a few gestures and said, 'On behalf of all the staff, Your Grace, I wish to say how happy we all are to have you in your rightful place at Cranleigh Castle,' and a hearty cheer went up.

The Duke was touched by this welcome. Although he had always been a popular member of the Stanforth family, it had never occurred to him that such a thing could happen. What he could guess, from seeing Titus's injuries first hand, was that the servants had suffered badly at the Earl's hand. 'Thank you one and all for your good wishes,' he said, climbing into the saddle. 'I cannot tell you how delighted I am to be back at Cranleigh. But to give full credit, it was only the quick thinking of Park here who saved the day! Thank you all for your kindness and loyalty.' Riding off, the Duke felt rather moved at his reception and, over his shoulder, he could see Park looking embarrassed and a little pleased as he was now surrounded by a sea of expectant faces all demanding the full story—and the old butler's vital part in it.

NINETEEN

The Duke turned his horse towards the vicarage. Outside the tidy, little Georgian house stood the two gypsies who had ridden away from the camp the night before. After the Duke said a few brief words to them, they mounted their horses and rode off. The Duke knocked on the door of the vicarage and Mrs Keswick, the housekeeper, instantly threw open the door as if she had been hovering behind it—for she had. 'Oh, Lord Anthony—ah—I mean *Your Grace*, it's *really* you! We've heard the news!' she cried emotionally bringing the hem of her apron to her eyes and dabbing at them. 'Come in, Your Grace, do! Forgive me for keeping you standing there! Come into the parlour, do! And I will tell the vicar you are here!' and she dogged his steps like a friendly sheep dog until she had corralled him in the parlour. Dropping an elaborate curtsy, she grinned at him all the time as she slid out and shut the door.

The parlour was sparsely and ascetically furnished with book shelves covering almost every inch of wall space. Interspersed, between lovingly kept volumes, were worn portfolios bulging with forty years of sermons. Bustling through the door, Mr Compton was in a state of high excitement. 'There you are, dear boy! I've heard the news! It must have reached London by now!' He pumped the Duke's hand triumphantly. 'Thank you for ridding us of that perfidious Greystone! I never knew for sure how dreadful he was until today, but I always suspected that something was *not quite* right with him. What an evil man! *Oh dear*—I really should not say such things in my office, but I think in his case I will make an exception. But you have sustained an injury!' he gasped, noticing the Duke's bandage for the first time.

'It is very minor, Vicar, and I see you have not got away unscathed. You have acquired quite a black eye. Not serious I trust?' enquired the Duke, helping Mr Compton lower his elderly frame into a chair. 'Have you any other injuries?'

'No, I am glad to say that is my only medal of honour on the field of battle! But I have to say, I certainly wondered what was going on last night at Revelstoke's ball! I stepped away from the ball for a few moments to cross the garden to where the servants were having their entertainment—I had promised to have a tankard with some of my parishioners amongst them. I was *very* late as I'd been playing whist. From *nowhere* these three reprobates grabbed hold of me and started to *drag* me towards a carriage! At first I thought it was a couple of my parishioners, who had partaken of too much ale, just larking about. When I realized that I was being *kidnapped* I was terrified!—I don't deny it! My cries for help were drowned by the noise from the ballroom on the one side and the celebrations of the estate workers on the other. That's when they blackened my eye to try to silence me! *Abducted!* An old, worthless country parson like myself! Who could *think* of such a thing! Just when I was sure all was lost your two gypsy friends appeared, released me, and pounded the perpetrators into insensibility! What an adventure! Well—I have to say for all that—I haven't enjoyed myself this much in years!' His face glowed pink with delight. 'And then your two friends brought me home and they've been here every minute, standing guard, until you sent them away just now. But *what* was it all about? I can only suppose that it had something to do with Greystone. It did, didn't it?' Mr Compton's face shone with expectation.

'Yes. Last night Lady Angelica told me that you both knew that I was alive and that your conversation was overheard by Hibbard. I was concerned that Greystone's men would attack you, thinking you knew of my whereabouts, and try to force you to tell them, by whatever means necessary. I am only thankful that my friends arrived in time.'

'*Staggering!* Absolutely staggering!' Mr Compton exclaimed still revelling in the excitement of his narrow escape. 'But...forgive my poor befuddled brain—' he said clasping his head in his hands and shaking it, '—I had very little sleep last night and I'm in a state of confusion...but did you say *Lady Angelica* told you *last night* about our conversation in the picture gallery? I *thought* the dear child was unwell and confined to her bed at Cranleigh?' When the Duke told him that Angelica had spent the night with the gypsies, Mr Compton's mouth dropped open in surprise and gaped like a railway tunnel expecting a train.

The Duke said, 'Lady Angelica is quite well and safe. But there isn't time to give you the details at the moment,' and he departed, leaving the old vicar feeling even more astounded.

As he rode away from the vicarage, the Duke's thoughts returned to Angelica; she had consumed his every waking moment and visited his dreams for the last days of his exile. Now he could hardly come to grips with the reality that he was free at last to pursue his life as he wished. And what he wished for most in the world was to marry Angelica and make her the Duchess of Stanforth. He remembered their declaration of love only a few hours before; he wondered if it had been only a fabrication of his imagination, or worse, if she had spoken only out of confusion, fright, or even pity. If she found him acceptable, did Cranleigh hold too many terrible memories for her, all connected with the Earl? As he rode towards the gypsy camp, he knew one thing for certain: he had never met anyone who had Angelica's disarming frankness and genuine modesty. They were qualities that made her shine out from the collection of society beauties he had courted in the past. He knew, too, that his hopes for happiness would be shattered if she refused him. With these thoughts chasing one another across his mind, he arrived at the path in the woods leading to the gypsy camp.

Standing at the edge of the clearing was Angelica, her eyes restlessly scanning the path. The Duke caught sight of her first and rode towards her. When she saw that he was injured, she cried out and ran towards him through the wood, oblivious to the brambles that caught at her skirt and scratched her hands. 'You're hurt!' she said in a frightened whisper as he dismounted and stood before her.

'It's nothing,' he said, his eyes exploring her face, hoping that her look of anxiety held something akin to love. 'Angelica, my dear, everything is as it should be. Greystone has confessed to his crimes and he is now in custody.'

'Oh, thank God—' she breathed, '—it's all over—' But not daring to believe that Fortune was ready to smile upon them, fighting panic she repeated, 'But you are hurt—are you badly injured? Please tell me—I must know!'

'No—truly it is nothing, I swear it,' and noticing that her hands had been caught by the sharp thorns, he gently grasped her wrist; he could feel her pulse racing as he lifted it to his lips. He could put off the moment no longer; he had to delve for the truth of her feelings. Looking down at her, he finally said, 'My darling—was I having a wonderful dream last night, or did you really say you would abandon everything and come away with me?'

Angelica's gaze was steady and with a small smile she answered softly, 'Yes, and I still shall, if it is what you wish.'

Drawing her into his arms, he held her slight, unresisting form to him for a moment while letting his lips explore her shining face and golden hair; then he held her in a kiss that spoke deeper than words.

When he released her from the kiss, he continued to hold her in his arms and smiled down at her with the look of someone who could not quite believe his good luck in capturing a treasured prize. Lightly tracing the outline of her lips with a fingertip, he said, 'My darling, will you abandon forever all thoughts of a gypsy life and settle for a more conventional existence at Cranleigh by marrying me?'

She was smiling slightly mischievously up at him. 'Which one of you would I be marrying?'

He gave a surprised laugh. 'Well...a combination of all...but you would have to be known at court as the Duchess of Stanforth.'

He paused to marvel at the joyful expression in her eyes. 'Say yes.'

'A thousand times *yes.*'

'I had forgotten the world could be so right,' he laughed and kissed her again.
the still, sun-lit wood, they spoke of many things and of their future together. The Duke said, 'There is a matter which I have not yet dealt with. I have not spoken to Lord Avery of my offer for your hand—but I suppose, as he has already given his blessing for you to marry a bogus Duke of Stanforth, he will not object to you marrying the real one.' As they laughed at this notion, it was as if their troubles had never existed.

After much urging on Angelica's part, the Duke finally gave her a rather sketchy description of what had happened at the castle to bring about Greystone's defeat. He emphasized Park's key role but omitted to mention that a combination of his own impulsiveness and Vaigatch's tardiness had almost cost him his life.

Returning eventually to the gypsy camp, they found Vaigatch showing off a spirited chestnut horse he had just bought; it reared and bucked at the end of a rope which took two men to hold. Vaigatch gestured towards the horse while smiling broadly at the Duke. 'Well, what do you think of this fine sleek beast? It will beat your Prospero any day in a race! We will have a wager on it!' he bellowed in his usual fashion.

'I shall be too busy for racing, old friend—' and before the Duke could finish, Vaigatch trumpeted, 'So! Your *bori rani* will have you, will she?' and to Angelica, he boomed, 'You will have a fine husband there if he is *already* talking of giving up his sporting life! May you both have all the happiness in the world!'

Angelica had wrapped the diamond brooch in a lace handkerchief. Taking it from her pocket, she placed it in one of Vaigatch's hands and folded his great fingers over it so that it remained unseen. 'Please, dear friend, accept this gift from me—it has brought us so much luck, and I hope it will do the same for you and your people—always. It is to say "thank you" for all that you have done for us, and for protecting Anthony so well from his enemies.'

Vaigatch, hearing this and knowing that he had almost let his old friend be killed, due to his slowness in getting to the castle, stole a look at the Duke's face to see if this was some sort of jest. Seeing the Duke looking just as perplexed as himself, he was delighted with the genuineness of the sentiment. 'My dear Lady Angelica!' he roared in his fortissimo, 'I am touched and honoured by your kindness,' and he bowed gallantly over her hand.

When the Duke and Angelica finally returned to the castle, Lord and Lady Avery greeted them warmly. Lady Avery had been instructed by his lordship not to question Angelica too closely about the events of the last twenty-four hours in hopes that she might never discover all the details. When they were told of the Duke's offer for Angelica's hand, they were ecstatic, and as Lord Avery put it, 'Delighted beyond measure, my dear Duke! Delighted! We could not wish for happier news!' Any confusion in Lady Avery's mind about the events of the last day was instantly forgotten as she turned all her attention to wedding plans.

Shortly afterwards, Mr Compton arrived, out of breath having almost run from the vicarage, bursting with a piece of news. He carried a letter which he had found amongst the papers of the late vicar, Mr Quince. At first he was too breathless to speak, but the Duke poured him a little glass of cordial from a decanter on a nearby sideboard to help calm him. Mr Compton downed the cordial and scanned their attentive faces. 'I have just come across the *most remarkable* piece of information,' he gasped, holding up the old faded letter. 'This is a letter addressed to me by the late Mr Quince, and written some nine years ago according to the date. In it he reveals the most remarkable tale. There were rumours—about ten years ago—that Lord Greystone had—' Mr Compton wanted to use the word *seduce*, but in deference to Lady Avery, he said, 'rumours that Lord Greystone had *taken advantage* of a pretty young serving girl by tricking her into a secret and false marriage ceremony at Crowood. And the issue of that liaison was a boy—named Titus—who worked as a boot black first at Crowood and now here at Cranleigh. It was only rumour that the boy was Lord Greystone's son—they say the mother died when she discovered she had been duped—but again it was only supposition, as the girl never made public the name of her child's father.

'*Well,*' continued Mr Compton, after fortifying himself with another cordial that the Duke had poured for him, 'according to this letter from Quince, the rumours were remarkably accurate. The ceremony—it is revealed in this letter—was to be staged by The Reverend Quince using a young travelling clerk dressed as a vicar to perform the ceremony. The only reason Quince agreed was because Greystone held over him the knowledge of some indiscretion Quince had committed in his youth which would have ruined the old vicar. As Quince tells in this letter, he could not bring himself to trick the girl in such an evil way so he defied Greystone by having the ceremony performed by a young vicar of his acquaintance who was staying briefly in a nearby village en route to his first parish which was in India—and of course Greystone thought the young vicar was only a travelling clerk—and Mr Quince never told him differently.' One by one, Mr Compton looked at the astonished faces of his audience to see if they had understood the significance of the letter. He went on, 'You see—that means young Titus is the *legal and lawful* son of Lord Greystone. Greystone was *legally married* to Titus's poor wretched mother! This letter proves that Titus is his legal heir and that means Titus will inherit everything from Greystone—*title—fortune—everything!*'

Lord and Lady Avery knew nothing of Titus and they would have been astonished to know that he, the nine-year-old heir to the Earl of

441

Greystone was, at that very moment, having a cheerie tea with their servants at the big oak table in the servants' hall at Ickworth. But Lady Avery, who had thought after the revelations of the day nothing could ever surprise her again, loved a plump piece of gossip and her mouth had fallen open, and she had her chubby hands plastered to her face, distractedly kneading it like dough. Lord Avery shot his cuffs and said thoughtfully, 'I wonder if the *dear boy* would like some financial advice from a wise old uncle, like myself.'

The Duke and Angelica were silent for a moment and then he turned to her and said quietly. 'Titus will need a great deal of help and guidance—shall we have him live with us until he is ready to take on the responsibility of running his own estate?'

Angelica slipped her arm through his and smiled softly up at him. 'Oh, yes—I was hoping that!' Her expression clouded a little. 'Poor Titus! What a mixed blessing for him... If that letter had never been written he would have inherited nothing and been poor and maybe happy in the ignorance of his father's identity. But now he will know the truth, and he will know how evil his father is. Titus will need all the love we can give him.' She looked up into the Duke's eyes and she realized that there was no further need for words.

That evening, after peace had descended upon the castle, the Duke and Angelica found themselves in the long gallery lost in talk. The gypsy's prophecy had come spilling back into her mind and had tumbled into place with the unfolding events of the last few days. She turned to the Duke and asked with a half smile, 'I suspect you are guilty of telling me something which was not true.'

'I?' he said, feigning innocence. 'What *absolute* particular did you have in mind, my dear?'

'I don't mean about hiding your true identity—I understand perfectly all your reasons for that, of course, but I have been thinking about the gypsy woman's prophecy. You told me that there was nothing in it—but you knew it would all come true.'

'I wanted to spare you worry.'

'All that she predicted has come true, but I was blinded into thinking you were the *poor man*—the poor man is Lord Greystone—he now has nothing.'

'Yes, he resides in Newgate Prison...and is soon to hang, or as the prophecy said, "soon to die." '

Angelica trembled. 'Yes, those were the fortune-teller's words.'

A smile tugged at his mouth. 'Now that you have caught me out in one lie, I have another confession to make.' Angelica looked at him, as any bride-to-be would at the sound of these words; she was innocent but not lacking in imagination; was he about to announce that he already had a gypsy wife and seven children? She laughed at her flight of fancy when a glance at his face reassured her that his expression was untroubled.

The Duke began, 'When I came across you in

the wood that first day, it was not an accident. What I mean is, I did not want to frighten you by riding after you, so...I'm afraid my confession is that Prospero and I played a trick on you.'

'What can you possibly mean?' asked Angelica, amused by the guilty grin he was struggling to control.

'Well, when I was a lad, all the young chaps round here used to hold informal race meetings. And I taught Prospero to limp—as if lame—at the sound of a skylark's song. It was a trick Vaigatch taught me. I did it because I could make the call of the skylark before a race and the betting odds would be in our favour as the other boys would think Prospero had gone lame. As we always raced in a meadow, no one thought twice about hearing a lark. Fortunately Prospero could tell the difference between my whistle and the real skylark song, otherwise he would have been in a terrible state of confusion. My father heard about my dubious trick and made me promise never to use it again. I kept my promise to him up until the moment I saw you in the wood. I was astonished that Prospero remembered after so many years. You see, I knew you would stop to check if Prospero had picked up a stone, and it would give me the chance to speak with you.'

Angelica tried to restrain her laughter. 'That is outrageous!' she giggled. 'I've never heard of such a thing. Thank goodness the old Duke kept a stern watch on you. And I suppose that's why our paths kept crossing in the wood—a tawny owl had been calling Prospero.'

444

The Duke smiled warily, 'All part of the ruse... I hope you are not angry that I employed such a stratagem on you...?'

Angelica was smiling, 'Not in the least—after all, if you had not, we might not be here now.'

They soon came to the painting that had held the secret of his identity. From his pocket he produced a delicate ruby and diamond ring and slipped it onto Angelica's finger. 'I hope you will wear this. It was my mother's and has been worn by the Duchesses of Stanforth for generations. If you look closely, you can see she was wearing it when this portrait was painted.'

'It is beautiful. I shall wear it always.'

Seeing the painting again, after his long absence, brought a rush of memories back to the Duke. He looked at the sloe-eyed wolfhound in the picture and said, 'That old Irish wolfhound had a passion for lime marmalade and would corner Park in the butler's pantry until he parted with some.'

They laughed lightly for a moment and then slipped into an easy silence.

Contentment surged through Angelica as she and the Duke stood gazing at the painting, her hand resting so naturally and securely in his. As she looked at the picture once more, a little spark of clarity almost made her jump, and she saw at last what it had been trying to say to her all along. It seemed so obvious to her now that she wondered how she could have missed it; looking into the dark, kind eyes of the happy family in the picture, she could see her destiny.

The publishers hope that this book has given you enjoyable reading. Large Print Books are especially designed to be as easy to see and hold as possible. If you wish a complete list of our books, please ask at your local library or write directly to: Black Satin Romance, Magna House, Long Preston, North Yorkshire, BD23 4ND.

This Large Print Book for the Partially sighted, who cannot read normal print, is published under the auspices of

THE ULVERSCROFT FOUNDATION

THE ULVERSCROFT FOUNDATION

. . . we hope that you have enjoyed this Large Print Book. Please think for a moment about those people who have worse eyesight problems than you . . . and are unable to even read or enjoy Large Print, without great difficulty.

You can help them by sending a donation, large or small to:

**The Ulverscroft Foundation,
1, The Green, Bradgate Road,
Anstey, Leicestershire, LE7 7FU,
England.**
or request a copy of our brochure for more details.

The Foundation will use all your help to assist those people who are handicapped by various sight problems and need special attention.

Thank you very much for your help.